Praise f

LONGLI ... ME
NOVEL OF T ... AR 2

"Gripping ... KEEPING

"A ter ... GUNN, SCOTSM

"Absorbing. This is a ... run and run." SHIRLEY WHITESIDE, SUNDAY HERALD

"Warm, witty, thoughtful, and thrilling." ALISTAIR BRAIDWOOD, SCOTS WHAY HAE

"An utterly riveting and often unexpected read, absolutely brilliantly done." LIZ LOVES BOOKS BLOG

"You should make time to get to know Maggie and Wilma." LOUISE FAIRBAIRN, SCOTSMAN

"Strong advocacy of and for women... that's what makes this such an engrossing read." LIVE AND DEADLY

"Incredibly gritty and compelling... absolutely superb writing." THE QUIET KNITTER

Praise for *Cross Purpose*

LONGLISTED FOR THE MCILVANNEY PRIZE FOR
SCOTTISH CRIME BOOK OF THE YEAR 2017

"A brilliant new talent for the lover of crime...a vibrant crime partnership and sound forensic expertise." SUE BLACK, DBE, FORENSIC ANTHROPOLOGIST

"A refreshingly different approach to the private investigator genre... a fast-paced tale." – SHIRLEY WHITESIDE, *HERALD*

"[A] fantastic new crime novel...a gritty book with a surprisingly warm theme of female friendship." *THE LIST*

"MacLeary's prose is assured and engaging, bursting with the liveliness of the Aberdonian vernacular... an impressive debut." RAVEN CRIME READS

FALKIRK COMMUNITY
TRUST LIBRARIES

ALSO BY CLAIRE MACLEARY

Cross Purpose
Burnout

RUNAWAY

Claire MacLeary

CONTRABAND

Contraband is an imprint of Saraband

Published by Saraband,
Suite 202, 98 Woodlands Road
Glasgow, G3 6HB

and

Digital World Centre, 1 Lowry Plaza
The Quays, Salford, M50 3UB

www.saraband.net

ISBN: 9781912235438
ebook: 9781912235445

10 9 8 7 6 5 4 3 2 1

Printed and bound in Great Britain by Clays Ltd, Elcograf S.p.A.

MIX
Paper from responsible sources
FSC® C018072

Claire MacLeary has lived in Aberdeen and Fife, but describes herself as "a feisty Glaswegian with a full life to draw on". Following a career in business, she gained an MLitt with Distinction from the University of Dundee. *Runaway* is her third novel and continues the Harcus & Laird series. *Cross Purpose* was longlisted for the McIlvanney Award 2017, and *Burnout* was longlisted for the Hearst Big Book Award 2018.

Claire MacLeary has lived in Aberdeen and Fife, but describes herself as a Glaswegian with a fair bit of dame of. Following a career in business, she gained an MLitt with Distinction from the University of Dundee. Runway, is her third novel and continues the Harcus & Laird series. Cross Purpose was longlisted for the McIlvanney Award 2017, and Burnout was longlisted for the Heart Big Book Award 2018.

I

Emergency

'Emergency. Which service do you require: police, fire or ambulance?'

On the other end of the line there was nothing but ragged breathing.

'Which service, caller?'

'Police.'

There was silence, then, 'Police Scotland,' their control picked up. 'What is your emergency?'

'It's my wife.' The man cleared his throat. 'She's gone missing.'

'Can I have your name, please?'

'Scott.'

'And your last name?'

'Milne.'

'Have you any reason, Scott, to suspect your wife has come to harm?'

'Not really.'

Yet another call that should have been directed to 101. Patiently, the operative responded. 'Try to stay calm. I'm going to put you through to our service centre who can take this forward.'

'Hurry up, will you? I'm…' He swallowed his words as he was put on hold.

'Hello, Scott.' A female voice this time. 'How can I help?'

'It's my wife, she's gone missing.'

'What makes you think she's missing?' The young call handler smothered a yawn. If she had a penny for every missing from home that was called in and turned up safe she'd be a millionaire by now.

'She wasn't at home when the kids got in from school. She didn't turn up to make their tea.'

'Has this happened before?'

'No. Well, she's run a bit late, sometimes, if she's been shopping and that.'

'Let me take down some details. Your wife's full name?'

'Debbie, I mean Deborah Anne Milne.'

'Maiden name?'

'Esslemont.'

'Date of birth?'

'12th April 1986.'

'Place of birth?'

'Aberdeen.'

'Home address?'

'66 Belvidere Street.'

'Do you have the postcode?'

'AB25 2… Christ, I can't remember.'

'Not to worry. What district is that?'

'Rosemount.'

'Can you tell me where Deborah…?'

Scott cut her short. 'She answers to Debbie.'

'Can you tell me where and when Debbie was last seen?' She launched into her routine.

'Today, in the kitchen at home. It would be the back of eight, I'd say, when I left for my work.'

'And her physical description?'

'Tall. Five foot eight.'

'Build?'

'Not thin.' He paused. 'Not fat either. Curvy, I suppose you would say. Brown eyes. Dark hair.'

'Can you tell me what Debbie was wearing when you saw her last?'

On the line there was silence, then, 'I dunno. Some sort of house-coat thing.'

'Did your wife have any plans for the day?'

Another baffled silence. 'Who knows what Debbie gets up to when the kids aren't around? Women's stuff, I suppose.'

'And what frame of mind was she in, would you say?'

'Look, do you really need all this?' he demanded. 'Can you not just send someone out to look for her? I'm at my wits' end.'

'What I'm going to do, Scott,' the call handler said calmly, 'is send a police unit out to your home address. Is someone there now?'

'Me.' His voice dropped an octave. 'I came straight from work when the kids phoned to say Debbie wasn't there.'

'Good. But first,' she repeated, 'I need you to tell me what frame of mind Debbie was in when you saw her last?'

Scott sighed. 'Bit quiet. But that's not unusual, what with seeing the kids are up and dressed, getting the breakfast, packed lunches, all that.'

'Just say she was planning to go out somewhere,' the handler persisted. 'What would Debbie wear do you think?'

'Jeans? Boots? Jacket? Or a coat, maybe.'

'Does your wife have her own transport?' she asked, one eye on her crib sheet.

'Yes, but her car's still sitting in the drive.'

'Does she own a mobile?'

'Of course.'

'Has she been answering it?'

'No. That's another thing. Phone's switched off, and that's not like Debbie. Usually, it's never far from her hand.'

'Well, you stay put. I'll circulate your wife's details to all police units over the radio so they're alerted. A uniformed response team will be with you as soon as they can.'

The Beginning and End of It

''Scuse the mess.' Wilma ducked into the foot-well of her red Fiesta, grabbed a clutch of empty Coke cans and crisp packets, and chucked them into the back.

'No probs.' Maggie wrestled with her seat belt. 'I'm grateful for the lift. It's a lifesaver. Can't believe I didn't notice the time, nor put petrol in my car.'

'Too much on your mind.' Wilma gunned the engine, shot out of the drive.

'Steady on.'

She turned. 'Thought you were in a hurry.'

'I am. Only I'd prefer to get to my meeting in one piece.'

Barely losing momentum, Wilma nosed into a stream of traffic.

She turned, again.

'Keep your eyes on the road.'

'Okay,' Wilma fixed her eyes straight ahead. 'Where are we heading?'

'Carden Place.'

'Hang on.' She floored the accelerator and jumped the lights at North Anderson Drive, taking a left onto the ring road.

'Wil-ma.'

'What?'

'You just went through a red light.'

She grinned. 'So?'

In the passenger seat Maggie stiffened. 'Wilma Harcus, it's not a laughing matter. You're breaking the law.'

'Look...' Wilma turned, once more, to face Maggie. 'Do you want to make that meeting or not?'

'Sorry,' Maggie answered, chastened. This meeting was important: a new and potentially lucrative corporate client. If she didn't make her appointment, she might not get another chance. Not that it should figure, not the way she was feeling about the agency right now. She'd been ready to throw in the towel when their last major case – in which a woman, Sheena Struthers, had accused her husband of trying to kill her – had fallen apart. Maggie had gone against Wilma in taking on the client in the first place, and the ensuing furore had caused the two women's relationship to fracture. Ever since then, Maggie had questioned not only her own judgement but her whole *raison d'etre*. Still, she'd agreed a temporary stay of execution, so she should show good grace. After all, Wilma was doing this out the goodness of her heart. Just like the day she'd run Maggie to the mortuary to identify her dead husband – the day Maggie's life had changed forever.

'Now I've got your attention,' Wilma's voice broke her train of thought. 'Let me tell you, I've hardly slept the whole night.'

'Why is that?'

'The business.'

'Oh, Wilma!' Maggie let out an exasperated sigh. 'We've already been through all that. I've agreed to give the agency another six months, then…'

'Six months?' Wilma broke in. 'That's no time at all,'

At the Seafield Road roundabout, the small car shot out in front of a massive artic, causing horns to blare.

Maggie fingers sought purchase on the fake leather seat covers, knuckles white.

Wilma extended a steadying hand.

'Don't!' Maggie shrilled.

Wilma withdrew, changed down to second, accelerated past a stream of cars.

'Whatever.' Maggie regained her composure. 'In the meantime we'll stick to the routine stuff. At least until…' *We're back on an even keel.* She was loth to acknowledge the damage that could have been done to the agency's reputation – far less her friendship with Wilma – by a debacle of her own making. Maybe her instincts were true: the damage was irreparable, it was time to call it quits.

'Aye, except,' Wilma pursed her lips. 'If we shut up shop, you can pick up more hours at Seaton or go back to being a legal secretary, but what about me?'

'I'd be hard-pressed to achieve either of those things,' Maggie retorted. 'Resources are tight enough at school as it is, and we both know I'm not sufficiently up to speed on the IT side to get a secretary's job. As for you, you'll do what you've always done: make it up on the hoof.'

Wilma grinned. 'I'll take that as a compliment. All the same...' There was a wistful note to her voice. 'If we keep the agency going, I could really make something of myself after all these years of doing shite jobs.'

Maggie's conscience pricked. After Struthers, she owed Wilma one.

The small car sped up the outside lane of the dual carriageway. The city's show of spring flowers had withered and gone and the roses studding the central reservation were yet to bloom. But the trees bordering the road were lush with new foliage, albeit they passed in a blur of lime green.

'And,' Wilma didn't let up. 'Are you not the one that's aye banging on about integrity: doing the decent thing?'

'I am. And I'm not wrong either,' Maggie said with an admonitory frown. Her head swam with the numerous other incidences where Wilma had flouted the law.

'Well, that justifies my argument: you shouldn't rush to jack in the business. You need to give it a bit longer.'

'Listen, Wilma, let's not fall out again. We've only just...'

Reaching Kepplestone, the Christmas tree air freshener suspended from the rear-view mirror swung wildly, its aroma adding a pungent top-note to Wilma's scent, as the Fiesta whizzed right into Queens Road.

Maggie gritted her teeth. She thought she was going to be sick.

'Is it because you're a bit touchy, still, from the Struthers...'

Maggie bristled. 'I am *not* touchy.' Though her mind tumbled with images of the day, earlier that year, she'd tailed Gordon Struthers – alleged wife slayer – from his office in this very road to his club at Holburn junction.

'Then tell me,' Wilma persisted, 'you'll give it a bit longer.'

At Queen's Cross, they joined the tail end of a queue of traffic.

By this time Maggie was glued, rigid, to her seat. Her thighs, unaccustomed to being confined in tights, were clammy with sweat.

Wilma leaned across. 'What do you say?'

'I'm saying,' Maggie's shoulders sagged. 'I'm tired, Wilma. Tired of juggling two jobs. Tired of keeping erratic hours. Tired of dealing with poor, sad folk I can't do anything for.'

The line crept forward.

When she reached the roundabout, Wilma stepped on the gas.

The car rocketed ahead, narrowly missing a knot of youngsters who were trying to cross. 'Move your fuckin' backsides,' she muttered as she made Carden Place.

Maggie checked the time on her phone. 'Next block on the left,' she gestured. She'd make it with only minutes to spare.

'Gotcha,' Wilma acknowledged. 'Want me to drive up to the door?'

'No,' Maggie shot back, rather too hurriedly. Bad enough she was in a lather without someone clocking Wilma's banger. Then, shamed by her snobbery: 'You crack on,' she offered, gratefully. 'Just drop me here.'

The Fiesta screeched to a stop.

Maggie opened the passenger door and swung her legs onto the pavement.

Wilma extended a restraining hand. 'About the business.'

'Look,' Maggie lost her rag. 'If it will shut you up, I'll give it a year.'

'A year's not long enough,' Wilma began.

'A year,' Maggie repeated, poker-faced. 'And that's the beginning and end of it.'

Belvidere Street

'Does your wife have mental health issues?' Police Constable Dave Miller looked up from the Missing Persons *aide memoire* on his knee.

'Certainly not,' Scott Milne retorted, his face a study in mortification.

They were in the spacious, bay-windowed front room of Debbie Milne's home: a five-bedroom Victorian granite mid-terrace in the popular Rosemount district of Aberdeen. An original tiled fireplace in a heavily carved oak surround dominated one wall, which was painted in a modish shade of dove grey, while the looped carpet, deep-buttoned sofas and Roman blinds evidenced serious outlay.

PC Ian Souter made a mental comparison with his own home. The entire footprint of his chalet bungalow in Bridge of Don wasn't much bigger than this one room. Not for the first time, he wondered if he was in the wrong job. 'What my colleague is trying to establish,' he threw his colleague a black look, 'is whether there are any medical issues that might make Debbie vulnerable?'

'Like what, for instance?' Scott shot back, maintaining the affront.

'Diabetes, for example.' Souter worked to placate the man. 'Or asthma. Or suicidal thoughts,' he slipped in at the end.

'None of those,' Scott retorted. 'Aside from the occasional hangover, my wife is the picture of health.'

'She's not alcohol-dependent, then?' Miller volunteered, in a voice that spoke more of hope than expectation.

'No.'

Miller ticked the next box on his list. 'Drug-dependent?'

Weary voice. 'That neither.'

'And she doesn't have dementia?' His pen hovered, expectant, over the form.

'I think that will be a "no",' Souter rushed to answer, giving his partner the full evils.

'Righty-ho.' Dave Miller made a laborious tick in another box.

'You last saw your wife at breakfast time today?' Souter continued.

'That's correct.'

He jotted a note in his police pocket book. 'What sort of mood was she in, would you say?'

Scott Milne bristled. 'What do you mean?'

'Happy? Sad?'

'We haven't had a row, if that's what you're getting at.'

The two constables exchanged looks.

'Does your wife work?' Souter changed the subject.

'She did. Fashion boutique in Thistle Street, but the place went out of business, and part-time jobs are hard to find, the ones that fit in with school hours anyway.'

'Do you have any idea what Debbie's intentions were? How she planned to spend her day?'

'Much like any other weekday, I should imagine: housework, shopping. Maybe meet a friend in town. Then home in time for the kids getting in from school, give them their tea.'

'You've told us she kept her mobile phone close by, and that it is currently turned off?'

'That's right.'

'Did she have access to a computer?'

'We share a laptop. She has an iPad of her own.'

'Where is it now?'

'Upstairs in our bedroom? I didn't think to check.'

'If she *had* gone out, would she have taken her car? I gather it's still here.'

'You'll have walked past it,' Scott waved an arm towards the front window. 'No, she wouldn't have taken it, not always. Debbie wasn't confident at parallel parking. She'd have taken the bus if she went into town.'

'Would she have had money on her?' Miller fingered the form in his lap. 'Access to funds: credit cards, bank account?'

'We have a joint account with the Clydesdale. Debbie can spend what she wants.' Scott hesitated. 'Within reason, of course. There's the mortgage. And the kids, well, they're growing…'

'You've given our service centre a brief description,' Souter stepped in before his partner could put his foot in it again. 'Does Debbie have any distinguishing features: scars, moles, strawberry marks?'

'Nothing like that.'

'A recent photograph would be helpful, if you have such a thing.'

'I'm not sure,' Scott Milne furrowed his brow. 'Debbie doesn't like getting her photograph taken, says they make her look fat. There's our wedding photos,' he deliberated. 'But, what with the move and all, I don't know where they are.' He rose to his feet, cast around hopelessly. 'Wouldn't know where to begin looking, even.' He crossed to a wall unit, began to rummage in a drawer. 'Debbie, now, you ask her for something, she'll lay her hands right on it.' His voice cracked with emotion. Brusquely, he brushed away a tear. 'There's this,' he unearthed a dog-eared snap and held it out.

'Thanks.' Souter looked down at a smiling, dark-haired woman, clutching two pre-school children to her breast.

'It's a few years old, taken on holiday. But it's a good likeness, I reckon.'

Souter passed the photo across to Miller.

'Quite the looker, your wife.' Miller's grin was borderline lascivious.

Scott started forward, his face contorted.

'With your permission, Mr Milne,' Souter rushed in. 'We'll circulate this photograph on our North East Police Division Facebook and Twitter accounts. Nowadays, that's often the fastest way of getting a response.' *Thank God for social media. Might even do the job.*

'What about the newspapers?' Scott suggested, mollified.

'The press, too,' Souter added, silkily. 'In due course.'

'Not right away?'

He met Scott's anxious gaze. 'If Debbie is still missing after seventy-two hours, our investigation will be stepped up.'

'But...'

'Let me reassure you, the vast majority of missing persons turn up safe and well within a couple of days.'

Scott threw up his hands. 'And while I'm sitting here for seventy-two hours, what am I supposed to tell my kids? Plus, I've my job to consider. It's already...' He broke off, reddening.

'Mr Milne,' Souter began.

'Scott.'

'I know this is difficult for you, Scott, but I guarantee you, we'll do all we can. First off, I'd like...' He yanked his head at Miller, who was using the cuff of his uniform jacket to give his shoulder numbers a polish. '...with my colleague, to conduct a thorough search of the house and attic, together with any garages or outbuildings you may have.' *Better make it good.* Souter was still smarting from the reprimand he'd received after missing a pack of sleeping pills by a comatose woman.

'What's the point of that? I've already looked everywhere. First thing I did. And it will only waste...'

'I understand your frustration,' Souter conceded.

'Do you?'

'Trust me,' Souter came straight back. 'We have experience in dealing with...'

'I'm sorry,' Scott's face was the picture of misery. 'I didn't mean...'

'That's okay. As I was saying, we'd like to have a look around, with your permission, of course.' Pulling a pair of blue nitrile gloves from his pocket, he gave Miller the nod. 'And I'll need Debbie's mobile phone number.' He got to his feet. 'I'd also want to have a look at that computer and iPad you mentioned. Do you know one another's passwords?'

'Yes, but I don't see...'

'Write them down for me. Debbie's internet history may tell us if she's bought a ticket somewhere, booked a hotel room...'

'Why on earth would she do that?' Scott interrupted.

Souter ignored this. 'Spoken to anyone on social media.' They'd look at the motivation once they'd established the facts.

One thing he didn't mention: Debbie might have written a suicide note.

Trifle for Afters

Wilma breezed through the back door.

'Forget something?' Ian asked, pointedly, from his seat at the kitchen table.

'Don't panic.' She dumped her handbag on the worktop. 'I've made mince and tatties for your dinner.' She reached to light the gas under the pan on the hob. 'Won't take minutes to heat through.'

'Where have you been?' he persisted.

She turned. 'Ran Maggie into town.'

'Why didn't she take her own car?'

'Wouldn't start.' The lie tripped off Wilma's tongue.

'She could have caught a bus.'

He's tired! In his job as a motor mechanic, Ian had an early start. By the time he got home and showered he could sometimes be cranky.

'Come on.' She crossed to his side and playfully elbowed his shoulder. 'Maggie was late for a meeting. I made the offer. End of story.'

His lips compressed. 'You're at that woman's beck and call.'

She turned back to the stove. 'That's not true.' She was determined to keep her cool.

'Isn't it?' he demanded, not letting up.

She rounded on him. 'You know bloody well it's not.'

'Looks pretty one-sided from where I'm sitting.'

On your fat arse! 'What do you mean by that?'

'You do the donkey-work, she gets the glory.'

'Gets her nose rubbed in it, more like,' Wilma retorted. 'Since me and her teamed up, it's been Maggie has gone out and drummed up new business.'

'While you sat up half the night running credit checks and I don't know what.'

Just as well! Along with Maggie, Wilma hadn't the least intention of telling Ian what she got up to.

'No pain, no gain,' she observed. 'If I'm going to better myself…'

'I'm not good enough for you since you got in tow with that snotty bitch, is that it?'

'Maggie Laird is not a "snotty bitch", Wilma insisted. 'She's a decent, generous–'

'Generous? That's a joke. Woman doesn't have two pennies to rub together. And think of the unpaid hours you put in before she thought of paying you a wage.'

'It was all she could do at the time.'

'And the gear you've bought…'

You don't know the half of it! 'My choice.'

Ian sighed. 'Whatever. You know what I think of your so-called detective agency.'

'Aye,' Wilma planted her hands on her hips. 'And I know why. It's because, Ian Harcus, everything isn't falling into your barrel anymore.'

'It's not…'

'And that's because, after years of suiting other folk, I've a life of my own.'

'There was nothing to stop you,' he began.

'Mebbe. Mebbe not. But I'll tell you this for nothing, I like what I'm doing.'

His lip curled. 'Sitting for hours in front of a computer? Nosing after ne'er-do-wells?'

'It's a whole lot more satisfying than taking cheek from drunks and wiping old men's bums.' Although she'd cut back on her hours, Wilma still held down two part-time jobs: as a barmaid in a Torry pub and a clinical support worker at Aberdeen Royal Infirmary.

'I'll grant you that.' Hungrily, Ian eyed the steaming pan. 'But…'

'What?' Wilma demanded.

Warily, Ian regarded his wife. 'Since you've been working with her, you've changed, Wilma.'

She squared up to him. 'How, exactly?'

'Oh,' he backtracked, 'it's hard to put a finger on. Just, I don't remember when we started out you were quite so…' He pondered for some moments. '…upfront.'

Confident! Wilma interpreted. And not before time. Darren, her first husband, had hammered her into submission. And he wasn't the only one. By the time Wilma got in tow with Ian Harcus, she'd had a bellyful of blokes telling her what to do.

'Must be marrying you that did it.' She elected to humour him. This wasn't the moment to spoil for a fight.

He made puppy-dog eyes. 'Plus, you've shrunk.'

'Shrunk?' She grabbed hold of her love handles.

'Not shrunk, exactly, more…' He struggled for the word. Failed. 'If I'm honest, I liked you better when you were bigger.' Cupping his hands in a weighing motion, 'A fella likes something to get a hold of.'

'Still plenty left.' Grinning, Wilma thrust out her boobs. Then stuck her nose in the air. 'Christ! The tatties have caught.' She ran to the hob, snatched the pan off the gas. Gingerly, she lifted the lid. A cloud of acrid steam filled the air. 'Caught in the nick of time,' she fibbed. She'd just about manage to rescue a plateful. 'And,' she mustered a megawatt smile, 'there's trifle for afters.'

Brian

Brian Burnett sat on his bed-settee, eyes glued to the open laptop in front of him.

He zeroed in on the thumbnail. Read the caption: Nikki, 32, smiling for the camera, slightly protruding front teeth, two curtains of long blonde hair framing her overly-made-up face. Pretty, but a bit on the young side. Plus, he couldn't be doing with all that slap.

He clicked the mouse on the coffee table in front of him: Irene, 39. Round face. Dark bob. Looked a nice enough woman, but at that age probably came with a heap of baggage. Bit like him. With a sigh, he snapped the laptop shut.

Following his dalliance with a young civilian officer by the name of Megan, Brian had registered on a couple of Aberdeen dating sites. Free sites. His acrimonious split from former wife Bev had left him not just homeless but damn near penniless. He'd been devastated when he learned of Bev's affair, doubly so when it became obvious he was the last to know, for it was common knowledge among Brian's fellow officers that Bev played the field. She'd dallied with more than one of his colleagues, it transpired, and for months been consorting with a toy-boy personal trainer. That there had been no children of the union to compound the hurt was a Godsend. During the long, lonely hours spent in his bedsit, Brian had speculated whether things might have turned out differently had there been a family for Bev to take care of. Now, his divorce was in the final stages. He sighed. More expense, and bad enough he'd been driven to going online in the hope of forming a new relationship without paying for the privilege. Nor was there any point in searching further afield. His job as a detective sergeant in Police Scotland's Aberdeen Division left little enough time for relaxation. There was no way he was going to spend it hiking up and down the country in search of love.

He'd agonised over his profile. Play it down and you come over as a wuss, big it up and you run the risk of attracting the wrong sort.

Wrong sort! Brian could write the book. He'd wanted to join the force ever since he could remember, but there were days – more days since he'd been living on his own – he wished he'd chosen another career.

With a despairing look, he took in his surroundings. The bedsit on Urquhart Road hadn't improved since the day he'd first picked up the keys. If anything, it had gone seriously downhill: the carpet crunched with trampled-in grit, the thin curtains hung off one end of their rail, the coffee table was pock-marked by innumerable take-away cartons. Brian no longer bothered to tidy away his bedding of a morning. In consequence, the bed-settee bulged with his duvet and pillows and he had to change his seating position at regular intervals to prevent doing himself an injury.

He'd long since resigned himself to the racket from his upstairs neighbours. The students were nice enough lads, but blithely impervious to his occasional strictures to keep the noise to an acceptable level. And besides, the tenants changed at suspiciously frequent intervals. Brian would pass the time of day with someone on the stairs, but rarely – or so it seemed – the same face twice.

Right on cue there was a bang from overhead, followed by a burst of raucous laughter. Brian tensed. What had happened to his New Year resolutions: find somewhere decent to live, a companion to share it with? Then there was his career. He'd been stuck at sergeant long enough. He'd raised the idea of promotion with his immediate superior, Detective Inspector Allan Chisolm, but it appeared to have gone no further.

Brian closed his eyes. Almost halfway through the year and he'd achieved eff all.

And whose fault is that? He had to hold his hands up, he'd let himself get stuck in a rut: at home, at work. As for his love life, his thoughts turned to Maggie Laird. If he hadn't put off time there, got himself embroiled in her PI business, who knows what progress he could have made? Brian had carried a torch for Maggie ever since he and his best mate, George, had trained together at Tulliallan. Watched from the sidelines as the two courted, then married, produced two children and settled in a neat bungalow in Mannofield. He'd been gutted when George opted for early retirement rather than face a disciplinary panel after a major drugs trial had collapsed amid accusations of perjury and police corruption, devastated when his friend had been found dead. Brian's subsequent wooing of the widowed Maggie had been a catalogue of errors: over-eagerness on his part, connivance on hers. Or so he saw it. In her headlong rush to build George's struggling business, she'd used Brian shamelessly: milking him for inside information, picking him up and dropping him at will.

Tears pricked his eyelids. He'd been well and truly shafted, first by Bev, then by Maggie. But all that was behind him. He'd consign Bev to history. As for Maggie, he'd maintain the friendship, for George's sake if nothing else. But at a distance. Offer practical support when called upon, as he had when the boy, Colin, had got himself in trouble, but no more.

Thumps resounded from above.

Brian opened his eyes.

He performed a few neck rolls, stretched his arms and stood up.

Rubbing his lower back, he ambled through to the tiny kitchen. The worktop was crammed with unwashed crockery and purchases from his rare shopping trips – tins of tuna chunks and value baked beans, a carton of Bran Flakes, a bottle of own brand tomato ketchup – which somehow he never got around to putting away.

He filled the kettle, switched it on, changed his mind.

Opening the fridge, he reached for a beer. Not that there was much else: a days-old sandwich, a small carton of milk, a Greggs' sausage roll.

He flipped the cap off the bottle and took a long draught.

Time to get your finger out!

He squared his shoulders, strode back through to his living-room and resumed his position on the sofa-bed.

Brow furrowed, he re-booted his laptop.

Bugger the dating sites. He Googled 'Aberdeen letting agents'.

Once he had a decent roof over his head, the rest would follow.

Too Little Too Late

'Too little, too late.' The guidance master raised his eyes from the desk.

'But I thought…' Maggie began.

'…that he'd pulled his socks up? Yes, and no.' Will Mackie turned to Colin, who sat, head bowed, on a high-backed chair. 'You've given it your best, I accept. But I'm afraid, given the number of days you were absent from school last year, you've left it far too late to make up the ground.'

Colin raised his head. A pink tide-mark rose from his shirt collar and crept slowly upwards.

He looked to his guidance teacher, then his mother and back again.

He opened his mouth to speak. 'I…I…' Thought the better of it, lowered his head again.

'But surely,' Maggie came to his rescue. 'We won't know where we're at until the results of this year's Highers are out?' She'd requested this meeting for an up-date on her son's progress. Col was unforthcoming at the best of times, but since he'd received a police reprimand for cannabis possession, his responses to her questions had been monosyllabic.

'Quite so, but Colin's prelims have given us a fair indication.' The guidance master paused to let the significance of this sink in. 'And I'm afraid it doesn't augur well.'

She squirmed in her seat. Awkward enough being on the 'wrong' side of the desk when she was accustomed to being the one in control. Worse still to be the receiver of bad news.

'He only just scraped the marks required, and the school took a chance presenting him for Highers at all. To be frank, it's unlikely the UCAS applications we've lodged will have much chance of success. Indeed, if he were to go up to university, I doubt he'd get through his first year. Now, if Colin were to lower his sights, consider something more…' He hesitated. '…vocational.'

'There's no question of that,' Maggie shot back. 'For the meantime at least.'

She'd been proud as she accompanied her son through the entrance archway that afternoon. Felt their sacrifice – her and George's – in sending their son to be privately educated fully justified. She'd set her heart on seeing Colin follow his sister to university. Both children, as she saw it, set up for life.

'If Colin were willing to commit to a sixth year,' the guidance master ventured, 'that might allow him space to build on the gains he's made.'

Maggie knew that made sense. Colin was young, yet – immature – unlike Kirsty, who'd been collected from the day she started nursery. And angry as she was with him for lying to her about his school attendance record, there were mitigating circumstances. After the trauma of his father's death, another year at school might, indeed, settle him. But there was one obvious downside. She'd assumed Colin would move seamlessly on – as Kirsty had – from fifth year to university, his tuition fees paid. Inured herself to the thought of an empty house should he decide to go away to uni. But a further year's school fees would set her back over £12,000, and that's before she had to dip into her pocket for the uniform and the books and the after-school activities. Maggie made frantic mental calculations. The arrangement with the mortgage company she'd set up after George's death was still in place, so that gave her some leeway. But even given the agency's improved cash flow and her modest salary from the Seaton job, she was stretched to the limit, what with the business and the household expenses and Kirsty's accommodation.

She felt hot, all of a sudden. Raised a hand to her brow, felt it beaded with sweat. Said a silent prayer that it wasn't the start of her menopause.

She hazarded a sideways glance at Colin. Cheeks flushed, chin on chest, he slouched – all arms and legs – on the upright chair.

In that moment, Maggie experienced such a surge of love for the boy she'd given birth to and nurtured and laughed with and agonised over, her eyes welled with tears.

She drew a deep breath. 'I appreciate your frankness, Mr Mackie, as I'm sure does Colin.'

From beneath a protective fringe of hair, her son hazarded a wary look in the teacher's direction.

On unsteady legs, Maggie rose to her feet. 'Thank you.' She extended a hand. 'We'll give your advice careful consideration.'

Justice for George

She spied him at the deli counter. 'Jimmy?' She quickened her steps.

The man's head swung around. His eyes flickered recognition. He didn't smile.

'You don't look overjoyed to see me,' Maggie joked, gaining his side.

'I'm not.' Craigmyle responded, grim-faced. 'If Vera catches me with you, I'm a dead man.'

Maggie scanned the throng of late-afternoon shoppers. 'Where is she?'

'Checking out the clothes. Sent me ahead to get Scotch eggs for the tea.' He threw a nervous glance over Maggie's shoulder. 'I've not long moved back in and, well...' He shrugged. 'It's early days.'

'I understand.' Maggie rushed to reassure him. She was stung, nonetheless. George's long-time partner on the force, and he didn't want to know her. Not that it would be the first time. Maggie had long stopped counting the acquaintances who averted their eyes, turned their heads, even crossed the street since George retired under a cloud from the police rather than suffer the awkwardness of an encounter.

'You've started the new job, then?' One of Vera's preconditions for a reconciliation had been that Jimmy give up his security job at business magnate James Gilruth's clubs and find employment with regular hours.

He nodded. 'Couple of months ago.'

'How's it going?'

He cast another glance over Maggie's shoulder. 'So far so good. The kids are over the moon. Vera, well...' he pulled a rueful face. 'It'll take time.'

'I'm pleased for you, Jimmy,' she forced a smile. 'It's been...'

'Water under the bridge.' Scowling, he cut her short. 'Look, I don't want to be rude, but this whole business…' He broke off. ' I've paid one hell of a price.'

Maggie's blood boiled. *He's paid a price?* Was this the same man whose back George had covered for years: a copper who'd chanced his arm, flouted the rules, and when the ship was sinking, dragged his partner down with him?

The queue shuffled forwards, the two of them with it.

She drew a calming breath. 'I was only…'

'I've done what you asked: held my hands up it was me turned off that tape. There's no more I can do for you, Maggie.'

'Does that mean…?' Her heart plummeted into her shoes. Maggie's whole purpose in life since her husband's untimely death had been to clear him of the allegations that had led to the collapse of a major drugs trial. And it was as a conduit to achieving justice for George that she'd been persuaded to take the reins of his ailing detective agency.

'Of course not. What do you take me for? If they re-open the case – and I doubt that will happen, not now – I'll testify to my statement that it was me turned off that interview tape.' He grinned, suddenly. 'I know you don't have a high opinion of me, but I'm not a complete shit.'

She laid a hand on his arm. 'I know. And thanks for that.' She gave a wry grin. 'It's better than nothing.'

Only just, a small voice said inside her head. Since his discharge from hospital after a near-fatal assault, Bobby Brannigan, whose perjured testimony led to George's disgrace, had, once again, gone to ground, so Maggie was still a long way from achieving her objective.

They neared the head of the queue, Craigmyle's eyes darting back and forth, his agitation visibly heightening. Then, 'There's Vera,' he pointed.

Maggie followed his finger. Sure enough, Vera was working her way down the opposite aisle, pausing every few steps to pick an item off a shelf or check out a label. She looked well, Maggie thought:

trimmer, more relaxed than when… Well, she would, wouldn't she? Maggie allowed herself a smile. Dark days. Please God, they were almost behind her.

Craigmyle grabbed hold of her arm. 'You better go,' he hissed. Or else…'

Maggie decided to cut her losses. It was a cruel twist of fate that they should have met at all. Her local supermarket was at Bridge of Dee. It was only because she'd had some errands to do at that end of town and remembered there was nothing for Colin's tea when he came in from rugby training, that she'd dropped into the superstore in the Beach Boulevard Retail Park.

'I'll let you get on.' She turned and walked away.

Kirsty

'Kirsty!' Maggie caught her daughter by the arm as she exited the kitchen. 'Can I have a word?'

It was only the end of May, but Kirsty's classes had finished for the semester and her exams were behind her. Maggie marvelled at how the time had flown: one minute it was Easter, the next her daughter was home for the summer. Then she felt a familiar wave of guilt. She hadn't taken the kids out to visit her folks since Christmas. Nor had she been out to Oldmeldrum more than a handful of times, making do instead with a weekly phone call.

'A word?' This was accompanied by a dark look. 'What d'you mean?'

'Now you've eaten, I thought we could maybe sit down together, have a chat.'

'What about?' Slouching onto a chair, Kirsty said, 'You're not still banging on about my false pregnancy, are you?'

Maggie sat down opposite. 'No, not at all.' She tried not to think about about the worry Kirsty had put her through the previous year. 'Though I wish it hadn't happened.'

Kirsty sighed, dramatically. 'You and me both.'

'All the same, I hope you've learned from the experience and you'll be more careful in…'

'…future.' Kirsty finished the sentence. 'And I hope, next time I have a hiccup, you don't over-react.'

Over-react? Inwardly, Maggie fumed. Bad enough Kirsty had brought home that lout of a boyfriend, Shaz, without then getting pregnant by him. If it was him, the thought suddenly occurred. 'An unplanned pregnant is rather more than a hiccup.' She worked to keep her voice steady. 'Think of the implications. For your studies, for your job prospects, for…'

Kirsty leapt from her seat. 'I'm just through the door and I'm getting the third degree.'

'You are nothing of the kind,' Maggie retorted. 'And, besides, you've been home for nearly a week.'

'Whatever.' Kirsty turned on her heel. 'I shouldn't have let you talk me into coming back here. I should have stayed in Dundee.'

'You'll be better able to revise at home.'

'That's arguable. But I won't be able to get a decent summer job in Aberdeen, for sure.'

'Of course you will,' Maggie insisted, though her voice lacked conviction. The oil downturn had had a knock-on effect, and even casual jobs were more difficult to come by. 'And there's no need to jump down my throat. Sit down. I only wanted to ask you about your digs for next year.'

'Same as this year.' With bad grace, Kirsty reoccupied her seat. 'Landlord said we can stay on. Lease runs right through.'

Money down the drain, Maggie thought. She buttoned her lip. 'Thing is,' she chose her words with care, 'I have concerns about the area.'

'Magdalen Yard? It's fine, as Dundee goes anyhow.'

'That's just it. You know your dad was worried about you going there to university, and not without reason.' *You want to hear the stories that come out of West Bell Street.* Maggie could remember George's exact words.

'Leave my dad out of this.'

'And although I backed your decision, when you and Sarah moved out of halls, it was on the clear understanding that you would stay somewhere...' Maggie scrabbled for the right adjective. '...safe.'

'Not smart enough for you, is that it?' Kirsty sneered. 'You're such a snob, Mum, you know that? And since you took over the business you've got worse.'

Maggie reddened. 'I don't know what you mean.'

'Since you got in tow with that...creature next door, you've been completely up yourself.'

'I have not.'

Kirsty leaned in. 'Yes, you have. You think you're some ace private detectives, you and her.' She thrust her face into Maggie's. 'But you're kidding yourselves. All you are is a pair of sad, middle-aged housewives.'

Maggie's blood boiled. 'Don't you dare talk to me like that, Kirsty Laird. While you're under my roof I'll ask you to show some respect.'

'It's Dad's roof. It was him paid the mortgage.'

Not anymore.

But wasn't that just typical? One minute, Kirsty was insisting her dad be kept out of the conversation, the next she was throwing him back in Maggie's face.

'It was he who...' She couldn't help correcting her daughter's grammar.

'Didn't I say?' Kirsty spat. 'You're totally up yourself. And you've just proved my point.' Said over her shoulder as she rose and stormed from the room.

II

Mad Mike

'Jeannie?'

The voice was frighteningly familiar.

'Mikey?' She squinted through the security spyhole. 'That you?' She hadn't been expecting him.

A distorted face glowered back. 'Who the hell dae ye think it is, Clint fuckin Eastwood?'

'N-no,' she faltered.

'Well, open the fuckin door.'

Jean Meston eased the door a fraction. She peered through the crack.

'*Now*.' The safety chain strained under the man's weight.

Jean unlatched the chain from its housing. 'Och, Mikey.' She opened her arms, a tentative smile on her lips. 'Ye canna be too sure. No these days.'

Mike Meston stormed past his wife.

Gingerly, she pushed the door to, followed his dark shape down the hall.

'Fuck's sake,' he whirled to face her. 'This how ye've been living?'

Covertly, Jean ran her eyes over the disordered settee, the stained carpet, the ashtray overflowing with cigarette butts. 'I've no had the time, what wi one thing an…' Her voice trailed off.

'I'll gie ye time,' Mike thundered. 'Wean in bed?'

'Naw.' How to explain Willie's absence? 'He's at his Gran's.'

'Get us a beer, then. Ah'm gaspin fur a swallow.'

She stood, immobile.

'Go on.'

There was silence, then, 'There's nae money fur beer.'

He cast her an evil look. 'An ye ken why.'

Jean struggled for an excuse. 'Benefit's no in.'

'Benefit my arse.' Mike stood, hands on hips, legs straddled. 'I'll tell you why there's no fuckin beer. My income's gone up in smoke.'

'Well,' she ventured, 'if you'd stuck wi what you were used to...'

'Puntin the odd nicked phone or carton o fags? Widna keep a roof ower our heids. Too many other punters on the game.'

'But... drugs, Mikey?'

'That's where the money is. An it's no as if it was heavy stuff, like, heroin or naethin. Onywye,' his lips formed a thin line, 'it's your fault it's gone down the tubes.'

'Mine? How?'

'Fur no keepin a tight rein on thon laddie o yours.'

'Yours an aw,' Jean shot back.

'Aye.' Long pause. 'Mebbe.'

'You've a neck.' She drew herself up. 'The way you sent the loon roon pub doors, an him the age he is.'

'Bastard might as weel be occupied if he's no at the school.'

'He wullna go tae the school.'

'That's at your door an aw. He widna get the chance tae skip school if you wurna fuckin blootered in the mornings.'

'Ah wisna blootered. The wean widna get oot o' bed. An wi nae man in the hoose Ah couldna mak him.'

Mike flexed his biceps. 'Ye couldna get a wee loon on his feet, is that what ye're tellin me?'

Jean took a backwards step. 'Aye, that's the God's honest truth. If Wullie's set his heid against it, naebody could. No me. No the teacher. No the Schools Inspector. No the Social. An...' She was grasping at straws, now. 'Ah dinna ken how ye're layin the blame at ma door. Wisna down tae me ye landed yersel in the jail.'

'Dinna even go there, ya idle cunt.'

'It's down tae thon Fatboy,' Jean moved to mollify her husband. 'If Willie hudna got in tow wi him, nane o this wid huv happened.' When, the previous year, Mike had been sent down, he'd dispatched ten-year-old Willie to act in his place as runner for local drug dealer, Christopher Gilruth, who went by the name Fatboy.

'Aye. Weel, he'll no be botherin onybody fur a while.'

'How d'ye ken that if ye jist got oot?'

Mike puffed his chest. 'Jungle drums.'

Jean quailed. If her husband knew about the outcome of the Fatboy affair, what else had he heard? She cosied up to him. 'Hiv ye hud yer breakfast?'

'Naw. Couldna wait tae get doon the road.'

'Come in aboot.' She took him by the sleeve, led him through to the kitchen. 'Ah've no long made a fry-up.'

'Is that what ye'd call it?' Mike Meston eyed the plateful of food. 'Twa eggs an a puddle o beans? Whaur's the meat?'

'There's nae money fur...'

'How d'ye fancy that fur a fry-up, then?' He grasped her by the hair, shoved her face into the plate of food.

She fought for breath as the congealed egg yolks filled her mouth and nose, the still hot beans scalded her skin.

'Be my guest.' He pushed down harder.

Desperately, Jean scrabbled for the edge of the table. She tried to brace herself, push back, but his grip was too strong.

'Fit ur ye sayin tae it now?' He yanked her head up.

She brushed the back of one hand across her face. Gobs of egg and clusters of beans dropped to the floor.

'Weel?'

She stuck two fingers into her mouth. Cleared her throat. 'Naethin.'

He threw her the evils. 'Canna hear you.'

She took a breath. 'Naethin.'

It was then he put the boot in.

Jean felt the searing pain as one of her ribs cracked. Maybe more than one.

She drew her knees up to her chest.

Covered her head with both hands.

A Surprise

'You're up early,' Maggie observed from her stance in the kitchen doorway. 'Are you all right?'

'Fine,' Colin replied, keeping his back to her.

There was something on the hob. 'What are you up to?' She moved forward.

Colin took a step sideways, obscured her view. 'Go back to bed,' he mumbled. 'It's meant to be a surprise.'

Maggie padded through to the bedroom. The king-size bed she'd shared with George was barely rumpled, only an indentation on one pillow and a neat triangle of folded-back duvet to show it had been slept in. Her heart took a little leap. It was at times like this that she felt the loss of her husband most, that and the occasions – increasing in frequency as her children grew more independent – she turned the key in the front door to an empty house.

Retracing her steps to the bathroom, she took a quick pee. Washing her hands, she took notice of the the dark circles under her eyes. That left eye looked normal, at least, not floating off sideways as it did, sometimes, when she was stressed. Maggie had been less aware this past while of folk doing a double-take when they met her for the first time, probably because she was more in control of her life. But her hair was standing out at all angles, the Titian curls sorely in need of a restyle, and her cheekbones jutted prominently. There was a time in her teens she'd have given anything for the hollow cheeks that were *de rigeur* in the modelling world, but this was taking things too far. She resolved to drink more fluids, reward herself with a couple of early nights.

She went back to the bedroom and crept under the duvet.

"A surprise," Colin had said. She closed her eyes, prayed he wouldn't take long. She had a full day ahead: her stint at Seaton

School, a couple of client meetings, precognitions to take, the inevitable pile of paperwork.

'Mum?' A voice in her ear.

Maggie's eyes snapped open.

Colin was standing by the bed, a tray balanced in both hands.

'What's this?' She raised her head from the pillow.

Awkwardly, he dumped the tray on her stomach. 'I've made your breakfast.' A crimson blush rose in his neck and climbed to the roots of his hair. 'Thought it would save you a bit of time.'

Holding the tray steady with one hand, Maggie wriggled up the bed to a sitting position. 'Thanks. What a treat!'

She eyed the items set out on the tray: a mug of milky tea, a glass of what looked like fizzy orange. A blue china egg cup held a boiled egg. On a plate sat a slice of brown toast, roughly cut into soldiers, a knife alongside. There was even a cloth napkin. Maggie couldn't remember when she had last used such a thing. Poor lad. He must have dug it out from the sideboard.

'I'll leave you in peace, then.' Colin backed away from the bed.

'You don't have to.' She patted the duvet.

He sat down. Jumped up again. 'I forgot something.'

He rushed out the door, returning with a teaspoon.

'Thanks.' Maggie smiled. 'That was a lovely thing to do.'

Colin looked down at his feet. 'I wanted to say sorry.'

'What for?

'Bunking off school. Flunking my exams. Giving you grief.'

She held up a hand. 'That's not your...'

'I know you're worried about money,' he cut her off. 'Me doing a sixth year, all that. I realise I've left it late, but I just wanted you to know I'll give the exams my best shot.'

'Oh, Col.' Maggie felt tears prick her eyes. 'I know you will.'

'One more thing.' He shot out of the room.

Maggie took a sip of tea. It was tepid and over-sweet.

She picked up the glass of juice, took a sniff. It was, indeed, Fanta. Bless! She recalled the first time George had brought her breakfast in bed: a bowl of soggy Kellogg's Corn Flakes. It hadn't been much better.

She sliced the top off the egg, reached for the toast.

Colin rushed back in. 'Ta da!' He waved aloft a bunch of flowers, deposited them under her chin.

'Where on earth did you get these?' She inhaled the delicate scent. The lilac freesias wouldn't have been sourced from a garage forecourt. He must have bought them in town.

'Secret,' he said, looking pleased with himself.

Chisolm

'Morning.' Detective Inspector Allan Chisolm's eyes swept the room.

'Morning, sir,' his squad responded from their workstations. By the window, Detective Constable Douglas Dunn broke off from studying his reflection.

'Well, jump to it,' Chisolm snapped.

One by one, they settled around the table: the sergeants yawning and loosening their collars, Susan Strachan tugging at her skirt, Douglas carefully hoicking up his trouser-legs before he sat down.

'What have we got?'

'Assault, burglary, and a missing from home,' DS Brian Burnett reported.

'Scintillating,' Chisolm sighed. 'Let's start with the misper. Give me the background, will you Burnett?'

'Deborah Anne Milne, aged 32. Reported missing by husband at 17.13 on Tuesday after she'd failed to collect her kids from school. Unit dispatched to home address.'

'And?'

'Husband Scott Milne was interviewed and a search made of the property. Seems the wife left in a hurry. As far as was established, Debbie, as she was known, took only the clothes she was wearing, together with her handbag and mobile phone.'

'Won't the phone signal give us her last location?' As usual, Dunn, the token graduate recruit on the team, was first to jump in.

'Switched off,' Brian answered. 'Either that or the battery's run down.'

'Does she have cash? Credit cards?'

'Affirmative.'

'Response officers?' Chisolm demanded.

'Souter and Miller.'

The expression *as thick as mince* came into his head. He'd torn a strip off the pair of them during the Struthers case, hoped they hadn't ballsed-up this time. 'And Debbie was last seen when?'

'Tuesday morning.'

'Hmm.' Scowling, Chisolm eyed his team. 'Thoughts?'

'Marital dispute?' Dunn came back in.

'Husband says not,' his sergeant slapped him down. Brian Burnett still hadn't forgiven Douglas his part in failing to wrap up the Struthers case, where the husband had walked away from an attempted murder charge, and the wife – well, he'd never know what game the wife had played. In consequence, the squad had failed to secure a conviction for either husband or wife.

'Well he would, wouldn't he?' Douglas shot back, undeterred.

'Sounds to me,' Duffy growled, 'like she went off in the huff.'

'Some huff,' Douglas again. 'She's kept it going coming on four days.'

'Four days is nothing,' Duffy retorted, 'when it comes to women. My wife…'

'Cut it out,' Chisolm snapped. 'Could Debbie have run home to mum?'

'Negative,' Brian said. 'No contact there.'

'Friends?'

'Them neither. Seems she was a bit of a homebody, our Debbie. Life revolved around the house and kids.'

'Still, woman must have had friends.'

'Plenty. Other mums, plus she attended a couple of evening classes, but nobody special.'

'The kids, how old?'

'Ten and eleven.'

'Not completely dependent, then.'

'No. The daughter – Chloe she's called – is in first year at Grammar. Jack, the wee boy, attends Gilcomston. He's due to join his sister after the summer.'

'Still,' DC Susan Strachan offered, 'they're young yet, especially the boy.' She fixed Douglas with a challenging look. 'Takes them longer to mature.'

'Is the dad holding the fort?' Chisolm enquired.

'He was, initially, but when Debbie didn't turn up after the first couple of nights his mum moved in.'

'Why not her own mum?'

'Lives in sheltered housing in Midstocket. Another reason Debbie moved to Rosemount. The husband died not long ago and she doesn't keep good health.'

'You all know the stats,' Chisolm drummed his fingers on the table. 'Approximately half of missing persons are found at their home address, the next quarter at friends, the balance walking in a public place. If the misper hasn't come home and she's not with friends, is she on the move? Which begs the question, does she have a passport?'

'Still in the house.' Brian again.

'Access to a computer?'

'Scott and Debbie share a laptop. She has her own iPad. Souter had a look-see, didn't find anything.'

Around the table doubtful looks were exchanged. They all knew of the response officers' cock-up in the Struthers case, when they'd failed to spot a blister pack of pills close to a comatose body.

'Does Debbie have her own car?'

'It's still in the drive and she hasn't taken the keys.'

'Would it be worth to placing a marker on the PNC,' Susan volunteered. 'If she's still in the vicinity, there's nothing to stop Debbie nipping back for it while the husband's at work.'

'Good thinking.' Chisolm jotted a note. 'Is it probable she's in an open space right now: the street, a park, the beach?'

'According to Souter, the only protective clothing she took was a light quilted jacket so, I'd say not.'

'If she's outside, she'll be dead by now,' Duffy observed, glum-faced. 'Aberdeen gets bloody cold at night, even in early summer.'

'In the absence of a body,' Chisolm said, pointedly, 'we'll proceed on the basis that isn't the case. Do I take it we've notified the National Missing Person Unit and posted Debbie's details on social media?'

Brian consulted his notes. 'Yes sir.'

'And a description circulated to all units?'

'Affirmative. Bus and taxi drivers as well, together with hospitals and the ambulance service.'

'And she's in good shape? Medical history sound? No mental health issues?'

'Appears so.'

'Right, folks.' Chisolm shuffled his papers. 'According to the risk assessment, there's no indication Debbie Milne is in danger, so where do you suggest we start?'

'With the family,' Douglas shot back. 'That's always the first place…'

'Yeah, yeah,' Duffy intervened. 'Do you think we were born yesterday?'

Chisolm silenced them with a hard look. 'We need to get tasks assigned and a timetable agreed. Susan, I want you to interview Scott Milne again, dig deeper into the background. Douglas, you go along.'

Douglas smirked.

Susan threw him the evils.

'Have another dekko at that computer and iPad,' Chisolm continued. 'But, be warned, no stepping out of line this time.' That last occasion, when Douglas had hacked into an eminent accountant's computer, was still fresh in Allan Chisolm's mind. 'And both of you, take another good look around.'

'Right, sir.' Susan leapt to attention.

Sulky-faced, Douglas Dunn made no attempt to move.

'Duffy, get yourself down to the school gates, find out who Debbie was chummy with, when they last spoke, how she appeared?'

'Sir,' Sergeant Bob Duffy said without enthusiasm. In normal circumstances, these tasks would have fallen to his fellow sergeant, Dave Wood. But Wood was on sick leave, claiming a bad back. In

Duffy's opinion, the miserable bastard was using every trick in the book to coast up to his retirement date.

'And check out CCTV opportunities in the area.'

'Sir.'

'Burnett, look at the husband's background: job history and so on.'

'Yes sir.'

'Okay. We've spent enough time on this for now.' He closed the folder, set it aside. 'Who's going to brief me on these burglaries?'

Seaton School

The Seaton School staffroom had emptied and Maggie was making the most of the peace and quiet when Glen Mason sidled up. 'Fancy a drink?' He towered over her.

She'd secured a part-time position as a teaching assistant there in the face of George's opposition. Exposed to the full force of the North Sea, the Seaton district of Aberdeen, on the opposite side of the city from Maggie's home in Mannofield, is divided from the university campus in Old Aberdeen by King Street, the arterial route north. Comprising a mix of pre-war council four-in-a-block flats and featureless high rises, the area is marked by severe deprivation. But, despite George's fears for her safety, Maggie had applied for the post. It had been a good move. Although she worked only a few hours a week and had to deal with some distressing situations, after years as a stay-at-home mum Maggie had grown in confidence. When George died, the job had proved a lifeline.

'A drink?' she echoed, now, looking up from the lesson plans she'd been studying.

Glen Mason had been drafted in to Seaton School on a supply basis to cover the sudden departure of Maggie's colleague, young teacher Ros Prentice, who had fled from a controlling husband back to the parental home in Edinburgh. Maggie was saddened by the loss of her friend and ally. She'd been heartened when Ros joined the staff the previous year: buoyed to find someone on her own wavelength, grateful for back-up when the old guard got too much. But there was no denying the introduction of a male member of staff had lightened the atmosphere in the staffroom. And taken the spotlight off pupil support, for which Maggie was thankful.

'No.' She indicated her half-empty mug of tea. 'I'm good.'

'Hah, hah!' He settled his large frame on a seat alongside. 'Seriously, though...' He leaned in close. '...can I take you out for a drink sometime?'

'Well,' Maggie felt a flush rise in the nape of her neck, said a silent prayer it didn't show. She was surprised she'd even registered with the new man, far less made an impression. Teaching assistants – together with caretakers and administrative staff – were generally considered nothing more than 'mum's army': fit only for washing paint pots and wiping noses. 'I don't know.'

'Come on. It's just a drink I'm talking about. Won't hurt.'

'No.' Maggie summoned a weak smile. 'I can see that. But…' Her mind raced. Glen was attractive enough: just short of six feet tall, with a rugby player's build and an unruly thicket of dark hair. And recently divorced, she'd gleaned from staffroom gossip. He'd moved up from Glasgow, and had already charmed the older members of staff with his good-natured banter.

But it had been so long since anyone made a pass at Maggie. Decades. If you didn't count Brian, the thought occurred, but Brian was old news. And then there was Allan Chisolm. Maggie could no longer deny the frisson she felt in the DI's company. In her cold, lonesome bed, she'd replayed more than once their fleeting embrace. But the inspector had seen his move as a lapse of judgement. Hadn't he admitted, "I overstepped the mark"? She resolved to dismiss both detectives from her thoughts. They were too closely connected to her professional life.

Glen Mason was another story: newly single, presentable, good fun. Plus, he'd made clear he found her attractive. Maggie had been ploughing a lonely furrow for long enough. Wasn't it time she got a life of her own? Then prudence took over. *Don't shit in your own nest!* The old adage was vulgar, but true. Negotiating school politics could be tricky enough at the best of times without getting romantically involved with another member of staff. And, besides, Maggie had stretched the boundaries since she'd taken on the agency: ducking out early on more than one occasion, conducting business in school time. She couldn't afford to jeopardise her income stream by drawing attention to herself.

'I've got a lot on at the moment,' she ad-libbed. 'Can I…'

The door flew open. 'Anne here?' a voice asked. 'No, obviously not.' It banged shut again.

'…take a rain-check.'

Glen helped Maggie out. 'Sure. Only don't leave it too long.' He straightened, grinning. 'I might get snapped up.'

Tell Me Something New

'Milne case,' DI Chisolm led the daily briefing. 'We'll kick off with you, Brian. Anything to report?'

'No, boss,' Brian responded. 'Leastways not as of 22.00 hours last night. We did get something in yesterday from Missing Persons: female answering to Debbie's description found in a confused state somewhere near Kilmarnock. Turns out the woman had mental health issues, wandered off from a supported unit.'

'Classic,' George Duffy observed. They'd all seen the fallout from care in the community, where adults with often complex mental health problems were discharged from hospitals to live in supervised accommodation.

Chisolm ignored this. 'Did we get anything from CCTV in the Belvidere Street vicinity?'

'We're still working through that.'

'What about social media postings?'

Brian grimaced. 'Just the usual head-bangers.'

'Anything from you lot?' Chisolm turned his attention to the rest of his squad.

'I managed to get hold of the husband.' Susan Strachan was determined to get in before Dunn. 'Took a while. He's a project manager with an oil services company. Took an age to pin down.'

'And?' Chisolm's tone screamed impatience.

'He confirmed what's in Souter's report: that everything's hunky-dory in the marriage, Debbie seemed happy enough, disappearance is completely out of character, and…'

'Yes, yes,' Chisolm interrupted. 'Tell me something new.'

Susan picked at her nail polish. She'd so wanted succeed in the Struthers case, been gutted when it went down the tubes. This was a fresh opportunity to make her mark. She drew a deep breath. 'I got the feeling Scott Milne was holding something back.'

'As in?'

Susan felt a flush creep up the collar of her blouse and suffuse the roots of her hair. 'Hard to say,' she stammered.

Chisolm tuned to Douglas. 'What's the computer whizz got to contribute?'

'Not a lot,' Douglas muttered. 'When I called at the house there was nobody in but the granny.'

'That was a problem?'

'She couldn't lay her hands on the iPad,' he fidgeted. 'Sorry, sir.'

Chisolm raised his eyes to the ceiling. 'You'd better get back there. And pronto.'

Dunn studied the table-top. 'Sir.'

'I hope you've made more progress, Burnett.' Chisolm turned to his sergeant.

'Done a load of digging. Scott Milne's HR people were very helpful, once I'd explained the situation.' He cleared his throat. 'Data protection and that. Confirmed he's been in continuous employment with them for the past seven years. No history of sickies, nothing. Hard worker. Gets on with most folk in the office. Seems the real deal. As to extra-mural activities, there's nothing to show Milne has any hobbies. He did play football, five-a-side, way back, but seems to have given that up. The financials…' Brian hesitated, '…were a bit trickier. Short of getting authority to go into his bank details…' And I take it we're not at that stage yet?' He looked to Chisolm for confirmation.

'Affirmative.'

'There's a limit to what I was able to find. However, what I can tell you…' He perked up. '…is that the Milnes have a large mortgage with Santander on their house in Belvidere Street. They also have a charge account with John Lewis and store card with Debenhams.'

'Good work, Burnett,' Chisolm nodded, approvingly.

'What I also gleaned from a quick chat with one of Milne's colleagues, is that the company has embarked on a cost-cutting exercise.'

'Par for the course,' Chisolm came right back. 'Can't be alone, not in Aberdeen.' The collapse in the price of oil had depressed not only the job market but housing sales and all manner of ancillary businesses. 'All the same, let's see if we can press him on that.'

'You next.' He addressed Bob Duffy.

Duffy re-settled his large frame on the moulded plastic seat. 'Been to both schools, first thing and end of the day. Spoke to a fair few mums. They'd nothing but praise for Debbie Milne. Nice woman. Always willing to pass the time of day. Kids turned out smart, never spoke back.'

'What about the husband? Did his name come up?'

'Only that he was a good provider. They'd not long moved into the Rosemount property, started out in a chalet bungalow in Craigiebuckler. She's a real wee home-maker, Debbie, by the sound of things. Meanwhile,' Duffy rolled his eyes, 'he's working all hours to pay for it.'

'Nothing new there,' Chisolm observed, with what might have been a trace of bitterness. 'Anything else?'

'Only that Debbie mentioned someone called Sam.'

Douglas piped up. 'Male or female?'

Duffy scowled. 'Didn't say.'

'Well,' Chisolm retorted. 'Since you've so helpfully posed the question, that's another thing you should be keeping in mind when you examine that iPad.'

'Sir.' Douglas blushed scarlet to the tips of his artfully gelled hair.

In Our Prime

'Good day?' Wilma turned from her stance at the sink.

'Not great,' Maggie replied, leaning back against Wilma's massive fridge-freezer. 'I got torn off a strip at school.'

'What for?'

'Coming in late. You?'

'I've seen better. Ian's been kicking off again about the hours I've been keeping.' She made a tragic face. 'Why else do you think I'm standing here peeling tatties?'

'The way to a man's heart.' Maggie couldn't help but smile. 'All the same, he has a point.'

'Agreed. Not that I'm going to admit it.'

'Something has to be done,' Maggie insisted.

Wilma dropped the last of the potatoes into a pan. 'You said it.' She wiped her hands on a tea towel. 'I couldna hack another separation, that's for sure.' Referencing their falling out earlier that year when her husband had given her an ultimatum and she'd fled back to Torry. 'And Ian's been sounding off...'

Maggie cut her short. 'No more Ian. I've had it with men for today.'

'Ooh,' Wilma's eyes popped, 'tell me more.'

Maggie grimaced. 'New man at school asked me out.'

'And?' Wilma pressed. 'What did you say?'

'Turned him down.'

'You never did.' She let out a long exhalation. 'You're such a wuss, Maggie Laird. Fella comes on to you, and you run a mile.'

'I did not "run a mile",' Maggie protested. 'I said I'd think about it.'

'Ah.' Wilma said with a knowing look. 'Now we're getting to it.'

'We're not "getting to it" at all, Wilma Harcus. So you can wipe that look off your face right now.'

'Don't you fancy him, like?'

Maggie sighed. 'I've never thought about it. I work with him, that's all.'

'Glen from Glasgow,' Wilma teased. 'Has a ring to it.'

'If you say so.'

'Hot, is he?'

Maggie shrugged. 'How would I know?'

'You'll never find out if you don't give it a go. Ever since you've been on your own, all you've done is work and more work. You're a fine-looking woman. Isn't it time you got a life of your own?

'I'm a forty-something widow with a two kids and a mortgage.'

'So,' Wilma countered, 'Look at me: a forty-something divorcee with two kids and...' She thrust out her stomach. '...a corporation.'

Despite herself, Maggie giggled.

'Seriously, you're looking good, Maggie.'

She blushed. 'You think?'

'I do. When I think back to when we got together first. Christ,' she rolled her eyes, 'the stuff you used to wear: wee granny blouses; trousers hanging off your arse. And them Hush Puppies? I mean, who would...?'

'They were not Hush Puppies,' Maggie interrupted. 'They were Footglove. There's a difference.'

Wilma shrugged. 'Whatever.'

Talk about the pot calling the kettle black? Maggie's mind jumped back to the day Wilma rolled up on her doorstep – all fake tan, low-cut top and sprayed-on leggings – to moot the idea of taking on George's business. Thanked her stars Wilma had toned down her own appearance. Tactfully, she kept her counsel.

'The way I see it,' Wilma asserted, 'the two of us can still pull with the best of them.'

'I beg to disagree. You can "pull" maybe. You're different from me in that regard.'

'Not so different,' Wilma came straight back. 'Where the fellas are concerned, we're two bonny quines.'

'Bonny *old* quines,' Maggie joked.

'Bollocks! Wilma dismissed her. 'We're in our prime, I'd say. Aye,' she cupped a breast in each palm, gave them a jiggle. 'In our fuckin prime.'

Whatever

'Mrs Meston?' A face popped through the cubicle curtains. 'I'm Doctor Jayawardena. I've come to have a look at you.' The white-coated figure glanced down at his notes. 'Are you okay with it if I call you Jean?'

The woman lying on the trolley regarded the young man with hostile eyes. He couldn't have been much more than twenty. Jean wondered where they got their qualifications, these foreigners. If they had any.

'Whatever,' she responded, her voice heavy with resignation.

'Before I examine you,' the doctor went on. 'Can you tell me how you came about your injuries?'

Jean Meston lifted a feeble hand from the sheet, let it drop. 'Fell down two sets of stairs.'

'You live in Seaton, is that right?'

'If you say so.'

'But the address I have here,' Dr Jayawardena consulted his notes once more. 'They're four-in-a-block flats. Correct me if I'm wrong.'

'Yes,' she winced in pain. 'You're right enough. It's a flat I live in. An *upstairs* flat.' She emphasized the word.

'But,' the doctor came back, 'two flights, didn't you say?'

'I fell halfway down.' She affected a huge sigh. 'Then I got up and fell down the rest.'

He threw her a quizzical look. 'Quite.'

'Are you going to examine me now?' Her voice was full of impatience.

'In a moment. Bear with me, if you will.' Limpid brown eyes sought her own. 'I'm required to put these questions to you, Mrs Meston. I'm sure you understand.'

Jean did. She'd made so many visits to A&E, the staff had stopped asking. This guy, she sighed again in resignation, must be new.

'So,' he continued. 'Your fall…'

Jean raised her eyes to the ceiling. She'd rehearsed her story, knew not to go into too much detail. 'I was coming down the stairs with the washing and I fell.'

'And that was when?'

'Yesterday morning.'

'But you've left until today to come into hospital?'

She shrugged. 'Had a headache.' She raised her head off the pillow. 'Now…' Rattled, she lapsed from polite English into her native Doric. 'Ur ye gaun tae examine me or ur ye no?'

Gently, the young man prodded Jean's face: cheeks, nose, jaw. His hands moved downwards to her ribs.

She flinched as his fingers explored.

He straightened. 'There doesn't appear to be anything broken, but we'll do an X-ray, just to make sure. Then there's the headache. We'd best keep you here overnight, just to be safe.'

'But,' Jean argued, 'my man, he'll be needin his tea.'

Dr Jayawardena smiled. 'I'm sure he'll manage – just this once – don't you?'

'No,' Jean wailed, a look of abject terror on her face. 'Mikey's fussy aboot his food. An he's no long oot the…' She broke off.

There was a long silence, then, 'I see.'

Val

Maggie was typing invoices on her laptop when her FaceTime pinged.

She pressed 'Accept.'

Val's face filled the screen. 'Are you free to speak?' she asked.

'To you?' Maggie responded, shoving her paperwork to one side. 'Always.'

A couple of years had passed since Maggie's closest friend had gone to live abroad, and she missed her terribly.

A shadow crossed Maggie's face. 'Is everything okay? It's just…'

'I know. It's been too long. Sorry about that. Don't know where the time has gone since Mum came out here. I don't seem to have a minute in the day.'

'I can understand,' Maggie sympathised. Val's mother suffered from Alzheimer's disease and needed constant attention. When Phil, Val's husband, had been sent by his oil company on a short-term contract to Dubai, they'd taken Val's mum with them rather than put her into residential care. 'How is your mum?' she offered up a silent prayer of thanks her own parents were in good shape.

'Happy as Larry. She hasn't a care in the world, thank God. And of course she's waited on hand and foot.'

Maggie felt a small stab of envy. Val had said they employed servants. What Maggie wouldn't give to have even a few hours' help in the house.

'And you? How are things?'

Val shrugged. 'Much the same. There's not a lot to do here.' She made a comic face. 'Not unless you like shopping. Other than that, it's all work-related. If we're not entertaining we're out being entertained.'

'Sounds very glamorous.'

'The reality,' Val grimaced, 'is anything but.' She hesitated.

'However, I didn't ring to talk about me. It's you I'm worried about. How are you, Maggie?'

'Oh,' Maggie kept her voice neutral. 'Doing away.'

'The kids?'

She groaned. 'Don't go there. Colin's fluffed his exams. As for Kirsty, we go head-to-head all the time.'

'History repeating itself,' Val observed.

'How do you mean?'

'Same as you and your own mum. Kirsty and you have the same temperament, so it's hardly surprising sparks fly.'

'Oh,' Maggie responded, lamely. 'I hadn't thought of it like that.'

'Speaking of your folks...'

'Both fine. At least...' Maggie felt a rush of guilt.

'Give them my best.'

'I will.'

'And the agency? You must be a fully-fledged private investigator by now.'

Maggie summoned a smile. 'I'm working on it.'

'Whatever, you're looking good.'

Maggie patted her curls. 'You think?' She'd kept the short hairstyle she'd got at Gilruth's fancy salon, although shortage of funds had sent her back to her local hairdresser.

'Definitely.'

'To tell the truth,' she blurted, 'I'm having second thoughts.'

'About the detective agency?'

'Not the business so much. That's running pretty well now the systems are in place. No, it's the...' She floundered.

'Staff?' Val offered.

'Sort of.'

'That's one thing I don't miss,' Val said, emphatically. 'People don't want to work anymore, not in the UK. Whereas here...'

'It's not a question of commitment,' Maggie rushed to correct her. 'If anything, it's the other way.'

Val frowned. 'I don't get you.'

'It's my partner, Wilma,' Maggie confided. 'From the day George died, she's been an absolute rock. And don't get me wrong, I've been thankful for her support. But she's so full-on. I feel she sweeps me along, doesn't give me space to think.'

'That's no use,' Val said, firmly. 'You want to sort that out before it becomes a real problem.'

'I know,' Maggie said. 'But how?'

'You need to be more assertive.'

Maggie sighed. 'That's easier said than done. On the few occasions I've argued my case, we've ended up having a real ding-dong. Last time, we nearly fell out for good.'

'You need to distance yourself. Start by backing off a tad. Take it in stages. See how it goes.'

'I'll try.'

'Sounds like you're too wrapped up in the business, Maggie. When you're as immersed as you seem to be, you don't make good business decisions. Maybe it's time you broadened your horizons. Nothing major: see a few more people, give yourself a treat now and then.'

'You're right.' Val's advice confirmed what Maggie had been thinking: Wilma had a big heart, but she wasn't invested in the business to the same degree: neither dependent on the income to pay the bills nor motivated, as Maggie was, by a higher purpose.

'Look, I'm sorry,' Val said, 'but I really should go. I can't leave Mum for long or she gets agitated. But I was thinking of you, and…'

'I'm glad you rang. I've been thinking about you, too.'

'You could always ring me.'

'I know. But I'm spread so thin these days,' Maggie complained. 'I never get a minute to myself. And, besides, I don't like to, in case it's the wrong time of day, or you're in the middle of something, or…'

'I'm never too busy to talk to you. That's your problem, Maggie. You spend too much time thinking about other people. You need to do what you want for a change.'

'You're right.' Maggie made a mental resolution to ring Dubai once a month at least. Val was someone in whom she could confide her innermost thoughts: things she couldn't do with her children or even with Wilma. Especially with Wilma, she realised, now.

A Coincidence

'We'll start with the domestic,' Chisolm announced. Get that out the way before we tackle the others.'

'Talk about our daily penance!' Bob Duffy rolled his eyes. Not a day went past without one or more domestic abuse cases landing on their desks. 'It was bad enough trying to navigate your way through one of those before the new legislation. Now you'd have to be a fucking mind-reader as well as a marriage counsellor.'

'And don't let's get started on the MeToo and Time's Up movements,' Douglas Dunn chipped in, never one to miss an opportunity to make mischief. 'Talk about escalating a situation.'

'Ever the misogynist,' Susan sniped. 'If you hadn't been so blinkered on the Struthers case...'

'And you'd followed the protocols.'

'May I remind you,' Chisolm cut them short, 'Police Scotland treat all cases of domestic abuse with the utmost seriousness.' He selected a folder from the pile in front of him, flipped it open, scanned the top sheet. 'Christ,' he groaned. 'Not again.'

''Fraid so, sir,' Brian remarked. 'Neighbour complained of hearing shouting.'

'In Seaton?' Duffy joked. 'Never.'

Brian ignored him. 'Seems Mad Mike came down the road from Peterhead spoiling for a fight.'

'Figures.' Douglas said.

Mike Meston was well-known to the team. A known fence and repeat offender, he'd last crossed their consciousness when he'd been banged up for dealing in class B drugs.

'We've taken statements, but the wife won't press charges.'

'What's new?' DC Susan Strachan had lost count of the number of domestic incidents she'd attended where the spouse had refused to co-operate.

Chisolm ran his eyes down the top sheet on his file, 'Has our misper turned up? Burnett?' He engaged Brian.

'No sir. I've had another chat with the husband, not that he told me anything I didn't already know other than put a name to Debbie's pal: Samantha Clark, aged 33.'

'Living where?'

'Aberdeen, for the time being at least.'

'Have you got an address?'

'No, sir.'

'Phone number?'

'Negative. All Debbie's contacts are on her mobile. Which…'

Chisolm finished the sentence. '…she took with her.' He turned to Dunn. 'Did you lift anything off that iPad?'

'Nothing significant. When she wasn't seeing to her kids, seems Debbie filled her days either sewing or watching soaps. Which would account for her password.' He tittered. 'Hollyoaks32. There wasn't a dickey-bird from Sam, that's for sure.'

'Isn't that a bit odd,' Susan remarked. 'A friend you think enough of to mention at the school gates, yet you don't have a single email?'

'If you were more clued-up,' Douglas shot her down, 'you'd know they'd have their conversations on Facebook.'

'And if you weren't so full of yourself,' Susan rejoined.

Chisolm cut her short. 'Do we have a photo of this Sam?'

Several heads ducked at once.

'Douglas, you've set yourself up as the techie, can I take it you've gone into Debbie's Facebook page?'

He puffed out his chest. 'I have, indeed.'

'And?'

'She shut it down the night before she disappeared.'

'But, surely,' Susan interjected, 'if her oldest friend had come back on the scene, she'd have posted that on Facebook, photographs as well.'

'I told you,' Douglas rounded on her, 'I already checked: Snapchat, Instagram, the lot.'

'Don't you think that's weird?'

He sniffed. 'Your word, not mine.'

Chisolm sighed. You're like a couple of kids. He turned. 'Duffy, anything from you?'

'No sir.'

'Wood still on a sickie?'

Around the table, covert looks were exchanged. With dwindling resources, they were all hacked off with their sergeant's protracted absence, but no one was going to shop him for malingering. He wouldn't be the first police officer to suffer workplace fatigue and hide behind a sick note from a sympathetic GP.

'I take it that's a "yes". Anyone else have anything to contribute?' He directed his interrogatory gaze towards Strachan, Dunn and the uniforms who were present.

'My money's still on the marital angle,' Dunn insisted.

'There's no evidence,' Susan countered.

'Sez who?' Douglas came back with a sneer. 'Weren't you the one said the husband was dodgy?'

'Yes, but…' She stopped, mid-sentence. She'd find that evidence, she resolved. Stuff it down Douglas's throat.

'Pack it in,' Chisolm snapped. 'You pair would argue with your bloody shadows.'

Douglas smirked.

Susan hung her head.

'This friend,' Brian threw in, 'could Debbie have shacked up with her?'

'What?' Duffy started from his seat. 'Lezzies, like?'

'No,' Brian protested, 'that's not what I'm suggesting. More that Debbie's been cheesed off for some reason, and Sam has provided a shoulder to cry on.' He shrugged. 'There doesn't seem to be anyone else.'

'There's no evidence for that, either,' Douglas asserted, his pink shirt swelling with self-importance. 'This Sam creature seems to have flown in from nowhere. She could as easily have flown back out.'

'Bit of a coincidence, though, don't you think?' Brian came back in. 'Debbie's not long moved into her dream house, kids are in good schools. Then Sam rolls up and Debbie goes AWOL.'

'Any advance on that?' Chisolm eyed the others, in turn.

Nobody spoke.

Chisolm furrowed his brow. 'It's unusual not to have a single lead at this stage in the game, so we'll have to settle for hypotheses. Which are?'

'A marital upset?' Douglas was sticking to his guns.

'Debbie has run off with her friend Sam?' Brian suggested.

'Or,' Susan ventured. 'Both.'

Chisolm nodded his approbation. 'Quite possibly. So, we have two main lines of enquiry: the family and Sam. Strachan, I want you to address the marital aspect. Get back to Belvidere Street, talk to the granny, the neighbours, see if you can add substance to that gut feeling of yours. And while you're there, do another sweep of the property. God only knows what those uniforms could have missed.'

'Right you are, sir.'

'Burnett, pay a visit to Debbie's mum, see what you can dredge up.'

'Sir.'

'The rest of you concentrate on Samantha Clark. I need chapter and verse on that woman: what she does, where she's living, when she last saw Debbie Milne and under what circumstances?'

'Sir.' Several voices echoed.

'Duffy, run Sam Clark's name through the system, see what it throws up.'

'We've already done that, sir.'

'Well, do it again. 'See if you can find anybody by that name who fits Sam's profile. Draw on DVLA records, cross-checked against the passport office, whatever. Germane to that is to source a likeness.'

'And if that doesn't work?' Duffy asked in a doom-laden voice.

'Then,' Chisolm allowed a pregnant pause, 'we run it through HOLMES.'

A ripple of apprehension ran around the room. They all knew the Home Office Large Major Enquiry System would spew out a stream of extraneous information that might bog them down for days.

'I don't think we're quite at that stage,' Brian added, diplomatically.

'Then you'd better find me a photo of Sam Clark some other way.'

'Debbie's phone?' Duffy suggested. Anything for a shortcut.

'She's taken it with her, eejit,' Brian made light of his colleague's slip-up.

'Go back to the husband?' Susan suggested. 'He might have one on his phone.'

'Not bloody likely,' Douglas smirked, 'if he hated the woman's guts.'

Susan rounded on him. 'They could have asked Scott Milne to take a photo of the two of them together.'

'They'd have done that on their own phones, either that or taken a selfie.'

Susan coloured. 'I suppose.' Unwilling though she was to agree with Douglas on anything, she had to admit he was right.

'Scott might have a holiday snap of the pair of them,' Brian volunteered.

'Won't that be ancient, though?' Duffy grumbled. 'Thought they hadn't been in touch since they were teenagers.'

'Right enough,' Brian conceded.

'Whatever. Get a recent likeness of that woman. And get it pronto.' Chisolm's thoughts turned to his DCI, who would soon be chasing him for a progress report. 'This has gone on long enough.'

A Cocktail Waitress

'Ta-da!' Face alight, Kirsty burst through the front door.

'Oh, hi,' Maggie was making her way downstairs with a pile of washing. 'I didn't expect you back so soon.'

Kirsty beamed. 'I've got a job.'

'That's great,' Maggie deposited the dirty laundry on the bottom step. 'Come on through,' she led the way into the front room, 'and tell me about it.'

Kirsty plumped onto the sofa. 'As a cocktail waitress.'

'A cocktail waitress?' Maggie echoed.

That's right,' Kirsty ran on. 'In that new place in Belmont Street. Didn't think I'd stand a chance. There were scads of people up for it and I've no experience, but they said they'd give me training.'

'To be a waitress?' Maggie queried. She failed to see how serving drinks could be that complicated.

'It's more involved than you think. You need to know the licensing laws, be able to pull a pint. Then there's the different cocktails: which glass to use, the measurements, the method, the garnish.'

'Oh,' Maggie assumed what she hoped was a positive expression. 'What sort of hours?'

'Twenty to start. Four-hour shifts, evenings and weekends, but there's the opportunity for sickness cover, may be a bit of overtime, and…' Her words tailed off. 'You don't look too impressed.'

Maggie's mind raced. The job would be minimum wage, she was sure. And if this bar were open into the small hours… Mentally, she calculated the cost of a taxi. She'd hoped Kirsty would land something full-time, manage to save something towards the next semester, or at least help with the cost of her keep. She was a picky eater, preferred to 'graze' as she called it, rather than sit down to a cooked meal like her brother. And the avocados and exotic fruits that went into her smoothies had already escalated the cost of

Maggie's weekly shop.

'I'm pleased for you, pet,' she summoned a smile. 'It's just, I thought you'd be going for something more…' Her thoughts scrambled. '…vocational.'

Kirsty scowled. 'Like what?'

'A lawyer's office, something like that.'

'Not upmarket enough for you, is that it? You're such a snob.'

Kirsty had a point, Maggie had to concede. A cocktail bar, to her mind, was no place for a young girl. She drew a calming breath. 'I'd prefer you put your law studies to use, that's all.'

'What? Do an unpaid internship like last year?'

'If need be. I'd rather take on extra work rather than see you slave in some dive for a pittance.'

'You can talk,' Kirsty cut in. 'Wiping kids' bums half the week, chasing dirty scrotes the other.'

'If it was good enough for your dad,' Maggie came right back.

'Leave my dad out of it.'

Here we go again! Maggie drew a calming breath. It didn't seem to matter what she said or did these days, she was always in the wrong.

III

Life and Death

The young man pushed his cup to one side. He rose from the table. 'Scott Milne.' He extended a hand.

Maggie Laird proffered her own.

'Can I get you something?'

Maggie shook her head. 'I'm fine.'

'Thanks for agreeing to meet me at such short notice.'

'No problem.' She made a mental note of his physical features: five foot ten, stocky build, dark hair cut in a fashionably spiky style, fair complexion, hazel eyes. He was dressed in a two-piece grey suit, brown pointed shoes, white shirt open at the neck, no tie. Maggie registered the red ID lanyard swinging from his neck, the old scratches on the backs of his hands. Her eyes sought his. 'Life and death, you said.'

'Well, I…'

Damn and blast! As she took a seat, Maggie's eyes dropped to the old pair of jeans she'd pulled on when she came off the phone that morning, the bobbled jumper showing its age under her business jacket. She'd run a comb through her hair, shot out of the house without a scrap of makeup, run a couple of red lights to make it to their meeting. And now the prospective client was about to back-track. She could feel it in her bones.

'It's my wife,' Scott Milne sat down, leaned across the table. 'Debbie. She's disappeared.'

'I'm afraid,' Maggie began. Then, catching her reflection in the mirrored wall, brought herself up short. Her right eye was in focus, her left floating, as it did, sometimes, when she was pushed. She cursed her naivety for turning out on what was obviously a wild goose chase when she could still have been happily tucked up in bed.

His face crumpled. 'You're going to turn me down. I expected as much. That's why…' He broke off, agitated.

'…you were so circumspect on the phone?'

He nodded. 'Thought you'd tell me to go to the police.'

'Quite right,' she acquiesced. 'The police should always be your first port of…'

'I've done all that.' He cut her short. 'Rung 999. Got passed from pillar to post. Eventually, the police sent a unit out, took down the details, searched the house.'

Under the table, she noticed his right knee spasm. Maggie had seen it many a time, that almost hypnotic jiggling. *Elvis Leg*, she called it.

'Do they think anything untoward has happened to your wife?' she asked.

He hesitated. 'Not as such.'

'Well, then. My advice, Mr Milne–'

'Scott.'

'My advice, Scott, is to go home and wait for news.' A thought occurred. 'You have left someone in the house, I take it?'

'My mum. She's holding the fort.'

'Good. Well, you get yourself home…'

'Only she's not able.' Scott threw Maggie an anguished look. 'She's had a hip replacement. And the kids – Jack and Chloe – they're a handful.'

'I understand. But I'm sure it won't be long before…'

'Seventy-two hours, that's what the constable said. Only,' his fingers worried the cuff of his suit jacket, 'their seventy-two hours are up and nothing's happened.'

'How long has it been since you saw Debbie last?'

'Four days, give or take.'

'I can see that you're worried sick,' Maggie hastened to reassure him. 'But the majority of people who are reported missing turn up safe and well within a few days.'

He sniffed. 'That's what the police said.'

'And that's one reason,' Maggie's smile oozed sincerity. 'But only one, why my agency doesn't take on missing person cases.' Another being that Harcus & Laird had never been asked before, nor would she and Wilma know where to start. 'Aside from which, your approach to my agency is premature. Had the police exhausted their lines of enquiry…' She broke off, abruptly.

Shut up, Maggie, you're over-compensating!

'But that's just it.' He clutched at her sleeve. 'The police haven't come up with anything. And it's so out of character. If you knew Debbie…' His voice wavered. 'She's that house-proud. Such a home-body, she'd never walk away from everything she's…' He corrected. 'We've built up. Never mind abandon her kids, especially when…' He welled up. '…Jack's worried about going up to big school. He wears glasses, says he's afraid he'll get bullied. He's been having nightmares,' he elaborated. 'Debbie's had to sleep in his bed these past few nights.'

'Poor wee lad,' Maggie murmured. She could well remember the plaintive cry in the night of her own children when they were small, the bundle of heat sliding into her bed.

'But four days? It doesn't bear thinking about. Any damn thing could have happened to her by now.'

'I hear what you're saying,' she observed, with practised detachment. 'But, equally, there could be a perfectly simple explanation for your wife's absence. And, as I've said, most people turn up safe and well within…'

'My Debbie,' Scott set his chin. 'Is not "most people".'

'I understand, but…'

'That's why I rang you. We're a team, me and Debbie. We've worked so hard to get where we are and…' He welled up. '…I'd be lost without her.' He increased the pressure on her arm. 'Say you'll think about it, at least.'

Maggie looked down. Scott's knuckles were white, his hand trembling.

'My wife has been missing for days,' he rushed on. 'God knows where. The kids have been asking for their mum. I couldn't get them to sleep. We none of us slept, come to that. And they're only young. They need her.' He released his grip. 'I need her.' He slumped back in his seat.

Poor soul! For a moment Maggie wavered. Then she took a deep breath. Wilma would have her guts for garters if she took on another bleeding heart case.

She squared her shoulders. 'I'm sorry, Scott, truly I am.'

Maggie shut her ears to the torrent of pleas that came after.

When, finally, Scott Milne ran out of steam, she said, 'The best I can do is repeat what I've told you already: go home and wait for news.'

Loosen Up

'Right, team, updates.' Chisolm looked around the table. 'Who's going to start?'

'I will.' Brian opened his briefing pack. 'First off, we've had a large number of sightings in the Milne case.'

Heads jerked to attention.

'Which we've narrowed down to seven possibles.'

'Good stuff,' Chisolm granted.

'Of which,' Brian went on, 'only two are viable.'

This was met with groans of disappointment.

'Let's have it, then,' Chisolm urged.

'Number one: a woman answering Debbie's description was seen on Tuesday's 9.07 Megabus service to Dundee.'

'That sounds promising,' Bob Duffy observed. 'Fits our timescale.'

'But does it?' Susan countered. 'She'd have been pushed to make that if she took her kids to school.'

'It was a dry day on Tuesday,' Duffy argued. 'Maybe they walked.'

'Or our witness got the time wrong.'

'Okay. But either way why Dundee? Does Debbie have connections there?'

'Not that we know of,' Brian responded.

'And, even if it was Debbie,' Douglas stuck his oar in. 'The fact she caught a bus to Dundee doesn't mean she ended up there. She could have travelled onwards to Glasgow, Edinburgh, just about anywhere, really.'

'Good point.' Chisolm offered a rare smile. 'Burnett?'

'Number two, a similar woman was seen, in the company of an older man, in the in the bar of the Berkeley Hotel.'

'When was this?'

'Around 20.00 hours on the Thursday, five days before she went missing.'

There was a collective sigh of disappointment.

'The witness, reliable is he?'

'It's a 'she' sir, a Mrs Muriel Catto. Retired pharmacist. Not one to go making exaggerated claims, I'd say.'

'You've taken her statement?'

'Yes, sir. Fits Debbie to a 'T'. All except – according to Mrs Catto – she was dressed to the nines and clarted with make-up.'

'Doesn't sound like the woman Scott Milne described to us.' Susan again.

'No, indeed,' Chisolm concurred.

'The guy,' Brian went on, 'looked to be a business executive of some sort, possibly staying in the hotel. I've had them circulate Debbie's photograph around the staff, but I'm not holding my breath. 'That photo is years out of date and most of the staff work shifts, plus there's a high turnover. Still,' he added, ever hopeful, 'you never know.'

'Did you check out the restaurant?' Douglas put his oar in.

'No. Why?'

'They could have booked for dinner.'

'Come off it,' George Duffy stepped in. 'If Debbie Milne was playing away, she'd most likely have had…' He made a lewd gesture. '… room service.'

Chisolm silenced him with a stern look. 'Stay on top of it, will, you, Brian?'

Brian? Burnett's eyes stood out on stalks.

It was uncommon, these days, for a DI to address his squad by other than their first names or, conversely, for the squad to call their superior officer anything other than DI, boss or guv. But, when Allan Chisolm had transferred from Glasgow, he'd made it clear that – in this respect, at least – he was firmly of the old school.

'Sir,' Brian responded, then hastily looked away.

Chisolm suppressed a smile. He'd been on the defensive when he first arrived in Aberdeen: pride injured, emotions wrecked, looking to lash out at all comers. But now? They were a decent lot, his squad.

Did their best. He wouldn't make mention of the protocol, nothing so overt. No. Insinuating the occasional forename into the conversation would do the trick. Time to loosen up.

A First Time for Everything

'Lord!' Maggie flopped down onto one of Wilma's cane chairs. 'What a morning I've had.' She checked her phone. 'And it's not gone eleven o'clock.'

'Better make you a cup of strong tea,' Wilma eyed her from the kitchen doorway. 'You don't look your usual collected self, right enough.'

'Neither would you, if you'd had to run out at the crack of dawn to an emergency.'

'Nee-naw. Nee-naw.' Wilma did an impression of a police siren. 'What got you out your bed this time?'

'Young guy with a runaway wife.'

Wilma groaned, 'All in a day's work,' easing herself into the chair opposite, all thoughts of tea forgotten. 'She's likely in the sack with some bit of beefcake. And–'

'Before you say another word, I turned the case down.'

'That's okay, then. No harm done.'

'Other than wasting my time.' Maggie kicked off her shoes, tucked her feet onto the chair. 'Not that I didn't have a minor wobble, especially once he mentioned his kids.'

'Kids?' Wilma perked up. 'How old?'

'Eleven and ten.'

'Poor bairns.'

'Bairns nothing!' Maggie dismissed her out of hand, Val's strictures still ringing in her ears. 'Children are pretty self-sufficient at that age.' She had a sudden vision of Willie Meston's Seaton gang: street-wise ten-year-olds who'd got themselves mixed up in a murder. Swiftly, she dispelled it. 'It's not as if they're babes in arms.'

'Aren't you the sarky one?' Wilma countered. 'Get out the wrong side of the bed?'

Maggie smothered a yawn. 'Low blood sugar, that's all.'

'The husband, he's sure she's done a runner?'

'Didn't hang around long enough to get the details. Pleaded with me, too, poor man. Said the police hadn't done a thing and his wife could be dead by now. He even…' She rolled her eyes. '…flagged up a tenuous connection with some aunt of yours.'

'You got a name?'

'"Auntie Fanny", he said.

'Now you're winding me up.'

'I'm not. Honest.'

Wilma chewed her lip. 'I did have an auntie right enough, Franny we called her. Frances was her right name.'

'Where is she now?'

Her mouth widened into a grin. 'Six feet under. When you think about it, though, them bairns…'

'Scott Milne's kids will be fine.'

'I dunno. Seventy-two hours is a long time without your mum.'

'Oh, come on,' Maggie argued. 'The granny's holding the fort till Scott gets home from work. And, anyhow, Debbie Milne will be back long before then.'

'Sez who?'

'Statistics.'

'But what if she's not?'

'Then,' Maggie said, decisively. 'It's up to the police.'

Wilma changed tack. 'Did he show you a photograph?'

'No. Why?'

She shrugged. 'Just saying.'

'Oh, Wilma, you're trying it on. You don't 'do' innocent.'

'Wondered if the case was worth another look, that's all.'

'Give me one reason.'

'Cash flow?'

'Forget it,' Maggie moved to close the subject. 'Money's one thing, ignorance is another. May I remind you we've never done a missing from home before?'

'May I remind you,' Wilma mimicked Maggie's accent, 'there's a first time for everything.'

'Yes, but…'

'Half the agency's time is spent trying to find people. If it's not debt, it's insurance fraud. If it's not insurance fraud, it's telephone scams. And if it's not telephone scams it's…'

Maggie held up both palms. 'Enough. Admitted we have experience in chasing up debt, but this is completely different.'

'How?'

'It just is. Debbie Milne could be anywhere. Or she could walk back through her door in Belvidere Street at any moment.'

'She could be dead,' Wilma intoned with a dark look.

'That, too. Regardless…' Val's words of warning rang in Maggie's ears. 'It's simply not within our remit, Wilma. End of.'

'Fella not come across as credible, is that it?' Wilma carried on, oblivious.

Maggie sighed. 'Not at all. It was a genuine cry for help, that's for sure.'

'That Struthers dame still bugging you?'

'No.' Caught in the lie, Maggie felt her face flood with colour. 'Well, a bit,' she conceded. 'More than a bit. So much so, I've been re-thinking our conversation the other day.'

'About the business?' Wilma shrieked, starting forward in her seat. 'You're joking.' She saw her plans for bettering herself go up in smoke.

'Seriously.' Maggie un-tucked her legs and planted both feet on the floor, the better to argue her case. 'I'd thought it all through. Concluded we've given it our best shot. I was clear in my mind the end of this year should be make or break time.' She grimaced. 'Until you browbeat me into making a concession, that is. But I've come back to my first way of thinking.' She steeled herself for what might come. 'Another six months is quite enough time for us to prove ourselves.'

Wilma shot out of her chair, grabbed Maggie by the wrist. 'After all the work we've put in.'

'That's just it.' Maggie shook herself free. 'The way I see it, we've been knocking our pans out for nothing.'

'That's not true.'

'It is true. And today's a good example. I've wasted a morning and let my son put himself out to school for no…'

Wilma cut her short. 'Colin's old enough to look after himself.'

'Granted. But I jeopardised my Seaton job chasing after a two-bit drug dealer, and in the end all that happened was he got off scot free.'

'That's only one case out of dozens.'

'Then I let myself be led up the garden path by a deluded woman.'

'There's no evidence she was deluded,' Wilma argued.

'That's my point,' Maggie wagged a finger. 'We didn't get a resolution of any description. And that's before we come to the crux of the matter: I'm no nearer getting justice for George than I was when you talked me into going down this road in the first place.'

Wilma's face set. 'It's all on me, is that what you're saying?'

'No, not at all. Simply that if you look at the facts, we've managed to stay afloat – and that only just – by handling a mountain of routine. Anything more than that we've made a complete mess of. And just look at the downside. Taking on the agency has alienated my kids. It has near cost you your marriage, and…'

'Think how much we've learned along the way.'

'That's just it: a whole load of shady stuff we'd have been better off not knowing.'

Wilma struggled to her feet. 'Why don't I pour you a wee snifter?' She extended a comforting arm. 'Perk you up?'

Maggie batted her away. 'I don't need a drink. Not that sort of drink, anyhow.' She summoned a smile. 'Whatever happened to that cup of tea?'

There's a Thing

'We'll kick off with you, Strachan,' Chisolm announced. 'What have you got on the Milne case?'

'Made some progress, sir.'

All eyes turned to Susan.

She fixed Douglas with a triumphant stare. 'I found Debbie's engagement and wedding rings.'

'Now, there's a thing,' Bob Duffy said, grinning. They all, even the recent recruits, were familiar with the 1998 Fraser case, where missing housewife, thirty-three-year-old Arlene's, rings were found hanging on a peg above the washbasin days after she vanished from home, leaving two young children. Her husband, Elgin fruit and veg wholesaler Nat Fraser, was ultimately convicted of her murder, despite the absence of witnesses or a body. No trace of Arlene was ever found.

'Where were the rings?' Chisolm asked.

'In a bedroom drawer.'

'Was the husband at home?'

'Not when I discovered them. He got back later.'

'What did he have to say?'

'He forgot.' Susan gave a small shrug. 'That was his excuse, anyhow.'

'You reckon he's bumped her off?' Duffy looked, now, like the cat who'd got the cream.

'You're adding one and one and making three,' Chisolm rebuked his sergeant. 'Stick to the facts. However, this put's a different complexion on things altogether.' He paused. 'Anything from Debbie's mum?'

Brian shrugged. 'Negative. Husband died last year: oil-related accident. Mrs Esslemont was a bag of nerves, couldn't give me straight answer to a straight question to the extent I wondered if she was in the early stages of dementia. Regardless, we're wasting our time there.'

Chisolm turned to Susan. 'What did you get from the other granny?'

'Nothing constructive. Told me everything had been hunky-dory until…' She hesitated. 'To be honest, I didn't find her all that helpful.'

'That doesn't surprise me,' Bob Duffy butted in. 'She's the mother-in-law, don't forget. Bet the sun shines out her son's arse.'

'…friend Sam appeared on the scene.' Susan finished, unflustered. 'Then, according to Mrs Milne senior, Debbie's behaviour "deteriorated" to use her own words.'

Chisolm frowned. 'I assume you pressed her on that.'

'I did, but she wouldn't be drawn. Kept insisting, Scott was the model husband.'

'Model husband?' Duffy sneered. 'Where have I heard that one before?'

This was met by vigorous nods of agreement. They'd all worked on cases where the distraught husband had proved to be the perpetrator, most recently the instance of Gordon Struthers, respected accountant and member of Aberdeen's prestigious Royal Northern & University Club, who had subjected his wife, Sheena, to decades of sexual abuse.

'If she is to be believed,' Susan ignored him. 'Scott gave Debbie free rein. Probably,' she grimaced, 'in the hope Sam would disappear as fast as she appeared.'

'On the subject of which,' Chisolm turned to Susan, 'do we have a photograph yet of Sam Clark?'

Susan blushed to the roots of her hair. 'No, sir. Scott was vehement he didn't have a photo. DVLA didn't give us anything, seems Sam has never held a driving licence. I'm still waiting to hear from…'

'Chrissake,' Duffy interrupted. 'Woman could be dead and buried by the time.'

Chisolm silenced him with a sharp look.

'What about the kids?' Susan came back in. 'They're old enough to have their own phones. Could be one or other of them has taken a snap or two, especially the girl, if her mum was dressed up to go out.'

'Good thinking,' Chisolm remarked, 'though we'd have to tread carefully. We could only check out the kids' phones with the express permission of their father.'

'Unless we had a warrant.' Douglas was always quick to quote procedure.

'We don't have the grounds,' Chisolm slapped him down.

'Not yet,' Douglas came back, quick as a flash. He caught the steely glint in his DI's eye. 'Sir,' he added.

'So,' Chisolm moved to wrap up the meeting. 'Actions. Let's concentrate on Scott Milne. Pull him in for questioning, on a voluntary basis at this juncture. You deal with that, Burnett.'

'Sir.'

'Duffy, keep working on Debbie Milne's contacts. Check out these classes she goes to.'

'Yes, sir.'

'Dunn and Strachan, get yourselves back to Belvidere Street. If uniforms missed those rings, who knows what else they've overlooked. Dunn, you keep your focus on the comms: telephone, internet, social media.'

'Okay.'

'Susan, we need more on this Sam person. If, as Burnett says, Debbie's mum is a lost cause, see if the other granny can fill you in on when and where the Clark and Esslemont families were neighbours. If we can establish that, we'll get uniform round there to do a door-to-door, assuming it's within our jurisdiction. If not, well we'll worry about that when we come to it.'

'Sir.'

'And, squad?' He surveyed his team. 'Jump to it.'

A Bad Penny

'For the benefit of my colleague.' Maggie took the lead. 'Can you run through the chain of events again?'

They were back in the same cafe, another early morning meeting before Scott Milne started work. Against Maggie's better judgement. She'd been clear in her head that Scott Milne's missing wife was no concern of theirs. Worse, she had a nagging suspicion that Scott was being economical with the truth. But Wilma had worn her down. First, by appealing to Maggie's maternal instincts: two children left without a mother. The parallels with her own situation weren't lost on her. Finally, when that fell on deaf ears, because Maggie – post Struthers – owed Wilma a favour.

And now Wilma was calling it in. With some reluctance, Maggie had agreed to set up another meeting. Not, she told herself, out of weakness. She was perfectly capable of defending her corner. But out of pragmatism. The six months she's given the agency might be too short in Wilma's eyes, but it would be an eternity if they weren't getting along.

Now, sitting alongside, she nodded encouragement.

Scott put a hand to his brow. 'The alarm was set to go off at seven. Debbie got up first. She went through to the kids.' He offered a rueful smile. "They can take a while to get moving. Then she went downstairs to see to the breakfast. She sets the table the night before.' Another smile. 'She's very organised, is Debbie. Sees to us first, then nips back upstairs to get dressed.'

'And you?' Maggie prompted, swallowing a reviving mouthful of coffee.

'Slow in the mornings, more so this past while.'

'Why is that?' Wilma, scoffing a bacon roll, was in there like a bullet.

'Things have been a bit full-on. At work, I mean.'

'In what way?'

'Oh,' he picked at his fingernails, 'this and that.'

'What are you not telling us?' Wilma probed.

Scott fixed his gaze on the far wall.

'I have to remind you,' Maggie asserted, 'that we'll only be able to help if you're completely honest with us.' It hadn't escaped her that Scott's Americano sat, untouched.

He flushed. 'Truth is,' his eyes sought hers, 'my job's on the line.'

Bingo! In her seat, Wilma straightened. Nothing like putting the screws on. 'Does your wife know?' she demanded.

'Not yet. She's a worrier, Debbie. I didn't want to say, in case, well, there's nothing certain as yet. Only they've flown in some big-shot troubleshooter from the States. Looking to make 'cost savings'. What folk are saying, in the office, is shed jobs.'

'How would that affect...?' Maggie began.

Scott cut her short. 'It would ruin everything, all we've worked for: the new house, the kids' schools.' His voice cracked. 'That's part of the reason we moved: to be in the right catchment area.'

'Could Debbie have found out about your job, do you think?'

'I don't see how. She doesn't come into the office, and the kids being the age they are we don't socialise that much, at least not with folk from work. The only thing I can think of is, I've been working all hours. Well, more hours than usual.' He grimaced. 'Trying to make myself indispensable, I guess. And it's because of that I missed Chloe's parents' evening.'

'When was that?' Wilma spoke through a mouthful of food.

'Last Wednesday. Went right out my head.'

'Was your wife upset?' She swallowed, noisily.

'Tell me about it. We attend together, always have. And it being Chloe's new school and all...' He sighed. 'You can imagine.'

Both women could.

'And afterwards?' Wilma took a slurp of her tea.

'We had a bit of a back and forth. Nothing major.'

Wilma leaned forward, thrust her face in his. 'Not enough for

Debbie to leave.'

'No,' he recoiled. 'Definitely not. We're sound, me and Debbie. We may have the odd disagreement. Show me one married couple that doesn't. But we didn't row. That's what I told the police.'

'Those scratches on your hand,' Maggie let the words hang in the air.

Wilma's eyebrows shot up. Maggie hadn't made mention of any scratches.

Scott looked down. The livid red marks had faded to into magenta lines. 'Those?' He uttered a strangled laugh. 'Got them in the garden: raspberry canes. House belonged to an old lady, needed a lot of work. That's how we were able to afford it. And the garden, you should see it. When…'

Maggie cut him off. 'And you've still no idea where Debbie could have gone?'

'No. I rang her mum to check if she'd been in touch. Not that I let on. I wouldn't want to alarm her, not unless…'

That's very sensible.' Maggie interjected.

'My mum's been living in since.' He fumbled in his trouser pocket, drew out a tissue, blew his nose. 'And I've phoned everyone I can think of: the couples we see regularly, the mums Debbie hangs out with at the kids' schools. I've even tried to contact her mate, Sam.'

'Who's that?' Wilma got straight in there.

'They grew up together,' Scott explained. 'Then the family moved away and the friendship fizzled out. But they got back in touch not that long ago.' He wrinkled his nose. 'Facebook. And shortly after that Sam turned up.' He frowned. 'Like a bad penny.'

'Why do you say that?' Wilma drained her cup.

'She's not my favourite person, is all.'

Her eyes narrowed. 'Now we're getting to it.'

'Could they have gone off together, do you think?' Maggie jumped in, fearful that Wilma might further inflame the situation.

'Doubt it,' he responded. 'Debbie's been trying to get hold of her for days, but no joy. She's a rolling stone, Sam. I wouldn't be surprised if she's moved on. Talking of which,' he checked his watch. 'I've got to go.' He scraped back his chair, got to his feet.

'One more thing,' Wilma shot from her seat. 'We'll need a photograph. Am I right in thinking you'll have given one to whoever responded to your emergency call?'

'Correct.'

'Who was that?' she asked. 'Out of interest.'

'Couple of bobbies. Souter, I think one of them was called. Can't remember the other.'

Maggie looked on, admiringly, as Wilma filed this for future reference. Wished she were as quick on the draw.

'Gave them a holiday snap,' Scott Milne continued. Bit dated. Kids were young at the time, but it was all I could lay my hands on.'

'You'll have something more recent on your phone,' Wilma insinuated.

'No. Debbie doesn't like getting her…'

'Come on.' Wilma gave him a playful nudge. 'Have a look.'

Scott started back. For a moment, it looked like he was going to refuse. Then he pulled out his phone, scrolled through his photostream. 'This do?' He flashed it in Wilma's face. 'She'll be mad if she finds out.' He looked like he was going to cry. 'I took it when she wasn't looking.'

'Perfect. Here's my email.' She held up her mobile.

'Thanks.' She watched as Scott messaged her, a satisfied smile on her face. An up-to-date photograph would give Harcus and Laird a clear advantage over those dozy wooden-tops.

Deep Shit

Miller took a swig from his bottle of Irn Bru. 'We're in deep shit.' He wiped off the orange moustache with the back of his hand.

'How?' Souter asked.

'The misper,' Miller answered, dour-faced.

Their panda car was parked up a dead-end at Nigg Point. From there, the two constables would have had a fine view of Aberdeen harbour, had it not been pitch dark outside and pelting with rain. Instead, the ships' lights dissolved into ghostly shapes in the gloom. Still, it was a good place for a skive in the middle of their nightshift, one of several they repaired to when things went quiet.

'Why so?'

'Wife's rings turned up in the house.'

'Whereabouts?' Souter puzzled.

'Bedroom drawer.'

'Not on our heads,' Souter retorted. 'It was the wife we were charged with looking for, not checking the husband's socks were paired.'

'Try telling that to the boss?' Miller came back. 'You and me, we're already on borrowed time.'

'Aye,' Souter ferreted in the cardboard tray balanced on his knee, stuck a chip slathered in curry sauce in his mouth. 'Reckon we're in line for a Reg 9.'

'Minimum. And another thing,' Miller grumbled. 'DI took issue with the fucking photo. According to my source, he said it was a decade out of date and you couldn't see Debbie Milne for her kids or her face for the hair.'

'Christ!' Cheeks bulging, Souter spattered the windscreen with sauce. 'Another effing stick to beat us with.'

'Steady on,' Miller protested.

'Sorry.' Souter scrubbed at the mess with a paper napkin, only making it worse.

'What d'you make of it all?' Miller asked, biting into his burger roll.

Souter tugged the ring-pull from a can of Coke. 'I reckon the wife's dead.'

Miller chewed for a bit, then, 'How do you arrive at that?'

'Think about it,' Souter slid a battered sausage into his upturned mouth. 'Woman leaves her rings, her kids, her home – fancy new home at that. If we'd been able to afford a place like that: nice, quiet cul- de-sac, enough bedrooms that the kids didn't have to share, garden front and back. My Shirley would give here eye teeth for that. Then you've direct access to Victoria Park, shops around the corner, good schools…' He broke off.

'Christ.' Miller gulped down a mouthful of minced meat. 'You sound like a fucking estate agent.'

'All I'm saying is,' Souter waved a fat chip, 'Debbie Milne had all the things you'd think would matter to her. Matter to any woman in the world, come to that. No, my money's on the husband. Why else would she go missing?'

'Aye.' Miller took another swig of Irn Bru. 'Right enough.'

'You mark my words,' Souter warmed to his theme. 'It's a bit too perfect, thon set-up: her with her home-baking and her night classes and her sewing-room, and him – Scott Milne – squeaky-clean. It's not normal, that. My Shirley…'

'You reckon he done her in?' Miller was quick to interrupt. He'd heard enough of Shirley to last him a lifetime.

'Wouldn't be surprised if they're excavating the back garden any-time soon. Remember thon case in Inverkip a couple of years back,' he expanded, referring to the disappearance of Margaret Fleming, a thirty-six-year-old woman with learning difficulties not seen since 1999. Ms Fleming's carers, Eddie Cairney and Avril Jones, were accused of fraudulently claiming £182,000 in state benefits and subsequently charged with her abduction, assault and murder. 'Had the diggers in there, took the place apart…' His next words were drowned by the crackle of his Airwave radio.

'Responding.' Souter spoke into his shoulder.

He stashed his can between the seats, thrust his sausage supper at Miller, switched on the ignition and threw the car into gear.

'Four minutes.' Said as he belted up.

He depressed a dashboard-mounted 999 button.

On blues, the panda car screamed into the night.

Somewhere to Sleep

'What are you doing?' Maggie stopped in her tracks as she passed the open door.

'What does it look like?' Kirsty spat, bending to stuff a pair of jeans into her backpack. 'I'm going back to Dundee.'

'But, your job,' Maggie protested.

She shrugged. 'Got the sack.'

'How come? I thought you were enjoying it.'

Kirsty straightened. 'How would you know?'

Maggie felt a twinge of conscience. She'd hardly had sight of Kirsty since she started her bar job, far less had a conversation about it. But after the day she'd had, she wasn't in the mood to take cheek from anyone. 'Look, here,' she marched into the room, grasped her daughter by the arm. 'I know it's no fun having to work through your holidays, but that's the way it is.'

Kirsty shook her off. 'Don't I know it? Ever since Dad died it's been nothing but, "We can't afford this" or "you can't have that".'

That's a downright lie. Maggie had jumped through hoops to ensure whatever privations she faced didn't impact on her children. But she wasn't going to rise to the bait. 'It's hard, I know.'

'Hard?' Kirsty shrilled. 'Hard doesn't begin to describe it.'

'Well, at least when you're staying at home…'

'That's a joke. This dump…' She waved her arms. '…isn't home anymore. It's just somewhere to sleep.'

The barb scored a direct hit. Since Maggie had taken on the business, she'd neglected the bungalow, and it was looking decidedly shabby – paint flaking off the windows, loose tiles on the roof – especially by comparison with its pristine mirror-image next door. And that was just the outside. Maggie didn't want to contemplate the cost of redecorating, far less replacing the worn carpets and dated furniture. Nonetheless, she held her own. 'That's not fair.'

Kirsty ignored this. 'And that's because you're never here. You've got no time for anything but your precious agency.'

'Is that right?' Maggie responded. 'Who do you think does the cooking and cleaning and washing and ironing around here? The tooth fairy?'

'Very funny! You've had a one-track mind ever since you chummed up with that...' Her eyes bulged. '...*person* next door. You're so blinkered,' her voice wavered, 'you can't see past the end of your nose.'

'Unlike you.' Maggie had heard enough. 'You're a vain, self-obsessed, nasty little...' She broke off.

'Go on,' Kirsty goaded. 'Say it.'

Maggie chewed on her lower lip. She wouldn't give her daughter the satisfaction, even she could be a bitch at times. She drew a deep breath. 'I'd no idea you felt that way,' she said, stiffly.

'That's because you never asked.'

'No?' Maggie lost it. 'Like when I trailed down to Dundee because I was worried sick about your pregnancy?'

'False pregnancy,' Kirsty corrected.

'Regardless. Didn't it occur to you to let me know it was a false alarm?'

Kirsty shrugged. 'Whatever.'

'In my book,' Maggie didn't intend to let up. 'That was hugely irresponsible.'

This was met with a sneer.

Maggie sighed. This was going nowhere. 'What brought all this on?' she asked.

'Same old: money. I'm stressing over losing the job.'

'You shouldn't be worrying about money.'

'No? Isn't that at the root of all this: where I can afford to live, whether I go out or not, what I do in the summer holidays, even if Colin can do a sixth year or not?'

'Well...'

Kirsty cut her off. 'No point telling me otherwise. Isn't money

– or the lack of it – why you're running round in circles with that fat eejit next door playing at private detectives?'

'We are not "playing" at anything.'

'No?' Then if you're serious, why aren't you making a success of it?'

Maggie counted to ten. Kirsty had a point. For all their minor – and they were minor – triumphs, she and Wilma had experienced more than their fair share of failures: failures for which she, as senior partner, was wholly responsible.

She drew Kirsty down to sit on the edge of the bed. 'The job, do you want to tell me what happened?'

Kirsty shrugged. 'It was the trainer. We didn't get on.'

'But, surely…'

'Adam. Does the rounds of the clubs, bars and stuff, bringing the new staff up to speed.'

Maggie waited.

'He started coming on to me. Nothing I couldn't handle, not at first, anyhow. Guy's full of himself. Tries it on with all the newbies, I'm told. It was after I had to smack him down in front of some permanent staff that it got personal.'

'In what way?'

'He began making remarks about the police: general stuff, then more pointed. I knew what was coming. It was to do with Dad.'

Maggie caught her breath. *You don't think about your good name until you've lost it.* She'd thought the slights and the innuendo a thing of the past. But not only had they not gone away, they had followed her children. That made her blood boil. 'Oh, pet,' was all she managed.

'I didn't say anything, just took it.' Kirsty's chin wobbled. 'I took it for days and then…' Her eyes brimmed with tears. '…I told Adam to shove his job up his arse.'

Maggie burst out laughing. 'I'm sorry.' Her shoulders heaved. 'I know it's not funny. I'm laughing because I'm so proud of you.'

Kirsty turned a puzzled face. 'You are?'

'You bet.'

'You're not mad I packed in the job.'

'Not a bit. I thought all along you could do better than a cocktail waitress.'

'Not in Aberdeen, not these days.'

'Perhaps not.' Maggie was serious again. 'So you're set on going back to Dundee?'

'The flat's sitting there, rent paid.'

'But, Sarah, isn't she in Greece?'

'That's right.'

'So, won't you be lonely living there on your own?' Maggie said a silent prayer Shaz, the boyfriend Kirsty had brought home, and who might have been responsible for her pregnancy scare, was miles away.

Kirsty smiled. 'Not a problem.'

'Well, it's your decision.' Maggie's heart wrenched. Dundee was a dangerous place. Since her daughter first started uni, Maggie had been fearful for her safety. Added to which, she loved having her wee girl back home in the upstairs bedroom across the landing from Colin. It made the house feel whole again. Well, almost.

'And I didn't mean what I said about the house.'

'No.' Maggie wondered if a judicious lick of paint would brighten the place up. Then, where would she find the time? And, besides, paint was such a price these days. 'If you're not in a rush,' she forced a smile, 'why don't you let me make you a mug of hot chocolate, warm you up? Then we can take it from there.'

Interview Room

'Will you explain to me how two rings,' Brian Burnett glanced down at his notes, 'a gold wedding band and a diamond solitaire,' he looked up, engaged the man seated opposite, 'came to be in your sock drawer?'

Scott Milne shifted in his seat. 'When I got home – after I got the call to tell me she hadn't picked the kids up from school – I tore around the house looking for Debbie. When I went into the bathroom, they were the first thing I saw: lying on the shelf above the basin. That's where she always leaves them when she…' His voice wavered.

'Take your time.'

'It was then Chloe came in behind me, wanting to know what to give Jack for his tea. I hadn't heard her come upstairs, and I panicked, I suppose. She's of an age. Well, they both are…' He broke off, distracted.

'Go on,' Brian prompted.

'I scooped the rings off the shelf, palmed them till she'd gone. Then…' He drew a weary hand across his forehead. '…I put them in the first place that occurred to me.'

'And that was?'

'The top drawer of the chest by the window: the drawer I keep my socks in.'

'Can you confirm that the two rings you concealed…?'

Scott cut him short. 'I didn't "conceal" them.'

'We won't split hairs,' Brian soothed. 'What were your intentions when you placed them in that drawer?'

'To put them out of sight of the kids.'

'Was that the only reason?'

'I don't know what you're getting at.' Scott leaned forward. 'What other reason would there be?'

Brian ignored this. 'Can you confirm they were your wife's wedding and engagement rings?'

'I can.'

'Why didn't you mention this to the officers who responded to your emergency call?'

'It went right out of my mind. I mean,' Scott gave a helpless shrug, 'there was that much going on.'

Crooking an eyebrow, Brian said, 'You've just reported your wife missing and you don't think to mention she's left her rings behind?'

Scott flushed. 'I know it looks bad, but…'

'Can you describe to me your reaction when you first spotted the rings?'

'I felt sick. Thought she'd left me.' He looked to be on the verge of tears. 'Not that she had any reason, not unless…I've been working all hours. And my job – project management – the way things pan out, even when I'm home, I'm never off the phone. Maybe Debbie felt I was neglecting her. But that doesn't account for…'

Brian waited.

'She hasn't been herself. I put it down to the move. She was chuffed to bits at first, but lately – now I think about it – she's been a bit off.'

'In what way?'

'Tired. Snaps at the kids. Me too, though I let it run off me. Women!' He offered a conspiratorial smile.

Tell me about it! Brian could have written the book.

'Have you had any thoughts since…?'

Scott finished the sentence. '…she left.' He grimaced. 'Plenty. As you can imagine, I haven't been getting much sleep.'

Loving husband or guilty conscience? Brian strove to keep an open mind.

'First conclusion I came to it was down to her pal, Sam.'

'Why so?'

'Timing, I suppose. What with the new house and all, Debbie should have been hunkering down, pulling things together. And she was, at first anyhow. Manic, the way she went at it: painting walls, sewing curtains.' He passed a hand across his brow. 'They don't call it nesting for nothing.'

Brian's thoughts turned to his bleak bedsit in Urquhart Road. The dump he'd meant – but not yet managed – to move on from.

'But once Sam Clark came back on the scene, Debbie couldn't settle to anything. There's stuff lying all over her sewing room, one of the bedrooms is half painted, the paintbrushes gone hard. She's even been dishing the kids up ready-meals…' He broke off. 'She's always prided herself on her home cooking.'

Brian didn't say a word. Since his split with Bev he'd survived on a diet of Chinese and Indian takeaways.

'I mean, it was one thing during the flitting,' Scott ran on. 'But now? It's like Debbie's always saying about the kids…'

Brian cocked an eyebrow. 'What's that?'

'Their minds are on other things.'

'Would you care to expand on that?'

Scott shrugged, hopelessly. 'It's like she's living in another world.'

Big Mistake

Maggie watched as Glen Mason, the supply teacher from Seaton School, crossed from the bar. She'd felt a mixture of emotions as she set off from home. Nervousness. Aside from her sporadic assignations with Brian, she hadn't met with a man in a social setting for a long time. And a sense of happy anticipation. She'd enjoyed pulling clothes out of the wardrobe she hadn't worn in an age, taking time over her hair and make-up. Now, at last, she was doing something for herself.

'Merlot for madame.' Glen set a wine glass in front of her, placed a foaming pint alongside.

'Thanks.' She drew a calming breath. He was a decent bloke. It was going to be fine.

He'd caught her unawares: a chance encounter in the school corridor.

About that drink, he'd said, pinning her between himself and the wall.

Yes, she'd answered, whether out of sudden bravado or the fear that they might be seen. As the agency business had gained momentum, she'd picked up on snide comments in the staffroom about her "other job": the demands it made on her time, the adverse publicity it had attracted on occasion. Didn't want to provide ammunition for further gossip. On the other hand, didn't becoming more assertive mean making her own choices? A casual drink was hardly going to endanger her business, and both she and Glen had enough baggage to be discreet. *What do you suggest?* she'd asked.

They'd batted back and forth the pubs within spitting distance, settled for the Newburgh Inn – commonly known as Briggies – in the pretty coastal village of Newburgh. A discreet distance from school, the village was a long-time favourite of Maggie's: on many a summer evening, she and George had driven out from Aberdeen.

There they'd have a stroll on the beach, a leisurely drink in the Udny Arms. When George's shift pattern allowed, that was. When George was alive. The hotel had been closed for some years, and although planning permission had been granted for redevelopment and expansion, it was yet another thing in Maggie's life that would never be the same.

Her body tensed as he slid behind the table. She'd expected him to take the chair opposite, but what of it? The banquette would be roomier, she supposed, for a big chap like him.

'Are you with me?' Glen's voice broke her train of thought.

'I'm sorry,' she stammered. 'You were saying?'

'You're looking glam.'

'Thanks.' She coloured at the compliment, simultaneously wondering if she'd overdone her outfit. Anxious not to turn up in school rig-out of trousers and flat shoes, she'd opted for heels and a pencil skirt. *Bad idea!* The shoes had pinched her toes from the moment she put them on, and it was just as well she'd parked close by, for the constraints of a tight skirt made walking any distance well-nigh impossible.

He raised his glass. 'Cheers!'

'Cheers!' She joined him in the toast, swallowing a greedy mouthful for Dutch courage.

'First of many, I hope.' He flashed a smile.

Maggie caught a whiff of beery breath. Resisting the urge to wrinkle her nose, she put her glass down, sat upright in her seat. *Give the guy a break!* She returned a nervous smile.

'You're a private eye, I hear,' he opened the conversation.

Maggie's heart sank. Her companion hadn't been at Seaton School for more than a month and already probably knew everything there was to know about her. No matter, she rationalised. They were only having a casual drink. And, anyhow, as a supply teacher, he might not stay that long.

'That's right,' she mustered, taking another gulp of wine.

'Seedy business, is it?' He moved in close. Too close, in Maggie's opinion.

'Pretty run-of-the-mill, actually.' She deflected the question, reluctant to talk business with a complete stranger.

'Oh, come on,' he edged sideways, his thigh making contact. 'You must have some cracking stories to tell.'

'Even if I had,' she moved smartly away, making no attempt to mask her annoyance, 'I wouldn't tell. I've a reputation to protect.' Nervously, she crossed her legs, then, catching Glen's downwards glance, tugged her skirt over her knees.

'There's no need to be sniffy about it.' He put a placatory hand on hers. 'I was only asking.'

She shook his hand away. 'I'm sorry if that sounded rude. I try to keep my business life quite separate from school, that's all.' *What an idiot! He asks you a perfectly innocent question, and you overreact.*

'I get it,' he said, mollified. 'It's just, I thought you'd be more...' He hesitated. '...up for this.'

Mistake! Maggie grasped the enormity of her misjudgment. *Big, huge, giant mistake*! She'd rehearsed, in her head, how their meeting would go. Had assumed, in the light of his divorce and her bereavement, Glen would have been more circumspect. She didn't respond.

'Have I read this wrong?' he persisted. 'You *are* single, aren't you?'

'I suppose.' Divorced, widowed, separated, it all boils down to the same thing.

'Well, then.' He flashed another smile. 'Relax. If you're not keen to talk about your shady goings-on, we can talk about something else.'

'I'm sorry.' Frantically, Maggie scrabbled for an excuse, failed to come up with anything that would extract her from this predicament. 'You're a really nice guy. And I thought I could do this. But...' She reached for her handbag. '...it's too soon. For me, at any rate.'

Glen started forward. 'You're not leaving.'

'I am.' She said, decisively. And with that she picked up her glass and drained the rest of her wine.

'But,' he protested, looking a lot less cocky than when he'd arrived, 'we've only just got here.'

'I know,' Maggie shrugged an apology. 'But I'm not ready for this. That's obvious.' She managed the ghost of a smile. 'To me if not to you.'

She rose to her feet. 'Sorry,' she said, again.

Be My Guest

'I'll take the upstairs,' Douglas announced, as he and Susan Strachan stood in the hallway of the Milne home in Belvidere Street.

Susan blocked his path. 'I thought the boss told you to concentrate on the comms?'

'Plenty time for both,' Douglas countered, silkily, squeezing past her.

Classic! It was all Susan could do not to knee him. Dunn hadn't forgiven her for finding those rings. *Well, good luck there, mate!* She'd done a thorough search, was convinced he'd get no joy.

'Fine by me.' She turned on her heel and marched into the sitting room. Scott Milne's mum had retreated to the kitchen and the kids were at school, so the two detective constables had a clear run.

For the next hour, she worked her way methodically through drawers and cupboards, pausing only to deflect inquiries from the granny on her progress or whether tea or coffee would be required. There was little of interest, for Susan knew from her previous visit that many of the Milne's possessions remained sealed in the removal company's stout cartons in one of the spare bedrooms, Debbie having gradually unpacked only the necessities whilst the house was being decorated and the family settled in. But, tedious as the search was, Susan knew from experience that dedicated policing brought results. Hadn't the long hours she'd spent at Sheena Struthers' hospital bed ultimately proved rewarding?

From time to time, she'd hear a dull thud overhead as Douglas conducted his own search, the sound of a door banging open or shut. *Typical!* Like others of her male colleagues, Douglas felt the need to big up everything he did, while she went about her duties quietly. Other than that, the house was eerily silent, only the hum of traffic at the end of the cul-de-sac and sporadic birdsong to be heard. Susan's thoughts turned to her own flat, a cramped space on a busy road. What she wouldn't give for a lovely house like this. Not for the first time, she speculated on what it would take for a young woman to walk away from her dream home. Not only that, but walk away from her kids. A man she could understand. She'd been in enough relationships to know how love could turn to loathing. But vulnerable young children? That was beyond her comprehension. If Debbie did walk away, a question mark formed in Susan's head. Her heart had flipped when she found those rings. Scott Milne hadn't struck her as an abuser. But, then, neither had the diminutive and mild-mannered Gordon Struthers.

Nothing upstairs.' Douglas interrupted her train of thought.

Told you! Susan couldn't help feeling a small thrill of satisfaction, but responded only with a shrug.

'I'm just going to have a look around the garden.'

'Why?' she demanded. 'Uniform already checked it out.'

'They might have missed something.'

Fair point. She couldn't resist. 'Like what?' she scoffed. 'A recently dug grave?'

His eyes flashed defiance.

'We're needed back at HQ,' Susan persisted, just for badness.

Colouring, Douglas tugged at his shirt collar. 'Give me ten.'

'Oh, go on, then,' she conceded. 'Be my guest.'

A Plan

If we're going to have a go at the Milne case,' Maggie engaged Wilma across the breakfast table. 'A proper go, we'll need to have a plan.'

'Couldn't agree more,' Wilma mumbled through a mouthful of warm rowie. She shifted position. Maggie's spindly Ercol chairs weren't what you could call comfy. She wished she was in her conservatory next door.

'For all your arguments about us finding people, this is uncharted territory. That being the case, we can expect it to test our initiative and competence as PIs.'

'Right,' Wilma nodded. She was always in awe when Maggie came out with the big words.

'Given the time frame I've set,' Maggie continued in full senior partner mode. 'This may well be the agency's last major case.'

'But…' Wilma protested.

Maggie ignored her. 'If we succeed in locating Debbie Milne, it will be a huge feather in our caps.' *And restore our reputation.* 'Either way, we sink or swim.' She looked Wilma straight in the eye. 'Agreed?'

Wilma nearly choked on the giant piece of morning roll she'd just stuffed in her mouth. 'Agreed.'

'Plus, this time, we'll work together from day one. I've learned my lesson from Sheena Struthers. We'll make joint decisions. And this time, there's to be no skullduggery,' she threw a stern look. 'No sneaky moves behind my back.'

Chewing furiously, Wilma could do nothing but nod. Then, 'We're already behind the loop.' She brushed flaky crumbs from her mouth with the back of her hand. 'From what I've boned up on misper cases, the first twenty-four hours are critical, so we've missed the boat. The filth – sorry, police – will have already searched the house, spoken to the neighbours, whoever. Plus, they'll have circulated Debbie's description. A photo, too, most like.'

'So,' Maggie took a sip of her tea, where do you suggest we start?'

'Social media,' Wilma shot back.

'Oh,' Maggie put down her mug with a clatter, 'that's your answer to everything.'

Wilma grinned. 'And I'm not wrong either. If you tot up the credit checks I've run, the background reports I've verified, the fraudsters I've nailed.'

'Enough.' Maggie held up her hands in mock surrender. 'Agreed, that's as good a place as any to begin. See if Debbie has given any indication of her plans, her frame of mind, whether there has been any recent activity.'

Wilma gulped down the last of her roll. 'I'm on it. I'll start with Twitter, Facebook, whatever. Then, if they don't throw anything up, I'll try Missing People, Runaway Helpline, the Sally Army.'

'How do you know about all those?'

'Don't ask.' Wilma tapped the side of her nose. She reached for a second breakfast roll, lathered it with butter. 'I'd lay it on the husband,' she spoke through a full mouth.

'How do you work that out?'

'Seven-year itch.'

'Ten's more like.'

'Near enough.' Wilma smacked her lips, reached for her mug of coffee. 'Plus, he came across a bit sleekit, that Scott, don't you think?'

'What makes you say that?'

'The way he talks, for a start. Corporate-speak, isn't that what you call it?'

'Oh, come on. He's no different from any other guy his age, especially one that works for a US company. They have all the buzzwords. Bit like you when we started out: hitting me with all that guff from The Apprentice.'

'No need to rub it in,' Wilma said in a peeved voice. 'Plus, he's a bit shifty, doesn't meet your eye.'

'I didn't get that,' Maggie countered. 'You probably scared the life out of him.'

'And what was all that about scratches?'

'Oh,' Maggie said, 'just something I picked up at our first meeting. Doesn't signify.'

'Still and all, I'd put money on they've fallen out, him and her.'

'Mum,' Colin burst through the door. 'I need fifty pounds.'

Maggie craned her neck. 'What for?' Her son was over six feet tall and still growing.

'Rugby tour.'

Frowning, she reached for her handbag. 'I'm not sure I've got fifty.'

'But, mum,' Colin complained, 'I told you last week. I have to pay the deposit today.'

'Here,' Wilma produced her purse. 'You get on. Your mum and me will sort it out.'

'You didn't need to do that,' Maggie remonstrated as the front door banged.

'Mebbe. But we've enough on our plates without a domestic incident. Talking of which,' Wilma polished off the last piece of roll on her plate, 'back to Scott Milne and his marital problems.'

'Or lack thereof,' Maggie wasn't going to back down so easily.

'Worth digging, though?'

'Agreed.'

'Looks like we can rule out both sets of parents. From what Scott's told us, Debbie's mum isn't in good shape, and the mother-in-law stepped in smart-ish, so they don't look to be at loggerheads. What about the kids, though? Could it be they've given Debbie grief? Or are they a bit young for that?'

'Hardly. You're lucky with your boys. Girls are manipulative from a very young age.' Maggie said, with feeling. 'Seems like Kirsty and I have been head-to-head from the day she was born.'

'How could we talk to the kids on their own, though?' Wilma pondered. 'I know. Call in when they get back from school, before

Scott's home from work. One of us can keep the granny occupied, whilst the other…'

'There's laws against that sort of thing,' Maggie remonstrated. 'Maybe I could check if anyone at Seaton knows their teachers, get the lowdown that way.'

'Hmm.' Wilma didn't look convinced. 'Waste of time going down that road, in my opinion. We'd be better off looking at Debbie's routine: plotting her movements on an average day, speaking to everyone she'd come in contact with.'

'That could take forever.'

'Doesn't follow. Her life wasn't exactly a blast, by the sounds of it. Seems her weekdays were taken up with school runs and shopping, so we're only talking a couple of neighbours, few mums at most. The rest of the time she'd be at home, cleaning and…'

Maggie ran a finger along the rail of her chair leg, held it up. 'Don't remind me. I haven't done a deep clean since I don't know how long.'

Wilma ignored this. 'It's decided, then. We'll target Debbie's contacts, her friends.'

'And let's not forget her motivation. Marital relations aside, Debbie Milne could have run for any number of reasons: anxiety, depression, whatever.'

'Ach,' Wilma scoffed, 'what did she have to be depressed about? Good-looking husband, two healthy kids, muckle great house, no job to get up for of a morning. Bloody woman had it made in my opinion.'

'Stop right there,' Maggie sat up straight. Given her diminutive height, she reckoned she conveyed more authority sitting down. 'You're acting on assumptions, Wilma. What we need are facts.'

'I get you,' Wilma scowled, abashed at the reprimand. 'All the same…' She was determined to have the last word. '…it sounds to me like Debbie Milne did a bunk out of sheer fucking boredom.'

Shaz

Shaz wove a zigzag path. He'd had a heavy night: kicked off in the Union, continued down the Perth Road, ended up in some club – he couldn't remember which. Or where.

He'd been okay till he popped that couple of tabs. He extended an arm, steadied himself against a wall. He'd always been able to hold his booze – born of a hard Scouse background – but now he was spaced out.

He crept forward, using the tenement for support. It was solid, reassuring.

Whoops! He lurched into a doorway, crumbled to a crouch.

He let his head fall forward, hugged his knees. Stayed there for some minutes, trying to clear his head.

He was out of cash. Spent his last few quid on a kebab. Bad move. He concentrated on his breathing, fought the urge to be sick.

He'd have missed the last bus. With a shaking hand he brushed snot from the end of his nose. Should have kept his digs in town, but he'd been on his uppers and Carnoustie seemed a bargain at the time.

He could cadge a bed. Pete? Mike? Four Eyes? He worked his way through his mates, but they all lived a distance away.

He tried to think straight. Kirsty, maybe. Last he knew she was renting down Magdalen Yard. Not that they were shagging, but Shaz reckoned she fancied him, still.

He fumbled for his phone, scrolled down his contacts. Kirsty wouldn't be too pleased. And that flatmate of hers, Sarah was it? Boot-faced at the best of times. Still, he'd have settled for the sofa. Or the floor, come to that.

He was about to press 'call' when he remembered. It was the end of the semester. They'd both have gone home.

Bile rose in his throat. *Fuck!* He coughed it up. Spat an arc onto the pavement. Wished he hadn't binned that half-empty bottle of water.

He leant back against the heavy door, slid down into his jacket, tugged the collar up around his ears. His head was still swimming, his stomach churning. He sighed. Best stay where he was.

With a wrench, the door opened. He toppled backwards into the close.

'Fuck off.' A burly workman in a Hi-vis vest stood over him.

'Okay,' Shaz wrestled to an upright position, 'I'm going.' He grasped the door handle, hauled himself to his feet. 'Sorry mate.' He lurched onto the pavement.

The man disappeared into the early morning haar.

Shaz cast around. In the disembodied glow of the street lights, tenements cast blank faces. Overhead, the iron skeleton of the Tay rail bridge loomed black.

He lurched from one door to the next. None offered shelter.

Then, halfway down the street, a builders' skip beckoned.

Shaz staggered towards it.

Steadying himself with both hands, he peered over the side.

It was half-full: a bedrock of broken masonry and plasterboard topped by bulging bin bags, randomly tossed.

His eyes fought to focus. There was a piece of carpet, a broken desk lamp, a bunched-up duvet – the detritus of student life.

Fingers splayed, he edged around the rim.

Finding the lowest point, he leant over, tumbled inside.

He lay for a few moments, resisting the urge to vomit. When he'd decided this was a good idea, he hadn't factored in the smell.

He shifted position, trying to find a comfy spot, then reached for the duvet.

It was damp, and reeked of piss. Still, beggars couldn't be… He retched, swallowed a mouthful of bile.

Trembling with cold and nausea, Shaz tugged the quilt towards him, tucking it in as he went.

He was almost done.

A couple of hours' kip and I'll be brand new, he was telling himself, when, *Christ!* He jolted upright as his right hand settled on a human arm.

IV

Black Ops

'Did you see this?' Wilma held out the newspaper. Unusually, she and Maggie were in Wilma's front room, Wilma having not long mopped her kitchen and conservatory floors when Maggie came to the door.

'What?' Maggie spoke through her nose, in a futile attempt not to inhale more of Wilma's scented candles and air purifiers than she had to.

'It says here,

Fears are growing for mother-of-two Debbie Milne, who has been missing from her home in the Rosemount district of Aberdeen for several days. Debbie (32) was last seen at the family residence in Belvidere Street at breakfast time on Tuesday. There, a woman answered the door to our reporter, but refused to comment. One neighbour, who declined to give her name, said, "Debbie was a doting mum. This is a friendly neighbourhood. I can't tell you how shocked we all are."

A spokesman confirmed the matter is now the subject of a police investigation. "Anyone who thinks they may have seen Debbie, is asked to contact us on…"

She broke off. 'Blah, blah, blah.'

'Oh, well.' Gingerly, Maggie set down her mug of tea on a marble coaster. 'That's that, then.'

'What?'

'If uniform have passed it onto CID, we'd better back off.'

'Why should we?' Wilma demanded. 'It was Scott Milne came to us. We didn't go chasing his business. Not like them what-div-you-call-them folk on the telly.'

'Ambulance-chasers?' Maggie hazarded a guess.

'That'll do.'

'Yes, but…' The leather sofa squealed as she sat forward.

'Got it.' Wilma assumed a triumphant look. 'You don't want to upset your pal, Allan.'

Maggie bristled. 'It's not that at all.'

'Brian, then.'

'Neither. But the fact remains, we've landed in the middle of a high-level police investigation twice already.'

'We?' Wilma teased.

'Okay, I hold my hands up. But…'

'Fatboy, I'll grant you. It was you decided to go after thon nutter. But the Struthers quine, that was different. It was her come to us screaming for help.'

'Accepted. And look how that ended.'

'Whatever.' Wilma wasn't going to back down. 'We wis there first.'

There was no arguing with Wilma when she got her teeth into something, but as Val rightly said, it was high time Maggie held her own. She took a deep breath. 'We may well have "been there first" as you've pointed out, but we came in a very poor second.'

Wilma huffed. 'Don't know what you mean.'

'Let's face it, we had no chance of unravelling the Struthers case. We simply didn't have the resources: the authority to check phone records, internet activity, bank accounts.'

'Not legal, like,' Wilma tossed in.

Maggie gave her a sharp look. 'Not at all.'

'Okay,' Wilma held up her hands in surrender, 'I get the message. We mebbe couldn't have done more there, but where Debbie Milne is concerned we've advantages the police don't have.'

'Such as?'

'We can be quicker off the mark. More flexible.' Said with a sly grin.

Maggie stiffened. 'If you're referring to those gizmos you've employed behind my back, let me make it clear, once and for all…'

'Yes, yes,' Wilma dismissed her. 'But we've one thing no policeman,' She winked. 'Not even your clever Inspector Chisolm has.'

'And that is?'

'We're women. Mums, just like Debbie.'

Maggie frowned. 'I don't...'

'The way I see it,' Wilma interrupted. 'The police will already have collected a mass of data, taken photographs, conducted interviews. Our best chance is to concentrate on the personal angle: get inside Debbie Milne's head, find out what makes her tick.'

'I suppose,' Maggie allowed. She wasn't convinced.

'Put yourself in her place,' Wilma persisted. 'What would you do if you were Debbie? Run home to mum?'

'I doubt it,' Maggie responded, decisively. She could imagine her mother's reaction: *You've made your bed, now lie in it.*

'What, then?'

'Depends. From everything we've heard, home and kids were the two most important things in Debbie's life, so I'm struggling with her motivation, to be honest.'

'Say, for the sake of argument, she was hacked off, wanted to give her man a wake-up call? She's likely shattered from the move, remember. Needing support. And Scott said himself he's been working all hours.'

'If money were no object, I'd spend the night in a nice hotel.' Maggie pulled a wry face. 'More probably I'd look for a bed and breakfast. But you'd be better a better judge, Wilma. I've never been in that position.'

She chuckled. 'Lucky you.' Then, seeing Maggie's crestfallen expression, hastily readjusted her features.

'What would you do?' Maggie enquired.

'Check into a women's refuge.'

'Even if you hadn't been abused.'

Quick as a flash, Wilma came back. 'I'd shoot them a line.'

Maggie let this go. Lately, they'd been getting along better after their rift over the Struthers case. Another ding-dong with Wilma now was all she needed. 'And if there wasn't a place available?'

Wilma shrugged. 'I'd sleep rough.'

'You wouldn't last the night.'

'You reckon?'

Mentally, Maggie added this to the list of experiences Wilma had over her.

'All I'm saying is, once we know what floats Debbie Milne's boat we'll get the answer to why she did a runner. And there's a good chance that will lead us to her, regardless of whether she's holed up in some outhouse or someone has given her shelter. We might even,' Wilma's eyes shone, 'manage to beat the polis at their own game.'

'I'm not with you.'

'Think on it. If we were to get there first – find Debbie – would that not make you feel a whole lot better about the agency's future?'

Maggie's mind teemed with conflicting thoughts: reluctance to compromise yet another police investigation, compassion for Debbie Milne, concern for the agency's future. She'd been mortified when the Struthers case had come to nothing, and that coming hot on the heels of her humiliation at the hands of defence lawyer Louis Valentine during the Fatboy trial. Then there was Wilma. What was her motivation in arguing Debbie Milne's case? Most likely trying to exert undue influence again in the hope of winning a reprieve for the agency. She swithered. 'I don't know.'

'It would give you a boost, Maggie,' Wilma continued. 'Restore our reputation. Plus, it would be great publicity. Trust me.' Her baby blue eyes looked into Maggie's own. 'We might have got burnt by the Struthers dame.' Uttered with magnanimity. In her own mind, Wilma was convinced she'd been right about Sheena Struthers from the very start: that Sheena had set her husband up in revenge for years of sexual abuse. 'But,' she grinned, 'virgin territory or no, if we set our minds to investigating Debbie Milne's disappearance, this time we could bloody nail it.'

'Perhaps.' Maggie hoped she wasn't letting herself be talked into this for all the wrong reasons. But, no, she reminded herself. Wilma's instincts were sound. It was Maggie's lack of faith that had almost caused their partnership to founder.

'Think of the hours we've already put in,' Wilma went on.

'True.'

'And the experience it would hand us.'

'Yes,' Maggie conceded. 'But…' *Sink or swim.* The words reverberated in her skull. One more major case and she'd review the entire operation.

'We'd work on the QT, goes without saying: a covert operation.'

Black Ops! Wilma's imagination worked overtime. Already, she could picture how it would all play out: the shady internet purchases she could bring into play. Since she'd become involved in the PI business, Wilma had invested any spare cash she could muster in building up a small arsenal of surveillance equipment. Of course, Maggie wouldn't sanction their use, but what she didn't know wouldn't hurt her. Look hard enough online, and she could turn herself into Torry's answer to James Bond.

Wilma had a quiet chuckle to herself. What sport she was going to have!

Maggie sighed. 'Okay.' Bottom line, she owed Wilma one.

A Receipt

'Milne case.' Chisolm announced, entering the room. He had come straight from a meeting with his DCI, where he'd had his ear roundly chewed.

There were groans around the table.

He drew up a chair, turned to Brian. 'What did you get out of the husband, Burnett?'

'Says he was only putting the wife's rings out of sight of the kids.'

'Did he give a reason?'

'According to Scott, he'd torn a strip off his daughter. Chloe had mislaid her school sports hoodie and needed it for PE the following day. She insisted someone must have nicked it. He reckoned she'd been careless and left it in the school changing room after the previous lesson. They'd had words, anyhow, and Chloe hadn't spoken to him since. So when she came into the bathroom, rather than risk another confrontation, he grabbed the rings and put them in the first place that came to hand.'

'Not because he'd done the wife in?' Duffy added, morosely.

'The voice of doom,' Douglas joked.

One look from Chisolm was enough wipe the grin from his face.

'No. If he's to be believed, it was because he didn't want another scene.'

'Anything else?' Chisolm demanded. 'What about you, Bob?'

Bob? Duffy knitted his brows. That was a new one. 'Nowt to report.'

'You two,' he eyed Douglas and Susan in turn, 'did you get anything at Belvidere Street.'

'Sir.' Douglas jumped in before Susan had time to open her mouth.

'Ladies first,' Chisolm turned to Susan. 'What about this Sam woman? Do we have a photograph yet?'

She shook her head. 'Still working on it, sir.'

'Did you get anything out of the granny?'

'An old address in Dyce, but I haven't had time to...' She cursed Dunn's tardiness at Belvidere Street. If he hadn't insisted on covering the upstairs, hadn't gone into the garden, they'd have had time to nip out to Dyce.

Chisolm cut in. 'Well, then, since all you've managed to turn up is a couple of rings...'

Significant rings. Susan was irked she hadn't got credit for finding them in the first place. Judiciously, she kept her mouth shut.

'Sir.' Dunn's hand shot into the air.

'What?' Chisolm scowled.

'I found a receipt.'

Bastard! Susan threw Douglas a black look. First she'd heard. 'Where?' She didn't want to give him the satisfaction, but the question was out before she could bite her tongue.

'In the Milne's bedroom,' he responded with a smug look.

'That right?' Her tone echoed disbelief.

'Yup. Seems it's not only uniform that miss crucial evidence.'

'Crucial?' she sneered, wondering what could top Debbie Milne's wedding and engagement rings.

'Let's have it, then,' Chisolm interceded.

Out of his folder, Douglas slipped an evidence bag, waved it in the air. 'B&Q,' he announced with a triumphant grin. 'The weekend before his wife went missing, Scott Milne purchased a spade.'

So that's why you were so keen to go in the garden!

'Told you,' Duffy growled. 'He done her in.'

Chisolm ignored him. 'Give it here.'

Douglas passed the evidence bag over.

Chisolm scanned the contents, then, 'A fork, a spade, a climbing plant and a packet of weed-killer. Doesn't look that sinister to me.'

'No, but,' Douglas began.

'Could be perfectly innocent,' Susan was fuming at Dunn's sleight of hand. 'Fella's just moved house.'

'Yes, but...' He protested. '...weedkiller's poisonous. And then there's the spade...'

'That will do.' Chisolm slapped his palm on the table. 'You lot have given me plenty theories, but damn all evidentially, so whether this latest piece of information is of significance or not is a moot point. But taken together with the rings, it's looking increasingly suspicious, especially with absence of proof of life.' He ran fingertips around his chin, where a rash of dark stubble was itching to be scratched. 'But, as you all know, suspicions aren't enough, so let's start again. Facts. What do we know?'

'Not a lot,' Douglas muttered under his breath.

'I hear you,' Chisolm shot back. 'Perhaps, for the benefit of the team, you'd care to list "not a lot" on the investigation board.

With a show of defiance, Dunn scraped back his chair and ambled over to the back wall, where Debbie Milne's photograph was already displayed, along with her description.

For a few moments he stood, toying with a marker pen. Then, 'I'll help you out,' Chisolm barked. 'What don't we know?'

'What Debbie was wearing when she left the house,' Susan offered. Loth as she was to rescue Douglas, her professionalism prevailed.

Dunn scrawled, CLOTHING.

'Only indications are that she'd be dressed much the same as she usually was on a weekday,' Susan elaborated. 'Jeans, boots, some kind of top, maybe a padded jacket. Nothing distinctive enough to give us a break.'

'Anything else?'

'Her direction of travel.' This from Duffy.

Laboriously, Douglas added DIRECTION OF TRAVEL to the list.

'Again, no specifics,' Duffy added. 'Debbie Milne could have headed anywhere.'

'Except, as far as we know.' Brian came in, 'she was on foot. That would limit our search radius.'

'Not necessarily,' Duffy responded. 'She could have arranged to meet someone with transport, caught a bus, train, plane. The possibilities are endless.'

'Keep it coming,' Chisolm urged.

'Her mood,' Brian added with a grimace. In the lead-up to his separation from Bev, he'd become an authority on mood swings.

'Good point, Burnett. As you're aware, we'll have to treat this more seriously if Debbie Milne was in a negative frame of mind.'

'She wasn't, though.' Douglas insisted. He was hacked being made to stand at the whiteboard like the school dunce. 'Not more than anyone else first thing in the morning,' he qualified.

'That's just one day in Debbie's life you're talking about,' Susan argued. 'She could have been worried, depressed.'

Douglas snorted. 'The age her kids are at, it's a bit late to go shouting post-natal depression.'

'I didn't say "post-natal", Susan contested. *God help whoever who lands up with him,* was what she was thinking. 'She's just moved house, and no doubt incurred extra expense in the process, her husband's under pressure at work, her mother's not well, and her dad has not long died. Is that enough for you?'

For once, Douglas was lost for words.

'For all Debbie's outward calm,' Susan continued, 'things could have been building up inside for a long time.'

This was met by nods of agreement. They all knew it didn't take much to tip someone over the edge.

'On a more positive note,' Chisolm put an end to the back-and-forth, 'the stats tell us that around ninety percent of missing persons will be found within forty-eight hours.'

'Of which Debbie Milne,' Douglas couldn't help himself, 'isn't one.'

Chisolm silenced him with a look. 'Just short of a hundred percent within a week. But, given the closed Facebook account, the absence of mobile activity, the fact no funds have been withdrawn, two hypotheses are emerging: one that Debbie Milne has been the victim of foul play, two, that for reasons best known to herself, she doesn't want to be found.'

'That last doesn't chime with what looks like a hasty departure,' Susan commented. 'Rings apart, as far as we can establish Debbie didn't take any luggage: no spare clothes, no toiletries, no make-up.'

'Doesn't sound like any woman I know,' Douglas said.

Sexist pig! This observation was met with a scathing look from Susan.

'Debbie watched a lot of TV, did she not? Maybe she picked up tips off that...' Duffy scratched his bald pate. 'It has gone right out my head.'

'*Hunted*?' Brian supplied.

'That's the one.'

'We can do without the facetious remarks,' Chisolm snapped. 'Either way, it's time we got ourselves a warrant, had a look at the Milnes' finances, together with that laptop and Scott Milne's telephone records.' He paused. 'Does their house have a landline?'

'Yes sir,' Douglas rushed to answer, 'though I understand it's hardly used.'

Chisolm threw him a curt nod. 'That too. As to the husband, get him back in will you, Burnett, under caution this time.'

'Sir. I should mention,' Brian thought he'd better get this in quick. 'Scott Milne has been making noises about search parties.'

Chisolm snorted. 'We've the press to blame for that.' In his head he totted up the projected cost in overtime, not to mention the police helicopter, the divers. How would he get that past his superior officer? 'No, given we've no concrete evidence of foul play, we've a way to go yet before we can justify a full-scale search.'

'Yes sir.'

Chisolm readied himself to leave.

'There is one more thing,' Brian volunteered.

'And that is?' Chisolm snapped, riled by the late interruption.

'It has come to my attention...' *Best get it over with.* He cleared his throat. '...that in the intervening period between Scott Milne being interviewed by uniform and the case being passed to CID, he retained the services of a firm of private investigators.'

'I hope you're not going to tell me,' Chisolm threw Brian a thunderous look, 'we're talking about a firm of *female* investigators.'

''Fraid so, sir.'

A stunned silence ensued. Everyone in the room knew chapter and verse on Maggie and Big Wilma.

'They'll have been stood down when the case was escalated.' Chisolm's tone brooked no argument.

'I imagine so,' Brian replied, non-committal. He said a silent prayer that Maggie Laird had learned her lesson.

Sam

'This friend of Debbie's,' Maggie began. They'd agreed she should lead the interview.

Scott's face darkened. 'Samantha. Samantha Clark.' He'd been so reluctant to take time out from work, they'd made an early evening rendezvous at Starbucks in Union Square.

'Do I gather you don't approve?'

'It's not so much that. More...' That twitching knee again. '... they go way back, the pair of them. Families were neighbours. Sam and Debbie played together, started school together. They were that close.' He demonstrated by crossing his middle over his index finger. 'Like sisters. Christ, they even looked alike. Same build, same eye colour, same dark hair. There was a while back they even dressed the same. Like two peas in a...' He broke off, leaving the word hanging in mid-air.

The PIs waited.

'There was never a father.' Scott took a mouthful of coffee. 'Leastways not since I came on the scene. And Sam had two younger brothers and a sister. Can you imagine? Four kids to play with. Next door was like a magnet to Debbie, her being an only child. She was in and out of Sam's house. If the stories she'd told me are to be believed, her and Sam ran wild together.' He furrowed his brow. 'Still would, I reckon, if they got the chance.'

Maggie leaned forward. 'Could you elaborate on that?'

'They'd not seen as much of one another, not for a while. Did different subjects at secondary. Then, when we were going out together,' he offered a wry smile. '...Debbie didn't have as much time for Sam.'

'I understand.'

'It was about then Sam's family moved away.'

Wilma piped up. 'Do you know where?' She lapped a swirl of

cream off the top of her caramel hot chocolate.

'South. A new town: Livingston, maybe, or Cumbernauld.'

'Oh.' Licking her lips, she tried not to show her disappointment. Tracing Sam Clark could be a struggle. She bit into her cinnamon swirl.

'It's only been the past few months she's been back.'

Maggie's heart did a little flip. 'In Aberdeen?'

'Aye.'

'Are they in touch?' Wilma came back in.

'Sort of.' Said with a sheepish look.

Maggie's mind raced. This could be the lead she'd been waiting for. She took a judicious sip of her coffee, for she knew from experience that keeping her counsel would encourage her client to open up.

'According to Debbie, Sam turned up on our doorstep, right out the blue.' Under the table, his knee performed a little jig. 'Don't know how she found us. We've moved house a couple of times.' He grimaced. 'Though, later, Debbie let on they'd been chatting for a while on Facebook. Anyhow, I was at work at the time. The kids were at school. As Debbie tells it, Sam fell in the door and the pair of them sat the entire afternoon, gabbing like they'd never been apart. After that...'

Maggie held her breath.

'...they met up a few times. I wasn't that keen, I'll be honest with you. Debbie and I are settled. Nice home, two good kids. Sam, well, she fell pregnant when she was seventeen, put the kid up for adoption. Married not long after. Whereas Debbie and me, we waited until...'

Wilma was right in there. 'So Sam could be going under her married name.'

'I doubt it. Married young. Way too young, if you ask me. Older man. He was a decent enough guy, but the marriage didn't last. Never did find out why, but the rumour was, Sam was never at home. Debbie, she had more sense, always did have. Made me wait till she was twenty-one. Anyhow, according to Debbie, Sam's had a string of relationships since, nothing that's ever amounted to much. Plus, she's never held down a job, not a proper job. Seems to stagger from one temp contract to the next.'

Maggie wondered where this was going.

'What I'm trying to say is, Sam's idea of a good time wouldn't be mine.' He frowned. 'Nor what I'd want my wife to be doing.'

Whoops! Maggie raised a mental eyebrow, but managed to keep a neutral expression.

'Not that I'm a prude.' He smiled, grudgingly. 'Far from it. It's just, we lead a quiet sort of life: a family life. It's what Debbie always wanted. What we both wanted. And Debbie's a good wife.' His expression clouded. '*Was* a good wife.'

Alarm bells clanged in Maggie's mind. Should she read something into Scott Milne's use of the past tense, or was it a slip of the tongue?

'Proud of our home,' he ran on. 'Dotes on the kids. I just can't get my head around it.' He looked close to tears. 'It was Debbie wanted to move to a bigger house: somewhere the kids could have a room of their own and still leave a workroom for her. She's creative, see. Into sewing, interior design. She's even...'

'Thanks.' Wilma cut him short. She didn't need telling how important a stable home was. Hadn't she had her fill of dismal rented flats and draughty caravans with that bastard first husband, Darren? She sent a mental prayer of thanks to whoever was up there for her tidy bungalow in Mannofield.

'And it was all coming together,' Scott ran on, undeterred. 'Belvidere Street. Debbie fell in love with the house, was over the moon when our offer was accepted. It was to be our forever home, and she was full of enthusiasm: running up curtains and that. Then, when she came back on the scene – Sam, I mean – it was all clothes and clubbing.'

'Where was Sam living?' Wilma posed the question. She'd already made a mental note Scott hadn't mentioned his and Debbie's relationship.

'No idea. Debbie and her, they'd meet in a bar, one of those trendy joints: Orchids, Revolution, or sometimes in the Queen's Road.'

'Sam didn't come to the house?'

'No.' His eyes slid sideways. 'I didn't encourage it.'

'Was she in work?' Maggie, again.

'According to Debbie, Sam was temping.' He snorted. 'I find that hard to believe. You can't just walk into a job – even a temporary job – in Aberdeen these days. And even if she did, I wouldn't want to employ her.'

'Did she drive?'

'Don't think so.'

'Could they have gone off together, do you think?'

'No way. Debbie's too sensible for that. Running off, I mean, without a word. And, besides, what sort of woman would abandon two young kids?'

Their eyes met.

What sort of woman, indeed?

Humour Me

Brian and Susan were sitting alongside each other, Scott Milne facing them across the interview room table. Indignantly, Scott had declined representation.

'These rings,' Brian began, having run through the preliminaries.

Scott raised a hand to his forehead in resignation. 'We've already been through all that.'

Brian smiled, politely. 'Humour me, if you will.'

'I told you,' Scott said, 'I put them in the drawer out of sight of the kids, Chloe in particular.'

'And that was when?' Brian knew that, in the Arlene Fraser case, nine days had elapsed between the young mother's disappearance and the discovery of her rings. The time frame in this case was shorter, but still.

'Right after I found them, when Chloe went back downstairs.'

'You didn't see them before?' Brian persisted.

'No. Debbie was last in the bathroom. She gets dressed after us, puts on her make-up and stuff. I told you that, too.'

'Hmm.' Brian played for time. Putting Arlene's rings back had been one of the factors that had led to Nat Fraser's conviction. Detectives suspected Fraser had put them back in the house to make it look like Arlene had given up on the marriage and left him. Instead, following a violent attack by her womanising husband, Arlene had begun divorce proceedings. Fearing an adverse financial settlement and losing custody of their two children Nat had laid a trail of deception. He'd thought he could outwit the police, commit the perfect murder, but he'd overplayed his hand. His alibi was too perfect: so tight it had raised question marks among the seasoned investigating team. There again, Brian surmised, Debbie's rings were hidden from sight. He changed tack. 'Your marriage?' He let the question hang.

'Is sound.' Scott replied with a sigh.

Brian cocked an eyebrow. 'You've already admitted to having an argument with your daughter. Are you trying to tell me you and Debbie don't row?'

'Of course we do. Everybody does. But we didn't fall out last Tuesday.'

'When did you last argue?'

'I've no idea. Look, am I going to be here long, because I've a big project on the go, and if I don't get back…'

'I'm sorry to have called you in here again,' Brian soothed. 'But, believe me, I wouldn't do it if it wasn't absolutely necessary.' He engaged Scott with a conspiratorial look. 'We're both after the same thing: to get Debbie home safe and well, don't you agree?'

Scott nodded, miserable.

'So,' Brian glanced down at his notes. 'Your marriage,' he said, looking up. 'How would you describe it?'

'Sound. Debbie and me, we're on the same page.'

'About everything?' Brian's voice rose. 'I find that hard to believe.'

Especially after Bev, was what he was thinking.

'Well, no,' Scott responded. 'Not every single thing.'

'Can you give me an example of something you and Debbie didn't see eye-to-eye on?'

For a few moments, Scott was silent, then, 'My work, I suppose. I've been putting in extra hours these past few weeks, bringing work home. And what with the house move…' He broke off. 'She wasn't too happy.'

Brian nodded. He knew the situation only too well.

'It has taken the shine off the new house, that's for sure.'

'Enough to make Debbie want to leave you?' Brian posited.

'Me, maybe.' Guilt clouded his face. 'The kids? Never.'

'Or make you want Debbie to go?' Brian insinuated.

'No,' Scott's voice rose. 'No way.'

Susan slid an evidence bag across the table. 'For the benefit of the recording, I am showing Scott Milne a B&Q receipt. This receipt,' she addressed Scott. 'Do you recognise it?'

He picked it up. 'Yes.'

'You can confirm it's yours?'

'Yes.'

'And that you purchased the items listed?'

Scott nodded. 'Of course. What are you getting at?'

'I should think that's obvious, Scott,' Susan met his eyes. 'You go shopping for a spade, then your wife goes missing.'

'That's ridiculous.' He leapt to his feet. 'I've had enough of this.'

'Sit down,' Brian ordered.

Sheepishly, Scott took his seat.

'Can you explain to me,' Susan picked up where she had left off, 'why you purchased these items?'

Scott shrugged. 'Isn't that bloody obvious?'

'Not to me.'

'That was one of the reasons we moved house. The garden at Craigiebuckler was the size of a postage stamp,' he explained. 'And with the kids growing up…' He broke off. 'The tools I had were hand-me-downs from my old man. They'd had it, so I chucked them and splashed out on new. Not that I'm a gardener,' he grumbled. 'But Debbie said if she'd to cope with a bigger house, I'd to do the outside.'

'Mmm,' Susan gnawed on the end of her pen. She was likely heading up a dead end. But she'd been livid when Douglas had pulled that one on her. If she could get one over on him she's be a happy bunny.

'I made a start,' Scott elaborated, 'the weekend before she…' His voice wobbled. 'Dug out old raspberry canes. They'll still be there.' His eyes sought Susan's. 'You can check.'

'We will.' She put the pen down. 'There's just one thing I don't understand. Can you explain to me, Scott, how our officers identified in your garden shed a B&Q garden fork such as you've just described?' She fixed him with a penetrating look. 'But could find absolutely no sign of a spade.'

Scott sighed. 'Easy. It broke.'

'Really?' Susan raised an eyebrow. 'I would have thought it would be pretty difficult to break a brand new spade.'

He shrugged. 'You and me both. There must have been old paving stones or something where I was digging. But I kept whacking away.' He paused for breath. 'Debbie had been getting on at me. Then the shovel came away from the shank. Serves me right for buying the cheapest. But we've had that much expense…' He looked to be close to tears. 'I could have had the thing mended, I suppose,' he composed himself. 'But I couldn't be arsed.'

'Where is it now?'

'I was in such a rage, I chucked it in the bin.'

'Which bin would that be?'

He sighed. 'I can't remember.'

'Is that right?' Susan made a mental note to check it out.

'I even bought Debbie a wisteria,' he ran on. 'She's always going on about wisteria. The houses in those glossy magazines she reads are always dripping with it. Guy in the B&Q garden centre said it takes ages to get established.' His eyes welled up. 'Years.'

Distracted or devious? Susan was undecided whether to take this information at face value. The guilty – if they didn't go 'no comment' – tended to be economical with their answers.

She was saved when Brian stepped in. 'Are there any other factors relating to your wife's disappearance that you think might have come into play?'

'Factors?' Scott puzzled. 'Like what?'

'Debbie's friend Sam, for instance.'

'Look,' he leaned across the table. 'I might not like Sam. I might not want Debbie hanging out with Sam. But my wife works her butt off for me and the kids, and if she wants to hang out with bloody Sam I'm not going to be the one to stop her, especially when…' He looked to be on the verge of tears.

'Go on,' Brian encouraged.

He was met with silence.

'Especially when?' Brian urged.

Scott fixed his eyes on the table.

'Scott?' Brian prompted in a soft voice.

Slowly, the younger man lifted his head. 'I can't satisfy her,' he said, his voice full of bitterness. 'The worry, about the job I mean, has got to me.' He looked to Brian for comfort. 'I can't get it up.'

An Item

'Looks like the pair of them done a bunk,' Wilma observed. She and Maggie had agreed to rendezvous at the Inversnecky, midway between Seaton School and Wilma's scheduled meeting in town. Cheery and well-priced – for although Maggie was on top of the household bills she still had to watch the pennies – it also displayed a sandwich board, on which the daily pun never failed to bring a smile to her face.

'How do you figure that out?'

'Dunno. Only it's a bit of a coincidence: Sam turns up out of the blue. Next thing she's gone, her and Debbie both.' Her eyes glowed with satisfaction. *Right again!*

'But why? Sam I can see. But Debbie? She left two kids for God's sake.'

Wilma puckered her lips. 'Could have been an item.'

'A lesbian relationship, is that what you're saying? Don't be daft.'

'Stranger things have happened.' Wilma could picture, still, the faces of the two blokes she'd caught *in flagrante* in that caravan at Maryculter. 'Scott said they'd been close, way back. And kids experiment, you know they do. Maybe Debbie was depressed, unhappy in the marriage. Not even unhappy, just bored. Then Sam appears, all glammed-up, takes Debbie out on the town.'

'That bit I get. The rest…'

'Two halves of the same coin. Think about it: on the one hand you have an only child, on the other the product of a chaotic big family. They feed off each other. Then, later, one has security – all the benefits of family life – but she's trapped, whereas the other can act on a whim. Could be Debbie grounds Sam and Sam lends Debbie glamour. Like thon pair in the black and white movies, you know who I mean?'

'Fred Astaire and Ginger Rogers?'

'Aye. He gave her class, she gave him sex.'

Maggie's eyebrows shot into her hairline. 'Not literally, she didn't.'

Wilma snorted. 'You would know. Anyhow, what I'm saying is it's not beyond the realms their relationship could develop into…'

'Spare me the cod psychology.' Maggie interrupted. She'd been in two minds whether to bring up Scott Milne's use of the past tense in reference to his wife. Thought better of it. This latest theory of Wilma's was a case in point. If they were to succeed in solving Debbie Milne's disappearance, Maggie would need to curb her business partner's imagination. 'Don't you think, if Debbie was that way inclined, she'd have shown some indication way before Sam Clark re-appeared?'

'Doesn't follow. Debbie is an only child, remember. She's used to keeping her own counsel. It's not a huge jump from there to being secretive.'

'Oh, come on.'

'Sometimes it just starts with a cuddle,' Wilma persisted. 'Two lonely women…'

'Too much information.' Maggie cut her off mid-sentence. 'The way you're talking, anyone would think you'd been there yourself.'

Wilma cocked her head. 'I'm saying nowt. But from what we've heard, find Sam, odds on we'll also find Debbie.'

'And how, tell me, do we do that? We've got precious little off Facebook. As far as Scott knows, Sam doesn't have a car, so no registration number, even if we could sweet-talk someone to PNC it. We don't know where Sam was living before she re-appeared in Aberdeen, so we can forget the electoral roll, and there will be a trillion Clarks listed in the phone book. If it's Clark she's calling herself.'

'You heard Scott, the marriage didn't last a minute and she introduced herself as Clark the first time she rolled up to the house. We have to accept that as gospel.'

'Fair enough, but that doesn't take us forward.'

'You could check out the employment agencies.' Wilma gave Maggie a sly look. 'I think you have form there.'

'Don't rub it in.' Maggie shrank from revisiting the scene of the previous year's humiliation, when she'd failed to secure gainful employment as a legal secretary in the wake of George's death.

'I'm serious. If she's in work…'

'It's highly unlikely any agency is going to divulge details of her employer.'

'Even so, she'd need to call in now and again.'

'So we stake out all the employment agencies in town? Can't be done.'

'Fair enough. You got a better idea?'

'Find where Sam has been living since she came back here. If she and Debbie are "an item", as you call it, or even just out for fun, that's where they'll be.'

A Development

The Incident Room was electric with anticipation. They'd been summoned at short notice: Brian from a much needed haircut, Bob Duffy from his admin, Douglas from the gents' lavatory where he'd been dabbing at a spot of ketchup on a new Charles Tyrwhitt shirt, Susan from fetching a jumper from the locker room. She'd a cold coming on, either that or she was pre-menstrual. Either way, she felt like shit.

Chisolm strode through the door. Throwing an armful of folders onto the table, he gestured to his team to be seated.

'Listen up.' His voice brooked no argument. 'Tayside Division…'

Burnett and Strachan sat to attention. Duffy scratched his balls. Dunn adjusted the amount of cuff showing under his suit jacket. The uniforms looked at the floor.

'… have today reported the discovery of an IC1 female body.'

This news was met by a volley of questions:

'Who by?'

'What were the circumstances?'

'Is it Debbie?'

'Sorry, folks. All I can tell you at this stage is that the body was discovered in the early hours in the vicinity of the Perth Road.'

'Cause of death?' Douglas ventured.

He was met by contemptuous looks. There wasn't a pathologist in the world – outside of CSI – would put his reputation on the line without first establishing the scientific facts.

'How long before we get ID?' This from Duffy.

This was met with a dubious frown. 'How long is a piece of string? But, from what little I've gleaned, the remains were in bad shape, so it may take some time.'

'Bad shape, how?' Susan asked, images flitting through her head of the cadavers she'd viewed that were so badly damaged as to be unrecognisable. She stopped short before she got to the decomposed bodies. She'd learned to overcome her early squeamishness, but maggots still gave her the shivers.

'Beaten, I gather, so I wouldn't get your hopes up.'

Susan had a mental vision of Scott Milne wielding a spade. Although Brian, like their DI, hadn't attached great significance to the B&Q purchase, she'd asked uniform to check out Scott's story, prayed they'd beaten the bin men to it. A redeeming thought occurred. 'So,' she put the question. 'We could be looking at either of them, Debbie or Sam?'

'Or neither,' Douglas smirked.

'In any event,' Chisolm held up a silencing hand. 'Sam Clark may have gone off the radar, but she hasn't been reported missing. If she were, that's another story. If Tayside suspected the body was Sam's, and they were able to locate family members, they could obtain familial DNA which, in turn, could lead them to other confirmatory identifiers. Whereas, should their cadaver be Debbie, it will be relatively simple to obtain DNA from her home address and eliminate her from their investigation. Either way,' he flipped his file shut, 'that's all I've got at the moment.

'Would it be an idea, sir,' Susan ventured, 'to put a Family Liaison Officer in the Scott household? I mean, the Tayside murder may not yet be public knowledge, but these things don't take long to get out, not with social media.'

'But we've just agreed,' Douglas cast Susan a scathing glare. 'There's no evidence at this point to link Tayside's cadaver to the Milne investigation. And the budget...' He looked to Chisolm for approbation.

...is fucked. 'Fair comment,' Chisolm replied. 'But I do think Susan has a point.' He addressed his DC. 'I'll get back to you on that one. But for now,' he turned to Brian, 'where are we at with the husband?'

Anyone I Know

'Mum?' Kirsty called from the upstairs bedroom as Maggie was about to shoot through the front door.

'Yes?' she stopped in her tracks.

'Is it okay with you if I have a friend up for the weekend?'

'Of course.' Maggie checked her watch. 'Why wouldn't it be?'

'Just...'

Maggie sprinted up the stairs. Subsequent to the fallout from the bar job, Kirsty had been mercifully quiet, and there had been no more noises about going back to Dundee. Maggie took it as read Kirsty had been looking for other work, but hadn't wanted to raise the matter in case she'd been turned down. Stung by Kirsty's remarks about the house no longer feeling like home, however, she'd resolved to spoil both her children, over the holidays at least.

'Look,' she barged into the bedroom, dropped onto the foot of the bed. 'I know the job didn't work out, but it's not the end of the world. There are other jobs. Better jobs. It's just a matter of being in the right place at the right time.'

'It's not the job,' Kirsty surfaced from under the duvet in a pair of checked pyjamas and bed hair. 'You were right. It was a bum deal: working unsocial hours for minimum pay.'

Maggie kept her counsel.

'I'll call into a couple of employment agencies next week,' Kirsty continued. 'See if there are any office jobs going. Maybe ring round some solicitors as well.'

It was on the tip of Maggie's tongue to suggest a couple of her client firms. She thought better of it. Best leave her daughter to do her own thing. 'Good idea,' she said. Then, 'Anyone I know?'

'Huh?'

'This friend? Is it someone local?'

'No.' Kirsty yawned. 'From Dundee.'

'I thought Sarah was abroad.'

'She is. And it's not a girl, mum, it's a boy?'

Where will he sleep? was Maggie's first thought. 'Oh!' she said. 'Right.'

'He's had a bad experience.'

'Really?' Maggie affected polite interest. From what she'd gleaned since the advent of social media, a 'bad experience' covered everything from failing an exam to being unfriended on Facebook. 'I'm sorry to hear that,' she covered her back, just in case.

'I thought a change of scene would do him good,' Kirsty added.

'What day are we talking?'

'Friday lunchtime, I thought.'

Maggie's mind worked overtime. She had a heavy meeting with Harlaw Insurance scheduled for Friday morning, precognitions to take in the afternoon. Then there was Colin's rugby kit to put through the wash, and the weekly shop, and… 'Okay.' Hadn't she resolved to spoil her kids? She'd manage, somehow. She took a surreptitious peek at her watch. If she didn't get a move on, she'd be late for school. 'Is there anything this boy doesn't eat?' At that age, she knew, they were led by their stomachs.

'No, he's not fussy.'

'That's good to hear.' She smiled encouragement. Too many kids professed to have allergies: if it wasn't wheat it was soya, either that or peanuts. Maggie couldn't be doing with any of it. For once, she was thankful for Colin's hearty appetite and Kirsty's healthy eating. 'How about sleeping arrangements?' she ventured. Best get that out of the way.

Kirsty stifled another yawn. 'Dunno. We can worry about that when he gets here.'

Maggie speculated on the relationship: was it platonic, she wondered? If so, would the couch suffice? Or might Kirsty expect her guest to have a proper bed, in which case she could have the couch. Then, maybe Kirsty was planning to share a bed with this person, Maggie fretted. It wasn't uncommon for friends of different sexes to share nowadays, that much she'd been informed. She made a mental note to change Kirsty's sheets on Thursday. She was tempted to ask how long the friend would be staying, thought the better of it. 'How will he be travelling?' she asked, instead.

'Bus, I expect. But, don't worry, he won't need picked up.'

One less thing! Maggie checked her watch again.

'He's been before.'

Maggie stiffened. 'Here?'

'Yes. Shaz. Don't you remember him?'

Remember him? Maggie would never forget him, ignorant little runt that he was. She could picture him, still, trying to impose his will on her little girl, treating Kirsty with disrespect. 'Yes. Vaguely. Look,' her mind worked overtime. 'This weekend's not the best. Can we leave it off till another time?' With a bit of luck, Kirsty would forget all about it.

'Not really.' Kirsty's lower lip jutted. 'He's in a bit of a state.'

'Well, if that's the case,' Maggie said, grudgingly, 'Friday it is.'

She got to her feet. 'Look, I've got to run. You enjoy your lie-in. We can talk about it tonight.'

The Illicit Still

'What are you saying to it, Sarge?'

'Huh?' Brian started at Susan's question.

They – Duffy, Strachan and himself – were in the Illicit Still, a traditional pub in the city's Netherkirkgate. Dunn, citing a hot date, had ducked out. Now that the Athenaeum had been taken over by a chain, this pub – along with the Old Blackfriars in Castle Street – had become the go-to for Chisolm's squad. Not that pubs were high on their agenda. What with police cutbacks and demands on the domestic front, detectives these days were a relatively clean-living lot. Added to which, even one bevvy could render you foul of the drink-driving limits.

'Tayside cadaver. Think the Dundee quine is our misper?'

Brian shrugged. 'Wouldn't put money on it.'

'You're a negative bastard,' Duffy said.

That's rich coming from you! 'Join the club,' he retorted. Bad enough what twenty odd years policing did to a man without the added ignominy of being cuckolded.

Duffy laughed. 'You for another?'

'No.' Brian nursed his pint of Caledonia Best.

'Come on,' Duffy gave him a nudge. 'Push the boat out. We're off the clock.'

'Thanks.' Although his bedsit was within walking distance, he was trying to cut back. 'I'll stick.'

'Susan?'

'Not for me. I've a bus to catch.'

'Ah weel, I better lay off, I suppose,' Duffy said. 'Meeting the wife for late-night shopping. Then we'll have a bite to eat before we head home.'

Home? Brian had a mental vision of his bleak bedsit. Wondered if he'd ever have a proper home again.

'Not that you haven't got a point,' Bob Duffy took a swallow of his Tennents. 'On the Tayside case I mean. The one single thing their case has in common with ours is that the subjects are both female.'

'You saying you haven't heard anything on the jungle drums?' Susan asked, incredulous. The older sergeant was the go-to for station gossip.

'Blunt-force trauma,' he stated in a disappointed voice.

'Who does that remind you of?' Brian floated the question.

'The Law Killer.'

'I remember,' Susan acknowledged. She took a careful sip of her drink: vodka and tonic with fresh lime. For the umpteenth time – her system sluggish from a regimen of sedentary work and junk food – she'd embarked on a healthy eating kick.

'Aye,' Duffy nodded. 'Robbie McIntosh. Battered a dog walker near to death with a dumbell. Left her unconscious. Bastard was already banged up for stabbing another woman to death. He was on home leave from Castle Huntly when the second attack happened. Victim was left permanently disfigured and impaired.'

'Where's McIntosh now?'

'That's the problem,' Duffy answered. 'Banged up again, evil wee scrote that he is. Five years, minimum, the sentence was, with a lifetime restriction. Bastard will still be inside.'

'Where does that leave us?' Susan again.

'In the dark,' Brian responded.

'And I caught the boss cracking his knuckles today,' she went on. 'Sure sign he's stressed.'

'He'll be getting stick from upstairs,' Brian defended their DI. 'Not that it's going to go away anytime soon. You have to admit, guys, we're getting nowhere fast. As for Tayside's body, it could be anybody: a prostitute fallen foul of a john, a drug addict done in for a debt, a student out clubbing chose the wrong dance partner. Take your pick.'

'We'd better pick quick,' Duffy observed, gloomily, 'before the Feds' – referring to Police Scotland's centralisation policy – 'come up the fucking A90.'

A Verbal Warning

'I won't beat around the bush,' Anne Shirrefs, the head teacher, indicated the chair opposite. 'I've called you in today because there have been a number of lapses this term, which...'

'I can explain,' Maggie cut in, her ears burning.

'If you'll let me finish,' Anne continued. '...have not gone unnoticed by me or, sadly, by your teaching colleagues.'

Maggie squirmed in her seat. Working the Milne case had eclipsed all else in her diary. She'd been pushing her luck, she knew, burning the candle at both ends, hoping she wouldn't get caught out. That morning's session with Kirsty had caused her to be late again for her Seaton job. And now here she was, feeling like a five-year-old. Inwardly, she cursed herself for not being ahead of the curve. She, who prided herself on her organisational skills, should have seen this coming.

'You've been through the mill, I know. But...'

The understatement of all time! Maggie thought: the drugs trial, George's disgrace and subsequent death. Then the birthing pains of the agency: student Lucy Simmons' tragic demise, Sheena Summers' later overdose and, now, Debbie Milne's disappearance. Anne Shirrefs was a decent sort: a divorced mum of three, she understood the daily juggling act that was the lot of working mothers. But, Maggie was painfully aware, she also had to maintain standards in the face of dwindling staff numbers and a series of budget cuts. Mentally, she posited myriad excuses: her health, her kids. No, she decided, better hold her hands up.

'I'm sorry.' She engaged Anne with an earnest look. 'I've had a lot in my plate this past week or two.'

'Bit more than a couple of weeks,' the head continued with a grim smile. 'Aside from which, story goes you've been spending time socialising with a male supply teacher. Would that be correct?'

'Yes,' Maggie conceded. Then 'No. We had a drink, admitted, but it was a one-off.'

'Not that your personal life is my business,' Anne Shirrefs allowed. 'Except insofar as it interferes with your duties here at Seaton. Do you understand where I'm coming from?'

Maggie nodded. She should have trusted her instincts, not allowed vanity to interfere with her judgement.

'And from where I'm sitting,' the head teacher ran on, 'looks to me like you're having difficulty fitting in your hours here at Seaton with your other…' She paused for a moment's reflection. '… commitments.'

Maggie held up her hands. 'Fair comment. I can only repeat…'

Anne cut in. 'Consensus is, your mind's not on the job.' She paused. 'You are still committed to your position here?'

Consensus? Maggie's first thought was the old guard had it in for her, then: *Who could blame them?* Her innate sense of fairness prevailed.

'Totally,' she responded, with more vehemence than she'd intended. 'In the time I've been here, I'd like to think I've made a useful contribution. And, ' her voice wobbled, 'I love the kids.'

'Yes,' Anne's smile was genuine, 'we all do, toe-rags that some of them are. However, to get back to the matter in hand,' she fixed Maggie with a troubled gaze. 'If you want to hold onto your job, you'll need to pull your socks up: tighten that time-keeping for a start. Consider this a verbal warning.' She scribbled a note on the form in front of her.

Maggie's cheeks blazed. Her Seaton job had been so hard won. Even George had been against it. And since she'd taken on his business, it had kept her grounded. Her work as a teaching assistant was fairly routine, and the relocation of the pre-additional support service from Seaton to the new Orchard Brae School had made her workload less onerous. Her working environment was safe, too, both these aspects the antithesis of the private investigation world, which was hand-to-mouth, erratic and – dealing as it did in people's misfortunes and the baser elements of society – sometimes downright dangerous. Were Maggie to relinquish her post, she'd be hard-pressed to find another, far less one that would fit in with Colin's school day. Plus, for all the inroads she and Wilma had made into making the detective agency a viable concern, Maggie still relied heavily on the small, but steady, income.

Her mobile pinged.

Not now! Thrown further off balance, she dug into her pocket, took a surreptitious dekko at the screen: a message from Wilma. Maggie wondered what had occasioned it. In normal circumstances, she'd have kept her phone switched off in school, at least outside of breaks. And, besides, Wilma knew not to cut across Maggie's classroom duties.

She looked up. 'Sorry,' she said, again, moving to stuff her phone back where it came from.

'Go ahead.' Anne Shirrefs cast a concerned look. 'Might be important.'

'No, really.' She was unsure whether the head was being sarcastic – yet more ammunition to damn Maggie with – or whether, as a working mum herself, Anne empathised.

'I insist.'

Maggie opened the message: *Dad in ARI.* Nearly fainted with fright.

'It's my father,' she gasped. 'He's been taken into hospital.'

Her mind churned: why was her dad in Aberdeen Royal Infirmary as opposed to his local hospital in Inverurie, what emergency had occasioned his admission, what if she wasn't in time? If he were to pass away, it would be more than she could bear. In her head she relived the day George died: the way the police had come calling, her frenzied dash to her new next-door-neighbour, the drive with Wilma to the mortuary. For as long as she lived, Maggie wouldn't forget the sight of her husband, lying discoloured and sightless on that viewing room gurney.

'Well, you'd better get yourself up there,' the head teacher said, rising. 'And do what's needed. I'll make sure your absence is covered.' Her voice softened. 'We'll keep this other thing between us for now.'

'Thanks.' Gratefully, Maggie scraped back her chair and shot out the door.

ARI

'What are you doing here?' Maggie demanded.

From the bed, her father offered a weak smile. 'I could ask you the same question.'

'That's not funny.'

'We didn't want to worry you,' he said, in an attempt to placate her.

Worry her? The minute she came out of the meeting with her head teacher, she'd run to the staffroom, grabbed her coat and handbag and sprinted to the car. With an agency appointment scheduled after school, she'd immediately called to make her excuses and driven straight to the hospital. She'd got in a lather trying to find a parking space. By the time she'd checked out admissions – where Wilma had spotted her dad's name as she came on shift – made enquiries, and located his ward, she was a wreck.

'And you think hearing second hand...' Her voice rose. '...that your elderly father has been rushed into hospital in Aberdeen isn't a matter for concern?' She broke off, trembling. Over the past few years, she'd seen a gradual deterioration in both her parents, but this was the first time she'd actually contemplated their mortality.

He regarded her calmly. 'I'm not that old. I wasn't rushed here. We drove. Quite a leisurely drive, in fact. And your mother was going to ring you.'

'When?' Maggie's throat hitched. 'When you were...' She broke off, imagining the worst.

'There's no need to get yourself het up,' he responded, unflustered. 'It's not anything serious.'

'Then why, tell me, are you in a cardiology ward?'

Her father held up a cautionary hand. 'I had a wee turn, that's all. Your mother was set on taking me into Inverurie. They insisted on sending me here. And this lot,' he waved an arm, 'want to keep me in while they run some tests.'

'What sort of tests?' She wondered what he was keeping from her.

'ECG, some other thing I can't remember. All routine,' he smiled. 'Nothing to worry about.'

'Where's mum now?'

'Gone downstairs to pick up a few things and have a cup of tea.'

'Right.' Maggie said, her body stiff with tension.

'Why don't you go down and join her? She'll be pleased to see you.'

'No.' Maggie shot back. Her father had been the peacekeeper in the old farmhouse all through her teenage years, when she'd gone hammer and tongs with her mum on what seemed, then, a daily basis. Even now, she didn't trust herself not to let her mum wind her up. 'I'll sit here with you for a bit, if that's alright.'

'Of course.' He patted the bedcover.

Nervous of being ticked off by the charge nurse, Maggie lowered herself onto the orthopaedic chair that sat by the bed. She leaned back, closed her eyes, trying to compose herself. A vision of Sheena Struthers flashed into her head. Maggie had sat in an identical chair when she'd sneaked into Sheena's room in the guise of a police detective in the hope of getting to the truth.

'Alright, pet?'

Her eyelids jolted open. 'I'm fine, Dad,' she smiled reassurance.

His beamed. 'Well, pet, if you're fine, then I'm a happy man.'

* * *

'Mum?'

Her head came up from the newspaper. 'Maggie.' Her face lit up. 'What are you doing here?'

Maggie shrugged. 'Dad just asked me the same question.'

'You've seen him?'

'Not two minutes ago. Got word from Wilma. Came straight here.'

'Sit down.' She moved her handbag from the adjacent seat. 'Can I get you something: tea, a sandwich maybe? You look as if you haven't eaten in days.'

Typical! Her mum's first thought was to feed Maggie up. Except she wasn't a kid, she was a grown woman. Then: *That's not fair. Didn't Maggie behave in the exact same way towards her own kids?*

'Thanks, but no. I have to get back to work.'

'Oh.' That one syllable spoke a lifetime of disappointment.

'Not right away.' Maggie dropped onto the seat. 'How are you, Mum?'

'Doing away.' The small frown lodged in her forehead spoke volumes.

'You must have got a fright.'

'Yes. Your dad is of an age – we both are – when…' Her voice wobbled.

'Oh, Mum,' Maggie exclaimed, 'you're not old.' *Not that old,* was what she was thinking. Her initial reaction on seeing her parents was how small they looked.

'No.' Her mother summoned a feeble smile. 'But you have to make allowances. I've been worried about your dad for a while. He's been complaining of pains: in his chest, his arms, his jaw. Breathlessness, too. And he's permanently tired. Yawns from morning to night. But he's cussed. Won't go near a doctor. That's why I insisted he get himself checked out after he took this last turn.'

'Last turn?' Maggie echoed. 'How often has this happened?'

'A few times,' her mother grudged. 'That I know about, anyway.' Abruptly, she changed the subject. 'How are the kids?'

'Great,' Maggie lied. 'I'm sorry we haven't been out for a while, but with one thing and another…'

Her mum cut in. 'You're working too hard.'

Maggie grimaced. 'Needs must.'

'Can't you ease off a bit? You'll be the one ends up in hospital if you carry on like you're doing. You won't be a lot of use to Kirsty and Colin then.'

'Don't exaggerate,' Maggie retorted.

'You always were independent-minded,' her mum ran on, undeterred.

For "independent" read "wilful". 'The agency's more manageable now than it was when I first took it on,' she fibbed, surprised at her new-found facility. 'And there's Wilma.' At whose elbow Maggie learned. 'She's been…'

'Ah, yes, Wilma,' her mum interrupted. 'Seems to me you rely too much on that woman.'

That woman. The inflection in her mother's voice said it all. First Val, and now her mum commenting on Wilma's influence. They couldn't both be wrong, could they?

'That's not fair,' Maggie sprang to her colleague's defence. 'Wilma's a hard worker. I couldn't run the business without her.'

'Couldn't you?' Her mother asked, her expression unreadable.

'No.' Maggie kept her voice even, although inwardly she seethed. Her mum was the product of a different generation: conservative, class-ridden. She thought of all those times Wilma had accused her of snobbishness. No marks for guessing where Maggie got it from.

'You could let us help.'

'Help?' Maggie echoed. 'How?'

'Paperwork, housework, shopping, gardening. There's umpteen wee jobs your dad and I could manage that would take the pressure off of you.'

'But,' Maggie protested, 'if he's not well.'

'Once they do the tests and prescribe whatever's needed, I'm sure he'll be fine.'

'Plus, you live miles away.'

'Twenty minutes. Wouldn't be a problem one or two days a week.'

'Oh,' Maggie said, quite lost for words. In the bleak months following George's death, she'd been so crisis-ridden, so driven in her quest for justice it hadn't occurred to her to seek succour beyond her home patch. Nor had she considered that her parents might be at a loose end since they moved from the farm. Lonely, even. She felt the old, familiar stab of guilt.

Her mobile vibrated.

'Sorry,' she fumbled in her bag, checked the screen. 'Duty calls.' She met her mother's eyes, the irony not lost on either of them. 'I'd best be going,' Maggie smiled an apology. 'Ring me when you get Dad's test results.'

A Connection

'DI Maguire?'

'Speaking.'

'DI Allan Chisolm, Aberdeen City.'

'What can I do for you?' The voice on the other end of the line was guarded.

'Your cadaver…'

'What about it?'

'You'll have been briefed on our misper.'

'And?'

'I wondered whether there might be a connection?' Said without conviction, for Chisolm had only placed the call in the face of increased pressure from upstairs.

There was silence, then. 'What makes you think that?'

'Long shot I know…' Chisolm played for time. He hadn't expected a joyous reception. Since the amalgamation in 2013 of Scotland's eight regional police forces into the unified Police Scotland, many officers harboured deep-seated resentment that major cases previously handled on a local basis became the remit of the centralised two thousand strong Specialist Crime Division, from which detectives were parachuted to the far ends of the country. That this wasted time and money and distracted from day-to-day policing was a commonly held belief, and made it more difficult to cement relationships. '…but I thought a call wouldn't go amiss, if only to rule your body out. What stage are you at with identification?'

'Nowhere near.'

Inwardly, Chisolm groaned. It could take weeks for identification to be positively confirmed, and he knew from experience it was pointless trying to hurry the process. 'Do you have anything at all?' he asked, in desperation.

'What I can tell you…' Maguire said, grudgingly. '…is our cadaver is a right-handed female aged between twenty-five and forty.'

Chisolm jumped on this. 'Fits the bill for our misper.'

'Aye,' Maguire conceded. 'Her and half of Dundee.'

'Fair dos,' Chisolm allowed, his mood plummeting. 'Will you keep us updated on the ID?

'If you insist.' There wasn't a trace of humour in Maguire's voice. 'Now if that's all…'

'Just one more thing. Sam Clark. Name ring a bell?'

'Who's asking?'

'She's a known associate of our misper.'

'That right?'

Chisolm thought he detected a note of interest. 'Moved up here from your neck of the woods. Got anything on her?'

'Might have.'

'Can I press you on that?'

'Nope. Not my remit.'

'Whose, then?'

'Not for me to say. Look, I've got to get on.'

'I understand,' Chisolm said, though inside he was seething. 'I'll keep in touch.'

A Bad Lot

'I told you the last time,' Scott Milne spread his hands in exasperation, 'Sam Clark appeared out of the blue and seems to have crawled back into her hole. Wherever that is,' he added with a curl of his lip.

'And you can't remember which new town her family moved to?' Maggie enquired. 'The woman had to be registered with a GP, a dentist, somebody.'

'No. It was years ago. And anyhow, they could have moved on from there. Plus, the mum could be dead by now.'

They were back in the Union Square shopping centre. Not Patisserie Valerie, Maggie noted thankfully. She'd had enough bad experiences meeting clients there. Not Starbucks, nor any of the other coffee shops. It was lunchtime, and the eating places were queued out, so they'd had to settle for a quiet corner just off the concourse, where the footfall was constant, the background music relentless. Scott had been reluctant to take even a short break from work, and in the absence of good news, she'd had to exercise all her powers of persuasion to engineer even this hurried assignation.

'When her and Debbie went out,' Wilma began.

She and Debbie, Maggie corrected in her head.

'Was there anywhere – a bar, a club – they went to on a regular basis?'

'Don't think so, not that they gave a lot away. They were forever in a huddle, whispering and giggling behind their hands. It was obvious they didn't want to include me, and I wasn't going to ask.'

Male pride.

'But the impression I got was they were doing the rounds, trying out this one and that. "Broadening her horizons", Debbie said, the one time I took her to task.'

'And Debbie never went to Sam's place? Sam always called at yours?'

'As I said,' he checked the time on his watch, 'Sam rolled up and off they went.'

'Debbie never stayed over?' Maggie this time.

Scott bristled. 'What do you think I am? She'd be late, I grant you, after midnight sometimes this past while. But she'd the kids to see to. And there's no way a wife of mine…' He took another glance at his watch.

'I understand,' Maggie soothed. 'And, believe me, I don't want to pry, but…'

'You're wasting your time,' he snapped. 'Like I told you, Sam Clark is a rolling stone. The woman's a bad lot, and if she doesn't want to be found you haven't a hope in hell of…'

'Other than you and your children, she may be the last person to have seen Debbie…' Maggie bit her lip.

'…alive?' Scott shrilled. 'Is that what you don't want to say? I don't know why I'm standing here. If Debbie had been a sixteen-year-old, the police would have had search parties out: sniffer dogs, helicopters with infra-red, you name it. And you pair,' he eyeballed Maggie and Wilma in turn, 'you're no better. All talk and no action.' He turned to go.

Wilma grabbed him by the sleeve. 'Now, you listen to me.'

'No,' Maggie prised Wilma's fingers free. 'He's right. I can't speak to the police investigation, but we haven't been sufficiently pro-active. And that's because we've had so little to work with. Now if there's anything,' she flashed an empathetic smile, 'anything at all Sam mentioned: a flat-mate, a neighbour, where she shopped, what bus she took? Anything that will help us narrow her location?'

'Couldn't tell you.' Scott Milne started to walk away.

'If you think of something,' Maggie called after him.

He paused, mid-stride. 'There was a boyfriend,' he called over his shoulder. 'Oiler.'

Maggie's heart took a little leap. 'Do you have a name?'

Scott turned. 'Only a nickname.' His forehead creased in a frown. 'Daft, it was: Bingo, something like that.'

'You sure?' she called across the heads of shoppers.

'No.'

Maggie slumped back against a pillar. She felt like a balloon someone had stuck a pin into. Wilma, she saw, had wandered off and was eyeing a fake leopard coat in a nearby shop window.

Then: 'Bongo.' Scott Milne was no longer distinguishable in the melee, but Maggie could have sworn she'd heard him right.

V

Refuge

It looked like any other house on the street: same panelled front door, same sash windows, same postage stamp of a front garden. But the windows were masked by vertical blinds, and above the door a CCTV camera blinked a watchful eye.

Jean Meston stirred in the narrow single bed. She opened one eye. The walls were papered in a floral pattern, the carpet patterned too. *Autumn colours.* Jean coined the phrase from another life: a life where her own mother still cherished her only daughter, Jean's parents having cut her off when she married Mike Meston, of whom they disapproved. And they were right. Jean contemplated the shabby furniture, the washed-out Polyester bedding. *Done*, her mum would have called that duvet cover. Jean's eyes welled with tears. Bit like her.

Squeezing both eyes shut, she relived the chain of events that had brought her to this place. How while Mikey was in Peterhead she'd run up debt just to feed and clothe her youngest and keep the electric on. How when Willie's wee arrangement with Fatboy had come to an abrupt end she couldn't service the loan. How the debt had been sold on to a loan shark. Still, Jean compensated, it wasn't her fault, not entirely. She'd been lonely when her husband was in prison. That's the main reason she drank: for company. That, and the warm, fuzzy space. And Mikey was the maker of his own misfortune. If he'd stuck to what he knew, steered clear of drugs, he wouldn't have been banged up, and her wean would still be at home.

Mikey had gone ballistic when he found out about the debt, and she'd been back more than once to the infirmary since her run-in with the young Sri Lankan, each time with escalating injuries. Each time the filth had been summoned. She'd given a misleading statement. Refused to press charges. Until this last time, when:

It won't do you any harm, the young PC had argued, *to take a break, spend a few nights' peace and quiet in a safe place, get your head together. Then, if you agree, the police will bring a case against your husband.*

This time, Jean had been too weak to argue. A night or two on his own would give Mikey time to calm down. Then, she could go back home. Home? She uttered an anguished sigh. She'd cast her two older sons out when they'd followed their father into a life of petty crime. She'd lost her youngest to the care of his gran. All she had left was a four-in-the-block council flat, and even that was in Mikey's name.

Jean had come to the refuge with only the clothes on her back, not even a toothbrush. The place was okay, but the shared kitchen and bathroom facilities meant privacy was at a premium, so for the first couple of days she'd been content to stay in her room. Besides which, the kids who capered in the dayroom brought home to her how much she missed Willie. On the rare occasions she'd seen him since he was removed from the parental home, he'd been withdrawn. Every visit, it broke Jean's heart to walk away. She'd give anything, she thought, now, to make a home again, just for the two of them. To have familiar things around her – not that her stuff was great, but it was her stuff. To hug her wee lad tight, never let him go.

There was a soft tap at the door.

'Yes?' She lifted her head from the pillow.

The door inched open. A grey head popped around. 'I've brought you a cup of tea.'

'Thanks,' Jean struggled to a sitting position.

'No problem.' The older woman – Jean would have put her in the late sixties – placed a mug on the bedside table. 'Didn't know if you took sugar, but I've put some in.' She smiled. 'Given the circumstances.'

Jean turned on her side, took a cautious sip. 'It's fine,' she blew on the surface. 'More than fine.' She couldn't remember when someone had last made her a cup of tea.

'There's a sitting-room downstairs, company when you feel up to it. Take your time,' her companion urged. 'Stay in bed for an hour, all day if you want. There are no rules here. Well,' she rolled her eyes, 'one or two, but mostly our rules are for the male of the species.'

At the mention of men, Jean grimaced. That's what had landed her there. Wherever "there" was. The hospital social worker had disclosed few details: merely that it was "safe".

'If you feel like talking,' the woman hovered by the bed, 'My name's Ella. I'm here to listen. We don't judge,' she added quickly, seeing the doubt on Jean's face.

'Not a lot to tell.'

'Try me. I'm a nurse,' she offered. 'Retired now, but you could say I've heard it all.'

'What the hell? Jean made her decision. The woman had a kindly face, right enough. Jean drained her mug. 'You'd better sit down.'

Back to the Drawing Board

Chisolm strode through the Incident Room door.

'What's the story from West Bell Street?' Douglas pounced, eager as a puppy.

'Disappointing,' Chisolm replied. He crossed to the whiteboard, where both Debbie and Sam's photos were now displayed side by side, the Passport Office having finally furnished a likeness. 'No ID on that body yet, I'm afraid.'

There was a collective groan.

'So that means…' Douglas started to speak.

'…it could be either of them.' Brian finished the sentence.

'Or neither.' In Wood's absence, Duffy had assumed the mantle of the team's naysayer.

'Will their pathologist be able to narrow the age window?' Susan asked.

'Possibly, though that will take time. Chronological age is more difficult to determine once the bones have stopped growing but before arthritis and tooth loss have set in.'

Catching Dunn's superior look, Susan nodded acknowledgement, wishing she'd kept her mouth shut.

'There is one more thing,' Chisolm added.

'What's that?' This from Duffy.

'The woman didn't walk with a limp.'

This received a mixed reception, the team unsure if their DI was trying to be funny.

'I was, however, party to one piece of useful intel, namely that Sam Clark was on Tayside's radar.'

'In what capacity?' Douglas again.

'That's as much as I know. DI Maguire, my point of contact, refused to be drawn.'

'He give a reason, boss?' Brian queried.

'For starters, Sam Clark isn't his case. Plus, whoever's handling it is not for sharing.' He raised his eyes to the ceiling. 'Hush-hush, by all accounts.'

'Even they did share,' Susan puzzled. 'That doesn't help us find Debbie, not unless Sam involved her in some way.'

'In what?' Dunn's lip curled. 'Got any bright ideas?'

'Shop-lifting for one. Debbie worked in a fashion shop. She'd lost her part-time job. If she wanted to go out on the razzle-dazzle with Sam and was strapped for cash, she might have been tempted to lift an outfit or two.'

'Oh, come on,' Douglas came back. 'That's preposterous.'

'Okay. Maybe not shoplifting but some other kind of misdemeanour.'

'Like?'

'Cuff it.' Brian lost his cool. 'Susan has a point. We know the two of them went out on the town together. Do you think they could have been up to mischief?'

'Not a hope.' Bob Duffy added his voice to the mix. 'Debbie's too much of a domestic goddess.'

'That scuppers our sightings,' Susan said, reflectively. 'Given what you've just told us, sir, it could have been Sam, not Debbie, our witness saw in the hotel. Same goes for the bus.'

'Fits,' Douglas conceded.

'You're jumping the gun,' Chisolm responded, resuming his seat. 'Making the circumstances fit the story rather than being evidence-led.' He cracked his knuckles, first one hand, then the other. 'It's facts we need.'

'Agreed,' Duffy said, morose. 'And we've damn few of these.'

'On the subject of which,' he zoomed in on Susan. 'Where are we at with this Dyce address?'

She reddened. 'Toiling, I'm afraid.'

'Well,' Chisolm urged. 'Stick with it.'

'We've a FLO in place at Belvidere Street,' Brian offered. 'Maybe she'll get us something.'

'How's Scott taking it?' Chisolm enquired.

Brian shrugged. 'Much as you'd expect.

Susan breathed a sigh of relief. Uniform had, indeed, missed the Belvidere Street refuse collection. And it was more than her life was worth to raise the subject with Chisolm again. Not until Tayside had identified their body, at any rate. A landfill search would involve a huge amount of time and resources, which Aberdeen Division could ill afford.

Getting back to Sam,' he continued, 'did DI Maguire have anything else to offer?'

'Not a great deal. Not our jurisdiction. You know how it is.'

The team exchanged glances. They knew only too well. An early casualty of Police Scotland's streamlining process had been the closure of Aberdeen's call centre. Despite call handling problems at Bilston Glen, command and control responsibilities had shifted to Dundee. One notable example of failures in communication had been when officers were dispatched to Great Western Road in Glasgow to attend a shop break-in instead of Aberdeen, a hundred and twenty miles away. In consequence, police arrived at the crime scene three and a half hours after the offence was reported.

'So I wouldn't get your hopes up,' Chisolm admonished. 'Or look to Tayside to solve Debbie Milne's disappearance. Until they ID their cadaver, I want to see some solid police work from you lot. So get yourselves out there. It's back to the drawing board.'

What's the Story?

Maggie was kneeling on the classroom floor, halfway through clearing a cupboard of teaching aids, when her mobile pinged.

Dammit! She fished the phone from her pocket and took a surreptitious peek.

A message from her mum. *Dad's results.*

Typical! No indication whether they were good or bad.

Mind whirling, she sat back on her heels.

'Will you be finished soon?' The tone was peremptory.

Maggie looked over her shoulder. One of the old guard was standing in the doorway.

'Yes,' she answered. Then, 'No.'

She leapt to her feet, scattering drawing materials in all directions.

'Where do you think you're going?' the older teacher asked as Maggie brushed past her.

'Out,' Maggie hissed.

'Out where?' The teacher consulted her wristwatch. 'The bell's not due to ring until...'

Maggie turned on her heel. 'None of your bloody business.'

* * *

'What's the story?' Maggie collared her mother in the hospital corridor. 'Are Dad's test results okay?' Notwithstanding her verbal warning from the head teacher, when she got her mother's message she'd decided her father's health was more important than any part-time job and driven at top speed to the hospital.

'Angina,' her mum replied, her expression doleful. She'd been sent off the ward whilst the nurses undertook some procedure or other.

'Oh,' Maggie reeled back. 'That's serious, isn't it?'

'Serious enough to bring on a heart attack or stroke. Just as well I made him get himself checked out.'

Right again! Maggie noted the satisfied look on her mother's face. 'But it's treatable?' she queried.

'He'll have to take drugs, a whole cocktail of them: aspirin, statins, whatever. And you know your father's not a pill taker. If they don't work...' The question hung between them.

Maggie waited for as long as she could bear. Then, 'Yes?'

'They can put in a stent, but that's short-term. Or there's open-heart surgery.'

'But,' Maggie protested, 'that's a major operation.' She racked her brains for what she could remember of the outcomes: irregular heartbeat, lung or kidney failure, memory loss. And those were apart from the primary heart attack or stroke that might ensue, the infections a patient could pick up in hospital. All these she's researched in the aftermath of George's death in an attempt to second-guess the contributing factors.

Her thoughts were interrupted by a cheery, 'You can go in now.'

'Dad?' She beat her mother to the bedside.

'You're a surprise.' He looked tired and frail, but his smile was wide. 'Thought you'd be off chasing some villain.'

Maggie tried hard to return his smile, but her emotions were all over the place: anxiety over her dad's prognosis, uncertainty with regard to her part-time job, guilt she'd neglected both her parents, not only since George died but long before, worry over her children. Then the agency. What did Wilma get up to when she followed up leads on her own? Were her activities legal? And how far was she a willing collaborator in the pursuit of Maggie's quest for justice, to what extent manipulating Maggie for her own ends? 'Never too busy to give my old Dad a hug,' she lied, bending to embrace him.

She straightened in time to catch a dubious look on her mother's face. 'How are you feeling?' she addressed her dad.

'I'm fine.'

Now who's fibbing?

'When are they letting you home?'

'In a day or two. Depends on getting the all clear from the consultant.'

'Your condition, it's manageable, then?'

'Sure,' he offered a reassuring grin. 'Common thing in somebody my age.'

'How long are you staying?' Her mum changed the subject.

'Just as long as.' Maggie said a silent prayer it wouldn't be more than half an hour. She found the atmosphere oppressive. Couldn't think of anything to talk about once they'd exhausted the obvious. Plus, she'd left the classroom in such a shambles it was sure to bring another reprimand, and she hadn't done anything about Col's dinner. 'Why?'

'I thought we might go downstairs in a bit, have a cup of tea.'

'You do that,' her dad chipped in. 'Not often you get a chance to catch up.'

Maggie's heart sank. After rushing off the last time they'd met, there was no way she could wriggle out of this one. She wondered if this was how it was going to be: her parents making increasing demands as they aged and their health deteriorated. 'If you're sure.' She looked from one to another in turn. 'Let's do that.'

Bongo

The Railway Tavern in Bridge Street had bugger-all to commend it. Painted a grimy shade of grey, its narrow fascia presented a blank face to the street, small windows obscured by etched glass, narrow doorway choked with a scattering of fag-ends.

Wilma pushed against the tarnished brass fingerplate and was hit by a warm fug. The pub, she'd already established, served as a staging post between the helicopter terminal at Dyce and the nearby railway station. Inside, the old-fashioned gantry was clad in layers of varnish the colour of treacle, the ceiling stained by decades of nicotine. The place was humming, even at ten in the morning. Small clusters of men squatted around tables crammed with beer glasses. Others stood behind, swilling and joshing. There wasn't another woman in sight.

She'd roared with laughter when Maggie floated the name:

Bongo, I'm sure he said. But what use is that? We don't know where he's from. We've no description, no occupation.

He's an oiler, didn't Scott say?

Yes, but, what sort: an engineer, a machinist, a driller? There are thousands of oilers on and offshore in Aberdeen.

With a handle like Bongo, it'll be a piece of cake.

Now, 'Dicks to attention,' a deep voice quipped.

I'd hack your dick off with my nail scissors, Wilma was tempted to respond, *and ram it up your arse.* Instead, she buttoned her lip.

'Bring on the talent,' a new voice offered.

Ignoring the catcalls that now came from all quarters, she shouldered her way through the scrum.

'Would you like to use my body?' A wee guy in a football strip barred her way.

Wilma gave him the once-over. From the glazed eyeballs to the stained crotch he was obviously tanked.

'Another time,' she said, amused.

He tugged at her sleeve. 'Aw, come on, pet,'

She shook him off. 'Get out my fucking road,' she hissed. 'Or I'll kick your bollocks so hard they come out yer fuckin lugholes.'

She made it to the bar, where even the staff were male. 'Vodka and tonic,' she demanded. No point in ordering a soft drink. Wouldn't go down well with this lot. And it's not as if she was driving. She'd come into town on the bus.

'Fancy a quickie?' Some wag shouted from the back wall.

'Later,' Wilma took a steadying gulp. 'I've business to attend to.'

'A prossie?' The wag persisted. 'Give us a hand job, then. Been a while since I knocked one out.'

There was a burst of raucous laughter.

Despite herself, Wilma's mouth twitched. You could hardly blame them, not after a fortnight offshore with filtered internet and no booze. Sleeping in a bunk bed and all, sharing a shower and toilet with some other bugger. Plus, they were a good bunch, the Geordies: cheery, hardy. Not like some of the local wimps she'd come across in her investigations. Sad gits.

'You wouldn't,' she cosied up to the man standing next to her, 'have come across a guy called Bongo?'

'Bongo? Aye. Due onshore today, pet. Should've been here by now.'

Wilma couldn't believe her luck. Till she looked at the clock. 'He's cutting it fine.' She'd already checked out the railway timetable.

'Nowt new there, darling. He's maybe still out at Dyce. You could try Spiders or Jury's Inn. There again, he might be in the bookies.' This was met by a burst of laughter.

'Right,' she acknowledged. A gambling habit would figure. From her enquiries thus far, Wilma had established Bongo owed money all over the place.

She debated whether to check out the nearest bookmakers, decided there were too many within spitting distance. And she daren't miss the subject. There wouldn't be another opportunity till his leave was up in three weeks. And by then anything could have happened.

A drink appeared at Wilma's elbow.

'Cheers!' she swallowed down the first, raised the second in a toast. It burned her throat. Choking, Wilma sniffed. The liquid smelled like neat vodka. Stung, she banged the glass down on the bar.

From behind, there was a rousing cheer, then a lone voice, 'Yer lady friend's at the bar.'

Wilma turned. He was a big fella: legs like tree trunks in ripped denims, biceps bulging under a fitted black T-shirt.

His face wore a puzzled look. 'Don't know her.'

More laughter. 'Either that or you forgot.'

He squared up. 'What do you want?'

Wilma took him on. 'It's a private matter.'

'Christ!' Some wag said. 'Forty if she's a day and he's got her in the family way.'

'Tell that one to the wife.'

Beneath his buzz cut, Bongo blanched.

For a moment, Wilma felt sorry for the guy. Still, looked like she'd got there in the nick of time. She cast around. At the bar the punters had melted away. She grasped her opportunity. 'Do you think,' she cupped an ear, 'we could go somewhere a bit quieter?'

'Now you're asking.'

Wilma ground her teeth. 'Have a chat.' She fixed him with a withering look.

Bongo took a shufti at his watch. 'It'll have to be quick,' he said, casting a sideways look at his mates, 'my train's in half an hour.'

'No probs,' Wilma ushered him towards the door. 'We can talk outside.'

* * *

'That's how we met,' Bongo took a long drag on his cigarette, blew out a steady stream of smoke. 'I'd nipped out the pub to lay a tenner on at Aintree. And there she was – Miss World – going hell for leather on the gaming machines.' His leathery face took on a dreamy expression. 'Next thing we were in the sack.'

Wilma batted the smoke away. She'd given up smoking, but after the couple of drinks she'd downed, she was dying for a fag.

Business first. 'Where was Sam living?'

'Bed-sit down Ferryhill. Bit of a doss-house it was, all sorts coming and going.'

'Like?'

'Foreign women. Eastern European, I'd say. Men too. Shady-looking buggers some of them. Didn't bother me.' He puffed his chest. 'Been in the army. Done a couple of tours in Afghanistan. After that, there's nothing much bothers you.' He took another drag.

'No,' Wilma murmured, I'm sure.'

'There were folk coming and going at all hours,' Bongo warmed to the subject. 'Not that they were a nuisance, mind. We probably made more noise than…'

'Did Sam have a job?' Wilma interrupted, conscious of time slipping away.

'Not that I know of. Whenever I got in touch she seemed to be available. And that's an understatement. We had good times, me and her. Loads of laughs, as well as the,' he cleared his throat, 'you know.'

Wilma nodded. 'I get your drift. How long did the relationship last?'

'Few weeks, couple of months, tops, then…' He took one last puff, nipped the end of his cigarette. 'One minute she was there, the next…' He shrugged. 'Came off shift, rolled up at her door and some other dame answered.'

'Who was she?'

'Couldn't tell you. Didn't speak English.'

'Any idea why Sam left?'

'Not a notion. I headed home, then, didn't have time to dwell on it. But later, once I was back offshore. Well, it's pretty boring out there in the North Sea.'

'And?' Wilma prompted.

'One time we were together this guy comes hammering on her door. Sam didn't ask him in.' He winked. 'Obviously. But they were arguing.'

'Did you hear what was said?'

'Only the odd couple of words. "Out of line" and "be back". Took it she'd crossed someone. When she came in the room she was scared. Big time. I'd have gone after the guy, only I'd a train to catch, and the missus…' He broke off, embarrassed. 'Look,' he checked the time again. 'I've got to go.'

'What's that Ferryhill address?'

'You'll get no joy there. Trust me, I've tried.'

'All the same.' Wilma produced a notebook and pencil from her pocket.

Bongo scribbled down the details.

'Do you have a mobile number for Sam?'

'I do.' He made a rueful face. 'But it's out of service.'

'Will you leave me yours? Then, if anything…'

'I'd rather not,' he answered. 'Ships in the night, you know how it is.'

Wilma did. She fished in her handbag. 'Here's my card.' She held it out. 'If you think of anything give me a call.'

Reluctantly, he palmed it, made to leave.

'One last thing, you wouldn't have a photograph?'

'Sure.' He flipped his phone, flicked through his photos. 'This do?' He waved it under her nose.

Wilma eyed the animated face, the sparkling eyes, that mane of dark hair. Small wonder men fancied Sam Clark. 'Perfect.' She watched as he read her mobile number off the card, tapped it in.

'Done. Now I really have to…'

Wilma clutched at straws. 'There's a woman gone missing. Her kids are pining for her. I gather you've kids of your own.'

'Too right. And if I miss that train, there will be hell to pay.' And with a perfunctory wave, he was gone.

A House Guest

The lights were on in the front room as Maggie pulled into the drive. *Waste of money!* she tutted. It didn't get dark this far north in early summer until after ten, and she'd brought her children up to know better.

She opened the boot and hauled out half a dozen bulging carrier bags. At the end of a week tidying up after small schoolchildren and keeping an investigation agency afloat, the supermarket shop was an unwelcome chore. More so when Kirsty was at home. She'd acquired exotic tastes since living in Dundee: not just in fruit and vegetables, but in flavourings and spices that were foreign to Maggie. Still, she reasoned, at least Kirsty was happy to cook for herself.

It was only as she turned the key in the lock Maggie remembered. Friday. Kirsty's friend, Shaz, would have arrived.

She pushed open the front door, dropped the bags that were already cutting into her fingers in the hallway. 'Kirsty?' She stuck her head into the sitting-room.

He was lying on the settee, feet – still in trainers – up on the armrest.

Kirsty sat, cross-legged, on the carpet by his head. In each hand she held a can of coke.

She looked up. 'Hi, Mum.'

Shaz eyed Maggie. He didn't speak.

Insolent little prick! 'You got here,' was all she could muster.

His lip curled. 'Looks like it.'

The silver stud was still in place, she noted, the brow piercing supplemented by another couple of rings. In his earlobes, two black plastic circles made exaggerated full stops. Or was the word 'period'? Maggie's mind went into reverse as she re-lived Kirsty's distress when she'd had the pregnancy scare, her own apprehension when she'd travelled to Dundee to ascertain the outcome.

'Can you give me a hand with the shopping?' she tossed in their general direction.

Shaz looked on, dispassionate, as Kirsty deposited the two cans on the coffee table and struggled to her feet. Picking up a clutch of carrier bags from the hall, she followed Maggie through to the kitchen.

'Is it necessary to have every light on in the house?' Perspiring from her shopping trip and seething with pent-up frustration, Maggie couldn't help herself.

Kirsty rolled her eyes. 'Don't exaggerate.' Methodically she set to unpacking the groceries and stowing them away.

'Well, really,' Maggie exploded. 'I leave you lying in your bed and come home to find my house invaded.'

'If you're referring to Shaz…' Kirsty started to say.

Maggie could take no more. 'That's exactly who I'm referring to.'

'But,' Kirsty protested, 'you said he could come.'

'Yes,' Maggie allowed. 'But I didn't say he could lie on my settee like a…' She struggled for the right word. 'Like a…' Settled for, '… turd.'

Where did that come from? Another example of Wilma's malign influence.

'Mum!' Kirsty stopped what she was doing, her eyes wide with shock. 'That's not nice.'

'No.' For once, Maggie was in complete agreement. She regained her composure. 'But neither is he, the way he behaved the last time he was here: calling you "Lardy", ordering you around. And that was before he got you pregnant.'

Kirsty rounded on her. 'He did *not* get me pregnant.'

'Who did, then?' Maggie couldn't stop herself. 'Or perhaps you don't know.'

'I'm going upstairs,' Kirsty spat. 'And I'll take Shaz with me. Out of your precious sitting-room and out of your way.'

'You do that,' Maggie retorted. They'd come looking when they got hungry. Which reminded her, Colin was due home from training any minute. 'Give you a chance to catch up,' she added. Then, seeing the wounded expression on her daughter's face, she weakened. 'He's had a bad experience, did you say?' She addressed the back of Kirsty's head.

'Yes.' Kirsty flung over her shoulder. 'He found a body.' And the door slammed behind her.

Ferryhill

The block of flats would have been smart enough when it was first built. Now, the pebbledash exterior was stained, the window frames in need of refurbishment.

Wilma mounted the short flight of steps that led to the entrance and ran a practised eye over the security entry system. As she'd expected, the grubby card inserts had been amended several times over. There was none in the name of Clark.

Her spirits sank. Then her gaze lighted on a service button.

Good-oh! A firm stab and she was in.

The pile on the hallway carpet was flattened, the walls smeared with scuff marks. A row of mailboxes overflowed with junk fliers. Running the width of the building, a corridor was punctuated by anonymous panel doors.

Wilma rapped smartly on flat number one.

No answer.

She worked her way down the corridor, first one side then the other.

No joy.

She retraced her steps through the hallway and started on the other side.

At the second door along, she could have sworn she heard a voice, swiftly stifled.

She knocked again, stood for a few minutes, ears twitching, but to no avail.

She made for the stairs.

Failed to raise anybody in the first couple of flats she tried on the first floor.

Wilma had just decided folk would be out at work and she was wasting her time when, from inside the third door she tried, there was movement, then a voice, 'Coming.' The scrape of a key in the lock.

The door inched open to reveal a female figure clad in a flimsy robe. The girl was slight, with blonde hair and high cheekbones, and didn't look to be more than seventeen.

She started back when she saw Wilma, a confused look on her face.

Bit of a doss-house. Bongo's words reverberated in Wilma's head. She wondered who the girl had been expecting.

Keeping her voice casual, 'I'm looking for a friend,' she said, with an ingratiating smile. She flashed her phone. 'You wouldn't have seen her by any chance?'

Fear flitted across the girl's face. She shook her head. 'No speak English.'

Wilma persevered. 'How long have you lived here?' she asked.

Another shake of the head. Then the door was shut in her face.

She was weighing her options when, further along the corridor, a door slid ajar.

A head peeked out. 'Looking for someone?'

This woman looked to be in her late forties, hair dyed black in a beehive, eyes rimmed with kohl. She was wearing a pink velour tracksuit, the top unzipped to display a pair of spherical silicone breasts.

'Sam.' Wilma flashed the photo once more. 'Have you seen her?'

Suspicion clouded the woman's face. 'Who's asking? You the fuzz?'

Wilma snorted. 'No way.'

The woman's features relaxed. 'You wouldn't have a fag on you?'

'Sorry. Given up.'

'Fuck. I've just had my last smoke.'

'Can't you nip out to the shop?'

'No way. I'm expecting a…' She hesitated. '…caller any minute.'

Wilma twigged.' Is that wee girl in number nine…?'

'Sure. They all are. Put up in dumps like this. Told how many, how much: oral, anal, full service, you name it. Not like the old days.'

She gave a helpless shrug. 'Time was, you did pretty much your own thing. Not that it was all hearts and roses, don't get me wrong, but you'd have your regular johns. Enjoy a bit of banter beforehand, get the client to relax. You'd feel you were providing a service. And you had a choice: if you didn't like the look of someone you could walk away. Now sex is just another transaction. And a set-up like this,' she curled her lip, 'it's run like a military operation: punters coming and going every twenty minutes some nights, and by the racket coming out of those rooms, Christ knows what they're doing to those quines. The minders, they're bad bastards and all. And here's me stuck here in the middle of it all with kids like her…' Toss of the head. '…for competition. And as if that wasn't bad enough…'

Wilma cut her off in full flow. She'd waited long enough. 'Sam,' she asked, again. 'Have you come across her?'

'Why do you want to know?'

She kept a straight face. 'Asking for a friend.'

'That right?'

'Flatted here, did she?' Wilma persisted.

The woman nodded. 'Wasn't here all that long.' She checked herself. 'Hang on. If you're a friend of hers you'd know that.' She backed away.

Wilma wedged herself in the doorway. 'I'm a private investigator.' She decided her best option was to come clean. 'Sam seems to have gone AWOL.'

'That right?' The woman inserted a careful finger into her beehive, delicately scratched her head. 'Come to think on it, I haven't seen her lately. Shame. She was out there. Would talk to anyone: the girls, the johns, the minders. Not like those effing Slovaks. Won't open the door to you, not for a fag or a teacup of milk and hardly two words of English between them. If you ask me…'

Wilma cut her short. 'Went by the name of Clark, did she?'

'No idea. Never got around to putting her name on the door.'

'How come Sam pitched up here, do you know?'

'Friend of a friend, from what I gather. As folk move out, the East

Europeans move in. I'd go myself, but I can't find a sodding thing, not in the city centre, rents are that high. But number six was waiting for repairs. Too scaffy even for the Slovaks,' she sniffed.

'Tough shit,' Wilma sympathised. 'So how did Sam pay the rent?' she fished. 'Was she in work?'

This was met with a contemptuous snort.

'She wasn't...?'

'On the game like the rest of us? Not from where I'm standing.'

'You didn't ever see her in company?' Wilma insinuated.

'There was a boyfriend. Oiler I think he was. Made good money, from what I gather. Maybe he kept her in sweeties.'

'What about women?' Wilma persisted. 'Did Sam flat-share with anyone?'

'No. She had this pal, mind, came round a few times. They'd get dolled up and head out together.'

Wilma pounced. 'The pal? 'She didn't go by the name of Debbie by any chance?'

'Don't remember,' she said with a shake of the head. 'I only saw her a couple of times. Dark hair; like Sam, but I never heard her mention a Debbie, that's for sure. Something real short, the pal's name was: Bea, maybe.'

'Can you describe her?'

'Nah. As I said, I only saw her in passing. Michaela's the one to speak to if you want more than that. Her and Sam were pally. Look, I better go.' She made to shut the door.

Wilma didn't budge.

'Where would I find this Michaela?'

'Upstairs. Flat fourteen.'

She cricked her neck. 'What number are you?'

'Nine.'

'Can I leave you my card? Then if you think of anything...'

'Okay.' The woman palmed it into the pocket of her trackie bottoms. 'But now,' she looked pointedly at Wilma's foot, which was keeping the door open, 'I really have to get on.'

'Thanks.' Wilma backed off. 'I'll give flat fourteen a…'

But the door had been shut in her face.

Catch You Later

'I'm not sure about this,' Maggie said from the big chair in the bay window. 'What if Dad takes another turn?'

'I'll be fine,' he responded from his seat on the sofa.

'Yes, but if I'm out at work and you're in the garden, Mum might not hear you if anything were to happen.'

'Nothing's going to happen,' he rushed to reassure her. 'The consultant said, just as long as I take my medication, the risks are low.'

'Yes, but any strenuous activity…'

'He said I've to keep physically active.'

'But…' Her parents were trying to be positive, she knew, but she wouldn't forgive herself if her dad were to take ill on account of her. Shrank, too, from further responsibility. If anything were to happen to him, how would her mother cope? How would she, Maggie, manage if either – or both – of them were to be incapacitated?

'…even something did happen,' he joked. 'I'm a lot nearer Foresterhill here than I'd be at Oldmeldrum.'

She frowned. 'That's not funny.'

'It's true.' He turned to his wife. 'You tell her, pet.'

'He's right,' her mum backed him up. 'And, anyhow, you can't plan for things like that. If God decides he wants to take you…' She broke off. 'I'm sorry, I didn't mean…'

Maggie closed her eyes. She'd nothing left to say to the god who'd reduced solid, decent, loving George to a shadow, then snatched him from the security of his family.

'That's okay.' She opened them again. 'I take your point. But, to get back to what I was saying, I'm not at all sure how the arrangement would work.'

'Why on earth not?' her mum puzzled.

'Well, it's one thing you coming to visit, quite another parachuting in to do odd jobs – unpaid at that – and bailing out again.'

Well-intentioned or not, she balked at the idea of them rolling up, unannounced. Had assumed, in the light of her dad's health scare, that their offer of help had gone out the window. 'Dad's supposed to be taking things easy for now. And there's the distance involved. Who's going to drive in and out? That road can be busy, and driving is stressful…'

Her dad butted in. 'We won't be travelling at peak times. And we're both still perfectly able to drive.' He looked to Maggie's mum for back-up. 'We can take it in turns.'

'Then there's Colin,' Maggie added. Something else she hadn't factored in. 'And Kirsty during the holidays. If you were here for the whole afternoon…'

'We wouldn't get in anybody's way,' her mother interrupted. 'We'd be in and out.'

'Yes, but what would you be doing, exactly?'

'Cleaning, gardening, bit of shopping. Whatever's needed.'

'That's way too much. Sounds more like a full-time job rather than a helping hand. And Dad shouldn't be doing any heavy lifting. Nor should you, come to that.'

Her mum laughed. 'We wouldn't be doing anything like that. Or doing it all at once. You could leave us a list.'

'Mmm.' Maggie had to admit the idea had some merit.

'There's things need doing I can see from here,' her mother continued.

Maggie's hackles rose. 'Like what?'

'Carpet wants shampooed, those shelves need a good dust, and your windows…'

'That's enough,' Maggie cut her off mid-sentence. She knew well enough her windows were a disgrace, especially when compared with Wilma's. But she kept missing the window cleaner, and didn't have the time or the energy to tackle them herself.

'Your mother doesn't mean,' her dad intervened. 'She…'

The back door banged. 'Anyone at home?'

Footsteps advanced through the kitchen.

'Oh,' Wilma appeared in the doorway. She addressed Maggie. 'Didn't know you were expecting visitors.'

'I wasn't,' Maggie replied. 'At least…'

'A flying visit,' her mother answered, stiffly. 'We've just dropped in to firm up some…' She hesitated. '…arrangements.'

'Ooh,' Wilma responded. 'That's nice.' Her eyes flashed alarm bells at Maggie. Despite having gone off-piste, Wilma was desperate to share Bongo's revelations and details of her trip to Ferryhill.

'Yes, well,' Maggie tried to close the door on the subject.

'Can I have a word?' Wilma beckoned.

'Can't you see she's busy?' Maggie's mum couldn't have been more direct.

'Right enough,' Wilma shot back, seemingly oblivious to the undercurrents in the room. 'But I've something I need to tell her.'

'Is it urgent?' Maggie's mum asked, pointedly.

'Kind of.'

Maggie's shoulders drooped. Here she was again, caught between a rock and a hard place: business and personal life, her family and Wilma. 'Can you give me a clue?' she asked, hoping Wilma would let her off the hook.

'Nothing that can't wait,' Wilma lied. 'Catch you later,' she threw Maggie a warning look as she backed out of the room.

In for a Penny

The service button was covered by an 'Out of Order' sign. Wilma swore under her breath. This was all she needed.

She'd ducked out ahead of time from an evening shift at the hospital on the off-chance of catching Sam's chum, Michaela. Ian was working overtime, so she'd time in hand except – the thought occurred – she hadn't done a dickey bird about his dinner.

She loitered in the doorway for as long as was practicable without drawing attention to herself, then decided to take a walk. She wandered around to the back of the building, but access was denied by the high rear wall of the adjacent tenement and there was nothing to be seen but blank-faced windows, most with curtains tightly drawn. *Figures!*

She retraced her steps, was about to call it quits when a taxi drew up.

A young girl alighted and mounted the steps to the front door.

Wilma quickened her pace and sprinted up the steps, was just in time to slip in behind her with a cheery, 'Hi.'

This was met by a puzzled look.

Wilma smiled inwardly. Worked every time.

She was about to engage the girl in conversation when, with a furtive look over her shoulder, the girl headed for the stairs.

Wilma followed.

Keeping close to the wall, she crept upwards.

At the first landing she stopped short, hearing a key scrape in a lock. She didn't dare stick her head around the corner lest she be visible to whoever might be standing in the corridor, but from the sound of the door as it clicked shut it seemed to be about halfway along. She resolved to check it out later.

Head abuzz, Wilma climbed upwards to the second floor. From what little she'd seen of Bongo, he was a decent enough guy, but not overly challenged in the brain department. She doubted he was holding down a high-level job. And even if he were a high earner, with a wife and family to support and a gambling habit to indulge, there wouldn't be much left in the kitty. This was underscored by the stories she'd been told about gambling debts.

Wilma speculated as to how Sam Clark could come and go at seemingly at will, how she could afford to rent a flat – albeit a modest one – in the centre of Aberdeen, how she could drink and dine out most nights. And how frequently she'd managed to rope Debbie in? Wilma doubted there was cash to splash in the Milne household. Why else would Debbie be running up her own curtains? She sniffed. She couldn't countenance such a thing.

Whoa! Wilma brought herself up short. She was already jumping the gun by going on the say-so of an avowed prostitute. Sam Clark – if Clark she was – might equally well have come into money, whether by nefarious means or not. As for Debbie Milne, there was no way of affirming that she was the 'pal' who'd visited Sam's flat, nor was it likely. For why would Sam invite her oldest friend – clean-living wife and mother that she was – into such a milieu? And, besides, hadn't Scott Milne been adamant Sam always picked Debbie up from Belvidere Street.

Number fourteen was second last on her right.

Wilma hammered on the door.

There was no answer.

She put her ear to it.

Nothing.

For a few moments she stood, willing someone – anyone – to appear. Then, *Bugger!* She swore under her breath. She'd made the sodding trip for nothing.

She checked the time on her phone. Ian would be home by now. He'd have had his shower, be wondering where she was. He'd go mental when she didn't have his dinner on the table for the second time that week. Still, *in for a penny in for a pound,* Wilma had no intention of letting her wee outing go to waste. She'd see if she could get anything more out of the quine downstairs.

She tripped down one flight, gave number nine's door a cautious tap.

No answer.

Fuckit! Wilma had assumed the old prossie was a fixture.

She knocked again, more loudly this time.

Nothing.

For some moments she stood there, at a loss.

Then, *If you snooze you lose.* She turned on her heel. She'd have another go at the door the East European had answered earlier.

She retraced her steps, gave a sharp knock.

From inside, there was scuffle. Then, 'What do you want?' The door swung open to reveal a stocky man. He was barefoot, dressed only in a loose vest and cotton boxer shorts. And completely bald, the light that bounced off his shiny pate vying with the gleam of the heavy gold medallion that nestled in a thicket of dark chest hair.

Wilma looked over the man's shoulder. There was no sign of the girl.

For an instant she stood, frozen, her business card fluttering in nervous fingers.

Then, fists balled, the man lunged forward.

Wilma sprang into action.

Another Sighting

Firmly, Brian knocked on his DI's door. He'd had nothing back from Chisolm on his request to be put forward to the promotion board and wanted to be seen as proactive.

'Enter,' came the brusque response.

Stifling his nerves, Brian strode into the room. 'You asked for an update on the Milne case actions, sir.'

Chisolm pushed aside a stack of burglary reports. 'Sit down.'

Brian lowered himself into the seat opposite. 'We've had another sighting. Cabbie came into the front desk last night. He'd had a fare from Ferryhill to a city centre hotel: two women answering the descriptions of Debbie Milne and Sam Clark.'

'When was this?'

'Three weeks ago.'

'And he's only just come forward?'

'Been on a fortnight's holiday, apparently: Benidorm. Fella's not into social media. It was his daughter picked up our Twitter post.'

Chisolm steepled his fingers. 'What do you think?'

'Worth following up,' Brian responded. 'It's not like we have much else, and if we can establish that Sam Clark was living in Ferryhill, it's quite feasible Debbie could have gone back there with her. My reservation is, this whole Sam thing could be a complete red herring. I mean…' Fearful of making a fool of himself, he was tempted to backtrack. '…by all accounts Sam Clark led an erratic lifestyle. She might have come back north for one reason or another, decided to look up her school chum, found they no longer had a thing in common and moved on.'

'Good point,' Chisolm remarked. 'Still, as you observe, we have little else. Get a full statement, will you, Brian?'

Brian? Again? He chanced his arm. 'Yes, DI.'

This was met by a quizzical look, closely followed by a sardonic smile.

'And get hold of that address, check it out.'

'Sir.' Brian reverted to type. If, indeed, Chisolm was easing up on the formalities, it could take a while

'Speaking of addresses…' Chisolm continued. 'Dyce.'

'Strachan has been out to the address where the Esslemonts lived. Only,' Brian hesitated, on the back foot now. 'That wasn't the house where Debbie was brought up. The parents bought a bigger place when her dad got a job in oil. And…' His nerve began to desert him. '…the folk who live there at the moment are only renting. The neighbours have moved away.' He offered an ingratiating smile. 'Everything's changed around there since…'

'Yes, yes,' Chisolm brushed off this catalogue of excuses. Not being local, he didn't know if his sergeant was spinning him a yarn or not.

'Well, use your initiative. Have you got any suggestions?'

'Social media?' Brian offered, tentatively.

Chisolm slapped him down. 'Saying what? If Sam Clark isn't missing and she still has living relatives we could look like numpties, never mind land ourselves in trouble.' The least of which would be stepping on Tayside's toes.

As if by osmosis, Brian piped up, 'If the woman's on their radar, why don't we leave that one to Tayside?'

'No way,' Chisolm snapped. He was still smarting from Maguire's brush-off. 'Is that the best you can do?'

'Sir.' Brian looked at his feet, quite lost for words.

'Then get on with it,' Chisolm snapped his fingers in a gesture of dismissal.

Seeing his hopes of promotion vanish out the window, Brian rose and scuttled from the room.

In Too Deep

'What happened to you?' Maggie gawped, when Wilma answered her knock.

Gingerly, Wilma touched two fingertips to her cheekbone. 'Had a wee run in with a car door.'

'You're shooting me a line. Did Ian…?'

'Dinna be daft.'

'Then how did you…?'

Wilma ducked the question. 'Tell you later.' She ushered Maggie into the hall. 'Come away in.' She wasn't readily going to admit she'd been working solo again after all the back and forth they'd had on the subject.

'I've been trying to raise you since yesterday,' Maggie complained. 'Didn't we agree we'd keep in telephone contact?'

'You can talk,' Wilma shot back. 'What about your dad's accident?'

Maggie sniffed. 'That was different. I was in a meeting with my head.'

'And how are you to know I wasn't "in a meeting" myself?'

'Oh,' Maggie knitted her brows, 'you never give up, do you, Wilma?'

'What d'you mean?'

'You always have to have the last word.'

'That's not true. Many a time you've…'

Maggie cut her short. 'Yes, it is. You run all over me like a steam-roller, talk me round in circles, wear me down.'

'I'm only trying to help,' Wilma justified.

'And you do,' Maggie answered. 'But I'm the principal in this agency. The buck stops with me, so I can't have you constantly calling the shots, don't you see?'

'How about…?' Wilma began, then bit her tongue.

Maggie's blood boiled. She was sure Wilma was about to throw

Sheena Struthers in her face. 'And another thing,' she wagged an admonitory finger. 'It's high time you did something about your language before I absorb any more swear words.'

Wilma pulled a rude face. 'Nobody's forcing you.'

'Perhaps not. But I found myself calling someone a turd the other day, so your influence must be subliminal.'

'Sub-what?'

'Oh,' Maggie scowled. 'Never mind.'

'So is this what you came round for?' Wilma queried. 'To tear a strip off me?'

Maggie relented. 'No, of course not. I came give you the latest intel. Something that has a bearing on…'

Wilma cut her short. 'And I came round to yours to give you my latest. But it'll keep.' She took Maggie by the arm, led her into the sitting-room. 'Now you're here, you can give me your opinion on my new rug.'

'But, Wilma,' Maggie protested. 'It's important.'

Wilma snorted. 'So's mine. But there's nothing so bloody important it can't wait for two minutes.'

Maggie looked down at the floor. Atop the grey fitted carpet lay a giant purple cow-skin. 'Wow!' she exclaimed, quite involuntarily. Wilma's taste was already over the top, but this took the biscuit. Added to which, with her farming background, the only place she'd ever seen a cow-skin was on the cow.

'What do you think?'

'I…I…' Maggie stuttered, quite lost for words. Then her lack of empathy shamed her. For despite their different tastes, didn't she and Wilma have the same end-game: making a home for their family.

Wilma took Maggie's silence for awe. 'Glad you like it.' Her grin was as wide as her hips. I've wanted one of these for ages. Wasn't sure about the colour, but it was such a bargain.' She propelled Maggie forward. 'Only ordered it on Saturday and it was delivered first thing. Go on,' she gave Maggie a shove. 'Have a feel.'

Maggie dropped to a crouch, extended a tentative hand. Just as she'd thought, the hide felt smooth when stroked in one direction, prickly in the other. She wondered if it would smell, resisted the urge to sniff her fingers.

'Sit you down,' Wilma urged. 'We can have a wee something to celebrate.'

'No.' Maggie struggled to her feet. 'I've something to tell you: the body that was found in Dundee…'

'The one in the skip?'

'Yes. It was Kirsty's boyfriend who found it.'

'What boyfriend is that?' Wilma demanded.

'Shaz.'

'The one you can't stand?'

'I didn't say I couldn't stand him, just that…'

'…he's working class.'

'No,' Maggie argued. Then, 'Yes, he is working class, but that's not why I don't like him.'

Wilma threw her a doubtful look. 'Whatever. Did you get this from Kirsty?'

'No, from the horse's mouth. Shaz is staying with us for the weekend.'

'That's a stroke of luck,' Wilma was right on it. 'We'll see what we can get out of him.'

Maggie frowned. 'I've already tried. And, besides, I doubt he'd be able to give us anything he hasn't already shared with the police. He's been hauled into West Bell Street, given a full statement. If he's to be believed…' Her lips thinned in disapproval. '…the interviewing officers used everything short of thumbscrews.'

'Still, you must have got something,' Wilma persisted.

Maggie's hackles rose. 'Of course I did.' She was getting cheesed off with Wilma treating her like the trainee. 'Good figure, shoulder-length dark hair. But the victim's eyes were closed and her face was smashed: nose broken, jaw fractured, so…'

'…it might be Debbie or it might not.'

'Precisely. So we'll have to wait for the police to complete the identification process.'

'Shame,' Wilma deliberated. 'He could have given us a leg up, that Shaz.'

Inwardly, Maggie shuddered at the very thought. She changed the subject. 'Did you manage to raise Sam Clark's boyfriend?'

'Bongo? Aye. Turned out to be an ex-drummer. Caught him yesterday when he came onshore.'

'Was it him gave you the black eye?'

Wilma threw a sideways glance. 'No. I told you…'

'No shady business, remember? No double-dealing. Give me the truth.'

Wilma's cheeks flamed. 'I got an address off the boyfriend, went to have a look-see.'

'But I thought we'd agreed…' Maggie hissed.

'Yes, I know. But the fella was running for a train, so I didn't get that much out of him, and happened Sam's digs were just down the road.'

'That's where you had your little accident?'

Wilma nodded. 'First time around I got a wee heads-up that Sam was pally with some dame, Michaela.'

'First time?' Maggie's voice rose. 'I hope you're not going to tell me you've been investigating solo more than once.'

'Nobody answered my knock, so I doubled back at the end of my shift in the hope of raising her.'

'And?' Maggie's curiosity was piqued.

'Still couldn't get an answer, so I thought I'd pay another visit to my informant, see if I could get a bit more out of her. I was doing great till this guy had a go. Bruiser he was, built like a bull.'

Maggie stifled a snigger. It shouldn't have been in the least funny, but what with the cow-skin…

'Came charging at me, took a swing, caught me right on the…' She had another feel of her cheekbone. 'I was keeping out of your road, to be honest, especially after the stick you've been giving me about doing everything together.'

Maggie nodded. So that's why Wilma hadn't answered her calls. ''What did you do?' she asked.

'What do you think I did? Kneed him in the balls. Then, when he was doubled up, whacked him over the head with my handbag. Knocked him sideways,' she said, with a satisfied smirk.

Maggie wasn't surprised. Last time she's had the misfortune to pick it up, Wilma's handbag had weighed a ton. 'You were lucky to get off with just a bruise.'

Wilma stiffened. 'Luck's got nothing to do with it. It's my boxing gym I've to thank.'

'Regardless, you shouldn't have been there in the first place.'

'You've got a nerve. Talk about the pot calling the kettle black.'

Maggie started to laugh.

'What?'

'Reminds me of the time you took me to your gym: the kettle-bells all lined up, and...'

'...Joe making you have a go on the punch-bag. Talking of which, it's high time you got yourself over there, did some training in self-defence.'

'Yes, well...' The smile vanished from Maggie's face. '...you still shouldn't have been there on your own.'

'I got a result, didn't I?'

'I wouldn't know. You've been too busy showing off your–'

'Forget about the fucking rug,' Wilma butted in. 'You're not the only one with a new piece of intelligence. I found out Sam Clark had a gambling habit. Full-on by the sounds of: FOBTs.'

'What?' Maggie cupped a hand to her ear.

'Fixed Odds Betting Terminals.'

'You don't think...'

'She got Debbie involved? Who knows? There's big money to be won. If Debbie saw Sam flashing the cash, and she was strapped...'

'Big losses, too, presumably,' Maggie cut her short. 'Seriously, you're not saying Debbie Milne, model housewife, spent her afternoons in bookies' premises?' Wilma's imagination was running away with her again.

'What makes you so sure? Have you ever been in one?'

'No, but...'

'See!'

Maggie held up her hands. 'You're at it again: having the last word.'

'Sorry I spoke.' Wilma stuck her nose in the air. 'But another thing, Sam was flatting in some shit-heap down Ferryhill.' She ran on, unabashed. 'Full of East European sex workers, it is, and according to one of the tenants she had a pal visited her there.'

'Oh, come on,' Maggie had heard enough. 'Are you trying to tell me, now, that Sam involved Debbie in sex work?'

'Probably not.' According to my source...' Wilma moved to redeem herself in Maggie's eyes. '...Sam wasn't on the game, at least not directly. But she was into something shady, that's for sure. The boyfriend told me she'd been threatened.'

'By?'

'Albanian hard men.'

'And it was one of them gave you that black eye?'

Wilma touched a hand to her face. 'What do you think?'

Maggie didn't know what to think. But Shaz's voice rang in her ear: "Her eyes were closed and her face was smashed: nose broken, jaw fractured."

One thing she did know: they were in way too deep.

VI

West Bell Street

'What can I do for you today?' enquired DI Gerald Maguire.

'Following up on our misper,' Chisolm responded. 'Debbie Milne.' He'd deliberated on the outcome of his telephone call to Maguire, concluded his best course of action was to visit in person. 'You'll have had the details.'

Maguire nodded acknowledgement.

'It is my understanding, DCI Maguire...' His reception at Tayside Police HQ that day had been cordial, but wary, and Maguire's open-ended question had put him on the back foot. *Two can play at this game.* Chisolm kept his words vague.

'Gerry, please.'

'Gerry.' He eyed his contemporary across the desk. Gerry Maguire was in his early fifties, he guessed. A small man – five eight at most – he carried the sandy hair and sharp features of what Chisolm recognised from his years in Glasgow as Irish heritage. Indeed, had he shed a stone in weight, he'd have passed for a jockey. With a name like Maguire, Chisolm took him to be a Catholic. Religious bigotry was another thing he hadn't been sorry to walk away from. Not that it was as virulent these days as when he'd first joined the force, not away from the football terraces at any rate. He picked up where he left off. '...your pathologist is still working to identify the Perth Road deceased.'

'Correct.'

'Debbie Milne's DNA...' He let the words hang in the air. 'The mortuary should have received that by now.'

'I don't need to tell you,' Gerry Maguire cut him off, 'pathologists do things in their own good time.'

'Quite.' Chisolm concurred, his tone emollient. 'I haven't come here to pressure you.'

'Then what is it you're after?' Maguire snapped. 'We could as easily have had this conversation over the phone.'

'Accepted. I'll be straight with you,' Chisolm said with a wry grin, 'I'm playing hooky from my paperwork. Thought a day out might clear my head.' That was at least partly true. The weather was dry and sunny, and he'd enjoyed the journey south: the spectacular views down the coast past Stonehaven, the soft arable acres of the Howe of the Mearns. Even Dundee, hitherto not a mecca for savvy Glaswegians, had undergone a makeover. As he'd made his way up the hill from the station, Chisolm had admired the re-landscaped waterfront, the tall masts of the sailing ship, *Discovery*, the craggy silhouette of the new V&A museum. He'd been brought back down to earth as he trudged uphill past Debenhams, turned right at the Lidl store by the roundabout, passed the Shell station and pushed through the doors of Tayside's police headquarters. The squat three-storey ridged box with its incongruous blue panels made his own base at Queen Street look positively glamorous.

'Now you're talking.' Maguire's face creased into a smile. 'Drive anyone round the bend. There's days I think even traffic duties would be better than this.' He waved a hand over the files that sat in untidy heaps on and around the desk.

'Not that I wasn't also hoping you'd help me progress our misper case,' Chisolm admitted. 'If Debbie's DNA is a match for your cadaver, then…'

'…we're looking at a murder investigation,' Maguire finished the sentence. 'Under Tayside's jurisdiction,' he added, with a warning look.

Chisolm sighed inwardly. Since the inception of Police Scotland, some officers guarded their patch with added zeal. Gerry Maguire was a case in point. No use arguing the advantages: specialist services – underpinned by financial savings – that would have been unheard of before, they clung to vestiges of the old framework. 'Lets us off the hook,' he made light, not wanting to alienate the man.

'And if it isn't a match?' Maguire asked.

'We have an ongoing headache, compounded by bringing the

powers-that-be down on our backs.'

Maguire grimaced. 'Tell me about it.'

'We've been pursuing another line of enquiry,' Chisolm volunteered. 'Friend of Debbie's, goes by the name of Samantha Clark. Long shot, but I thought since I'm here it might be worth a mention. She and Debbie had lost touch. Then Sam, as she's known, came back into the frame, and just as quickly dropped out the picture again. You mentioned, when I phoned, a Sam Clark was on Tayside's radar.'

'You're telling me this could be our corpse?' Maguire said, his voice disbelieving.

'No, just floating it past you. Clark doesn't have form, and she's moved around, so we haven't got much on her. Plus, she's not our primary line of enquiry. But anything you could add might move our case forward.'

Maguire narrowed his eyes. 'I don't know that I can help you in that regard. She's part of a long-running investigation to which I'm not party.'

It sounded to Chisolm as if the DI was choosing his words with care. 'To be honest…' Maguire seemed a decent bloke. Chisolm decided to throw himself on the DI's mercy. '…our investigation into Debbie Milne's disappearance is going nowhere, and she has left behind two young children, so I'd be grateful for anything you can share.'

'I'll see what I can do.' Maguire stood up. 'Give me ten minutes. While you're waiting,' he flashed Chisolm a cheeky grin. 'I reckon you could use a cup of coffee.'

* * *

'Bingo!' Gerry Maguire bounced back into the room. In one hand he waved a buff file. He slapped it down on the desk. 'People trafficking,' he announced. 'We've had a high-level inquiry running for the past eighteen months: Albanian gang. Claim to be Kosovan to gain asylum, then traffic young girls from Eastern Europe into the UK. They've been embedded in Dundee for some time.'

People trafficking? Chisolm's thoughts ran haywire. He'd superficial knowledge: Eastern European gangs trafficking women into Scotland to be sold to Asian crime groups and forced into sham marriages, Nigerian girls employed in sauna parlours, under-age Vietnamese children coerced into unpaid work in nail bars or cannabis factories, men with learning disabilities exploited as slave labour. And human trafficking wasn't confined to the nation's cities. There had been incidences reported in twenty-seven of Scotland's thirty-two local authority areas, stretching as far north as Orkney. But surely Debbie Milne – she of the sewing bees – couldn't have become embroiled in something like that?

'I've heard the rumours,' Chisolm remarked.

'As I said,' Maguire ran on, 'not my case. But given the circumstances, they're happy enough to give us a dekko.' He slid the folder across the desk. 'Just as long as it stays within these four walls.'

'Understood.' Chisolm flipped the folder open. For several minutes he leafed through it. He looked up. 'That's an eye-opener: injecting teenage girls with drugs to induce menopause.'

'Depo-Provera. It's not a factor in this case, to our knowledge, although there's evidence that it is used widely in Africa. It has a very high dose of progesterone. Stops their periods, so they don't get pregnant. The punters don't have the inconvenience of menstrual blood or mood swings. But there are long-term effects: physical changes such as infertility, mental problems, depression.'

But,' Chisolm knitted his brow, 'what has all this got to do with Sam Clark? She's not on the game, is she?'

'Not as such,' Maguire replied. 'According to my DCI, Clark has a gambling habit. Does a bit of escort work between boyfriends to fund it.'

Chisolm drained the last of the tepid coffee a young PC had supplied. He wondered where this was going.

'Only she ran up a debt. Big debt from what I gather. And got in tow – God knows how – with the Albanians. What our intel is saying is, there's one or two Slovak women working the high-end stuff. Real knockouts they are: great tits, legs up to here.' Maguire made appropriate gestures. 'Not that I have first-hand experience, you understand.' He leered. 'It was through them Sam Clark made the connection.'

'And?' Chisolm prompted.

'They've been using Clark to launder money.'

'In Dundee?'

'Spot on. Only she's not here now.'

'I'm aware of that,' Chisolm observed, not wanting to look a complete ignoramus.

Maguire ignored this. 'Sam Clark is a loose cannon, by all accounts. Big personality. Drew too much attention to herself. Managed to get barred from one betting shop after another.'

'Got you.' Chisolm reckoned he'd heard it all, but still, that was some story. With some difficulty, he pulled his attention back to his primary objective: Debbie Milne's disappearance. 'Your corpse?'

Maguire ran a hand through thinning hair. 'Could be any bugger. Clark hasn't got form, so we can't rule her out. We've no DNA on file. But from what I'm hearing on the grapevine regarding the injuries sustained, our body bears all the hallmarks of a punishment beating.'

'Christ!' Chisolm uttered an uncharacteristic oath. Although the language of his peer group was liberally peppered with swear words, he'd always tried to avoid at least the four-letter sort. 'So it could be Sam Clark, right enough?'

'Might well be. I won't go into detail,' Maguire continued. 'Wouldn't want to pre-empt the pathologist's findings. What I will say…' Confidentially, he leaned across the desk. '…is these Albanians are a violent lot.'

That Would Be Telling

'Hi,' Wilma breezed up to the counter of the betting shop. Once an elegant shopping destination, Aberdeen's Union Street had been reduced to a string of gambling dens and boozers. Not that it was alone. The growth of internet shopping had gradually eroded high streets up and down the country. It was only when she sat down to do some advance research online, Wilma discovered that Union Street – with twelve – had the third most betting shops in the UK. Small wonder Sam Clark had run up debt.

She flashed Sam's photo. 'This a client of yours?'

'Who's asking?' The woman behind the perforated security glass would have done well as a prison warder.

'She's a pal o mine.'

'That right?' The voice carried disbelief.

'Uh-huh.'

'She done a runner?'

Wilma winked. 'Something like that.'

'Even she was a punter,' the cashier commented, 'I wouldn't be able to say. Data protection.'

'Fair enough.' Wilma tried to soften her up. 'Just tell me if the face is familiar, then, will you?'

The woman shrugged. 'Maybe.'

'And say she was,' Wilma persisted. 'Could she have been, how will I say, regular?'

The cashier's mouth twitched. 'That would be telling.'

* * *

Wilma had started where Bongo had first met Sam, worked outwards from there. The shops all followed the same format: windows obscured by posters to tempt the punters in, interiors laid out so as to persuade them to stay. When she was married to her first husband, Wilma was a regular in the city's betting establishments, if only to deter Darren from further debt. Now, the shops were a sight more comfortable than she remembered: close carpeting, laminate flooring, upholstered chairs and occasional tables offering an ambience that could be enjoyed by both sexes. There were cold drinks for sale, tea and coffee on offer. Changed days from when placing a bet entailed a furtive dash in and out. And although the gaming consoles and padded high stools were a relatively recent addition, the bank of televisions hadn't much changed, the staff reading from computer monitors behind their security screens bore the same impassive expressions.

By close of business, she'd been round them all: Ladbrokes, Betfred, Paddy Power, Coral, William Hill. All within walking distance of Sam's flat in Ferryhill. Wilma had enjoyed a mixed reception: on Union Street, there were one or two flickers of recognition. Elsewhere, either the shop was busy, in which case the skeleton staff didn't have time to stop and chat, or they clammed up the minute she produced Sam's photograph and started asking questions. By the time she'd trudged the length of Union Street, worked her way along King Street and returned via George Street, Rosemount Viaduct and Schoolhill, she was fair wabbit. It was only as an afterthought she decided to make a detour down to Guild Street.

'Customer of yours?' She flashed Sam's photo.

Through the toughened glass screen, a male cashier looked her up, down and sideways. 'Aye.'

'Seen her lately?'

He keyed data into his computer. 'Hasn't played this week.'

'The machines?' Wilma yanked her head. 'That what floated her boat?'

'Look,' he backed away. 'I'm here on my own right now and I've phone calls to make. So, if you wouldn't mind…'

Wilma couldn't blame the guy. FOBTs were a touchy subject. Revenue from the machines, she'd learned, accounted for as much as half of betting shops' turnover. But with a proliferation of betting outlets located in the poorest areas and punters able to gamble up to £300 a minute, the resulting fallout from debt had been dramatic. So much so the Campaign for Fairer Gambling had successfully lobbied to reduce the maximum spin from £100 to £2, with effect from April 2019, thereby slashing the bookmakers' profits.

'No worries.' She flashed a dazzling smile. 'What did you say your name was?'

He gave her a guarded look 'I didn't.'

'Ooh,' Wilma puckered her lips. 'Don't be a stranger. I was just…' She thrust out her boobs. '…being friendly.'

He buckled. 'It's Dave.'

'Pleased to meet you, Dave.' She threw him an arch look. 'I'll pop back in another time.'

Quiet Coach

Allan Chisolm settled into his seat. He dug his phone from his jacket pocket, checked his messages. Was readying to log on to the rail line's wi-fi when he checked himself. Although the A90 south to Dundee was an easy enough drive, he'd opted to travel by train rather than drive in order to buy himself thinking time. God knows he needed it. Talk about bed-blocking. There was a stack of cases building up behind the Milne misper, and only so many hours in the day. He stowed the phone away and closed his eyes.

Before setting out, he'd overseen the morning briefing and dispatched a ton of admin. On the Scotrail service south, he'd caught up with his emails. The return journey would get him back to Aberdeen and into his office in time to wrap up for the day. He'd hoped his visit to West Bell Street would have gone some way towards resolving Debbie Milne's disappearance: either Tayside's cadaver was Debbie's or it wasn't. And if – as Gerry Maguire had confirmed – the process of identification was likely to be prolonged, Chisolm had hoped, by putting a face to his name, to speed it up. But that the body might belong to Sam Clark, that was another story altogether: a story that would put a completely different perspective on the case.

The train stopped at Carnoustie, jolting Chisolm from his reverie. He'd enjoyed a few rounds of golf way back in another life. Before it became too time-consuming. Before life became too complicated. He let out a long exhalation. Some days he missed his girls so hard his bones ached. He'd expected to be settled by this time: in the new job, in a place of his own, maybe even with a partner, though it was still early days.

The station had come and gone and Chisolm was nodding off when, in the seat behind, a mobile loudly warbled its ring-tone, a woman's voice proceeded to engage in animated conversation.

Startled, he turned and craned his neck over the headrest.

A teenage girl was sprawled full-length across both seats, her feet dangling over into the aisle. She was dressed in ripped denims and a puffa jacket, her phone clamped to one ear, the obligatory earphone wires dangling from her neck. On the table in front were scattered the detritus of a meal: an empty sandwich carton, a scrunched-up crisp packet, a half-drunk bottle of Irn Bru. On the window above her head, a sticker read, 'Quiet Coach'.

Chisolm pointed to it.

The girl looked up at it, looked back at him, turned her head away.

He was tempted to wave his badge, thought the better of it. The journey would take little more than an hour and she couldn't talk all that time. Or could she? Regardless, the life Chisolm was living, he was at risk of becoming an old fart. He slouched back in his seat, tried to shut out the noise, concentrate on making sense of what Maguire had told him.

Arbroath brought to mind parallels with another murder investigation he'd heard about: a woman bound, gagged, tortured, her body dismembered, the parts weighted with stones and dumped in Arbroath harbour. This woman had hailed from Eastern Europe, Chisolm recalled, the motive also money. Except, unlike Sam Clark, Jolanta – he thought that was her name – had been a hard-working, clean-living girl. He mined his memory for other, similar cases: Kimberley Mackenzie in Montrose, murdered and dismembered in 2016 by Gordon Jackson. Her body parts had been left in bins, her head stuffed into a black bin bag inside a suitcase and deposited in a shower cubicle.

He banished those images and tried to focus on the present. Could Tayside's corpse be Debbie Milne? That would fit with the Dundee bus sighting. But there was no evidence to suggest that Debbie was in danger. Might she have been the victim of a random attack? Statistically improbable. No, the likelihood was that of the two friends, Sam was the more vulnerable, more so in the light of what Maguire had told him. That's if the body were either woman. Chisolm sighed. Poor creature. Whatever she'd done, there was no life so worthless it deserved to end up discarded like a piece of garbage.

The Hollywood Cafe

'Any joy?' Maggie slid into the booth.

'Not a thing,' Wilma responded. 'You?'

'Likewise.' Maggie tugged at her coat collar.

They'd agreed to meet in the Hollywood Cafe, scene of Maggie's past assignations with Jimmy Craigmyle. The interior was warm, but despite this Maggie shivered. At the last port of call she'd had to stand on the doorstep for just shy of ten minutes whilst her credentials were checked and the security arrangements navigated. Although the rain had held off, an east wind had cut though the fabric of her thin coat. 'I've never felt so depressed in all my life.'

'Learning curve.' Wilma had got there early, had already ordered a cappuccino and a jam doughnut.

'And some.' I didn't realise these places would house such a cross-section of women.' Yet another of Maggie's preconceptions confounded. She'd assumed them to be the lot of the working classes.

Wilma raised her cup to her mouth, took a greedy slurp. 'Might come in useful one of these days.'

'I sincerely hope not.' Maggie signalled to the elderly waitress for another coffee.

Wilma had shed her jacket and her breasts strained under a stretch top. She crooked one elbow, sniffed an underarm. 'Thought I was being clever,' she contemplated the spreading damp stain. 'Legging it up from the beach. High time I was back at the gym.'

Maggie had expressed reservations about splitting the workload: *'I thought we'd agreed to do everything together this time.'*

'That was the plan, but we've a fair few refuges to get around.'

'How do we find out where they are? Their locations are supposed to be a secret, are they not?'

Wilma had winked. *'I could give us a heads up. As I recall, they're mostly quite central, though I'm mebbe not up-to-date.'*

'Sorry. I forgot you'd been through all that with Darren. Still, I'm not so sure.'

'If we want to get ahead of the police on this, Maggie, we'll need to move fast.'

'Yes, I know, but…'

'And if it's your personal safety you're worried about…'

'It's not.'

'These places have heavy security, Maggie. Trust me, you'll be fine.'

'You've a moustache on your top lip.'

Wilma brushed away the line of foam with the back of her hand, gave it a lick. 'All our efforts so far for bugger all.'

'Pretty much.' Maggie replied.

They'd already done a trawl of the city's major hotels, showing Debbie's photograph to doormen, bar and reception staff to no avail. Either they denied all knowledge or – in the couple of instances where someone thought her face looked familiar – couldn't pin it down to date or time. The bed and breakfast establishments proved even more unproductive, since the owners often went out after they'd served breakfast and didn't return until late afternoon. Plus, there were so many of them the PIs concluded they were a lost cause and opted to focus on the women's shelters instead.

'There is just one thing,' Maggie said. 'One of the women – Agnes I think her name was – said she'd come across someone who fitted Debbie's description. She'd been homeless, Agnes that is, sleeping rough until she got a place at the shelter.'

'Think it's worth following up?'

'I doubt it. Don't know how reliable the intel is. Woman's an alcoholic by all accounts.'

'Don't give me that face,' Wilma came right back. 'You'd hit the bottle and all if you'd to put up with some of the things those…'

'Sorry.' Maggie came back quickly. 'Didn't mean to be judgmental.' Her coffee arrived. She wrapped her hands around the cup for warmth. 'What now?'

'Last two and we're done.'

Maggie groaned. 'I thought we'd covered them all.' She lifted her cup, took a hungry swallow.

Wilma delved into a pocket, consulted a well-thumbed scrap of paper. 'Bon Accord Square or Union Terrace, take your pick.'

Maggie's shoulders drooped. Both lay in the opposite direction from Mannofield and she hadn't had time to shop for Colin's tea.

Get on with it!

She drank another mouthful of coffee, pushed her cup aside. 'Bon Accord will do fine.'

Colin

'Is it okay if I bring a friend home?'

Maggie's eye's widened. First Kirsty, now Colin. She wondered what was coming. 'Of course it is,' she answered. 'You know that, Col.'

He frowned. 'It's just, you're always so busy, Mum. I don't want to be a nuisance.'

'Come here.' She drew him into a hug.

He stiffened, awkward against her.

Maggie's heart performed a small somersault. It seemed no time since Colin was a baby, soft and pliant in her arms. And now here he was, all knees and elbows, a man, almost.

'I'm never too busy for you,' she said.

That's not true. Up until George died she'd been there in the morning to make Colin's breakfast, there when he came home from school. And now? He'd be lucky to see her in passing. She felt the familiar stab of guilt. Now she stopped to think about it, Colin hadn't had a friend round for months, preferring to visit his classmates' homes instead. He'd been keeping his head down, she was convinced, after the wheel badge incident. Why the change of heart, she wondered? Fervently, she hoped that the bad behaviour was behind them, and he'd finally come to terms with his father's death.

She'd been thrown the previous day:

'Mum?' He'd appeared at Maggie's shoulder.

'What?' Her head clogged with witness statements and billing hours, she hadn't looked up.

'Do we have any black bags?'

'What for?'

'Thought I'd tidy up my bedroom.'

'You what?' Her head shot up.

'Have a bit of a clear out.'

Maggie had regarded her son with suspicious eyes. First, breakfast in bed, now this. She'd wondered what had sparked the charm offensive? Perhaps there was some expensive piece of kit he wanted her to buy.

'What's this in aid of?' she'd demanded.

'Oh.' He'd shrugged. *'Just.'*

Maggie had realised, then, she was going to get nothing more out of him. *'They'll be under the sink,'* she'd said.

Now, 'When did you have in mind?' she asked.

'Friday. After school.'

'Let me check my diary.' She reached for her phone. Then, frowning, 'I've a meeting at four, but it shouldn't take more than an hour.' She pulled a wry face. 'I take it you'll both be wanting your tea.'

He flushed. 'That would be good.'

'Okay.' Maggie made a diary note. They'd be fine until she got home, playing computer games, whatever. Then she'd dish them up a meal. Something straightforward: burgers or baked potatoes. She gave a small smile. Boys were so easy in that respect. She could pick up something in the supermarket on the way home.

She looked up. 'That's a date, then.'

'Thanks, Mum.' He turned, made for the door.

'Anyone I know?' she asked, as an afterthought.

'No.' Said over his shoulder. 'Her name's Ellie.' And then he was gone.

Some Book

'That's some book you've got there,' Ian joked, coming through the conservatory door.

'Aye.' Wilma didn't look up from the deep cushions of her rattan chair. Sex or no sex, she hadn't forgiven the bollocking he'd given her the other night.

He stepped forward, leaned down for a closer look. 'Another of those private investigators' manuals, is it?' Along with her stash off semi-legal gizmos, Wilma had invested in a burgeoning library of self-help books.

'Get off.' Wilma snapped the book shut. 'You're stinking.' She batted him away, simultaneously stowing the book behind a seat cushion. 'Away and have a shower.'

'I'll go in a minute.' Ian persisted. 'Thought you might like a cuppa first.'

'I don't want tea. Had some not long since.'

'Coffee?' he ventured.

She shook her head. 'I told you. No.'

Ian headed through the kitchen. Wilma probably wouldn't say no to a beer, but he knew better than to start her on the booze this early. He stooped to pick up a scrap of paper. It was white, a couple of inches square, the sort of thing you'd find stacked in a box alongside a landline telephone. On it was written, in careful capitals, one word: SUBLIMINAL.

He turned and waved it in Wilma's direction. 'This yours?'

She leapt from her chair. 'Where did you get that?' She snatched it out of his hand.

He reeled back. 'On the kitchen floor. Is it yours, right enough?'

'Aye.' She wrinkled her nose. 'And now look what you've done: gone and got your oily paw-prints all over it.' She stuffed it in her jeans pocket.

'So?' He could keep his counsel no longer. 'What's so important about a wee bit of paper?'

Wilma gave him the evils. 'Never you mind.' How to explain she'd been mugging up on a dictionary she found in a charity shop. Ever since Maggie had thrown that word at her, Wilma had vowed to improve her vocabulary. Now, when she found a minute, she'd open a page at random, find a word that took her fancy and memorise its meaning. She'd write the word on a notelet and stow it in a shoebox, along with other bits and pieces she kept from Ian.

'Seriously,' he moved to defuse her wrath. 'If it's important, I'm sorry I got a mark on it.'

'Forget it,' she snapped.

'Funny word,' he ran a hand over his stubble. 'Not one I've come across.'

'Aye.' Wilma resumed her seat. 'Weel.'

'What does it mean?' he inquired, his curiosity piqued.

'Resulting from…' Wilma chewed her bottom lip. She'd had it off pat, not five minutes ago. Now, she was fucked if she could remember.

She concentrated hard, conjuring up a mental image of the shoebox with its store of treasures. *Gotcha!* 'Resulting from processes of which the individual is not aware,' she trotted out.

Ian's eyes stood out on stalks. 'Get you!' He hesitated. 'But what does it really mean?'

'It means…' Wilma measured her words, happy to have re-gained the advantage, '…doing something without thinking about it.'

'Right,' Ian grinned. 'Like me winding you up.'

'Aye,' she retorted. 'Or taking an effing shower.'

A Spot of Bother

'Let's be having you' Chisolm called his team to attention.

Bob Duffy stretched his arms above his head, His mouth opened into a wide yawn. Slowly, he unwound his bulk from his chair and lumbered over to the table.

Susan was already seated, pen poised, notes in a neat stack in front of her. She was joined by Brian, who threw her a surreptitious wink as he sat down.

'Where's Douglas?' Chisolm demanded.

'Having a facial,' Duffy shot back.

'You're having me on,' Chisolm threw him a thunderous look.

Duffy hung his head. 'Sorry, boss.'

Chisolm nodded tacit acknowledgement. 'We'll start without him.'

No mention was made of Dave Wood. Everyone assumed he'd keep his sick notes coming till he hit retirement.

'Quick update on the misper.' He glanced at his notes. 'I made a flying visit to West Bell Street. Thought I'd eyeball Maguire, that he might be more forthcoming that way.'

'And was he?' Brian ventured.

'Yes,' Chisholm responded. 'And no.'

The three waited, expectant.

'It appears Sam Clark has been on their radar in connection with trafficking.'

'Traffic?' Eyes wide, Duffy sprang to full alertness. The very word was sufficient to strike fear into a serving officer.

'Trafficking, you numpty,' Brian corrected.

'Who are you calling a numpty,' Duffy shot back, puffing his chest.

Chisolm rolled his eyes. 'Are you done?' He eyed each in turn.

'But,' Brian came back, 'we checked Sam Clark out. She didn't have form.'

'Not yet,' Chisolm responded. 'From what Tayside have told me, Sam liked a flutter, so much so she landed herself in a bit of bother. Debt. Bigtime. Then…'

The door opened and Douglas Dunn appeared, red in the face. 'I'm terribly sorry, sir, but…'

'Sit.' Chisolm barked. 'I'm not going to go through this again. You'll have to catch up.'

Douglas made a beeline for the chair next to Susan, but she was too quick for him, snatching her handbag up off the floor and depositing it on the seat with a thump. Instead, he sat down next to Duffy.

'As I was saying,' Chisolm threw him a pointed look. 'Sam was heavily in debt. Looks like she turned to escort work to pay it off. Or she may have been involved in that before she turned to gambling. Regardless, it wasn't enough.' He checked his notes again. 'Protocol doesn't allow me to divulge the details. They're the subject of an ongoing high-level investigation. What I can tell you is Samantha Clark ended up a mule for a gang of people traffickers.'

'But where does Aberdeen come into it?' Susan ventured. 'Is it likely Sam came up here just to keep a low profile?'

'And looked up her old friend, Debbie, when she was here,' Brian added.

'Who knows,' Chisolm replied. 'Initially, she was based in Dundee, but we think, for whatever reason, she ended up here.'

'Men or women being trafficked, sir?' Douglas spoke from under lowered lids.

'Women. We're talking pop-up brothels.'

'Right,' Duffy nodded. They all knew there was no longer any need for sex workers to walk the streets when they could move from one short-term lease to another and advertise their services on social media.

'In what capacity was Sam involved?' Brian asked. 'Moving the girls around or what?'

'Money laundering, it appears.'

'Got you,' Duffy grinned. 'That could tie in with the gambling habit.'

'But how does this involve us?' Brian queried. 'If it's Tayside's investigation?' He scratched his chin. 'Oh, I get it, they think their corpse is Sam Clark and want to know what we've got on her?'

'Not so,' Chisolm replied. 'According to Maguire, they're no nearer identifying that body than they were when it was first discovered.'

'Pathologists,' Duffy smothered a yawn. 'They're all the same.'

Susan rooted in her handbag for a tissue and dabbed at her nose. Even from the far side of the table, she found Douglas's after-shave overpowering. 'Where does that put us with Debbie, sir?' she deflected the line of questioning. She was no nearer to coming up with an address.

'For one,' Chisolm observed, 'it puts a new complexion on our sightings.' For another, we cannot now rule out that Debbie Milne and Sam Clark were acting together in some capacity.'

Susan's eyebrows shot up. 'You think Sam might have been using Debbie to launder money?'

'It's not beyond the realms,' Douglas countered, recovering his chutzpah. 'If the traffickers moved Sam up here because her face became too well-known, Debbie would have made the perfect stooge.'

'To swan into a betting shop?' Susan pooh-poohed. 'I doubt it. All the evidence suggests she was way too prim for that.'

'Hah.' Douglas came back at her. 'I'm glad you mentioned "evidence". We've no evidence to suggest otherwise.'

'Accepted,' Chisolm intervened. 'But what we do have is a window of time.'

This was met with bewildered looks. Hadn't upstairs been chasing their DI for a result?

'What crumbs Tayside have chosen to throw our way could afford us a golden opportunity,' Chisolm continued. 'This people trafficking investigation might be in their jurisdiction, but if Sam Clark is, indeed, a key player she's most recently been active in Aberdeen. Plus, she's closely linked to our misper, and---'

'Oh!' Douglas couldn't stop himself. 'I get it. While they're sitting on their hands waiting for ID on that body, we could wrap up their case.'

'Chance would be a fine thing,' Duffy muttered.

Chisolm ignored him. 'If we pull this off and help tie up a major undercover investigation, it will be a feather in our cap, no question. *And one in the eye for West Bell Street.* Chisolm hadn't forgotten that early, stilted phone call. 'So, team, let's put our best efforts into nailing this. With the intel we now have, we need to check out the gambling angle: casinos, bookmakers' premises. Re-visit these sightings: the hotel, the bus, the taxi driver. Check out the block of flats where Sam Clark was living in Ferryhill: tenants, visitors, CCTV opportunities in the vicinity. He paused for breath. 'Brian, draw up a list of actions.'

'Sir.' Brian acknowledged with enthusiasm. Another chance for him to show his mettle.

'Right.' Chisolm gathered his papers. He stood. 'Go to it.'

'Yes, boss,' his squad answered, almost, but not quite, in unison.

Union Terrace

'Ladies!' Ella raised her voice over the blare of the television. 'Can I have your attention?'

Heads turned.

'We have a visitor.'

Wilma's gaze took in the drawn blinds, the worn carpet, travelled over the knot of women huddled on the ancient sofa and pair of easy chairs, the kids squatting at their feet. A wide-screen television droned in the far corner, the atmosphere an amalgam of cooking and stale smoke. Sights and smells that were all too familiar. Not that refuges such as this one weren't comfortable enough, but kitchen and bathroom facilities were generally shared, privacy at a premium.

'Wilma's no stranger,' Ella went on. 'She's been a resident here, a victim of domestic abuse like yourselves, so you can trust her to keep anything you share confidential. Today, she's trying to locate a missing person. I'd like you to give her what help you can.' She turned to Wilma. 'I'll leave you to it.'

Wilma looked around. One of the women looked familiar. She did a double-take. But, no. The woman caught Wilma's stare and turned her head away. Wilma eyed the television. 'Would it be okay to turn the TV down,' she asked. 'Just for five minutes?'

'Nae bother.' One of the women crossed the room. To loud protest from the kids, she fiddled with the remote.

'Thanks,' Wilma threw her a smile. 'I won't mess about. I've suffered abuse from the day I was born. My dad was a drunk, beat the living daylights out of me just for looking at him the wrong way. A relative interfered with me from the minute I hit puberty, and my first husband was a bastard. You name it, he did it: fists, feet, teeth, lit fags. Anything that was handy was good enough for me.' She grimaced. 'And that's before I start on the womanising and the gambling and the dodgy mates.'

From around the room came sympathetic murmurs. Then, 'Make yourself at home,' a scrawny blonde patted the sofa cushion beside her.

'Thanks,' Wilma squeezed between her and a well-upholstered brunette.

'The blonde offered her hand. 'Please to meet you.'

'Likewise.' She looked from one to the other. 'I've been back and forth to refuges like this since I was just turned twenty, so I know what you're going through.' Her gaze took in the room. 'It's no fun being cooped up in a place like this.' She looked towards the children whose noses were now within inches of the TV screen. 'With or without kids. But, believe me,' she smiled encouragement. 'Just being here, you've taken the first step.' She hesitated. 'The hardest step to taking your lives back. You might think there are no happy endings, but I've a new husband – a loving husband – and a home to call my own.' She raised a clenched fist. 'I did it. And so can you.'

There was a muted round of applause.

Wilma dipped into her fake Gucci bag, embarrassed, suddenly, by her outburst. She extracted a photograph. 'If you've come across this woman, I'd like to know.'

The photo was passed around to murmurs of, 'Never seen her before.' 'Doesn't ring a bell,' and, 'Me neither.'

Shite! Wilma knew it was a long shot, checking the local refuges. If Debbie Milne had sought escape from domestic violence, she'd have been housed at a distance from her home address, where she'd be at less risk.

She got to her feet, 'I'll leave a card. If you think of anything – anything at all – I'd be grateful.'

As she left the room, all eyes were back on the TV.

* * *

Wilma was waiting in the lobby when she felt a tug at her sleeve.

She turned.

'Got a minute?' The woman who'd looked familiar stood close by her side.

'Well, I…' One of the residents had gone in search of Ella. It couldn't be long before she re-appeared.

'You're Maggie Laird's pal.'

'That's right?'

'Taught my kid.'

Wilma clicked. 'Jean, is it?' She smiled encouragement. Although Wilma had heard news of Jean Meston via Maggie, and caught the odd passing glimpse at A&E, the only time she'd actually seen her up close was at Fatboy's trial. Then, Jean had been dressed in her best. Now, she was wraithlike, her shoulder-length hair hanging in rats' tails, her bitten fingernails stained with nicotine. 'I've heard Maggie speak of you.'

'Didn't want to say anything in there,' Jean angled her head in the direction of the common room. Her hand strayed to her hair in a fruitless attempt at tidying.

'I understand.' By the time they reached a place of safety, these women closely guarded their anonymity. And given Mike Meston's history of violent behaviour, it was hardly surprising his wife didn't want her presence known.

'But I'll likely only be here for a day or two before they move me on. Mrs Laird's a decent woman,' she continued. Does her best for the kids.' Her voice cracked.

Poor soul! Wilma's heart went out to the woman. She knew from Maggie that Jean's youngest, Willie, had been removed from the family home.

Jean recovered herself. 'There's not many would be bothered.'

'Can I give Maggie a message?'

'No,' Jean replied.

Wilma's mouth turned down. 'Oh, well.'

'Not to do with your missing woman,' she continued. 'But there's something Mikey let on, something he got on the jungle drums at Peterhead.'

'Yes?' Wilma was all ears.

'Something I think Maggie Laird would want to know.'

A Gap in the Hedge

'What are they doing here?' Colin demanded as he stormed through the back door.

Maggie looked up from her paperwork. 'Giving me a hand.'

'Yes, but…' He dumped his backpack on the floor.

'What?'

'Have you seen the front garden?'

'Mmm,' she said. 'Grass looks heaps better.'

'But those orange things,' he persisted.

'French marigolds.'

'I thought you didn't like them.'

'I don't.' They took her back to her childhood: the old farmhouse, where the small square of garden was bordered by regimented rows of bedding plants, where life was pre-ordained according to the seasons. She'd married George to escape all that, and now here she was, back at square one.

'Then…'

'They're fine,' she soothed. 'Not a big deal.'

'What is there to eat?' He made for the fridge.

Maggie had a quiet smile to herself. The young were so easily diverted. She pointed a finger. 'Your tea's there, on the table.'

Colin headed for the dining-room. 'What brought this on?' He eyed the single place setting, the cling-filmed plate of salad in its centre.

'Your gran. She thought it would make a change from…'

He ripped the cling-film off. 'Tuna?' he sniffed. 'And hard-boiled eggs? Aren't there any burgers, or…?'

'Far better for you.' Maggie's mum materialised at his back, a duster in one hand.

He swung around. 'Oh!' He reddened. 'Hi, Gran.'

'Hello, dear.' She stretched to plant a peck on his cheek. 'How's school?'

'Okay.'

'When will you hear about university?'

He threw a panicked look at Maggie. 'Not sure.'

Poor lad! She ducked her head. Just through the door and he was already being interrogated.

'Will you be joining your sister in Dundee?' her mother continued, undeterred.

'No way,' Colin retorted. 'Bad enough having to put up with her for the holidays.' Then, catching his grandmother's disapproving look, he added, 'I might do a sixth year.'

'Why would you do that?' she demanded. 'Is there a problem with…?'

'Consensus is…' Colin pre-empted another inquest into his grades. '…it gives you an advantage. Later on,' he added. Then, seeing his gran's doubtful expression, 'Especially for boys.'

Turning to Maggie. 'Can you afford…?' she began.

'It's all still up in the air.' Maggie flashed her son a warning look. 'Colin, why don't you go and wash your hands?'

'Can you really afford to put that boy through a sixth year?' Maggie's mother demanded once Colin was out of the room.

'Well, I don't…'

The back door swung open. Maggie's dad stood on the back step, leaning on a garden fork. 'There's a gap in your hedge.' He gestured in the direction of the adjoining bungalow.

'Really?' Maggie feigned surprise. How to explain that Wilma had forced her way through the privet so often she'd made a permanent breach?

'I could try to patch it up if you like,' her dad continued. 'Might take a while, but…'

'No,' Maggie cut him short. Wilma would go mad if she couldn't raise Maggie at the drop of a hat. Then, 'Yes,' she changed her mind. 'That would be a help.' She smiled. 'Thanks, Dad.' Despite her best efforts, Maggie still felt in Wilma's shadow. If she really were to be less dependent on her friend and neighbour, restoring the hedge between their two homes would be a symbolic start.

Man Trouble

'About my pal,' Wilma said, opening the conversation.

Dave drew on his pint. 'She took off, you said?' He licked a line of froth from his upper lip.

'Aye. Without a by-your-leave.' Wilma made a sorry face. 'Man trouble.'

'Shame,' Dave responded, taking in an eyeful of Wilma's cleavage.

She felt a ripple of satisfaction. She'd worn a push-up bra for the occasion under a clingy Jersey top.

Dave made an hourglass shape with his hands. 'Easy on the eye, your pal. No many punters like her come in my shop.'

They were in The Fuddled Duck, two doors down from Dave's bookmakers. Wilma had 'bumped into' the betting shop manager as he was locking up for the night, spun him a story. It hadn't taken much to persuade him into the pub.

Wilma took a dainty sip of her wine. 'Regular of yours, was she?'

'I'll say. Came in three or four times a week. Never at the same time, mind.'

Wilma rolled her eyes. 'That's Sam. Canna depend on her.' She fluttered her false eyelashes. 'Did she have much to say for herself?'

'Never had the opportunity. She always seemed to turn up when we were at our busiest – lunchtimes and Saturdays – so there wasn't much chance of small talk.'

'Must have nipped out from her work,' Wilma said, disingenuously. 'Been worried if she took too long she'd get the sack.' She'd got the same story from three other bookmakers: Sam would appear, pass the time of day, then make straight for the machines. When she was done, she wouldn't hang about drinking coffee or talking betting speak with the other punters, but be off out of there like a bullet. In her mind's eye, Wilma saw a pattern emerging: either Sam Clark had a serious gambling habit or she was working some sort of scam.

She threw Dave a sly look. 'She still playing bigtime?'

'Tell me about it. The way she went at those machines, you'd think her life depended on it.'

Now, there's a thing!

Wilma wondered why – if Sam Clark was unemployed – she chose to frequent betting shops rather than bet online. And where did the money come from?

'They're popular, then,' she pressed, 'the machines?'

'Aye. Pay out massive wins.'

And produce massive losses.

'Plus, you can play all sorts on them,' he elaborated. 'Roulette, blackjack, slot games.'

'That right?' Wilma feigned avid interest.

'Aye. Then there's racing: horses, greyhounds, cockroaches.' Dave was in full flow.

'Cockroaches?' Wilma reckoned she'd heard it all. She took another slurp of her wine.

'That popular, you wouldn't believe. And then there's...'

Wilma's head tumbled with conflicting thoughts. It was common knowledge Fixed Odds Betting Terminals were used for money-laundering. She put two and two together and made five.

'Bulletproof are they?' She insinuated herself back into the conversation.

'What do you mean?'

'I heard them machines are used for money-laundering.'

Dave took a considered sip of his pint. 'Where did you get that?'

Wilma frowned. 'Can't remember. Might have read it in a newspaper.'

'I wouldn't believe everything you...'

'Go on, Dave,' she cosied up. 'Spill the beans. Just between you and me.'

'There's safeguards in place,' he ventured. 'Unless you've membership or get loaded up at the counter, there's a maximum bet. The screen gets locked if you go over. Plus, for every thousand pounds in, you'd have to play a minimum of a third or it would flash up in the office.'

'Ooh,' Wilma made cow-eyes. 'How interesting.'

'Don't get me wrong, it happens,' he conceded. 'Give you one example: our Newcastle shops get a ton of Scottish notes over the counter. Drugs money, most like.'

'That right?' Wilma puzzled. 'But why Newcastle?'

'Suppliers on their way south.'

'What about you?' She'd moved so close to Dave by now she was in danger of suffocating. 'Have you had any dodgy goings-on?'

'Nah,' he exhaled a waft of foul breath. 'You'd need to pay in half in my shop to get away with it.'

'Ever seen Sam do that?' Wilma asked, catching him hungrily eyeing her breasts.

He looked up. 'Can't say I have.'

Wilma decided this was as much intel as she was going to get out of Dave. 'You wouldn't have a contact number for Sam?' she tried one final ploy. Long shot. But if Sam had a membership card it was a possibility. 'Only this boyfriend, mad for her he was. Started to stalk Sam when she broke it off. She's had to change her mobile number, shut down her Facebook, the lot.'

Dave pulled away. 'If you're such good pals, she'd have got in touch, surely?'

'That's what I can't understand,' Wilma affected surprise. 'We go back years. But she's such an airhead, Sam. Silly cow must have wiped me from her contacts by mistake.'

This must have convinced him, for, 'Sorry to hear that.' His knee sought hers under the table. 'If she comes back in…'

Wilma cut him short. 'Christ,' she fingered her phone, 'is it that time already? I've got to go.'

'But,' Dave's face fell. 'We've only just got here.'

'I know,' Wilma said, knocking back the rest of her wine. She rose to her feet. 'Time fair flies when you're enjoying yourself.'

VII

Dossers

Maggie squatted on the pavement. 'Have you seen this woman?' She held out a flier Wilma had run off from her computer, showing the photograph of Debbie she'd downloaded from Scott Milne's phone.

'Fuck off,' a slurred voice droned from the depths of the sleeping bag.

'Sorry.' She shuffled backwards, struggled to her feet. 'Didn't mean to disturb you.'

At her back, Wilma fought to suppress a giggle. 'Come on.' She grabbed Maggie by the sleeve. 'Out of here.'

'But he's only…' Maggie protested.

'…the twelfth dosser you've approached,' Wilma supplied. 'Time,' she propelled Maggie down the street, 'for a new angle.'

'Okay,' Maggie huffed. 'I've been doing my best.'

'Granted. But there's some situations call for a bit more,' she flexed her free arm, 'muscle.'

'I don't agree. That poor man in the doorway was…'

'…out his skull.' Wilma finished the sentence. 'Looked like he'd just shot up. Didn't you spot the needle?'

'No.'

'See.' Wilma mouthed. 'You could have put your hand on it, and then where would we be?'

Maggie shook her off. 'It was your idea.'

'Well, what about your wheeze: targeting the geezers at cashpoints?'

'What about it?'

'You nearly caused a fist fight: the bank customers trying to shield their pin numbers, the beggars at their feet waiting to cadge a note, and you in between.'

'I wouldn't worry your head about that. The punters are used to it. As for the beggars, it's business. Goes to maintain a habit: drink, drugs, take your pick.'

'I know that.' Hadn't George said the self-same thing? Only there hadn't been nearly so many rough sleepers in his day. 'But while we're on the subject, why you felt checking out the Cyrenians was a good idea I don't know. Or turning up at all those other organisations: Social Bite, the Salvation Army, Peace House, St Vincent de Paul.'

'They dish out free food, clothes, sleeping bags. And–'

'Yes, yes. But we know Debbie Milne has access to cash.'

'Which she hasn't drawn on.'

'To our knowledge. And women's refuges are one thing, but homeless shelters, you need a social work referral for those.'

'Only some of them,' Wilma pulled her up. 'Which is why we've been doing the rounds of the dossers.'

'Who are almost all, without exception, men. And why they're on the street when there are professional outreach workers, proper facilities...'

'There you go again,' Wilma interrupted, 'off on your high horse. I'll tell you why they're on the sodding street: because they choose to be. Either they don't feel safe in the shelters. There's folk with mental health problems in there: PTSD and all sorts. Or they're worried they'll lose their pitch. Or they have a habit – drink, drugs, doesn't matter – they can't sustain in a shelter. And it's not even as clear-cut as that.' She was in full flow. 'There's folk in work who sleep rough. Get in arrears with their rent, lose the roof over their heads.'

'Thanks for the lecture,' Maggie sniffed. 'But it doesn't address my point: we've only come across a couple of females the whole time we've been out looking, and even those have paired up with men for protection. We're dancing in the dark, Wilma. We've no idea where to look. At least the police have up-to-date information. They patrol these folk day and night, whereas we...' She broke off. 'I told you this was a waste of time.'

Wilma shrugged. 'Nae bother.'

Maggie drew her into a hug. 'I'm sorry. That was mean. I'm tired. We both are. Two late nights on top of our day jobs, and I reckon we've combed every back alley and doorway in the city centre, not to mention the cemeteries and open spaces.'

'Tell me about it,' Wilma muttered. 'I better watch or Ian will be shouting the odds.' She disengaged. 'You're right, though. Time for a rethink.' She blew warmth into her fingers. 'Mind you,' her mouth curved into an impish grin, 'we might as well check out these last few folk on our way back to the car.'

Back to Square One

'Sir,' Brian rapped, then stuck his head round Chisolm's door. 'Anything new from Tayside?'

Chisolm's head shot up from the spreadsheet he was studying. 'Had a phone call not ten minutes ago. That's why you're here.'

Brian stood, jaw hanging open, anticipating a scoop.

Chisolm motioned him to a chair. Whilst Burnett's steadfastness was to be admired, his efforts to insinuate himself grated. When his sergeant was seated, he spoke. 'It's good news and bad news.'

Brian waited, expectant.

'I'll give you the good news first. Dundee's pathologist has run our DNA samples. They're not a match. Tayside's body is not Debbie Milne.'

'That's the good news?' Brian's mouth turned down. 'Gotcha,' he exclaimed. 'Bad news is we're no nearer to finding Debbie.'

Chisolm made no attempt to hide his irritation. 'Quite.'

'Do we know if the body is Sam's?' Brian enquired.

'Not yet,' Chisolm replied. 'Sue Black's people…' He broke off. Dundee University's Department of Anatomy and Human Identification was world renowned for its work, notably in Bosnia, and had proved a valuable resource to the force. But Sue – now Professor Dame Sue Black – had moved south to take up a new post in Lancaster. 'The folk at Dundee Uni,' he corrected, 'are working to eliminate Sam Clark from the picture, but it's early days.'

'Hope they have more luck than us. Do you have any further intel on Sam?'

'Only that her folks have been traced to Livingston.' Chisolm answered. 'That should help speed up identification.'

'If Tayside's corpse does belong to Sam Clark,' Brian pondered. 'Where's the motive for killing her?'

'Money,' Chisolm replied.

'You reckon she ran off with someone else's cash?'

'That's a possibility.'

'There could be something else.' Brian saw a chance to redeem himself in his DI's eyes. 'Something bigger. The CCTV we obtained from Ferryhill shows single men coming and going from those flats at all hours of the day and night. Precious few women. But those it does show are – with one exception – very young and of Eastern European appearance.'

Chisolm brightened. 'A knocking shop? That would tally with Tayside's intel.'

'Looks like it,' Brian confirmed. 'More than that, the activity appears to be on an industrial scale.'

'But is there anything to suggest these women aren't soliciting of their own free will?'

'Negative. But we know from the neighbour Sam was on at least nodding terms with men who looked to be Albanian,'

'Nodding terms, yes,' Chisolm conceded. 'But she wouldn't have been in Aberdeen long enough to have built up a business connection.'

'She could have been parachuted in from further south,' Brian argued, 'to act as a minder for the girls, a funnel for the proceeds. A fresh face, if you like.'

'That's a possibility. Regardless,' Chisolm grimaced, 'this is all speculative. 'What we need is hard evidence, so keep at it.'

'Yes, boss.'

Chisolm ground his teeth. 'And it doesn't move us forward any with Debbie Milne's disappearance.' Even his squad did bring off a territorial coup, they still had a wide open misper case.

'Not unless Sam roped her in.'

'And how likely is that?'

Brian couldn't meet Chisolm's eyes. 'Not very.'

'Bottom line is, we still don't know who Tayside's cadaver was or why that woman was killed.'

'So we're back to square one on Debbie Milne?'

Chisolm sighed. 'Looks like it.'

Mika

They'd walked past before it registered: a trainer sticking out from a mountain of cardboard.

'Get that?' Wilma gave Maggie a nudge.

She tugged at Wilma's coat. 'Come on. We've had enough hassle for one night.'

'No,' Wilma persisted. 'Hang on.' She dropped to a crouch. Gingerly, she lifted a corner.

The trainer twitched, the cardboard trembled as one denim-clad leg emerged, closely followed by another.

Then came a muffled voice. 'Who there?'

'It's okay,' Wilma leaned in close. 'We won't do you any harm.'

A flattened carton slid onto the cobbles, closely followed by another and another still. From the far end of the pile a head emerged, so tightly swaddled in woollen scarves it was impossible to distinguish age or sex. From the cardboard nest, a slight figure scrambled, eyes wide with fright.

Maggie started forward, then stopped, as the figure readied for flight. She held up a hand. 'Please don't go. We're sorry to have disturbed you.'

'No understand.' The voice sounded young, foreign, and decidedly female.

Maggie advanced a couple of steps. 'We're looking for a missing woman. Here,' she waved a flier with Debbie Milne's photo in front of the girl's face. 'Have you seen her?'

She shrugged. 'I don't know.'

'Can you tell us your name?' Wilma asked.

'You police?'

'No.'

'Immigration?'

Wilma snorted. 'Nae chance. Just two mothers looking for

another mum that's missing.'

Slowly, the scarves were unwound to reveal a pinched face. Then: 'Michaela.'

Wilma couldn't believe her luck. 'You haven't been living in Ferryhill?' she asked. If this was the same Michaela the old prossie had mentioned, it could be the breakthrough they needed.

'Flat,' Michaela answered. 'That way,' she pointed.

'Where are you from?'

'Slovakia.'

'If you have a flat,' Maggie reasoned, 'why are you sleeping on the street?'

Fear flitted across her face. 'Bad men.'

'You on the run?' Wilma again.

She nodded. 'Hide till night, then go bus.'

'Go where?' Wilma demanded.

'Glasgow.'

'Glasgow?' She repeated in an incredulous voice. She'd read the newspapers, heard the stories. In Wilma's opinion, Torry was one thing, Glasgow quite another: somewhere nobody in their right mind would willingly go.

'Slovakian consulate,' Michaela explained. 'Bad men take papers.'

'Oh,' Wilma conceded. 'I get it. Got a bus ticket?' she added.

Another shake of the head.

'Money?'

She dug under layers of clothing, drew out a dog-eared billfold. 'Some.'

Maggie and Wilma exchanged looks.

'Can we help?' Maggie offered.

'No. My friend, she come soon.'

'You look frozen,' Maggie persisted. 'Why don't you sit in the car with us till she comes?'

Michaela backed away.

'Don't be afraid. We want to help you.' She extended a hand. 'Truly.'

Trembling with cold, Michaela allowed herself to be drawn into a hug.

'There,' gently Maggie rubbed warmth into the girl's arms.

* * *

'Have you thought this through?' Maggie asked. They were sitting in her car, the heater sending a fug of warm air into the small space. Mika – for, shyly, the girl had intimated that's what her friends called her – was in the passenger seat, Wilma squashed in the back.

This was met by a perplexed look.

'What I'm saying is, Mika, I doubt even if you get to Glasgow, your consulate will be able to issue new documents right away.'

'No?'

'You'll need somewhere to sleep.'

'Sleep on street.'

'You could stay with me,' Maggie volunteered. 'Phone your consul, stay out of sight until your papers come through.'

Another shake of the head. 'No possible. I need go far from this place.'

Wilma nodded in agreement. After her encounter with what she assumed to be an Albanian gangster, she'd have done a runner too.

'But Glasgow is a huge city,' Maggie protested. 'It's a very dangerous place for a young girl on her own.'

'I go with friend.' This was accompanied by a stubborn look. 'We good together.'

'Your friend,' Wilma chipped in, 'is she on the run too?'

Mika nodded.

'Has she been staying in Ferryhill too?'

'No. Meet on truck. Bad men promise good job. Cocktail waitress.' Her face brightened. 'Show video: cocktail bar, so elegant. Nice flat where sleep.' Her mouth turned down. 'Tell big lies.'

'There wasn't a job?' Maggie pressed.

'One month lock in flat. Men come visit. Many men. Do bad

things. Dirty.' She shuddered.

'You weren't at liberty to go out?'

Mika shrank visibly. 'No. Bad men lock in room. Then if do what told, no lock.'

Maggie and Wilma exchanged horrified glances.

'And then?'

'Go out.'

'On your own?' Maggie asked, surprised.

'Go with mother.'

'Whose mother?' Maggie puzzled.

Wilma quelled her with a look. 'Betcha pound to a penny this was someone who'd been working there longer, earned herself the bosses' trust. Would I be right?' She addressed the question to Mika.

The girl nodded. 'We go shop, sometimes go park. Today big shop. Many people. When mother pay, I run.'

'Where to?" Maggie came back in. She tried to imagine what she would do in the same situation.

'Car park. Hide long time under van, then text friend.'

Wilma could imagine. 'Where is she now, your friend? Sleeping on the street, like you?'

'Not on street. She run last night. Find good place. Warm. But no space for me. She come soon, I think.' Mika started to rewind her scarf.

'After Glasgow,' Maggie again. 'When you get new papers will you go home?'

Mika shook her head. 'Slovakia, maybe. Home, no.'

'But your family,' Maggie began.

'Bad men.' For the first time that night, Mika's resolve faltered. 'Have sister. They take. Hurt.'

Maggie tried to put herself in the place of the girl's mother. She'd have had such hopes for her daughter, as Maggie did for Kirsty. Be worried sick if she hadn't heard from her. Plus, Maggie couldn't imagine a situation where home wasn't somewhere you could retreat to in times of trouble. 'Oh,' was all she said.

'Before you go,' Wilma thrust Debbie's photo under her nose. 'Are you sure you haven't see this woman?'

Mika furrowed her brow. 'I don't think so.'

'You know a friend of hers, I'm told. Sam is her name.'

'Sam? Yes.' Smiling. 'She kind. Try help.'

'Have another look at the photo,' Wilma pushed. 'I think this woman, Debbie, may have visited Sam in Ferryhill.'

Mika shrugged. 'I work. Daytime. Night time.'

Wilma grimaced. 'I understand.'

Maggie fumbled for her purse. 'Here,' she proffered a couple of notes. 'Take this.'

Mika mumbled her thanks.

'And this,' Wilma thrust out the agency's card along with a flier. 'Ask your friend if she's seen this woman.' It was a long shot, but they were desperate. 'It has both our contact numbers on it. If your friend has come across Debbie, or you remember anything, give us a call.'

'And Mika,' Maggie called as the girl clambered out of the car. 'Good luck.'

Ian

'What time do you call this?' Ian snarled as Wilma crept into the kitchen.

'Christ!' She staggered backwards. 'What a fright you gave me.'

'I'm asking,' Ian persisted, 'what you've been up to till this time of night?'

'Working,' Wilma responded, breezily.

'That right?'

'Aye.'

'Where?'

'Up town.'

'With your pal next door?'

'Right, again.'

'Doing what?'

Keep it vague! 'Following up possible witnesses.' There was no way Wilma was going to admit they'd been dredging through Aberdeen's homeless community 'Never mind me,' she tried to divert his attention, 'what are you doing sitting in the conservatory in the dark?'

He rose from his seat. 'It's you we're talking about.'

'It's about your dinner, is that it? Look,' she held up a pacifying hand, 'I'm sorry it wasn't on the table, you working overtime and all. But there was stuff in the fridge. You could have done your own...'

'...thing?' He advanced on her. 'A couple of cold sausages and an open can of beans?'

'Beans are good for you,' Wilma joked, in an attempt to lighten the atmosphere.

'Even if they've a skin of green mould on the top?'

She dropped her gaze.

'Didn't I tell you the last time?' Ian said, his voice weary. 'There was to be no more night-time outings. You've a job to hold down and a house to run.'

'I know that.' Wilma was tempted to tell him she was thinking of packing in her job at the hospital, thought better of it. 'But this was an emergency.'

Ian's lip curled. 'Three nights on the trot?'

'C'mon,' she snuggled up, 'don't be such a grump. I'm sorry about your dinner. I'll make it up to you.' She rubbed her boobs against his chest.

He disengaged 'You needn't think you can just…'

'No?' She flashed a grin, her hand working its way up the inside of his thigh.

'Wilma,' he remonstrated, batting her hand away.

'Since I married you, Ian Harcus,' Wilma cupped her other hand on his crotch, was rewarded with a stirring there. 'Never let it be said I've neglected my household duties.'

From his mouth came a soft moan.

She started to rub. 'Don't I keep a tidy home?

'You do, I'll grant you that.'

She rubbed harder. 'Turn myself out smartly?'

'That, too.'

'And the odd time your dinner isn't on the table don't you forgive me?'

He groaned. 'I suppose.'

'Well then.' She had the rhythm, now. 'We're sorted. So why don't we continue our conversation somewhere more…' She led him out of the kitchen and into the bedroom. '…comfortable? And I can give you a wee something to help you sleep?'

More Questions Than Answers

'Let's run through it one more time,' Maggie said, looking up from her notes.

'Do we have to?' Scott face was haggard, his hair uncombed. 'We've gone back over this stuff I don't know how many times and can't see what good it's doing, us sitting here having this conversation, when you could be out looking for Debbie. After all,' a muscle worked in his jaw, 'it's what I'm paying you for.'

Wilma's head shot forward. She was about to open her mouth, when,

'I understand,' Maggie beat her to it. A verbal spat was the last thing she needed. 'And we're concentrating all our efforts, believe me. But with so few leads…' She broke off. 'I won't lie to you, Scott, so far this case has thrown up more questions than answers.'

He sighed. 'I'm sorry. I didn't mean to be rude. It's just, I'm frantic with worry. And things are chaotic at home. The kids keep asking after their mum. Their gran, she's not really coping. And my job…' His head dropped into his hands. 'I shouldn't even be here. I only nipped out because I thought you might have news for me.'

They'd met in the Maritime Museum cafe. Grateful for a break and a sit down, Maggie had ordered a pot of tea, Wilma a Diet Coke. Not that the seats at the circular tables, with their slatted wood backs and spindly legs, were conducive to relaxation, but it was close to Scott's place of work in Salvesen Tower on Blaikies Quay.

'Right, well,' Wilma took over. 'If we can go back to the morning of Debbie's disappearance. She was wearing a housecoat and slippers, you said.'

He looked up. 'That's right.'

'What was she wearing the day before, can you remember?'

He furrowed his brow. 'Jeans and a jumper, I think.'

'Can you describe the jumper?'

Shaking his head. 'Just ordinary. Crew neck. Blue, I think.'

'Hmm.' Didn't look like that line of questioning was going to be productive. She changed tack. 'Does Debbie have any distinguishing features?'

'Such as?'

'Moles, scars, strawberry marks scars?'

'No.'

'Tattoos?'

He shook his head.

Desperately, Maggie tried to remember the missing person info she'd mugged up on. 'Is Debbie right or left-handed?'

'Christ,' Scott exclaimed. 'What's that got to do with it?'

'How did she look last time you saw her?'

Maggie ignored this. 'Happy? Sad?'

'Bit fed up. Goes with the territory: running after kids all day. If it's not the school run, it's birthday parties, sleepovers, sports training, ballet lessons…'

Wilma cut him short. She got the picture. 'She didn't look unwell?'

'On the contrary,' Scott flushed with pride. 'She looked great.' He hitched up his sleeve, made a show of checking his watch. 'Look, I know you're doing your best, but if you've nothing concrete to offer me…'

Wilma flashed warning signals at Maggie. Sounded like the client was about to give them their books.

'If there's anything else,' she shot back. 'Anything at all that might distinguish Debbie.' *A futile exercise,* was what she was thinking.

Scott looked down at his uncovered wrist, a bemused expression on his face. Then, 'She was wearing this thing on her arm. Yes, I remember now. I noticed it when she handed me my coffee that morning. Her sleeve rolled back, and…'

'What kind of thing?' Wilma interrupted.

'A string.'

Wilma thrust her face in his. 'Describe it.'

'Sort of threads woven together,' he puzzled. 'I don't know what you'd call it.'

'A friendship bracelet?' she suggested, unable to keep the satisfaction from her face.

'That's it.' Distractedly, Scott checked his watch again. 'I'd seen it before. The pair of them made the things before Sam moved away, but Debbie stopped wearing hers after a while. I'd forgotten about them, to tell the truth. Debbie must have kept hers, fished it out when Sam came back on the scene.'

'Can you describe this bracelet?' Maggie asked.

'Sort of plaited, like a pigtail. And thin, not much substance to it. Didn't look like much, to be honest.' He shrugged. 'They probably didn't make a good job. They were just kids.'

'What colour was it?' Wilma prompted.

'Red, mostly. A bit of white. Or could have been yellow, it was that faded.'

'Were they both the same, Sam and Debbie's?'

'I think so.' He scratched his head. 'Isn't that the point?'

Ellie

'Col?' Maggie tapped on the door.

She heard a scuffle, then, 'What?'

'Do you want some dinner?'

'No.'

'Okay.' Her shoulders relaxed. One less thing. The pile of paperwork on the dining-room table had been mounting daily. If she didn't have to cook, she'd make do with a sandwich and a cup of tea.

She'd turned to go when she thought she heard a stifled giggle. She wheeled. 'Colin?' she rapped more loudly. 'Have you got someone in there?'

There was another scuffle. The door opened a crack.

Colin stood in a pair of jeans and a tee-shirt. His feet were bare, she saw.

He eyed her accusingly. 'You said you were going to be late.'

'I know. My meeting was called off: this bug that's going about. So I did a shop. Thought I'd cook you something decent for a change.' She shrugged an apology. 'Too many ready-meals aren't good for you. But,' she broke off, suspicious. 'You haven't answered my question. Have you got somebody else in there?'

His face flamed. 'Well, I…'

Maggie twigged. Sod it! When Colin had first mentioned he had a girlfriend she should have anticipated this scenario, but she'd been too busy to take it on board.

'Make yourself decent.' She assumed a stern face. 'I'll see you downstairs.'

* * *

'Mum,' Colin hung back in the doorway, a bashful look on his face. 'Meet Ellie.'

From behind him slid a girl: tall, with a tumble of dark hair, and slender as a reed.

'Hello, Ellie,' Maggie said. She'd darted downstairs, shot through to the bathroom, repaired her make-up before scrambling out of her work outfit and into a pair of smart jeans. The jumble on the table she'd scooped into a Marks & Spencer Bag for Life and stuffed into the sideboard.

'I'm sorry,' Ellie began.

Maggie waved her away. 'Don't. If anyone owes me an apology it's Colin.' She threw him a baleful look, but his eyes were firmly fixed on the floor.

What do I do now? Maggie thought. *Throw the girl out? Tell Colin* he's *gated?* She wished – not for the first time – George had been there to back her up.

Oh heck! 'Good to see you.' She forced a smile. 'It would have been nice to meet under other…' She hesitated. '…circumstances. But you're here now. And I suppose you're hungry, the pair of you.'

Ellie nodded.

Colin wouldn't meet her eyes.

'Sit down.' She pointed to the table. 'I'll make you something to eat,'

A Direct Approach

On the Esplanade, the lone figure of Allan Chisolm maintained a steady pace. When his alarm had shaken him from sleep, he'd rolled out of bed, splashed his face and brushed his teeth before pulling on the well-worn running gear he'd laid out the night before on a chair by the bed.

From the floor-to-ceiling window of his sixth-floor rented flat in Bannermill, a modern development located between Constitution Street and the Beach Boulevard, he'd watched the sun rise over Aberdeen harbour. When he'd first arrived in the city, the harbour had teemed with activity, vessels jostling for space. Since the oil downturn, there was room to spare. In the foreground, the Shore Porters Society warehouse stood silent. Founded in 1498, six years after Columbus discovered America, the international removals company was one of the oldest co-operatives in history, its pantechnicons with their navy blue and scarlet livery a familiar sight, carrying the chattels of an itinerant population from one end of the UK to the other and far beyond. Chisolm hadn't needed to call on their services when he'd moved north from Glasgow. He'd walked away from the place he'd called home for so many years with little more than the clothes on his back and a heart full of regret.

He'd dismissed the thought. Purposefully, he'd stretched his limbs, taken a few deep breaths, rolled his head in one direction, then the other to loosen his neck. Then he'd uttered a sigh of satisfaction. Best time of the day.

It had been nearly a week since Allan had taken his last run, and his knees protested as his trainers hit the pavement. For the umpteenth time, he resolved to make an early morning jog a fixture in his timetable, knowing full well this would be yet another empty resolution. When he'd first arrived in Aberdeen, he'd intended to join a gym, both to maintain his fitness level and to meet new people. But his squad had got mired in a series of obtuse investigations and he hadn't got around to it, that and the other things that were to enrich his new life. The current misper was a case in point. In all his years in the force, he'd never come across a case so devoid of evidence. Granted, when people went missing, it was often because they didn't want to be found. But now, with the electronic trail left behind on their phones and hard drives, it was well-nigh impossible to disappear without trace. Allan Chisolm speculated, not for the first time, that Debbie Milne was dead.

He checked the app on his watch. It wasn't yet six, and the big Asda store, he knew, didn't open till eight. But the building was ablaze with light, lorries lined up in the loading bays shedding wheeled containers of stock into the store. His stomach growled. He could have done with another hour in bed, a cooked breakfast instead of the coffee and cereal bar he'd oftentimes grab on his way into work. Still, the run would clear his head, Chisolm rationalised. And at least it wasn't raining: the sky slashed grey-blue, the wind whipping the waves into peaks stiff as meringue.

As he reached the row of cafes that bordered the entrance to Codonas, he allowed himself a smile. The sandwich boards weren't yet out, but the Inversnecky was known for its pithy one-liners. Behind the Grampian Eye Big Wheel, the fairground's main attraction, Marischal College and the ugly tower block that was Chisolm's place of work were silhouetted against the skyline. Above his head a seagull wheeled, poised, then dive-bombed a stray chip. Bit like policing, he mused: the way you zoomed in on your target.

Tugging his woollen cap over his stinging ears, Chisolm jogged past the tall pylons of the Pittodrie football stadium. As he took the bend into Seaton, his thoughts turned to Maggie Laird. Her firm had been retained by Scott Milne, he knew. Maggie would have gone through the motions with Scott, her and/or the big Harcus woman. They'd have asked the same questions, got much the same answers as did uniform at the outset of the investigation. What the PIs had done since was an unknown. Chisolm assumed the business relationship with Scott Milne would have been terminated when the police investigation was escalated to CID. For, surely, Maggie Laird would have known better than to compromise a police investigation for a third time. Chisolm resolved to find out. But how? He could ask his sergeant. Brian Burnett was close to Maggie, how close Chisolm didn't want to speculate. Brian had dodged the question when it was put to him. Was that because he knew something? Chisolm dismissed the notion. After the reprimand he'd received in relation to the Fatboy affair, Burnett wouldn't want to blot his copybook if he hoped to gain promotion. No, best make a direct approach.

His last encounter with Maggie Laird had been less than satisfactory. Downright embarrassing if he were honest with himself. She'd looked so vulnerable, he'd let his feelings get the better of him, overstepped the mark when he'd taken her in his arms. But, the misunderstandings she'd occasioned and the accusations he'd thrown, he was full of admiration for the way she'd faced up to everything that had been thrown at her.

Crossing the road, the sea behind him, the rise in Allan Chisolm's blood pressure was palpable as he recalled their embrace.

Tyres squealed. A horn blared.

He pulled up short, raised a hand in apology as a white-van driver gave him the finger.

Regaining the relative safety of the pavement, he jogged up Seaton Road and turned left onto King Street. He'd give Maggie Laird a call, he decided, suggest they meet. Neutral territory. Nothing heavy, just a casual drink, sufficient to restore cordial relations. For, despite their past differences didn't they have a common objective?

The Milne case was going nowhere. It was a shot in the dark, but in the immediate aftermath of his wife's disappearance who knows what nugget of information Scott Milne might have divulged that the response team had overlooked. Harcus and Laird might just have the piece of the jigsaw that would complete the picture.

Yes, Chisolm gritted his teeth as he reached the home straight, he would kill two birds with one stone: smooth relations with Maggie Laird and at the same time mine her for information. Best get an update on Brannigan first, he chided himself. Maggie was bound to ask.

High and Dry

'Turn that up, will you?' Maggie gestured towards the car radio. 'We might get something on the news about that body.'

Accompanied by Wilma, she was driving to Ballater to take statements from witnesses in an agricultural fraud case: a latter-day incidence of cattle rustling, where the theft had been perpetrated, not in the open in the dead of night, but indoors and on paper. Maggie always enjoyed a drive out to Royal Deeside. She loved the countryside: the rolling hills and the forests of Scots pine and Sitka spruce, the fields dotted with fat sheep. They took her back to her childhood. She even loved the place names on the road signs that flashed past: Inchmarlo and Lumphanan. Dinnet and Tarland. Cambus O'May and Kincardine O'Neil. At this time of year, the silver birches by the roadside were in full leaf, the River Dee, when she caught a glimpse now and then, sparkling in the bright daylight. Despite the tawdry task in hand, the bounty of the landscape gave Maggie hope that her life might hold promise, after all.

'Good thinking.' Wilma leaned forward and twiddled the dial.

The national news came on. *Police have confirmed that the body found on Tayside is not that of missing Aberdeen woman Debbie Milne. No trace of Debbie, 32, who vanished from her home in the city's Rosemount district on Tuesday of last week, has been found, despite extensive coverage in the press and on social media. A police source, speaking exclusively to this newspaper, said, "We are pursuing several active leads."*

'That's a help,' Wilma said, sour-faced. She'd inveigled herself into Maggie's house whilst Shaz was installed, but despite repeated attempts, neither she nor Maggie had elicited anything useful from him. Then Maggie had come home one night to find Shaz gone. Kirsty wouldn't be drawn, and Maggie had deemed it prudent to drop the matter.

'Where do we go from here?' Maggie fretted, as they left Peterculter behind. 'We've followed our game plan: checked out the hotels and B&Bs, milked the women's shelters and homeless squats and run out of steam on Sam Clark. If Debbie Milne is still in Aberdeen, she must be holed up with someone.'

'Not Sam, that's for sure. From what I got out of the quine at Ferryhill, sounds like our Sam's done a bunk.'

'Where does that leave us?'

Wilma screwed up her face. 'High and dry.'

'We could get back in touch with the missing persons' organisations,' Maggie suggested. 'See if there have been any new sightings.'

'We're way behind the curve there.' Wilma dismissed her out of hand. 'The police will have run it past them at regular intervals from day one.'

'Do you want to call it quits?' Maggie asked, ambivalent. On the one hand, she'd been proved right. As PIs, they were completely out of their depth. On the other, Debbie Milne, stay-at-home mum of two kids, wasn't that removed from where Maggie had been not that long ago.

'Not yet.' Wilma prevaricated, picturing what might be the agency's last major case go down the drain.

'You sure?' Maggie persisted, passing Crathes Castle. 'We've clocked up a fair few billing hours. There's an argument for cutting our losses while we're still ahead.' She dropped her speed as she navigated the traffic through Banchory.

'Yes, but…' Still, Wilma played for time.

'Let's face it, we've exhausted all possible channels. Maybe it's time we held our hands up, admitted we're not very good at this sort of thing and left it to the police.'

'No!' Wilma's voice rose in panic. If the business folded, she might never see another chance to work her way up the career ladder. 'If we could only get a heads-up on the police investigation,' she said, more in hope than expectation.

'Not going to happen.' Maggie's last attempt at getting intel out of

Queen Street had resulted in a face-off with DI Chisolm.

For a few moments Wilma deliberated, then, 'You could always ask your pal, Brian.'

'No way. Brian's a busted flush.'

'Oh,' Wilma said, her expression arch, 'I don't know about that.'

'He didn't give me tuppence last time I tried.'

'Shouldn't stop you having another go.'

Maggie changed gear, pulled out to overtake a lorry. 'Drop it, will you?'

'Okay. But it was Brian helped you, don't forget, with Colin's wee adventure.' Shamelessly, Wilma dredged up the incident where Maggie's son, Colin, and a school chum had pilfered wheel badges from a car. 'And if we could only find out where the police are at, it would mebbe...'

"Pursuing several active leads." 'You've just heard it on the bloody news. And you know perfectly well what that means.'

Wilma groaned. 'They've got fuck all.'

The two sat in silence as they passed through Aboyne, its village green, home to the annual highland games, on their left, elegant granite villas to their right.

Then, Wilma laid a hand on Maggie's arm. 'We're not going to give up on Debbie Milne.'

Maggie shook her off, gripping the steering wheel tighter. 'We don't have a choice.' She asserted, refusing to be swayed by emotion.

'But them bairns,' Wilma wailed. 'If Brian Burnett's working the case, surely...'

'Surely, nothing,' Maggie snapped. 'I've already told you, Wilma, the Milne case has run out of steam.'

'We could start again,' Wilma pleaded. Take another look at the family.'

'To what end? I doubt we'll get much more of out of Scott Milne. As to those kids, short of abducting them...'

'Now, there's an idea, ' Wilma interrupted. 'I guarantee you that would bring Debbie Milne running.'

'Be serious for once, will you?' Maggie turned and gave her a sharp look. She turned back.

'I am being serious. From all the evidence, Debbie's a good mother. Not just conscientious: running her kids to school, the home-making stuff. But didn't Scott say the wee boy was worried about going up to secondary, that Debbie had been taking him into her bed.'

'I think it was the other way around: Debbie going to him.'

'Whatever. If she's doing that because her kid's having bad dreams, just imagine what she would do if…'

Decisively, Maggie cut her short. 'Wilma. We've been through all that. I'm not having you pull any more of your dodgy stunts.'

This and That

'Cheers,' Shaz raised the bottle to his lips.

'Cheers,' his companions echoed.

They were in Braes Bar on Dundee's Perth Road. Opposite the Tower Building, it was one of the nearest drinking dens to the university.

'Been a while,' Pete offered.

Shaz nodded. He'd been keeping a low profile since his heavy date with a mutilated corpse. For one thing he was skint, for another emotionally drained from his repeat visits to West Bell Street. Not – fuelled as he'd been by drink and drugs when he'd happened across Sam Clark's corpse – that he was suspected of any involvement. Rather that he'd been pissing himself waiting to see whether he'd be charged on account of the skunk they'd dug out of his wallet, further unnerved when he'd been passed up the chain of command until being interviewed by the specialist unit that was investigating the traffickers.

'What you been up to?' Four-eyes was on lime and soda.

'Oh,' Shaz took another swallow, 'this and that. He'd been warned by the police not to broadcast his experience until identification was completed and he'd been given the all clear.

'Where you dossing? Mike enquired. 'Still up the coast?'

Shaz shrugged. 'It's only temporary.'

'I thought you were shacking up with that dame?' Pete again.

'Julie?'

'No. Law student. What was her name?'

'Kirsty.' Four-eyes came back in, colour rising to his face. 'Kirsty Laird.' He'd had a crush on Kirsty since the start of second year. To hide his confusion, he looked down at the floor.

'That snotty cow?' Shaz affected disdain. 'No way.'

'But you did have a thing,' Pete insisted.

'Yeah. Yonks ago. When I was in first year,' he elaborated.

Pete nodded, sagely, as if that explained everything.

'I hear you've been up in Aberdeen.' Mike enjoyed a bit of sport.

Shaz choked on his beer. 'Who told you that?'

'What does it matter,' Mike teased. 'Were you?'

'Yes, as a matter of fact. It was Kirsty's mum gave me a bed. She's a private eye,' he added, for effect.

'That right?' Pete put the question.

'Yup! Shaz confirmed. 'Investigating a big case.'

'Spill,' Mike prodded him in the chest.

Shaz tugged on one of his flesh tunnels. 'Can't.' He was in danger of letting it all out. And that could get him in trouble. Big trouble. He conjured up a mental picture of being done for possession, of his uni course going up in smoke. 'Not at the moment, anyhow. But,' he moved to redeem himself in their eyes. 'The mum – Maggie's her name – talk about MILF.' He gave an exaggerated wink.

'No kidding,' Mike's eyes were out on stalks.

'Mother's a whole load more attractive than the daughter.'

His three pals looked duly impressed.

What Shaz didn't let on was that Maggie Laird and her skanky big neighbour had given him the third degree. As for Kirsty – who he still held a torch for – she'd made him sleep overnight on the settee, torn him off a strip in the morning for giving cheek to her mother, and sent him packing on an early morning bus.

Ardoe House

'Cheers!' Chisolm raised his glass.

'Cheers!' Maggie mirrored the action.

They were in Ardoe House. Only three miles outside the city, it is a world apart. Set in thirty acres of tranquil countryside, the 19th-century granite mansion, with its crenellated turrets and stepped gables, is a popular wedding venue, its pool and spa frequented by locals and visitors alike.

Allan Chisolm had agonised over their meeting place: in town or out, intimate or not. Had been reluctant to ask advice of his colleagues. In the end it was a toss-up between Ardoe House and the Marcliffe at Pitfodels, both a short distance from Maggie's Mannofield home, both far enough away from Chisolm's office at Queen Street. But the Marcliffe hosted a wide range of functions, not least of them Rotary, and he wasn't looking to be compromised, so Ardoe House it was.

At five-thirty midweek, the Laird's Bar was all but deserted, the hotel's residents either not back from their day's business or upstairs in their rooms catching up with emails or getting ready for dinner. Chisolm watched Maggie finger the stem of a small glass of wine. He'd been surprised when she'd ordered red, had decided sauvignon more her style. Just went to show how little he really knew the woman.

Maggie perched on the edge of a purple velvet banquette. She hadn't seen Allan Chisolm since the Struthers business, and Ardoe House wouldn't have been her first choice for the meeting. She'd driven out the South Deeside Road many a time, sometimes with George for a meal or a drink at Maryculter House or the Lairhillock Inn, often just for a run out with the kids. Until that day, she'd only known the hotel by reputation, but the ornate wood panelling, pillared arches and stained glass windows she'd clocked as she walked through the foyer were a bit florid for her taste. As was the bar she sat in, now, its walls papered in a pattern of giant thistles she recognised from a magazine as Timorous Beasties, its gantry dominated by a stag's head with a full set of antlers and lit by a row of fringed lampshades.

Wilma would be in her element! She cursed herself, then, for being so small-minded.

She eyed Chisolm across the table. His long legs were folded into a squat tub chair. The dark grey flannel suit was one she'd seen before, so he must have come straight from work. But he'd ditched the tie, loosened the top button of a cornflower blue shirt. He looked more casual, younger, his eyes bluer than the steel grey she remembered. And normal, not the dark, brooding ogre she'd conjured up.

An awkward silence followed. Then:

'The reason I…' they both said at once, then burst out laughing.

'You first.' He extended an arm.

'No,' she argued. 'You.'

He smiled. 'If you insist. I asked you to meet me this evening for two reasons. 'First,' he cleared his throat, 'to apologise, again, for my behaviour at our last encounter.'

Maggie blushed. 'There's no need.'

'So you say, but…' Since the *MeToo* movement of 2017, strict new police guidelines had been issued regarding sexual impropriety. '…I shouldn't have…'

'Forget it.' She cut him short. As she said the words, Maggie made a fervent wish she could be as clear-headed. For in her imagination she'd revisited their brief embrace many times.

She stole a covert look from beneath lowered lids. Had this man really held her in his arms? Kissed her hair, her forehead? Or had she blown up a minor lapse of judgement into something more significant?

She fiddled with her drink, wondered if her nervousness was making her squint more pronounced.

'The second reason,' Chisolm continued, 'is to update you on our friend, Bobby Brannigan.'

'Oh,' Maggie was taken by surprise. She'd assumed Chisolm would have forgotten all about him.

'It's bad news, I'm afraid. We still haven't succeeded in locating Brannigan, and upstairs have bigger fish to fry, for the moment at least. But be assured, I'll keep on...'

'I'm sorry,' Maggie broke in. 'I meant to ring you, but with one thing and another it went right out my head. Thing, is,' she ran on, 'I've recently received information... *Keep it vague!* ...Bobby Brannigan's assault was ordered, not by James Gilruth, but by a Scouser gang.'

'Your source, it's reliable is it?'

'I can't say.' She wondered how much she could give away without digging a hole for herself, decided Allan Chisolm was someone she could trust. 'Jean Meston, actually. She got the intel from Mike.'

'Who got it out of Peterhead, presumably.'

Maggie bit her lip. 'I'm not sure.'

'I'll have it looked into,' Chisolm threw her a quizzical look.' He speculated whether Maggie had kept in contact with Jean Meston on account of Willie, her ex-pupil, or whether she was still dipping her fingers into the Milne disappearance. 'It could put a different complexion on our drugs investigations.'

'James Gilruth, you mean?' Maggie asked, eagerly.

'No. Not that Gilruth's squeaky-clean. He's party to graft: property backhanders, that sort of thing. Prostitution, too, but it's borderline: lap-dancing, you know the type of thing?'

Maggie didn't. All the same, she nodded knowingly.

'He's not into protection rackets, Class A drugs. Maybe once, not anymore. The drugs his people deal in are recreational, peddled in his pubs and clubs. It's the hard stuff the drugs squad are after: heroin, cocaine.'

'Fentanyl?' Maggie offered, trying to look knowledgeable

Chisolm crooked one eyebrow. 'That, too.'

'So James Gilruth…' she began. Maggie wondered if she'd been barking up the wrong tree, her vendetta against Gilruth entirely misplaced.

'…is being investigated for money-laundering, principally,' Chisolm responded.

'Oh,' Maggie said in a small voice. 'I see.'

'However, I should caution you, even if Brannigan were to back up the tape admitting his perjury with a full statement, there's little appetite from upstairs for taking things forward. Even if they did, what's the best that could happen: picking over old bones, at huge cost to the public purse? And at the end of it there's not a chance your friend Craigmyle would be reinstated, not after holding his hands up to a flagrant breach of interview protocol. Nor will it bring your husband back. I've made you a commitment and I'll honour that, but too much time has elapsed, I'm afraid, to have a realistic hope of success.'

Maggie's spirits sank. So he was closing the door. She didn't respond.

'I know we've had our differences in the past,' Chisolm ran on. 'It irked me when your PI activities encroached on my police work. But we were both finding our feet, so to speak, and I sincerely hope we'll have a more…' He hesitated. '…collaborative relationship in future.'

Maggie felt the colour start to rise in her face. 'I hope so too.'

'I'm sorry for your loss. By all accounts, your husband was one of the good guys and well-regarded in the force.' He leaned forward. 'Don't take this the wrong way, but now your children are of an age and you've put your business in a sound footing, shouldn't you be looking to the future?'

Was this an overture if some sort? Maggie blushed to her Titian roots.

'You're a lovely woman, Maggie Laird. Forgive me, I know it's not my business, but I think highly of you. That's why I'm asking the question: isn't now the time, perhaps, to look forward? I'm not suggesting for a moment you abandon your cause, but do it for yourself, Maggie, you and your children.'

Swiftly, she changed the subject. 'Anything interesting on the go?' she asked, in her best PI voice.

'Same old,' Chisolm saw his opportunity to bone up on the Milne case. 'Other than this missing woman, Debbie Milne. I believe you were in at the beginning of that?'

'Yes,' Maggie said. 'Husband panicked, made an approach, but of course when the case was escalated...' She ducked her head, fearful she'd be caught in the lie.

'Quite so,' Chisolm said, his face a mask. 'I'll be frank. We're toiling on that one. I don't suppose...' He let the question hang. '... Scott let anything slip in his dialogue with you that would move us forward?'

Maggie sat rooted to her seat. She'd wanted to ask Chisolm the exact same question. Her brain scrambled. What did the police know that would help the agency? What did she know that she was prepared to give in exchange? 'It was early days.' She played for time. 'All that was discussed were the circumstances of Debbie's disappearance, her immediate family, her friends.'

'That would be Sam Clark?'

'Right.'

'You have a photograph, an address?'

'Yes to both questions.'

'So you'll know Sam was flatting in Ferryhill?'

Maggie nodded.

'And that she's not there now. Seems to have moved on.'

'That's what I don't understand,' Maggie said. 'According to Scott Milne, the two of them were close, even though they'd been separated by circumstances for so long.'

'Maybe,' Chisolm argued, 'they thought they could pick up where they'd left off, but were disappointed. Could be marriage had changed Debbie.' He broke off, uncomfortable. It had changed him, for sure.

'But that isn't borne out by the friendship bracelets,' Maggie blurted.

'What friendship bracelets?' Chisolm asked.

Ambushed

Wilma was walking down Crown Street minding her own business when a gloved hand gripped her shoulder, a leather-clad arm encircled her neck.

In a reflex action, she jabbed the man in the ribs. To no apparent effect.

He clamped her head in a vice and dragged her into a doorway.

She'd sent some mail Recorded Delivery from the post office within WH Smith in Union Street, the Mannofield branch having long closed. She'd a notion, then, to drop Debbie's flier into a few more B&Bs. Crown Street was thick with them, so in a short space of time she'd be able to cover a fair few.

'You pal Sam?' the man demanded in heavily-accented English.

'Not a pal, no.' Wilma croaked, clawing at his arm. She wondered if it was the same guy she'd had a run-in with at the Ferryhill flats, twisted her neck until she could hear the tendons protest, in a vain attempt to see his face. But his head was covered by a cap: navy waterproof material and flat, like an old-fashioned baker's boy's, the peak pulled down over his eyes.

'Why you look Sam?' She caught a flash of gold teeth.

'Asking for a friend', Wilma shot back.

'No joke,' he spat. 'You tell, or...'

She felt something hard dig into the small of her back. Wondered if he had a weapon. Or maybe he was just excited. 'Look,' she played for time, 'I don't know why you're so interested in Sam, and I don't want to know. But we're both after the same thing. So, if you don't mind...' Pointedly, she looked down at his arm, '...will you ease off a bit?'

With a grunt, he relaxed his grip, but left his arm in place.

'I really am looking for a friend,' Wilma assumed what she hoped was an innocent face. She knew better than to let on to this bawbag she had even the flimsiest connection with the law. 'They were at school together.' That, at least, was true. 'But they've lost touch.'

The Albanian – for so she assumed him to be – milled this over, then. 'Why no Facebook?'

'Sam seems to have shut down her account.'

'Ha,' he grunted, his grip tightening again.

'Look,' Wilma reasoned. 'It's obvious we're both after the same thing. 'So why don't you give me a contact number, and if I come up with anything…'

'Fucking clown.' he hissed, sending a shower of spittle onto Wilma's face. It landed on her temple. ran over her cheekbone and dribbled down her neck.

Face contorted in disgust, she whipped her head away.

He grasped hold of her chin, yanked it back to face him. Then, in a voice heavy with menace, he said, 'No mess with me.'

VIII

South College Street

Maggie spotted it at once. Not that it stretched her powers of detection. The *To Let* sign above the entrance was weathered and torn, and looked to have been there for years. Small wonder. Running under the south-heading railway line and home to a number of enterprises over the years, the Victorian railway arches had been refurbished to varying degrees. Now the property of Network Rail, they were rented out for storage or light industrial use. But whereas many of the business units had been cleverly converted, with plate-glass frontages or seamless roller shutters, others were more basic, the arches crudely in-filled with unpainted breeze blocks and narrow panel doors.

This one was a case in point. As she came close, Maggie eyed the rusting metal door. It was secured by a heavy bolt. A bolt that should have been held in place by a padlock, she observed, but which someone had slid back.

Pulse racing, she gave it a shove.

Mounted on coiled metal springs, it gave with little resistance.

She peered into the gloomy interior. 'Anybody there?' she called, her voice uncertain.

Anybody there…there…there? The question bounced off bare brick walls.

For a moment, Maggie stood, deliberating her next course of action. Mika's call had caught her in the middle of a presentation: a bid for new business from a national law firm. Flustered, she'd apologised profusely, switched off her phone. It was only when she got home and off-loaded the shopping that she'd picked up the voicemail: *Missing woman…* Mika's voice was drowned by a rumble of wheels. *…railway arches.* Then the line was cut.

She'd already done a recce of Palmerston Road. Scored a blank. There, the arches were well-presented and secured, probably because of their proximity to the Union Square shopping centre, where the passing rents would be sky-high. Even South College Street must be an attractive enough proposition, for there were few vacant units, and even those were in good nick. Other than this one. She decided to investigate.

The door banged shut behind her.

She groped for a light switch, found the electricity had been cut off.

Idiot! What did she expect?

She dipped into her shoulder bag, fumbled for her phone. Its torch function wasn't the best, but it would have to do.

Then, *Blazes!* Not for the first time, Maggie cursed her lack of professionalism. In her haste, when she'd texted Wilma from the car, she must have left her phone on the passenger seat.

Oh, well, nothing for it!

She crept forward, arms outstretched, fingers spread. Encountered nothing but empty space.

Her spirits sank. She'd been buoyed by the phone message, decided this was the breakthrough they'd been waiting for, her and Wilma: the stroke of luck that would put the agency ahead of the police, return Debbie Milne to her family. And if Mika's tip-off proved fruitful, Maggie would have done it on her own: saved face with Wilma after the Struthers shambles and restored Harcus & Laird's good name.

Then, *Don't even go there!* Hadn't false pride landed her in trouble before?

The space was larger than she'd envisaged. What had the letting board said? She racked her brains. 3,500 square feet, if she remembered right. And with vacant possession. For the space was completely empty, she confirmed, as she veered first in one direction, then another. And yet... From the back wall, she imagined she heard a soft scuffling sound.

Maggie started in fright.

Hello, she called. And, again, *Anybody there?*

She was met with silence.

Rats, she decided. The arches were near enough to the river.

For a few moments, she stood, trying to still her pounding heart. Then, cautiously, shuffled forward until she encountered the partition wall of what might have been an office.

She opened the door, stuck her head inside. The smell that assailed her nostrils told her that it was a toilet, long disused. Smartly, she pulled the door to.

She was about to call it a day when the scuffling came again, closer this time.

She shuddered. The thought of rats running over her feet was more than she could bear.

She sensed a movement close by.

Picked up the distinctive smell of weed overlaid with the rank odour of sweat.

Fight or flight? Multiple scenarios raced through her head.

But before Maggie could make a move, strong hands threw her against the wall.

Winded, she made out the thud of running footsteps.

Glimpsed a brief flash of daylight as the door opened and clanged shut.

Heard the scrape of a bolt being slid into place.

A Positive ID

'Listen up,' Chisolm addressed his squad. 'I've an update from West Bell Street.'

Heads snapped to attention.

'They have a positive ID.'

'And?' Douglas couldn't help himself.

'Confirmed by dental records as Samantha Clark.' Tayside had a phone-in from Livingston: a brother, still, in Craigshill, who was able to provide details.'

'So they'll be able to to back up their findings with familial DNA?' Douglas pressed.

'They will, indeed.' Chisolm had rung Gerry Maguire with news of the friendship bracelets, and he'd passed the intel on. But though Sam Clark had been wearing hers when she was killed, so savage was the attack it was soaked in her blood, and was currently in the hands of forensics.

'Have they established a motive, boss?' Brian asked.

'Money, from what I gather.'

'Connected to the gambling?'

'Correct: laundering the proceeds of crime through FOBTs.'

In the room there were nods of understanding. Fixed Odds Betting Machines were a favoured method for disposing of illegally obtained cash.

He turned to Brian. 'Have you turned up any evidence Sam was active in that regard on our patch?'

'No, DI. Sorry. We've checked out the local casinos and called on every bookmaker in the city centre, but if anyone knows anything they're not saying.'

Duffy's lip curled. 'That surprise you?'

Brian didn't take him up on this. In his view, it was a good thing that bookies would be squeezed by the drastic reduction in the minimum gaming machine spin. He'd seen the misery that had already been caused. But you couldn't blame shop managers – already under pressure to meet targets in the face of increased competition from their high street neighbours and online – if they weren't rushing to admit to turning a blind eye to money-laundering.

'And this is linked to the Albanians?' he asked Chisolm.

'Seems so.'

'Do you think they intended to kill Sam?' Susan queried.

Chisolm cracked the knuckles of one hand. 'Who knows?' May have been a punishment beating gone wrong.' He cracked the other.

'Where does Aberdeen come in?' Duffy again.

'According to Tayside, Sam got her face too well-known, which in turn drew unwelcome attention to her behaviour.'

'So,' Duffy scowled, 'they shipped her up to us.'

'Precisely.'

Duffy muttered, 'Effing great!'

'So that's how Sam pitched up in those Ferryhill flats,' Susan observed, 'despite having no known source of income?'

'Did you get anything there?' Chisolm queried.

'Not a lot,' Susan hung her head. 'Half the CCTV cameras in the vicinity were out of action, and whoever lives in those flats they weren't in a hurry to open their doors.'

'If we were to put that block under surveillance,' Douglas smirked, enjoying Susan's discomfiture, 'we'd be able to film the punters going in and out.'

'How does that help?' Susan shot back. 'Except maybe prove it's being used as a brothel. If, as Tayside suspects, the tenants are trafficked, they're unlikely to be floating in and out at will.'

'Quite possibly,' Chisolm commented. 'West Bell Street have informed the powers-that-be they're planning a raid, but when that will be I've no idea.' He saw his window of opportunity to wrap up Tayside's case narrow by the minute. 'And whether that will be joint with us is a moot point. Still arguing the politics.'

'Christ,' Duffy mumbled. 'You can't effing move these days.'

'Yes, well…' Chisolm wasn't going to rise to that one. 'But back to Debbie Milne. Now it has been confirmed Tayside's cadaver isn't her…'

Douglas came back in. 'Could Sam have involved Debbie in some way?'

Chisolm shrugged. 'Who knows?'

'I'll lay a tenner on she did,' Duffy threw in. 'Sound of things, the pair of them were thick as thieves.'

'Haha,' Douglas aped amusement. 'That's a tenner down the drain.'

'Don't mock,' Duffy came back. 'You mark my words, thon Debbie's ended up dead somewhere, just like her pal Sam.'

A Matter of Time

Maggie sat against the wall, arms hugging her knees, which were drawn up to her chin. She'd shouted for help until she was hoarse. Banged and kicked fruitlessly against the door.

The druggie, if that's what he was, had long gone.

Whatever chinks of light could have penetrated the ancient structure had long dissipated. And whereas, outside, it was early summer, inside – with its bare brick walls and concrete floor – it was damp and bitterly cold.

She let her head drop onto her chest.

For a few moments she let it rest, savouring the familiar scent of her clothing, the residual warmth of her breasts.

Foolish, foolish woman! she chided herself. What on earth had made her go taking another run at something, as she had with the agency's last two major cases? After all she'd been through in the run-up to George's death – and since – hadn't she learned a thing?

Wilma will kill me, was her next thought. That's if her captor didn't get there first. Leaving her phone in the car was a cardinal sin for a private investigator, one Maggie hadn't repeated since an early surveillance exercise when Wilma had torn a strip off her. And hadn't they had the conversation at all too frequent intervals: that they were supposed to be partners in their fledgling enterprise, consult one another? Maggie's flaunting of this cardinal rule had nearly cost her, not just a partner but a true friend.

A tear slid down one cheek.

With her cuff, she brushed it away.

Think! she urged herself.

Without her phone or the benefit of a luminous dial on her watch, she had no idea of the time. Still, Wilma would get her text message when she finished at the hospital and come looking for her. There again, she might not check her messages until she got home.

Or – perish the thought – until the morning.

No, Maggie told herself, *that won't happen*. Even if it did, she reasoned, Colin would raise the alarm. Or would he? These past few nights she and Wilma had kept late hours, and Colin, when – eventually – he went to bed, slept like the dead.

Her car would lead them to her. Or would it? It was, by now, second nature to park discreetly out of sight. Once again, Maggie rued her idiocy in leaving her phone on display. For all she knew, her Volvo, old as it was, could have been broken into by now.

If only she'd taken Wilma's advice and invested in a rape alarm instead of castigating her partner for using questionable gizmos, Maggie could have been out of there. Home, safely tucked up in a warm bed. The very thought brought a tear to her eye.

It's only a matter of time, she consoled herself. She'd come upon a jumble of bedding and some cardboard in the far corner where the dosser must have made his bed. And there was a toilet, she'd established. Worst case, she'd have to stay there till morning. She'd make a racket when the adjacent units opened for business.

What if they don't hear me? a small voice niggled. *I could die here. Never see my children again.*

Of course, they'd hear her. She quelled her imaginings. In the meantime, she'd occupy herself by finding something to slip that bolt with.

She rooted in the depths of her bag, hoping to come upon a pair of scissors, a makeup brush, an emery board, anything she could insert into the door frame and try to work the bolt loose. Instead, her fingers found only a lipstick, a few coins and a couple of elderly peppermints.

She dusted one off, popped it in her mouth. The other she carefully slipped into her purse. She'd save that, just in case.

In the near distance, she could hear the steady hum of traffic from Riverside Drive. Not that it told her anything. One of the main arterial routes from the city centre, it was busy whatever the time of day. Still, she drew small comfort from the thought of fellow humans, said a quiet prayer she'd be rescued soon. And if not, that there wouldn't be rats.

Her prayer must have been answered, because the traffic noise was drowned by the wail of a police siren.

Thank you, God! Maggie summoned a weak smile. She knew Wilma would come up trumps. Except… The siren grew louder, and louder still, then receded into the distance. …how would Wilma explain the continued involvement of Harcus & Laird in Debbie Milne's disappearance? No. Whatever else Wilma was doing, it wasn't likely to include the police.

Maggie must have dozed off, because a rumble of thunder jolted her violently upright.

Steadily, the noise increased in volume until she feared the roof above her head was about to cave in.

At her back, the wall vibrated.

Fearful, she lurched forwards, ending up on all fours.

For what seemed like five minutes she stayed there, paralysed with fright. Then, just as it had begun, the hellish noise receded and was gone.

Heart thudding in her chest, Maggie sat back on her heels. Her knees were aching from the hard floor, her palms studded with grit.

Her rational self said the infernal noise emanated from a passenger train. The arches were, after all, located underneath the south-running line of an operational railway.

Her emotions told her to scream at the top of her voice, tear her hair, weep until the tears ran dry.

Instead, she crawled back to her position by the wall.

A Sour Taste

'Moving on. Meston domestic.'

From around the table there were groans. After the Fatboy drugs case, when the police investigation had been compromised by PI duo Harcus & Laird and evidence shredded by Glasgow criminal lawyer Louis Valentine, they'd all had a bellyful of Seaton.

'Who's on it?'

Duffy piped up. 'Me. sir.'

'Do we have a case, Sergeant?'

Bob Duffy looked shamefaced. 'No, sir?'

'Why not? According to this report,' Chisolm looked down at the file in front of him. 'The wife has presented at ARI with multiple injuries.' He looked up.

'That's correct, sir.'

'And on multiple occasions.'

'Right again.'

'Injuries which were deemed by medical specialists to be non-accidental.'

Duffy tugged at his collar. 'Sir.'

'Culminating in said wife,' Chisolm riffled through the file. 'What's her name again?'

'Jean, sir.'

'Culminating in Jean Meston taking up residency in a women's refuge. Am I right, Duffy?'

The sergeant wiped the sweat from his brow. 'You are, sir.'

'So,' Chisolm thundered, 'what's the fucking problem?'

'Woman withdrew charges.'

'Christ,' Chisolm sighed. 'Where have I heard that before?'

'So we don't have anything to lay on Meston?' Brian asked. After son Willie's show of non-co-operation throughout the drugs trial, he'd have given a lot to see Mike Meston back inside.

'Not a thing,' Duffy grimaced. 'Evil wee fucker that he is.'

'So he's sitting pretty with all home comforts,' Susan Strachan observed. 'While she, poor soul, is nursing her injuries in some dump with a bunch of other unfortunates.'

Duffy rolled his eyes. 'It's always the way.'

'Not any more,' Douglas Dunn piped up.

'What d'you mean?' Duffy took him on.

'Jean Meston signed herself out this morning. With a bit of luck,' Douglas smirked, 'she'll be back by now in her husband's tender care.'

Duffy made fists of his hands. 'You're lying, you wee shite. I saw her there not last night, and she was well dug in.'

'Well, she's not there now,' Douglas retorted. 'Got that from downstairs. If you don't believe me…' He looked Duffy in the eye, '…go and ask them.'

'Trust me,' Duffy stared him out. 'I will.'

'Have you two have quite finished?' Chisolm snapped.

'Sir.' Duffy turned. 'Sorry, sir.'

Douglas studied his nails.

A Snap Decision

Wilma gunned the Fiesta along Riverside Drive.

She'd checked her phone messages the minute she came off duty. Maggie's text – *Debbie sighted in railway arches. Following up.* – had near given her a heart attack. Bad enough that her partner was wandering down the riverside late at night, but that she was doing it alone put the frighteners on Wilma.

They'd had their ups and downs since the day their destinies had collided, and Wilma had been gutted that day she'd got the new rug when Maggie accused her of being manipulative. Her disappointment had been tinged with excitement: that Tayside's body had been discovered by Kirsty's boyfriend. Still and all, Wilma had been hurt. What was the word Maggie had used? Wilma's head was that fuddled she couldn't mind. And she'd probably said it out of exhaustion. Wilma had noticed that eye giving her grief again

Then, *steamroller,* it came to mind. The minute Maggie was gone, she'd dug out her dictionary from the bottom of the wardrobe and looked it up:

A steam-powered vehicle with heavy rollers used for compressing road surfaces during road making.

Wilma snorted. She knew that.

An overpowering force or person that overcomes all opposition.

She shed a wee tear over that. She'd a big personality, everyone said so, but that was different.

That was then, this is now, Wilma told herself. For all the hurtful words that had been hurled in both directions, she'd give her life for Maggie Laird.

If the tip-off was kosher, they could be within sight of tying up the case. But Maggie could be in danger, so time was of the essence.

She'd rung Maggie's mobile repeatedly, but it had gone to voicemail. Wilma's mind tumbled with irrational thoughts. Then, *Get a grip!* She was dog-tired from a day working on agency business followed by her hospital late shift, and she wouldn't be much use to Maggie if she arrived in a state.

But where to begin? The railway arches ran all the way from the Palmerston Place Viaduct to the Queen Elizabeth Bridge.

Wilma shot through the Great Southern Road roundabout.

She passed the Duthie Park children's playground, where in happier times she'd pushed Wayne and Kevin on the swings.

At the bridge onto Palmerston Road she veered left.

As she sped down South College Street, a horrible thought occurred. There were two sets of railway arches: the South College Street arches were set back, amongst office accommodation, from the river, whereas the Palmerston Road arches were closer to the city centre. Maggie's text hadn't given any indication of which.

For some moments Wilma swithered. Chances were a dosser would want to be near the action, be it for shoplifting, begging or foraging for food.

She made a snap decision.

She'd start at Palmerston Road. Work her way back.

All Too Much

Maggie sat up in bed, her petite frame in its checked flannelette pyjamas swaddled by a double duvet. On the bedside table, a half-drunk mug of hot chocolate.

Brian had maintained a careful distance once he'd delivered her home.

'Get out of those clothes,' he'd insisted. *'I'll run you a hot shower.'*

With what dignity she could muster, Maggie had acquiesced. Where he'd found the pyjamas she couldn't begin to guess. Nice as Brian was, the idea of him riffling through her underwear drawer filled her with horror.

Perhaps they belonged to Kirsty, she hazarded a guess. Whatever, she'd felt like a five-year-old as she pulled them on. Felt even worse when he settled her in bed, tucked the duvet around her, presented her with a clumsily assembled sandwich and the aforesaid hot chocolate and commanded her to drink up.

'Now,' he demanded from his perch on the ottoman at the foot of the bed, 'will you tell me how you came to be locked in a railway arch at four in the morning?'

She ducked her chin. 'It's a long story,' she replied, her voice muffled by the bedcover.

Brian threw her a quizzical look. 'I've got plenty time.'

There was a long silence, then, 'I was looking for something.' Her head peeked from a nest of down.

'Like?'

Maggie's mind worked overtime. When Brian had rescued her from the empty unit, she'd been so overcome with gratitude she hadn't thought to quiz him on just how he'd got there. And all Brian had divulged was that Wilma, having failed to locate Maggie, had first roused Colin, then him.

'A dog.'

Brian raised an eyebrow. 'That right?'

'Yes. A puppy, actually. It went missing, and…' She broke off. Experience had taught her that, when you were telling lies, the fewer embellishments the better.

'Come off it, Maggie. You don't seriously expect me to believe that a) you're that desperate for business or b) that you'd go puppy-hunting in the middle of the night.'

'Well…' Frantically, Maggie tried to conjure up a more plausible excuse. There's no way Wilma would have spilled the beans, and whatever Maggie did she couldn't allow Brian to make a connection between her mishap and Debbie Milne.

'You were looking for Debbie Milne. That's it, isn't it?'

Maggie felt the colour rise to her face. 'No.' She ducked down again into the duvet.

Brian rose.

He crossed the intervening space.

'Listen to me,' he said in a voice that was filled with concern. 'This is a serious matter. A woman is missing. And I'll be straight with you, Maggie, the case is going nowhere. Debbie Milne could be lying injured somewhere. She could be dead. And all we need is you and your…' He broke off. '…friend, walking all over an active police investigation again. Do you understand?'

Miserable, Maggie could only nod.

'Look,' Brian leaned in. 'I know you and Wilma have been working the women's refuges, and…'

'How?' Incredulity was written all over Maggie's face, and her head was swimming, whether from mendacity or fatigue.

'Do you think I was born yesterday? We're in and out of those places day and daily. And before you ask, uniform keep track of the dossers too, so we know all about your activities on that front.'

'Oh,' she said in a small voice. 'So…'

'…we're perfectly well aware that your agency was approached by Scott Milne. Although what he hoped to gain…'

'You lot weren't doing anything.' Maggie re-asserted herself. 'Poor man probably panicked. And can you blame him: under pressure at work, two kids clamouring for attention? And all your lot have got to say is they'll think about it.'

Brian ignored this outburst. 'What we had hoped...'

'You and your boss DI Chisolm,' she supplied.

Brian ignored this. '...was that you'd have the good sense to back off once you were aware the case had been escalated to CID. More so, in the light of past misdemeanours.'

'Spare me the lecture,' Maggie groaned.

'Notwithstanding,' Brian continued, undeterred.

Maggie knew what was coming. He'd warn her off. Secure her commitment to no further involvement, a commitment she couldn't keep.

She wanted to weep. She was weak with hunger, her body screaming for sleep. She'd had a fright, she was willing to admit, now, in the safety of her own home. She'd never been more pleased to see Brian Burnett than when she heard that bolt scrape back, saw a torch shine in her face.

Tears welled in her eyes, spilled over and coursed down her cheeks.

Brian draped an arm over her shoulders. 'There,' he tucked the duvet snug around her. 'There.'

'I'm so sorry,' she sniffed.

'It's okay.' He dropped a kiss on the crown of her head.

Faint with exhaustion, she wiped her wet face with the back of her hand, leaned back into the pillows and closed her eyes. It was all too much: the drop-outs, the battered women. She should never have let Wilma talk her into taking on the Milne case. And that on top of her problems at school, her dad's illness, her children's relationships.

Then there was Brian, who that very night had demonstrated all the qualities she'd so admired in George: loyalty, steadfastness, simple decency. There was no side to Brian. And he cared deeply for her, that was undeniable. And yet...

She enjoyed Brian's company, in much the same way she might have enjoyed colleague Glen Mason's, had he demonstrated more patience. They'd laughed about their "date" since, had settled into an easy friendship, so much so Maggie wondered, sometimes, if things might not have developed had she not been so narrow-minded. But Glen was in a new relationship, and before long he'd likely be in a new job, so Maggie had burned her boats where he was concerned. As for Brian, his kiss hadn't stirred her, not in the same way Chisolm's closeness sent tremors through her entire body.

She was re-living their embrace as she fell into a deep and lasting sleep.

No More Excuses

'What the fuck were you thinking,' Wilma yelled as she stormed through the back door.

Maggie turned from the sink. 'Don't you start.' She'd not long risen after a fitful few hours' sleep.

'I mean,' Wilma caught hold of Maggie's arm, 'are you right in the head, woman? Seems to me you've totally lost the plot.'

'Look...' Maggie said, shaking her off. '...I've been up half the night, Colin's in the huff, and I've already been torn off a strip by Brian Burnett.'

'You can forget about Brian. He's a big sap.'

'Actually,' Maggie tossed her head. 'He was rather sweet.'

'Sweet now, is it?' Wilma huffed. 'Would that be before or after he gave you a bollocking?'

'After, if you must know. He made me a hot-water-bottle and...'

Wilma rolled her eyes. 'Too much information.'

'Anyhow,' Maggie countered. 'It was you rang Brian in the first place.'

'What was I supposed to do? Dial 999?'

'No, but...'

'I only phoned your fancy man after I'd run up and down Palmerston Road like a mad thing and got your son out his bed.'

Fancy man! Maggie bristled, but bit her lip.

'You go off on your own,' Wilma ran on. 'You don't tell anyone where you're going. You...'

'I did tell you,' Maggie interrupted.

'Aye,' she spat. 'Railway arches. Take your fucking pick.'

'There's no need to swear.'

'I wouldn't be fucking swearing if you hadn't fucking driven me to it.'

Maggie put her hands over her ears. 'I don't want to hear any more.'

'You'll hear me out,' Wilma pulled them away, 'if it's the last thing you do.'

Maggie groaned. 'Will you give me a break?'

'It's more than a break you're needing. Do you not see…?'

'Yes, yes.' Maggie shrugged. 'I get it.'

Wilma ignored her. 'Since we started out, you've been near savaged by dogs, branded by a sicko, and now…' She cast her eyes to the ceiling. '…if I'm hearing right, attacked by some druggie scrote.'

'I wasn't "attacked", exactly.'

'And all because you think, Maggie Laird, you can take on the world single-handed.'

Maggie rounded on her. 'I made a judgement call. I got it wrong.'

'See,' Wilma's voice rose, 'you bloody won't be told. If you'd only listen to me.'

'I did damn-well listen,' Maggie shot back. She'd had a bellyful of having her misdemeanours shoved down her throat. And she was the senior partner in the business, after all.

Wilma was hard-working, she allowed, well-meaning, had Maggie's best interests at heart. But she also had a dominant personality, as both Val and Maggie's mum had insinuated. If Maggie didn't take positive action now, Wilma would be running the show, if show there was after the year end. And that could be the end of Maggie's quest for justice.

She reasserted her authority. 'If Mika's tip-off had been sound and I'd found Debbie Milne in that railway unit, you'd have been all over me.'

'Granted.' Wilma allowed, grim-faced.

'One thing is abundantly clear,' Maggie continued.

'What's that?' Wilma feigned ignorance. She knew what was coming.

'We're on a hiding to nothing with this Milne case.'

'Oh,' Wilma played for time, 'I don't know.'

'Well, I do. We've wasted way too much time on it – at the expense of other clients I'll remind you – and...'

'...we'll get paid, won't we?' Wilma butted in.

Maggie's lips formed a thin line. 'That's to be seen.'

Wilma was on the cusp of arguing back when she remembered: a case early on in their PI partnership where the client had occasioned the duo to jump through hoops and then reneged on the bill. She swallowed her tongue.

'Admit it,' Maggie pressed. 'We're chasing our tails. This latest...' She scrabbled for a suitably anodyne word. '...incident is a case in point: One of us goes haring off on the flimsiest lead. A solid day later, we're no further forward.'

One of us? Wilma could contain herself no longer. 'It was you got your knickers in a twist.'

'I did not "get my knickers in a twist" as you so vulgarly put it.'

'Yes, you bloody did. You could as easy have waited until I was off shift. Wouldn't have made a whit of difference. But instead you have to go charging off on your own,' she huffed. 'Bloody classic!'

'There's no need to be sarcastic.'

'It's the God's honest truth. You're your own worst enemy, Maggie Laird. You've good intentions, but you keep on doing the fucking wrong things.'

'That just goes to prove my point: I'm not cut out for this job. I told you that from day one.'

A daft idea, she'd said, when Wilma first mooted the notion of taking on George's business. And she'd been right.

Wilma ignored her. 'You mebbe do things for the right reasons, but I'm sick and tired of having to cover your back.'

'Cover my back?' Maggie spluttered. 'You've got a nerve. Who was it didn't want to take on a missing person investigation in the first place?'

Grudgingly. 'You.'

'And who was it talked me into it?'

'Me. Are you happy now?' Wilma sniped. 'You know what?

You're damn right. You're not cut out for this job, Maggie Laird. You should have been a bloody schoolteacher, right enough. Suit you right down to the ground.'

'I wish!' Maggie retorted with feeling. 'Then I wouldn't have to put up with people like you.'

'And I could crack on with my life, instead of aye having to look over my shoulder.'

'You reckon?' Maggie challenged.

'Too right.' Wilma's mouth twitched, then widened into a grin. 'Fancy a drink?'

Maggie groaned. 'At this time of day? I don't think so.' Still, she couldn't help but smile.

* * *

'What are we going to do now?' Maggie asked. They were sitting side by side on her back step, soaking up the morning sunshine, two steaming mugs of black coffee in their hands.

'Press on.' Wilma said, decisively.

'But, Brian, won't he…?' She noted that the boundary hedge, which her dad had painstakingly patched up, was again exhibiting a gaping hole.

'…spill the beans? No way. Think about it.' Wilma took a slurp of her coffee. 'Breaking and entering? Assault? False imprisonment? Offences that your man has – so far as we know – failed to report. And that's just the druggie. We haven't even started on you.' She grinned. 'You reckon Brian's going to broadcast his wee adventure? I don't think so. If he'd followed procedure he'd have called it in, let them send a response unit out.'

'I see what you mean.' Maggie nodded her understanding. 'All the same.'

'We stick to our game plan.'

'But, Wilma, we've covered all the refuges, talked to umpteen dossers. And our only promising lead – which presumably came from Mika's friend – has bombed.' She raised her mug to her lips, took a tentative sip. 'Let's face it, we've run out of options.'

'Not necessarily. Didn't you tell me there was more than one sleeping bag in that warehouse unit?'

'Yes.' Maggie set the mug down. 'But…'

'So Debbie Milne could have been there at some point.'

'Accepted. But so could someone else. We know homeless people often pair up for safety.'

'We carry on with the homeless angle.' Wilma's voice was firm.

'And if that doesn't give us anything?'

'There's always Brian.' She threw a sideways look.

Maggie stiffened. 'Don't even go there.' Though in her heart she knew Brian's feelings had mellowed. 'After all he's done – running to my rescue, picking up the car, seeing I was okay – I'm not going to pester him for information.'

'Your DI,' Wilma persisted. 'Is he worth a punt?'

'Chisolm? Not in a million years.'

'You could go take a turn round the Queen Street local drinking dens, see what gems you could pick up. News is Blackfriars and The Illicit Still have taken over from The Athenaeum.'

'Don't be ridiculous,' Maggie said in a shocked voice.

Wilma shrugged. 'Just saying.'

'Those off-duty coppers,' Maggie continued, 'they'd spot me in a flash. And, anyhow, I doubt the police are much further forward than we are.'

'Then we go back to basics: re-examine the family. A large proportion of crimes are committed by the victim's nearest and dearest, and that's a fact,' Wilma said, smacking her lips. We get back to Scott Milne, ask if he'll let us check out the house, see what we can find, and…'

'Fat chance,' Maggie cut her short. 'Scott's under enough pressure as it is. Plus, last time we met, I got the impression he'd lost confidence in us.'

'He hasn't taken us off the case,' Wilma shot back.

'No, but…'

'Well, then.' Sly look. 'We're laughing.'

Maggie drew a deep breath. True to form, Wilma was trying to badger her into submission. 'I still don't see…' she protested.

Noisily, Wilma drained her mug. 'I'll set up a meeting with Scott Milne, if you're not keen. You can go see Debbie's mum.'

'That's not going to happen. Brian told me…'

'First it was Glen. Now it's Brian. Next thing you'll be having a roll in the sack with Allan Chisolm.'

Maggie bristled. 'Don't be so crude.'

'And don't you be so buttoned-up,' Wilma retorted. 'I was only having a bit of fun.'

'Sorry.' Maggie pressed her palms together in mock supplication. Perhaps she'd come on too strong.

She changed the subject. 'I don't know how you cope. Your place is always so tidy. She eyed her back garden. Her dad had put in a power of work, keeping the grass in check and clearing the borders of weeds, but still it looked forlorn.

'I don't have two kids under my roof for a start.' Wilma made a mental note to check what those loons of hers were up to.

'Yes, but still.'

'I don't mind the housework. Now I've got a proper home, I like to keep it nice.'

'I suppose,' Maggie said, a wistful expression on her face. She no longer felt like the homemaker she'd once been. Her own home had been fractured: her children no longer there full-time, her husband gone forever.

'I juggle things in the air, that's all,' Wilma grinned.

'Like three jobs and a husband,' Maggie shot back.

'Oh,' Wilma replied. 'A hospital shift and a few hours in a bar? Compared with what I've been used to, that's a walk in the park.'

'Really?' Maggie knew Wilma had left school at sixteen, life since then seemingly one long struggle to 'better herself', as she put it. Not that Maggie's journey had been much different: a strong work ethic instilled early by God-fearing parents. But she'd had life much easier, largely thanks to a safe marriage and a complete lack of grit. All that had been turned on its head: not just that she was a widow, now, but she'd had to trawl her inner resources, drain the barrel dry, just to keep a roof over their heads, she and her children.

Wilma's voice broke her train of thought.

'Aye, to begin with I worked at the fish. Wet, that was. In a laundry. Hot. At the petrol pumps. Smelly. Been a checkout operator and all. Nightmare!'

'Oh, Wilma,' Maggie started to laugh. 'Is there anything you can't do?'

'Aye. String a fancy sentence together.' She was still, secretly, working away at the dictionary. But the book was that big, and there were that many words. Wilma sighed. You could spend your life and still not get through it. She speculated whether there was a shorter version on the net.

'To get back to Debbie Milne,' she collected her thoughts.

'Forget Debbie Milne,' Maggie said, firmly. 'We've been channelling our combined energies into this one case to the detriment of other work, work that's our bread and butter. Now we've reached the end of the line.'

'But.' Wilma protested, 'think of the leg-up it will give the agency when we solve it.'

'If we solve it,' Maggie's voice rose. 'And you have to admit, it doesn't look promising. We were going to get ahead of the police investigation, if I remember right.' Said with more than a hint of sarcasm. 'Instead, all we've done is scrape the bottom of the barrel, come up with nothing.'

Wilma saw her golden future disappearing down the sink. 'The way I see it...' Her mind worked overtime. 'Who knows Debbie best in the whole world?'

'Her mum, I suppose. But as I've told you before, Brian said he got damn all there.'

'Bugger bloody Brian,' Wilma shrieked. 'You get in there. Use your head. You're a professional private investigator, Maggie Laird, whether you like it or not. I'll bet you a pound to a penny you winkle stuff out that woman Brian never got near.'

Maggie was tempted to rise to the challenge, but still she resisted. 'That will take time. We've put so many hours in already and we're no further forward. It would be hard not to conclude we're out of our depth.'

'Total garbage,' Wilma insisted. 'We have a clear plan, which we're following.'

'With finite resources. The police…'

'Yeah, yeah. Are better resourced, but they have a scatter-gun approach. You wait and see. As one door closes, another will open. Haven't we seen that time and again?'

'Yes, but…'

'You're not going to see two bairns left without a mother?'

That old chestnut! Maggie thought, sourly. She was tired of being manipulated by Wilma. Still, her heartstrings tugged. What would she feel in the same situation? Her mind jumped back to the railway arches, that moment she thought she might never see her kids again.

'No,' she responded. 'But…' She'd call Wilma's bluff, put a finite timetable on closing the Milne case.

'No more excuses.' Seizing the moment, Wilma jumped in. 'As I said, we stick to our plan.'

A Study Plan

'Colin?' Maggie rapped on his bedroom door.

There was no answer.

'Colin?' She knocked again, more loudly this time.

This was met by complete silence.

Her heart hammered in her chest. After the previous episode, where Colin had emerged, dishevelled, with that young woman – Ellie – in his wake, Maggie had fretted constantly. Not that she didn't welcome the development. It was inevitable that Colin would find a girlfriend one day. Nor had she anything against Ellie. The girl was bright and well-mannered, quite unlike that lout, Shaz, who'd turned up again like a bad penny.

No, if anything Maggie was worried the relationship would develop into something serious, distract Colin from his school-work. Or worse. Kirsty's pregnancy scare had been a wake-up call, coming as it did on the heels of her self-harming. And Colin was so laid-back. It would be catastrophic if he were to get careless, land some girl in trouble.

Throwing caution to the winds, she barged in.

Colin and Ellie were sitting at his computer, their backs to the door.

As Maggie entered the room, she could see that under the small desk their knees were jammed together. It was only when she came up close she noticed the buds in their ears, the trailing headphone wires.

She flapped her hands to attract attention.

Colin removed his earphones.

'Hi, Mum,' he said, affably.

'What are you doing,' Maggie demanded.

He pointed to the monitor. 'English essay.'

Maggie squinted at the computer screen. Sure enough, she could see references to Muriel Spark.

'Oh.' Her heartbeat slowed.

'Ellie's helping me,' Colin added.

'Yes.' The girl turned. 'We're going to work out a study plan, support one another.'

'You're doing a sixth year, Ellie?' Maggie asked, surprised.

'Her dad says students do better at uni if they stay on at school,' Colin butted in. 'Either that or do a gap year.'

'He teaches at Aberdeen University,' Ellie added by way of explanation.

'Oh,' Maggie said. 'Right.' She didn't know whether to laugh or cry. On the one hand, Ellie might be just what was needed to make Colin buckle down. On the other, it now looked as if another year at Robert Gordon's – and a corresponding set of fees – was an inevitability.

Her mind seethed with conflicting thoughts: should she give up her Seaton job, take on extra corporate work? But her part-time job provided a steady, albeit, tiny income, whereas the agency's cash flow was erratic.

Should she downsize to a flat? The bungalow needed money spent, where something more modern would be more easily maintained. Except she'd need to smarten the place up before she could present it for sale. And that would take money, money she didn't have.

Might Colin apply for a bursary? There were bound to be some available. Only the competition would be stiff. She filed that away for future investigation.

With a jolt, Maggie brought herself back to reality.

'Have you had something to eat?' she asked.

'Yes,' Colin replied. 'We made ourselves a sandwich when we came in.'

'I'll leave you to it, then.'

She backed onto the landing and closed the door.

Foxy

It was Wayne gave her the idea. Wilma had been feeling bad since her row with Maggie. After all, as Maggie said after she'd slept off her ordeal, if the lead had been sound and she'd found Debbie Milne, it would have been a different story.

Wilma had lain awake wondering how to make it up to Maggie. Then she had a beezer idea. Her younger son had a birthday that week. She was long past celebrating her offspring's anniversaries, nor had she ever baked a cake. All things being equal she'd have emailed a voucher: Amazon or some such. This time she decided to do something more creative.

Since his discharge from hospital, Bobby Brannigan had dropped below the radar, and despite Maggie's overtures the police response had been at best lukewarm.

Old habits die hard. Wilma was convinced Brannigan was still somewhere in Torry: lying low, or being shielded by somebody. It was all he knew. The one thing Wilma could do for Maggie would be to flush out Bobby Brannigan. Idle fuckers that they were, Wilma's loons had been invaluable in extracting Bobby's confession. And they could be useful again.

Wilma decided she'd take both her boys on an outing and further Maggie's cause while she was at it. Now Jimmy Craigmyle had given a statement, if she could get Brannigan down the nick to back up what she'd obtained on tape, it would be job done. And with Maggie's quest for justice out the way, it would be plain sailing for the agency.

Wilma felt bad about the railway arch incident, reckoned she'd maybe come on a bit strong. It wasn't Maggie's fault, after all, that Wilma's mobile had been switched off. And if Maggie had gone against agency policy and followed up Mika's lead on her own, wasn't it because she was trying to do her best for everybody, Wilma included? Yes, she reminded herself, Maggie Laird was straight as a die, no side to her.

Wilma had stepped in, supported the poor woman in her hour of need. They'd come a long road since. And if the agency thrived, the world was their oyster. Wilma could already envisage giving up her crap jobs. Upgrading her car: something sporty. Buying new clothes. But their falling out over the Struthers affair had brought Wilma up short. And now she'd made things worse by pressing Maggie to persevere with the missing person case. She'd want to watch herself, take care not to overstep the mark. Her and Maggie Laird might be partners, but by rights it should be Maggie who'd be calling the shots.

Wayne and Kevin had jumped at the chance of a couple of hours at Codonas. Neither of them was in work, and their days were spent playing computer games and watching sport on telly. Wilma had looked on as they attacked the Vertigo Aerial Assault Course, screamed through the Dead Man's Drop Tower and got drenched on the White Water Log Flume, ending up high above her head on the Grampian Eye Big Wheel. She'd joined them on the Disco Waltzers, just to show willing. Not that she was feart, but the role of bystander gave her time to think her scheme out and, besides, the rides cost an arm and a leg.

Now, flanked by two chunky male figures, Wilma sat in the Sunset diner. As part of the package she'd offered her boys an all-you-can-eat meal.

'Thanks, ma,' Wayne mumbled through a mouthful of Margherita pizza.

'Aye.' Kevin wolfed another slice of his Americana. 'Cheers!'

'Nae bother,' Wilma scooped a gloopy gobbet of Mac 'n' Jack onto her fork. 'You wouldn't like to do a wee something for me?'

The boys exchanged suspicious glances. They should have known their adventure would come with strings attached.

'What sort of "wee something"? Kevin, as the elder of the two, took it upon himself to raise the challenge.

'You know how you pair watch sport?' Seamlessly, she dodged the question. *Do fuck all else*, was what she was thinking.

'Aye.'

'Ever seen a foxhunt?' she asked, slyly.

'Naw.'

'I seen one on the TV,' Wayne offered, nicking the last dough ball and stuffing it whole into his mouth.

'You're lying,' Kevin gave him a sharp nudge.

Theatrically, he reeled back. 'Fuck off.'

'Leave him alone,' Wilma intervened. 'Can you no get along, the two of you, just this once?'

'Okay.' With a sulky face, Wayne dug his spoon into the dessert. A communal bowl of goo, its doughnut base was topped with balls of vanilla, chocolate and strawberry ice-cream, the whole dish adorned with lavish helpings of whippy cream and sprinkles.

'Hang on,' Kevin added his own spoon to the mix, the pair pretend-fencing, sending sprinkles flying everywhere.

'Chrissake,' Wilma grumbled, 'Can I no take you any place?'

They grinned at one another, conspirators again.

'About them foxes,' Wilma picked up where she left off.

The boys stopped, laden spoons halfway to their mouths.

'You ken how they send the dogs after them?'

They nodded.

'Chase them into their dens?' She poked one fat finger into a swirl of cream, licked it with relish. 'Flush them out.' She dug her spoon into the bowl, speared a whole doughnut, lifted it high.

'Where you goin wi this?' Kevin puzzled.

'See thon Bobby Brannigan,' Wilma said, her face a blank.

Her sons regarded her with detachment. They didn't respond.

She went in for the kill. 'He look foxy tae you?'

This Isn't Working

Maggie stopped short in the kitchen doorway. She drew a steadying breath. 'This isn't working,' she said.

Her mother turned from her perch on a step-stool. 'What isn't working?' she asked, a puzzled expression on her face.

'You. Dad.' Maggie replied.

A small frown creased her mother's forehead. 'I was only...'

'...re-organising my cupboards.' Tight-lipped, Maggie finished the sentence. 'So I see.'

Her mum pushed the door of the wall unit to, clambered down from the steps. 'You *were* expecting us?' she insisted.

'Yes,' Maggie allowed. 'But when you offered to take the load off me, I didn't think you meant give my home a complete makeover.'

'I thought we were helping,' her mother contended, chin quivering.

'You are.' Maggie softened. 'You have, you and Dad both. Only...' How to explain the overwhelming reek of cleaning products, the items out of place, the total invasion of privacy. '...we keep different hours, have different habits, live differently from you.' She smiled, in an attempt to defuse the situation. 'I hate to admit it, but we've become set in our ways, me and Colin.' She didn't mention Kirsty, whose appearance was a thorn in her grandmother's flesh. No point in making things worse.

'In that case,' her mum huffed, 'you'd better give your dad a shout. We can be out of your hair before you know it.'

'There's no need,' Maggie backtracked.

Her mother drew herself up. 'There's every need.' She looked to be on the verge of tears.

'Come on,' Maggie crossed to her side, draped an arm around her shoulder. 'I didn't mean to upset you. Why don't I get Dad in from the garden and we can sit down and have a cup of tea?'

She stiffened. 'We had a cup of tea not long ago.'

'Well, have another one.' Gently, Maggie squeezed her mum's thin shoulders. 'Nothing like a cuppa,' she said, brightly. 'I'll be mother.'

* * *

The three of them – Maggie, mum and dad – were sitting at the table, three mugs of tea and a plate of home-made shortbread in front of them

'I don't know why we're sitting inside,' Maggie's dad complained, between bites of his biscuit, 'when it's such a lovely day out there. And your garden…'

'…is looking great,' Maggie injected her voice with false enthusiasm. 'Thanks, dad.'

'No bother,' he said, gruffly, never one to use a flowery sentence.

'I just wanted a quick word.' Maggie watched her mum out of the corner of her eye. You could have cut the atmosphere with a knife. 'I've been a bit concerned,' she continued, 'about the way the two of you have been going at it.'

Her dad gulped his tea. Her mother's eyes were downcast, her gaze firmly fixed on the table.

'I mean, you're not exactly spring chickens, either of you.'

This was met by a snort from her dad. 'We're not decrepit either.'

Damn and blast! Maggie should have known better than to insult his manhood.

'Granted. And it's not that I'm ungrateful.'

Her mum's head shot up. 'No?' she shrilled.

'No,' Maggie answered. 'Your efforts up till now have made a huge difference. You've sorted stuff I haven't got around to since George died, wouldn't get around to the way things are, not in a month of Sundays. And I *am* grateful. Truly. More than you'll ever know. But…'

Her mum jumped in. 'There's always a "but".

'You can't keep up this pace, not without damaging your health.

We have to face facts. Dad has a heart condition. One that can be managed, admitted, but only if he's careful. If ever there was a warning, that last turn he took was it.'

Her mum's lower lip jutted. 'That's us finished, then.'

'Look at it from my point of view,' Maggie said. 'Please.'

Curtly, her mother nodded.

'You've done a ton of work. And I thank you for that, both of you.' She looked from one to the other in turn. 'But how do you think I would feel if anything were to happen when you're beavering away on my behalf and I'm out at work? I'd never forgive myself. And that goes for you, Mum, as well as Dad.'

'There's not a thing the matter with *me*.'

'I didn't say there was,' Maggie rushed to placate her. 'All I'm proposing is we compromise.'

'How do you…?' her mum started.

'I don't know if this would suit,' Maggie interjected. 'But say we settled for one afternoon every other week, and that on a care and maintenance basis?'

'I don't understand,' her mother puzzled.

'Well, now the donkey work's done, I thought maybe Dad could keep the grass tidy, do whatever else he takes a notion to. But strictly no digging, no heavy lifting, nothing like that.'

'And where do I fit into all this?' her mother asked, accusingly.

'What would be ideal,' Maggie volunteered, in what she hoped was a diplomatic tone of voice, 'Would be if you could run round with the hoover, and…' She paused to frame the rest of the sentence. '…help me out with keeping the freezer stocked.'

'The freezer?' She was the recipient of a suspicious look.

'Absolutely. To be frank…' She leaned across the table, lowered her voice. '…it's a nightmare keeping Colin fed these days. Since I took on the business, I've had to rely on ready-meals for back-up.'

Her mum rose to the bait. Colin had long been her favourite. 'I thought he was looking a bit peaky. They're not good for you, processed foods. Full of chemicals and I don't know what.'

'I can make the time,' Maggie pressed on, ' to run a duster over the furniture or a cloth round the bathroom. But cooking is so time-consuming. Now, if you were to make a couple of tubs of those meatballs Colin is so fond of, or pizza bases, or chilli, or…'

'…we could do a shop on the way here,' her mother cut in, her voice animated.

'And I could square up with you,' Maggie offered.

'There's no need,' her dad chipped in.

'I could even do some baking,' her mum suggested, 'if there was time.'

'We'd be in heaven.' Maggie picked up a shortbread triangle, bit off a corner. 'Delicious!' she munched. 'This lot won't last long once Colin gets his eye on it.' She assumed a serious expression. 'How about it, then?'

'Just the ticket,' her dad replied. 'To tell the truth, I've been neglecting our own garden this past while. Plus, there's the bowling club. I haven't managed down since I don't know when. And I don't like to admit it, but I tire quickly these days. Doing more of what I fancy would be nice, especially now the Grim Reaper has come chapping at my door.'

Maggie threw up her hands in mock horror. 'I'll pretend I didn't hear that. You've years ahead of you.' She said a silent prayer it would turn out to be true. 'You, too, mum,' she turned to her mother. 'Well, what are you saying to my suggestion?'

Her mum offered the ghost of a smile. 'That will do nicely,' she said.

IX

Poldino's

Poldino's hadn't changed: same *faux* Travertine floor, same stucco archways, same Majolica plates dotting the walls. Must be ten years, Maggie mused, since she and George last celebrated an anniversary there, but the restaurant had lost none of its Italian charm.

Its surroundings were a different matter entirely. Since becoming pedestrianised, Belmont Street and the adjacent Little Belmont Street where the restaurant was located, were a cosmopolitan mix of bars and galleries and boutiques, their cobbled pavements dotted with craft stalls. Not that Maggie had either the time or the money to frequent the precinct, her recent experience being limited to the occasional snatched cup of coffee in Books and Beans.

Brian's call had caught her unawares.

She'd panicked when he'd suggested they meet in town for an early supper.

No, she hadn't eaten. And, *No, she didn't have other plans. Nothing pressing*, she'd hastened to qualify.

Colin was at a friend's, wouldn't be home till near bedtime. Kirsty had gone into town to shop on her way to work. Maggie had planned to do some admin, pig out in front of the TV while she had the house to herself.

A quick bite, Brian had said. *A chance to catch up.*

She'd balked at the thought of heading out again when she hadn't long got home, but the thought of someone setting a plate of food down in front of her that she hadn't had to cook was tempting. And it wasn't as if it was a formal dinner invitation, she reasoned. A couple of hours, a plate of something tasty, and then straight home. She'd still have time to spare before Colin got in. And anyhow, who was to know?

When Brian asked if there was anywhere in particular she'd like to go, she'd named the first place that had come into her head.

Now, the two were seated at a window table looking onto Little Belmont Street.

'How is it?' Brian eyed her plate of pasta.

'Delicious.' Maggie picked up her napkin, dabbed cream sauce from the corners of her mouth. She eyed the half-eaten plateful of prawn and scallop parcels. 'I can't believe I've demolished all that.'

'Won't do you any harm,' Brian teased. 'You could do with a bit of fattening up.'

She returned a rueful smile. It had been a long-standing joke between the three of them: that Brian and Maggie could eat anything they fancied and not gain weight, whereas George – poor George – just had to look at a cream cake and the pounds piled on.

'Seriously,' he reached across the table, covered her hand with his own. 'It's good to see you, Maggie.'

'You, too.' Time was, she'd have found the gesture unwelcome. Now, she wasn't so sure. When George was alive, Brian had been a constant in her life. She'd taken his loyalty and affection for granted. But when he'd turned his attentions to – Megan? Bethan? Maggie couldn't quite remember – she'd experienced a jealous rush that had taken her by surprise.

'We've had our differences,' he began.

That's what Allan Chisolm had said. Maggie felt a flush rise in the nape of her neck, hoped it didn't show in her face. She was physically attracted to Chisolm, no point in denying it, and their meeting at Ardoe House had shown him in a different light. But Brian was a known entity, decent through and through. And Maggie had played on that. He'd proved obliging. Obliging, that is, until she had pushed her luck and earned him a reprimand. Since then, however, Brian had shown strength of purpose: first in terminating his relationship with the young civilian officer, then in his decisive handling of Colin's run-in with the law. But that was before… Maggie's face suffused with heat, as she recalled her rescue from the railway arches. What had possessed her, she wondered, now?

'I can only apologise again.' She left her hand in place. She had no future with Allan Chisolm. Time to live in the moment. 'I didn't…'

Brian's voice broke in. 'I hope we can put all that business behind us.'

Gladly! After her unfortunate experience with cocky supply teacher Glen, Maggie was thankful to be in the company of a close and trusted friend. A known entity. Slowly, she felt the tension drain out of her body.

'I'm glad you rang.'

'Me, too.' Smiling, he gave her hand a squeeze.

Warmed by the food and the wine and the attentions of an attractive man, Maggie returned his smile.

* * *

'What's he doing here?' Kirsty ambushed Maggie at the foot of the stairs.

'If you're referring to Brian,' she jumped to the defensive, 'I asked him in for a coffee.'

Kirsty's voice rose. 'You've been out together? A date?'

Maggie dodged the question. 'I'd hardly call…' She hadn't mentioned her assignation with Glen Mason to the kids.

'Either you have or you haven't.'

'All right, then. I've been out with Brian Burnett. Though whether you'd call a quick plate of pasta "a date" is a moot point. And what business it is of yours…'

Kirsty cut her short. 'You didn't stop to think about Colin and me?'

'You've eaten, haven't you?'

Yes, but…'

'Well, then. And you can leave Colin out of it. Just because you're spoiling for a fight.'

'I am not "spoiling for a fight", just asking a straight question.'

'Which I've answered. Now,' Maggie side-stepped her, 'will you let me get on.'

Kirsty mirrored her action. 'I thought you didn't like Brian.'

'I've never said that.'

'Not in so many words.'

'Look, Kirsty, he's a friend, that's all there is to it.'

'Is that right?' Kirsty's eyes narrowed. 'Looks to me he's got a foot in the door.'

'He does not have...'

'No? Take a look.' She waved a hand in the direction of the open sitting-room door. 'He's even sitting in my dad's chair.'

Maggie drew a calming breath. 'The man has to sit somewhere.'

'He could have sat on the settee.'

'Well, he didn't.' She stalked through to the kitchen. 'So, as you're in the habit of saying, "get over it".

She picked up the kettle, turned on the tap.

'Is Brian staying over?'

Maggie whirled to face her. 'Don't be ridiculous.'

'You reckon? Not so ridiculous from where I'm standing. Do you think I haven't noticed the way he slavers over you? It was the same when Dad was alive.'

'You're seeing things that aren't there. And Colin hasn't...'

'Colin's half-dead. He wouldn't notice if it hit him in the face.'

'Look, Kirsty,' Maggie huffed. 'I don't know what I've done to put you in that frame of mind, but trust me, it's not attractive.'

Kirsty struck a pose. 'You would know.'

'Everything all right?' Brian appeared in the doorway behind her.

'Absolutely fine,' Maggie replied looking daggers at Kirsty.

Little bitch! was what she was thinking.

'I couldn't help but catch some of that.' He threw Kirsty an amused look.

Pursing her mouth, she gave him the evils.

'I really should be going,' he gave Maggie a surreptitious wink. 'I'll leave you girls to it.'

Joined at the Hip

'Joined at the hip.' The woman in the recliner chair smiled at Maggie. 'It was a standing joke.'

'Debbie and Sam?' With great reluctance, she'd acceded to Wilma's demand to give the Milne case one last go by seeing what she could ferret out of Debbie's mum. Now it was all on her.

Audrey Esslemont nodded. 'When they were little. Angus and me, we couldn't have more children. And Debbie, well, kids need playmates, don't they?' She looked to Maggie for confirmation.

'They do.' Maggie signalled agreement, though her own two were often at each other's throats. 'But am I right in thinking they lost touch after Sam's family moved away?'

'I… I'm not sure.' A shadow crossed the older woman's face. 'It was a long time ago.'

Not sure as in don't know or not sure as in can't remember?

'Doesn't matter.' She sneaked a glance at her watch. She'd been pressed to accept a cup of tea, twiddled her fingers in the airless sitting-room for all of ten minutes whilst Audrey Esslemont fussed in the adjacent kitchen.

Hope I never come to this! She said a silent prayer, for the room with its bland furnishings and vertical blinds was featureless save for a chunky enamelled grab rail and a pull cord dangling in one corner, the poky kitchen accessed by a wooden sliding door.

She wondered where the poor woman had lived before. How the loss of her husband and her home in short order had impacted her life. Then she saw the parallels with her own situation. Her parents had already undergone one displacement: from the farm that had been her father's life's work and her mother's source of pride, to a poky retirement bungalow. Her dad's health scare had given Maggie a reality check. What if anything happened to either of them? How would the other cope? And, selfishly, how would she? If the agency were to have a future, running back and forth to Oldmeldrum would be an impossibility. Could Maggie entertain the idea of having one or other parent under her roof? No, her home, modest though it were, was her sanctuary, hers and her children's.

She snapped out of her reverie, as Mrs Esslemont emerged from the kitchen carrying a tray. 'I understand Sam has moved back to Aberdeen.'

'Oh.' This was received with a blank look. 'That's nice.' She deposited the tea things on a side table.

'You haven't seen her, then?'

'No.' The older woman sat down. 'I don't think so. I mean…' A shaky hand strayed to her forehead. '…I wouldn't know her if I saw her, not now.'

Maggie cut to the chase. 'What about Debbie?'

'Debbie?' Her face lit up. 'That's my daughter.'

'Yes,' Maggie said smoothly. 'Have you seen her recently?' She knew Brian Burnett would have followed much the same line of questioning when he'd interviewed Mrs Esslemont, but saw no harm in covering the ground again. If nothing else, it would give the subject time to settle. In Maggie's experience, clients often took a while to loosen up.

'I…' Audrey Esslemont's gaze flitted around the room, settled back on Maggie. '…don't know the answer to that.' Her eyes held mute appeal. 'To be honest with you, since Angus died I've been a bit mixed up.'

Maggie could identify with that. In the days following George's death she'd alternated between blind panic and a state of numb paralysis, her body leaden, her brain in stasis.

Mrs Esslemont poured tea into two floral china cups. 'Help yourself to milk and sugar.' She settled back in her chair. 'I thought moving here would simplify things, help me…' Again, her eyes roved the room. 'But I get confused easily, especially when…' She broke off.

You're put on the spot.

In her role as a private investigator, Maggie had seen it many a time: the ruses folk employed to try and dodge a direct question. But this was different. Maggie wondered how much this woman's distress owed to bereavement or whether – although Audrey Esslemont couldn't have been much over sixty – she was looking at the early stages of dementia.

Whatever. She downed her tea. Brian Burnett had been right. She was going to learn little from Debbie's mum.

She tried one last ploy. Setting her cup and saucer back on the tray, she asked, 'May I use your bathroom?'

'Of course. First door on the left.'

'Thanks.' Maggie rose to her feet, walked through to the hallway, closing the door behind her.

Quietly, she turned the handle of one door after another: bathroom, hall cupboard, bedroom. She memorised the contents of the latter: single bed, bedside table, mirrored wardrobe. On the bed was a toy dog, on the table a reading lamp, a water glass, a hardback book.

Retracing her steps, she flushed the toilet, scanned the contents of the bathroom cabinet: a blister pack of anti-depressants, indigestion tablets, Steradent. Much as she'd expect. No extra toothbrush. No sign that Debbie Milne had been there, ever.

When she returned to the living-room, Audrey Esslemont was sitting as Maggie had left her, an open book on her lap. Her interest piqued. 'Do you mind if I have a look?' she squinted at the photograph album.

'No,' Mrs Esslemont handed it over. 'She said it would help, my health visitor. Looking at it, I mean. And,' she gave a small shrug, 'if nothing else, it passes the time. Living on your own, you get fed up looking at the television, such a lot of rubbish nowadays. And my eyes get sore if I read too much.'

'Yes,' Maggie sympathised, although it had been long enough since she'd enjoyed the luxury of a good book.

Idly, she leafed through the album. The first few pages were filled with tiny black and white snaps of what looked like Mrs Esslemont's antecedents, then followed larger colour photos, dozens of them: Mrs Esslemont, her husband, Debbie as an infant, Debbie growing up. Maggie's spirits sank. She was wasting her time. So much for Wilma's confidence in her.

She stayed her hand as she spotted Debbie together with Sam. 'That's a good photograph,' she flashed the page under the older woman's nose.

The girls must have been six or seven. They were standing in the front doorway of a house, their arms around each other. 'Is that where you used to live?' The words were out of Maggie's mouth before she had time to think.

'Yes,' Mrs Esslemont replied. 'I mean, no. Oh,' distress filled her face. 'I don't know.'

Dammit! Maggie swore under her breath. She should have known better than to hit the woman with a direct question.

'We lived at... Where was it?' Mrs Esslemont fretted. Her fingers fluttered in front of her face. Then, 'Dyce.' She seized on the word. 'We lived in Dyce when Angus worked offshore.'

Maggie pointed at the photo. 'Maybe you lived there before that.'

'No. 'That house is...' She looked away.

'Looks like a farm,' Maggie prompted. Her eyes took in a yard, what looked like a steading roof, a tall hedge.

'Could be.' Hopelessly, Audrey Esslemont shook her head. 'I think my parents might have farmed. There, again...'

Maggie leaned forward. 'In Aberdeen?' she asked gently.

'I don't...'

'If you could tell me where you went to school,' Maggie probed. 'Maybe that would...' She broke off. This could be her very last chance to find Debbie Milne. It wouldn't do to push too hard.

Angrily, Mrs Esslemont snatched the album from Maggie's hands, snapped it shut. 'I told you, I get confused.'

Chalk and Cheese

'Happy?' Brian asked.

'Mmm,' Maggie made suitably agreeable noises, but wondered if she'd ever be truly happy again.

They were sitting together on the settee, his arm draped loosely around her shoulders. Following the debacle with Kirsty, Maggie had rung to apologise and they'd fixed a date for a rerun. This time they'd eaten at Bistro Verde, a seafood restaurant on The Green.

Replete, Maggie relaxed into the soft cushions of her sofa. She'd made coffee for Brian, too sated herself to countenance anything more.

Brian bent in, nuzzled her hair.

For a moment she tensed.

Then, *what the hell!* It was over a year since she'd been in close proximity to a man. Not except for Glen Mason, and she didn't want to dwell on that. There was the night Brian had rescued her from the railway arches, she allowed. But that didn't count, their closeness borne out of comfort, not romance.

Snapshots of Allan Chisolm danced in her head: drenched on her doorstep; grim-faced as he cautioned her over the agency's involvement in an active police investigation; relaxed and smiling as they drank together.

Then that kiss.

In this very room.

Purposefully, she pushed the images away. There's no way anything was going to develop on that front. Hadn't Chisolm said himself it was a lapse of judgement?

Brian dropped a light kiss on her cheek. 'You've gone a bit quiet.' He eyed her, reflectively. 'Everything all right?'

'Just fine,' she smiled, thinking, *I could do worse than Brian: straight, decent, reliable Brian.*

He looked so at home sitting there. Hardly surprising. He'd shared their table many a time when George was alive: grateful for a warming bowl of soup after a long shift, a square meal of an evening. They'd drunk coffee afterwards in that very same spot in that very same room after his marriage had broken up. Maggie's thoughts ran away with her. If she and Brian were to get together, she could carry on with the business. They both worked odd hours, so that wouldn't be a problem. And the benefit would be mutual. They'd have someone to come home to, ask about each other's day, warm their bed.

Then she thought about her kids. Brian would be a father figure, a role model, support her in her decisions. But how would they react to him? Kirsty would go berserk. Maggie could see it now. But Kirsty already spent half the year in Dundee. And it would be no time before she was in permanent work, a long-term relationship, gone forever. As for Colin, he wouldn't care. Or would he? Underneath that laid-back exterior lurked a fragile and sensitive soul. But he, too, would be gone in the space of an eyelash.

The slam of the back door brought Maggie back to reality.

A few moments quiet followed, then, 'Can I eat those leftover sausages in the fridge?' Colin stuck his head around the door.

'Sure thing,' Maggie replied with an amused smile. Talk about a one-track mind. He'd behaved as if Brian wasn't there.

'Chalk and cheese, your two,' Brian observed when Colin had gone.

Maggie nodded her agreement. 'They couldn't be more unalike. Colin's equable, like George.' She felt a stab of guilt at the betrayal. 'Whereas Kirsty…'

Brian finished the sentence. '…needs a good slap.'

Maggie sat bolt upright. 'It's not for you to judge,' she leapt to her daughter's defence.

Brian dropped his arm from her shoulders. 'I didn't mean,' he began.

'That's the problem,' Maggie spoke through clenched teeth. Brian didn't understand, that was the long and short of it. How could he? Bev and him, they'd had no children. How could she begin to explain that, as a mother, she would forgive her child anything? Well, almost. In her mind, she projected Colin's mute defiance, the voluble bust-ups with Kirsty were Brian to move in.

Poker-faced, she pulled away. 'I think you'd better go.'

Netherley

It was the hedge that did it. Maggie had driven out of a sharp bend when it reared up in front of her.

She hit the brakes, drew into the verge.

For a few moments she sat, eyes closed, trying to visualise the photograph from Audrey Esslemont's album. She'd been sorely tempted to purloin it. Had reminded herself the petty act of theft would deprive a sick woman of yet another precious memory. And in any case, it might not be significant. But the image had lodged in her mind, so much so she'd rung Scott Milne, established that Debbie's grandparents did, indeed, have a small farm. That Debbie's mum had been brought up there. That, when the grandparents died, the grazing had been let. The farmhouse had lain empty since then, save for occasional use by a stockman.

The ideal place to hide out, Maggie concluded. Then, uncomfortable in the knowledge that there was no evidential basis whatever on which to base her assumption, she resolved not to share her hunch with Wilma.

Scott had been unable to furnish a postcode which – with the aid by her Satnav – would have taken Maggie straight there.

Only been once, he'd responded to her persistent questioning. *And that was with Debbie many years ago.*

It was the subject of a trust, he said, *handled by a firm of solicitors.*

Yes,' he confirmed, *Mrs Esslemont was a beneficiary of the trust, but neither she nor her deceased husband had demonstrated much interest in the place.*

Netherley. Can't tell you where, exactly. Things have changed such a lot around there.

They had, indeed, Maggie discovered when she embarked on her mission. The hamlets on both sides of the southbound A90 between Aberdeen and Stonehaven had grown exponentially with the advent of oil: sprawls of new housing and retail parks. The huge city bypass project, currently under construction, would change the landscape beyond recognition.

In other circumstances, Maggie's approach would have been methodical: obtain the name of the trust solicitors, place an exploratory call. But with time running out on her self-imposed deadline, she'd opted to take another leap of faith.

At the expense of Col's dinner, a small voice nagged inside her head, for she'd driven straight from school instead of heading to the supermarket as she'd planned.

Carefully pocketing her phone – the railway arches incident had taught her a hard lesson – she stowed her bag under the passenger seat and exited the car, locking it behind her.

She crossed the road.

Standing hard up to the hedge, she tried to peer through, but the foliage was too dense.

Cautiously, she crept around.

The house had that blank-faced look buildings acquire when they've lain empty too long. The paint on the front door was peeling off in curls. Across the front windows flimsy curtains were drawn.

In front lay what might once have been a cottage garden: two rectangles of lawn bisected by a path edged with angled bricks. Now, a small Vesuvius of molehills pockmarked the yellowing grass and the borders were waist-high in weeds. To one side, a potholed driveway accessed a rackety steading.

Maggie was convinced she'd come to the right place.

She made a decision: she'd start at the back, out of sight, work her way around. If there was no sign of life she'd call it quits and head home. She might even have time to pick up some shopping at Brig o' Dee.

The back of the building was even more decrepit than the front. Rusting machinery littered the yard. What looked like a bathroom window had been crudely patched with a piece of hardboard.

She tried the handle of the back door.

Put her eye to the keyhole.

Saw nothing but worn brown lino and another closed door.

Maggie worked her way around the building.

The gaps in the front curtains yielded little: one room was empty, the other furnished with a swirly patterned carpet and ancient moquette sofa.

The front door was secure, a scatter of fliers visible through the letterbox.

She turned her attention to the immediate surroundings. If the stockman used the place on a casual basis, it wasn't beyond the bounds he could have hidden a key.

Maggie upturned stones and flowerpots, ran her fingers along the lintel of the door. No joy.

Scolding herself for wasting time, she was set to leave when a thought struck her: that broken back window might afford a way in.

Breaking and entering? she reminded herself. *Don't even go there!*

Then, the window was already broken, so what would be the harm?

She cast around.

There was nothing in the yard but a rotting stick she recognised as the shaft of a broken scythe.

Maggie picked it up and stabbed at the window.

The board held fast.

She retreated to the steading.

Looked around for a hammer, a mallet, something more solid, but anything of value had long gone.

She was about to give up when she almost tripped over a metal object.

She groped in the half dark, found that it was an old flat iron, now covered in rust.

Maggie doubted it would do the job, but needs must.

She picked it up, crossed the yard, took a few swings.

The board gave but didn't break.

She tried again. And again, until her wrist was sore and her shoulder aching.

Criminal damage! She could imagine the repercussions.

Winded, she leaned back against the wall. There was patently nobody there, nor was she likely to learn anything that would help solve the case. She might as well give up and go home.

But now you're here, a small voice said.

Maggie resolved to have one last try.

She took a run at the window, swung the iron overarm.

The board buckled and gave with a loud crack, leaving Maggie with one arm up to her elbow in broken glass.

Gingerly, she tapped out the shards from the frame until the aperture was relatively safe. Then she climbed on an old lemonade crate she'd rescued from the steading and wriggled inside.

The smell hit her first: damp and mould and pee.

She cased the back porch, the meagre bathroom, where the pan was brown, the lavatory seat left up.

In the kitchen, an open tin of Heinz beans on an oilcloth-covered table testified to recent occupation.

In the front room, a corner of what looked like a newspaper peeked from under the sofa.

Slowly, Maggie teased it out. The date on the Press & Journal was Tuesday: the day Debbie Milne had disappeared.

Heart racing, Maggie slid it back into place.

Calm down! That doesn't prove a thing.

She took a few deep breaths, trying to slow her breathing.

Silly fool! Her nerves had been bad enough before, shot to bits since the railway arches. And now here she was, breaking and entering, and in broad daylight too!

Maggie told herself she'd done no harm. The trust would have needed to instruct a repair at some point to keep the weather out. And anyhow, even if a neighbour did pick it up and report it to the police, they'd put it down to kids up to mischief.

She allowed herself a small smile. Her little outing might not have borne fruit, but she'd eliminated the agency's final line of enquiry. And vindicated her own judgement. She'd been right all along about not dipping their toes into untested water. Now she and Wilma would be able to close the Milne case and concentrate on their core business for the rest of the year.

She looked up at the ceiling. She'd have a quick dekko at the bedrooms before she went out the way she'd come in. With a bit of luck, she might even be able to pull the piece of board after her, manoeuvre it back into place.

She retreated into the hallway.

Was about to climb the stairs when, overhead, a floorboard creaked.

* * *

Back pressed to the wall, Maggie edged sideways up the short flight of stairs. She didn't dare encroach on the bare treads lest whatever – whoever – was up there divined her approach.

Gaining the landing, she stood for a few moments getting her bearings. At either end a closed door. Bedrooms, she surmised, for in common with farm cottages of the period the only bathroom would be downstairs.

She crept forward to the first, pressed her ear against it.

Nothing.

With shaking fingers, she grasped the handle and turned.

The door gave onto a coomb-ceilinged bedroom. There were dark patches by the dormer window where damp had stained the wallpaper. Other than that, the room was a time-warp from another age: flower-sprigged walls, the same dark brown lino that she'd seen downstairs. On the iron three-quarter bedstead, wire springs spiralled from a ticking mattress. Alongside, a washstand with heavily patterned tiles sat askew, one of its china castors missing. Other than a few scattered mouse droppings, there was no sign of life.

Pulling the door behind her, Maggie backed through the doorway. The sound she'd heard must have come from the other bedroom.

Cautiously, she approached it.

Gripping the handle with both hands – for they were trembling so violently she didn't trust herself – she eased it open.

This room was a mirror of the first, but the floor was covered in cheap cord carpeting, the bed a modern, if undistinguished, double. Upon it lay a rumpled nylon sleeping bag and lumpy pillow. Atop the single bedside table sat a half-empty bottle of Fanta.

Maggie's first thought was that the stockman slept over from time to time, either that or napped during the day.

Then her PI instincts kicked in.

She dropped to a crouch, checked that there was no one hiding under the bed. Then she bent to the sleeping bag, slipped a hand inside.

It was warm to the touch.

She lifted a corner to her face, took a sniff. Like the rest of the interior, the overwhelming odour was of damp. This was underlaid with sweat. But there was something else: feminine, yet indefinable.

She dropped the sleeping bag as if it were red hot.

Stood stock still.

Closed her eyes.

Forget your hunches. Concentrate on the facts.

Someone had been in that house. And recently, perhaps earlier that very day. But they – whoever they were – weren't there now. Couldn't be, for hadn't Maggie checked all the rooms? There again, she was sure she'd heard a noise.

So what?

She knew from her parents' place in Methlick that old houses had a life of their own: that ill-fitting windows sighed, and Virginia creeper rustled, and loose boards creaked.

She racked her brains. There might be an attic.

She retreated to the landing, cast her eyes upwards. There was no sign of a trapdoor.

She lowered her gaze. Fixed upon a panel set into the eaves. No larger than a metre squared, it was covered in the same wallpaper that adorned the walls.

She squatted down, pressed her fingertips into the narrow gap, shuffled backwards as she prised the panel outwards.

It opened onto a void, tapering from front to back, which Maggie guessed ran the length of the landing.

She tilted forward onto her knees, squinted inside, could discern nothing but black space.

She fumbled in her pocket, extracted her phone, flicked on the torch function. The beam swung back and forth, finding nothing.

Sod it!

She sat back on her heels. All that time wasted for nothing.

Her stomach rumbled. High time she got back up the road.

Her thighs started to cramp.

She set down her phone, gave them a rub.

Then she heard it: a muffled crack, as if someone had shifted position.

She started forward, grabbing for her phone.

Played the beam this way and that.

Nothing.

Then she crawled into the space, turning first one way then the other.

She'd almost reached the far end when her torch illuminated what looked like the sole of a white trainer.

Maggie froze, her heart working overtime.

Slowly, she raised the torch.

Then, 'Debbie?' she ventured in a soft voice.

One Thing

'Well?' Wilma stood, feet apart, a wet cleaning rag in one hand.

Wayne and Kevin were under orders to report at the end of her shift to the bar where she still worked two evenings a week. They sat, side by side, at a table crowded with empty pint glasses.

Wilma eyed each in turn.

They fixed their eyes on the floor.

'You're not going to tell me you haven't flushed out that wee bastard?'

'Sorry, Mum,' Kevin mumbled.

Wayne busied himself re-tying the laces of one trainer.

'Did you even get off your fat arses?'

'Aye.' Wayne's head shot up. 'We've been round every pub within a mile of Torry.'

'Every bookies,' Kevin added.

'All the fuckin takeaways,' Wayne again. 'Chinese, chippies, the lot. There's nobody seen him.'

Wilma's eyes narrowed. 'Nobody that will put their money where their mouth is, more like.'

'We put the screws on, Ma, like you told us,' Kevin whined.

'That right?' Wilma sneered.

'It's the God's honest truth,' Wayne backed his brother up. 'Bobby Brannigan's no in Torry.' He shook his head. 'Canna be.'

Wilma's lip curled. 'A couple o big galoots like you pair an ye canna flush oot a wee turd like him.'

'We've had other stuff to do,' Wayne compensated.

'Aye? Like what? Playing computer games? Sitting in front of the telly?'

'It's ma asthma,' he whined. 'Canna over-exert maself.'

'Ye'd bring a tear tae a glass eye, you,' Wilma retorted. 'Ye hivna had asthma since ye wis nine-year-old.'

'Sorry, Mum,' Kevin said, again.

'I'll "sorry" you.' Wilma flicked the wet cloth and cuffed his ear. The one thing she could do for Maggie Laird and it hadn't even got off the ground.

'Ouch!' Kevin's hand shot up. 'That hurt.' He rubbed the rapidly reddening appendage.

Wilma ignored him. 'Couple o' useless fuckers,' she seethed, 'that's all you are. Couldna batter a fish supper,' she spat. 'Well, I'll tell you one thing, you needn't come running to me for anything – no handouts, no trainers, no eff all – until you've found that wee fucker. Do I make myself clear?'

Kevin stopped rubbing, but left his hand cupped protectively. 'Yes, Mum.'

Wilma turned on Wayne. 'You lost your fucking voice?'

'No.' He grinned. 'Can I have a pint?'

'Did you hear me?' Wilma bawled. 'I said don't dare ask me for anything until...'

'...we've found Bobby Brannigan.' They answered in unison.

'That's it.' Wilma rose from the table. 'Now fuck off out o' here.'

A Bit of Fun

'Have you been here all this time?'

Shaking uncontrollably, Debbie could only nod.

'Since last Tuesday?'

'Yes.' Said through chattering teeth.

They were sitting in Maggie's car, the heater going full blast. It had taken the best part of an hour and all her powers of persuasion to get Debbie Milne to leave the sanctuary of the house. Now, she sat swaddled in a smelly old tartan travelling rug Maggie had rescued from the boot.

'Do you want to tell me why you took off like that?' Maggie ventured.

Determinedly, Debbie shook her head.

'Why not?'

'Why would I?' Her eyes flashed resistance. 'I don't know you from Adam.'

Maggie extended a friendly hand. 'I realise that. But you have my word,' she met Debbie's eyes, 'I mean you no harm.'

'You're a private investigator, you said?'

'That's right.'

'So you work with the police?'

Whoops! In the light of past transgressions, Maggie didn't want to go there.

'Not necessarily,' she responded. 'Why do you ask?'

'It's complicated,' Debbie replied.

Maggie drew a breath. 'It might help,' she said.

'How?' Uttered with such vitriol Maggie started back in her seat.

'Just...' She struggled for a suitable response. '...get things off your chest.'

Debbie's mouth twisted. 'You reckon?'

What was so desperate, Maggie wondered, that this young

woman wouldn't open up to her? Her mind seethed with possibilities: drink, drugs, debt? The last seemed most likely. Or was Debbie Milne yet another victim of domestic abuse? There again, could her flight have been to do with her children? Were they the victims of abuse? Maggie's thoughts jumped to Seaton, where an illegal childminder with an alcohol habit had mistreated the children in her care. But, then, Debbie wouldn't have left them unprotected, would she, if were that the case?

She changed tack. 'How come you pitched up here?'

'After I left the house, I didn't know what to do. I wandered around for a bit, keeping away from the centre of town. Then I remembered this place. I caught the Stonehaven bus, walked the rest of the way.'

'But,' Maggie puzzled, 'your car...'

'...would have been too easily traced. I thought about hitching a lift – I'd grabbed a hoodie of Chloe's and covered my hair so I wouldn't be recognised – only there wasn't a thing on the road, not except for one tractor, and when I heard it coming I hid in some bushes.'

'The farmhouse, how did you get in?'

'There was a key hidden in the steading. Someone had been using the place, either the tenant or one of his workers, maybe, for shelter when the weather was bad.'

'How did you survive?' Maggie asked. 'There's no electricity, and...'

Debbie nodded. '...the water's turned off, too. I took some cereal bars from home – I buy them for the kids' packed lunches – and made them last. Then I found a few tins in a cupboard. They weren't that old. Past their sell-by-date, but I wasn't in a position to be fussy. Then I remembered the garden. There used to be a vegetable patch. I played there when I was a kid. But all I could find were sprouting cabbages and a few potatoes. There was nothing to drink except a bottle of juice I brought with me, so I rationed that and collected water from a butt out the back. Usually after dark, in case of a passing car. Mostly I've stayed in bed, to be honest, especially these past few days when I got really hungry. Serves me right.' She pulled a tragic face. 'I'm always moaning to Scott,' her voice cracked. 'I can never find the time to catch up on my sleep.'

Poor soul. Maggie's heart went out to the girl. She was still trembling with cold and – now Maggie saw her up close – hollow-cheeked, as if she'd caved in on herself, so different from the glowing, buxom figure in her photograph. Whatever she'd done, wherever she'd been since the previous Tuesday, Maggie couldn't help but feel sorry for her. With unwashed hair scraped back in a rubber band and a face devoid of make-up, she looked to be in her late teens rather than the thirty-something mother of two children.

Maggie thought back to when Kirsty was cutting: how sick with worry she'd been.

From the day you bring them into the world, you never stop worrying about them, her mum used to say. Maggie had sneered at the time. Now, she only too well the heartache a mother could feel. And what of Debbie? Hadn't she lost her own mother in all but name?

'Have you seen my kids?' Debbie ventured, her voice quavering.

'No, but they're fine. Your husband, Scott…'

'You've spoken to him?'

'Several times. His mum has been looking after them.'

'Oh.' Debbie's face relaxed.

'You must be missing them terribly.'

Her eyes welled with tears. She turned her head away.

'They miss you too.'

She turned back. Mumbled, 'I suppose.'

'So, tell me, Debbie…' With a gentle hand, Maggie lifted the girl's face to her own. '…what is it that's so terrible you can't make this right?'

'You don't know what it's like,' Debbie turned, her eyes beseeching.

Try me, Maggie thought. She knew from experience of taking statements, when somebody was ready to talk, best not get in the way.

'Stuck at home all day, cooking and cleaning. When I do go out, it's to ferry the kids back and forth, trail around Asda on my tod. It was okay when I had my job. You'd be talking to people.' She clammed up.

A long silence ensued. 'Bringing up two children isn't easy,' Maggie prompted, at last, in the hope of drawing the girl out. 'Trust me, I've been there.'

Still am.

There was no reaction.

'It's hard work.' Maggie persevered. She thought, fleetingly, of her fractious relationship with Kirsty, her fears for Colin. 'Relentless,' she went on. 'You plough a lonely path as a mother, even if you do have a loving partner. People don't understand that.'

This seemed to chime with Debbie. 'But, now, since the move…' She opened up. 'Don't get me wrong, I love the new house. But that's all it is at the moment: a roof and four walls. It could be months, years maybe, before it feels like home.'

'Moving house is a major undertaking,' Maggie counselled.

How do you know? You haven't moved in years.

'And it must be unsettling.'

'Plus,' Debbie ran on, I don't know anybody on the street, not yet anyhow. And Scott…' Another hiatus. 'I've been working so hard to make it perfect for us all.' Her eyes held mute appeal. 'But Scott hasn't supported me, not in the least. He's either not there – working late, he says – or he's miles away.'

Maggie waited for what was coming. Wished, now, she'd been more pro-active a year earlier when Ros Prentice had first vented her concerns about her controlling husband. At their meetings, Scott Milne had come across to her as decent, loving. But after what she'd learned from Ros, not to mention the Struthers case, Maggie was only too well aware nobody could tell what went on behind closed doors.

'We're a good team, always have been. But lately Scott doesn't want to know.' Her voice was bitter. 'He's gone right off me, and that's a fact.'

'He's under pressure at work,' Maggie was surprised to find herself defending Scott's corner. She hadn't warmed to him. But, still, to be left with two kids. She knew how that felt.

'Oh,' Debbie dismissed her, 'that's always his excuse. I thought at first he was having an affair. Somebody in the office. You know how it is. They get randy, men. Egg each other on. It's in their nature, I suppose.'

'Have you any proof?' Maggie prodded.

'No. How would I? Too busy seeing to his kids.'

'But…'

'I checked his phone, of course I did. Emails, the lot. Went through his wallet.'

'And?'

'Nothing.'

'Well, then.'

Tears spilled from Debbie's eyes and coursed down her cheeks. 'It was only meant as a bit of fun.'

'What was?'

But Debbie had clammed up again.

'What you need,' Maggie said, 'is a hot shower, a square meal and a good night's sleep in your own bed.'

Debbie lifted a stubborn face. 'I can't go home.'

'Why not?'

'Scott will be angry with me.'

'Why? You've not done anything to make him angry.'

Debbie whipped her head away.

'You haven't, have you?'

There was no response.

'You can tell me,' Maggie cajoled.

Debbie turned. 'It was the move brought it home to me,' she wailed. 'The sheer monotony of my life. I'd been happy up till then. Well,' she qualified, 'happy enough. Granted, I was stuck in a rut, but I imagined, when we moved to Belvidere Street, that would all change.'

'And it didn't?" Maggie prompted.

'No. If anything, it got worse. It's like I'm on a treadmill I can't get off. And Belvidere Street, nice as it is,' she broke off, a catch in her voice. 'It's just more of the same, only bigger.'

Maggie didn't comment. Now that Debbie had opened up, it was paramount she kept going.

'The house move turned my life upside down,' Debbie ran on. 'Not just moving stuff, clearing out. It made me take a look at myself, see how narrow my life had become. The first few weeks I thought I was just run-down. Plus, it takes a while to adjust: get your bearings, make new friends. Then I realised life would go on exactly like that if I didn't make an effort to break out.'

Maggie held her breath.

'Then Sam rang the doorbell.'

'And?' she breathed.

Debbie's head lolled. She had fallen asleep.

* * *

'You were telling me about Sam,' Maggie said in a soft voice. Almost an hour had passed before Debbie came to, an hour in which Maggie speculated feverishly on the young mother's flight. The tedium of motherhood she could understand, but there had to be more, and Sam Clark was the key. Maggie would have liked to have used her phone, but she was scared to make a move. Even texting Colin or Wilma might have spooked the runaway.

Debbie scrunched fists into her eye sockets. 'A real livewire. She's always been like that: likes to chance her arm, push the boundaries, see how much she can get away with.' She stretched her arms above her head. '*Life's no fun otherwise*, that's what she always used to say. And she was exciting to be with. Glamorous. And the glamour sort of rubbed off on me.' Debbie's mouth gaped in a yawn. 'She shone. Made me come alive. Do you understand where I'm coming from?'

Maggie didn't. She nodded all the same.

'First time, I only did it for a dare. I've always wanted to be brave, like Sam. Followed where she led when I was a kid. But this was my opportunity. She had this friend – several friends in fact – she used to meet for drinks and stuff. Businessmen. They'd be in Aberdeen for a day or two. Have meetings all day, be looking for a bit of company in the evening. Sam and me, we'd been chumming one another a couple of nights a week: clubs, cocktail bars. Scott didn't mind. Or if he did, he didn't say. Not that he was in a position to,' she insisted, her voice defensive. 'The hours he was putting in. Plus, the nights we went out I'd have been going to my classes, anyway, so it should have made no odds to him.' She looked to Maggie for approbation.

'I see,' Maggie said, non-committal.

'We'd have a couple of drinks. Somewhere nice, usually where they were staying. Dinner, occasionally.'

'That's all?' Maggie couldn't help herself.

'Well,' Debbie answered. 'Sometimes Sam would go upstairs with them.'

'You?'

'I'd take a taxi home.'

'If that's all you're worried about,' Maggie began.

Debbie ignored her. 'After that first time,' she ran on, 'I found I enjoyed it: the attention. Gave me a buzz. I don't get that at home,' she said, bitterly. 'Not anymore.'

'Are you talking about sex?' Maggie enquired, her voice gentle.

'That,' Debbie allowed, 'and everything else. Got to the point sex with Scott was the only excitement I could look forward to in my day. Then, when that fizzled out...' Her voice cracked. 'He couldn't get an erection. Either he wasn't interested or he was getting it somewhere else.'

'So did you...?'

'Get in the sack with those guys? The answer's no. Not that I wasn't tempted. They were nice-looking, most of them: European. American. Good teeth. Dressed well. Had plenty to talk about. And they were interested in me. They'd ask me questions about myself, actually listen to the answers. It was company they were after. It must be lonely staying in hotels. And Sam said that was the deal: keep them company, anything more was up to me.'

'I see.' Maggie didn't, but it filled a space.

'It was an escape,' Debbie justified. 'I could forget about home – cooking, cleaning, all that – become someone else.'

'Assume a different persona?' Maggie prompted.

'That's it exactly.'

'Under a different name?' she fished.

Debbie brightened. 'It was Sam suggested it, said it would save me feeling guilty, thinking about the kids. She said to keep it simple, so I didn't tie myself in knots. That's how we hit on Dee.'

The jigsaw pieces clicked into place. Wilma had mentioned a "Bea" after her visit to the Ferryhill flats, but Maggie hadn't made the connection.

Debbie deliberated for a moment, then, 'Sam even gave me a spare phone, so the clients…' She flushed. '…could ring me direct.'

A burner. Maggie had all the jargon. 'And cash?' she queried.

Debbie grinned. 'There was no shortage of that.'

Bloody hell! Maggie thought, now she was well down the road with the PI business, she'd be inured to surprises, but this took the biscuit. Still, she rationalised, providing it was couched in careful language, Debbie's escapade could surely be presented less as desertion than an act of rebellion.

She took hold of her hand. 'Let me take you home.'

'No.' Debbie snatched it away.

'But, why? You haven't done anything wrong, and your husband, he's worried sick.'

'I said, no.'

'Your children,' Maggie played her trump card, 'they're distressed, and…'

'I can't.' Debbie turned away.

'Why not?'

She turned back, eyes wide with fear. 'It's too dangerous.'

Moving On

Having a clear out?' Brian's upstairs neighbour, Stuart, enquired, picking his way through a jumble of cardboard boxes on the stair head.

'No,' Brian answered, 'I'm moving out.'

'You serious?' Stuart's face registered disbelief. 'Thought you were in with the bricks.'

That's the problem! What had started out as a temporary measure had become a way of life. And what a life! Since he'd signed the lease on his new place in Spring Garden, Brian wondered how he'd stuck it out for so long in the shit-hole the letting agent had the gall to call a studio flat. Inertia, he supposed. By the time Bev and he had managed to have a civil conversation and the marital home had been put on the market, he'd had neither the energy nor the inclination to shop around, and had settled for the first thing that was, a) affordable and b) within spitting distance of Queen Street.

'When are you going?'

'End of the month.'

'Jeez,' Stuart whistled through his teeth, 'we'll miss you, man.'

You kidding? Brian had been driven almost to breaking point by the constant barrage of noise from upstairs. If they weren't playing loud music, they were yelling at the tops of their voices or tramping back and forth across the laminate flooring in their Doc Martens.

He smiled. 'Nice of you to say.'

'Going for something bigger?' Stuart lingered, seemingly keen to talk.

'Two-bedder.' Brian shuffled his feet, anxious to crack on.

'You got plans?' he persisted.

'Nope,' Brian shot back. After his old friend and colleague George Laird died, Brian had harboured romantic notions of courting Maggie, his widow, and eventually moving in. Over-eager, He'd got off to a rocky start. That she'd used his police connections to further her business hadn't helped. But she'd been more approachable of late, and Brian had seen his chance. All that had changed, whether irrevocably or not Brian couldn't tell. What he did know – as borne out by her summary dismissal of him the previous week – was that Maggie Laird's children were more important to her than any man.

'Just saying.' Stuart grinned. 'Gathered you weren't a party animal.'

That's the understatement of all time!

'I'd better crack on,' Brian said, pointedly, backing into his doorway. He was hot from packing the few possessions he'd managed to rescue from the ashes of his marriage.

He ran a finger round the collar of the new Next shirt he'd bought with other items online in the hope of making himself more attractive.

He was tired from putting in time on an investigation that was going nowhere.

And he'd had it with women, that's for sure.

Full House

Debbie Milne lay on the settee, buried under an old-fashioned eiderdown, only her face with its halo of dark hair peeking out.

'Better?' Maggie enquired, kneeling on the floor by her side.

Debbie nodded.

It was after she had almost passed out – whether from hunger, exhaustion or the fug in Maggie's car – that she'd agreed to go back to Mannofield with Maggie. Resolutely, she'd maintained her insistence that returning home was not an option. And the meeting on neutral ground that Maggie mooted, Debbie discounted on the basis she might be recognised by a member of the public, since her photo had been widely shared. Nor would she countenance being driven to a police station. In the end, Maggie had been thankful for the suburban anonymity of her bungalow. It was, she'd concluded, the least-worst option.

Trust me, she'd said. *I know what to do.*

Only problem was – she checked her watch – they'd spent so much time sitting in her car, she was in danger of being caught out. Colin could appear at any moment, and having plied her house guest with the best of what the fridge had to offer, Maggie would have to resort to raiding her meagre store cupboard in order to cobble a meal together.

Worse, Wilma might descend. The PIs consulted one another at frequent intervals, all the more after their falling-out. Not half a day went by when one or other of them didn't breeze into the other's kitchen, and it wasn't unknown for Wilma to barge into the bathroom when Maggie was in the bath. She sent up a silent prayer of thanks that Kirsty, in her new job at a west end estate agent, wouldn't be back till evening.

Judging this as good a time as any to draw Debbie out further, she said, 'This danger you mentioned…' She kept the implicit question wide open, her eyes glued to Debbie's face, waiting to judge her reaction.

A flicker of alarm registered, followed by a confused look. Debbie didn't speak.

'What was that about?' Maggie zeroed in.

There was silence, then, 'Sam called me.'

Maggie surged with adrenalin. 'Where from?'

'I don't know. The line was bad. Lots of traffic noise in the background. Lorries, I think. Buses, maybe.'

'When was this?'

'Tuesday.' Small pause. 'Not this Tuesday, the one before.'

'And?'

'I'd gone upstairs to get dressed.'

'This was breakfast time?'

'Yes. Scott was downstairs with the kids. I was in the bathroom doing my face when my mobile rang. It was Sam. She was in a state.'

'A state?' Maggie's head buzzed with possibilities. 'Can you explain?'

'We only spoke for a couple of minutes. Sam sounded as if she was in a hurry. And,' Debbie's voice hitched. 'I've never known Sam be afraid of anything, but she was scared. Really scared.' Her eyes welled with tears.

'Here,' Maggie dipped into a pocket, proffered a clean tissue.

Her head swivelled as the back door banged.

There was a muffled thud, followed by footsteps, and Colin's head appeared round the sitting-room door.

'Is there anything to eat?' he addressed Maggie, seemingly oblivious to Debbie's prone figure. 'There isn't a thing in the fridge.'

For once, Maggie was thankful for her son's disinterest. 'I'm sorry,' she struggled to her feet. 'Been a bit of a heavy day.'

He rolled his eyes. 'Join the club.' He followed her through to the kitchen.

Maggie burrowed in a cupboard.

'There's baked beans,' she backed out, triumphant, waving a can.

'There might be baked potatoes in the freezer.'

He wrinkled his nose. 'How long will that take? I'm starved.'

'Not long,' she said, brightly, knowing she'd best not leave Debbie Milne on her own. 'I can stick them in the microwave.'

'Okay,' he grudged. 'Can you make me a sandwich or something till they're ready?'

'Sure,' she said, lifting the lid off the bread bin. Then, 'Oh, Colin, I completely forgot. We're out of bread.'

'For God's sake,' he retorted, face beetroot. 'I've been running around a rugby pitch, and…' His words were interrupted by the front doorbell.

'I'll be right back.' Maggie shot out of the kitchen.

Lord, what a sight! She caught her reflection in the hall mirror as she trotted past. Her face was streaked with smut, her hair sticking out at all angles. She'd been so busy seeing to Debbie Milne's wellbeing, she hadn't taken a minute to tidy herself up.

Gingerly, she opened the front door.

Allan Chisolm stood on the doorstep. He was dressed in jeans and a grey polo neck sweater that mirrored the colour of his eyes. He looked laid-back, Maggie thought, and wildly attractive.

'You wanted to see me?' he said, with a mischievous glint.

'Y-yes,' Maggi stuttered. She'd debated phoning Brian Burnett, but had been way too embarrassed. Kirsty's outburst had set her and Brian back, no question, just when Maggie thought the relationship might, after all, have a future. And after the way she'd behaved, cynically soaking him for information, it would hardly be fair. Plus, she'd landed him in hot water before: those Seaton kids. She shuddered as she recalled the row of small boys sitting side by side on Brian's bed-settee. Added to which, there was the small matter of the railway arches. What if that got out: that Harcus & Laird had been pursuing Debbie Milne's disappearance all along?

In the end she'd gone straight to Chisolm.

Can you come round?'

What, now?

No matter he'd tear her off a strip. Deservedly so. Their assignation at Ardoe House had debunked the myth that Allan Chisolm was some sort of bogeyman.

'Well,' he flashed a disarming smile, 'aren't you going to ask me in?'

'Yes,' Maggie said.

He stepped into the porch.

'But before you come through,' there was a tremor in her voice. She recalled the last time they'd stood in such close proximity. 'There's something I have to tell you.'

* * *

'So,' Allan Chisolm said from the big chair by the window, 'let me get this straight: Sam told you to run because she thought you were in danger?' He'd broken the news of Sam's death as gently as he could, stepped out of the room while Maggie consoled the weeping woman.

'Me. Her,' Debbie whispered from the depths of the settee. 'I don't know. She told me she'd done something really stupid. Done it with good intentions, but there would be serious repercussions. Said it was to do with the flats. That people would come after her. Bad people. And because I'd been at Ferryhill with her and we look a bit alike, she was worried they might target me by mistake.'

'These "people" you mention. Who are they?'

'A gang. Don't know the details.'

'Did you ever meet anyone in this gang?'

'No. Not to my knowledge, anyhow.'

'Did you meet anyone at all, during the times you were with Sam, anyone except…?' He broke off, casting a sideways glance at Maggie, who was sitting on the floor.

She dipped her chin, unwilling to meet his gaze.

This was followed by an embarrassed silence. Debbie had already opened up to her dalliance with the world of escort services.

'Only a couple of girls at her digs, Polish I think they were. But

I only saw them in passing, and they didn't speak much English. There was one man. Albanian, I think Sam said. He came to her flat once. I only remember because they had a row.'

'What about?' Chisolm delved.

'Sam didn't say.'

'Could you help our artist put together a likeness, do you think?'

Debbie responded with a shy smile. 'I could try.'

'Right, then, Debbie.' Chisolm leaned forward. 'First thing we need to do is let your husband know you're safe and well.' He made to rise.

'No.' She sat bolt upright. 'I'm not going home.'

'But,' Maggie interceded, 'your children...'

'Don't you get it?' Debbie's voice rose. 'It's to protect my kids I ran in the first place.'

'Understood,' Chisolm sat back. 'And it's to protect your children and others like them that I'm going to ask for your help.'

'Help?' she puzzled. 'How?'

'To bring the gang that killed Sam to justice.'

'Gladly.' Her eyes welled up. 'But I don't see...'

'You've done what you thought was the right thing at the time. And that was incredibly brave. Now, let the professionals take over. With your input, we'll be able to go after these thugs, and...'

The rest of his sentence was drowned out by another bang.

Oh to hell! Maggie had completely forgotten about Colin. She gathered he'd given up waiting, had gone off in search of a carry-out. More money out the window. Still, it couldn't be helped.

Animated voices resounded from the kitchen.

Maggie strained her ears.

Oh no! She tried to make herself small.

Resplendent in silver leggings and Dayglo top, Wilma filled the doorway.

For what felt – to Maggie – an eternity, she surveyed the scene.

Then, 'Jesus Christ!' Her kohl-rimmed eyes narrowed. 'What the fuck is going on?'

X

Mika

Mika was woken by a persistent drumming on the window. Rain. Always rain.

She raised her head from the grubby polyester pillow. Through the flimsy nylon curtain the sky was a watery grey, whether day or night it was hard to tell.

She let her head fall back, closed her eyes.

Imagined she was in another place, another time.

It is early morning. Mika lies snug in her own bed, her little sister Kristina curled alongside. One small foot has escaped the goose feather quilt. Mika tucks it in and wraps a protective arm around Kristina's waist. From downstairs she can hear the first signs of life. Her mother is already dressed. She'll fetch kindling from the woodshed, set light to the stove. Then she'll put a pan of water on to boil and go back out, with an old coat over her nightdress, to feed the hens.

Mika missed the familiar sounds and smells of home so desperately: the steady toll of the bell on the village church, the sweet tang of wood smoke, the folk song her mother liked to hum as she went about her domestic chores. The heat that came off her sister's small body, the scent of her soft hair.

A tear formed in the corner of Mika's eye. It felt like a parasite was nibbling at her innards, slowly eating her up.

It was raining harder, now, squalls whipping the panes, making the curtain billow in the drought.

Mika prised herself from the bed.

With heavy limbs, she crossed the room and struggled to close the sash, to no avail.

Sighing, she dropped onto the padded stool that sat in front of a makeshift dressing table.

The face reflected in the mirror was a lifetime removed from the girl who had been plucked from her home village not many months before: cheekbones more prominent, dark circles under her eyes. Her skin had lost its rosy bloom. Her lips were parched. But it was the eyes that revealed the most. Behind the false eyelashes and heavy kohl eyeliner they were empty voids.

'There was a sharp tap on the door. A woman's voice. 'Monica?"

'Two minutes.'

On top of everything else she'd lost – her home, her family, her unworldliness – Mika had been cautioned to change her name.

'Okay.'

She heard footsteps recede down the corridor.

Her mother would be worrying. Wondering why she hadn't heard, when the money was coming? Life had been more difficult than ever since her father died.

With hurried motions, Mika ran a brush through her hair.

She rose, crossed to the bed, straightened the covers.

She checked the contents of the bedside table: condoms, lubes, wet wipes.

Soon, she vowed.

She'd send the money very soon.

Their Problem

'Brian!' Chisolm answered his knock. 'Come in. Take a seat.'

Brian did as he was bid. Three times in as many days the boss had addressed him by his first name. Maybe there was hope for that promotion after all.

'Milne case.' It wasn't a question.

'Sir.'

'Let's have it, then.' Chisolm swept a bundle of files to one side, fixed Brian with a questioning gaze.

That sounded more like DI Brian knew. He reminded himself not to get his hopes up. 'You'll have had my report,' he began.

'Yes, yes,' Chisolm snapped. 'You've given me all the guff. Now give me the lowdown.'

Under his collar Brian's skin pricked. 'Yes sir.' He cleared his throat. 'I can confirm that Debbie Milne has been examined by a doctor. Other than a degree of malnourishment, she seems to have suffered no ill effects from her ordeal. Physically, that is.'

'And psychologically?'

'Who knows? Her mental health is fragile at the moment.'

'Not surprising. Your old school pal comes back into your life. Next minute she's dead.'

'Anything more from Tayside, sir?'

'Samantha Clark's brother has made a formal identification, but it could be a while before the body is released for burial. I've seen the pathologist's report. Catalogue of injuries: broken nose and jaw, fractured cheekbone, cracked ribs, broken fingers, deep cuts and abrasions.'

'Sexual assault?'

'There's no evidence of penetration. Whatever. Looks like she put up one hell of a fight.'

'Fits the picture. By all accounts Sam was a spirited lass. It's a blessing the mother's dead,' he added, reflectively. For all the years he'd been in the force, Brian still found the duty of breaking the of a loved one's death the most distressing.

Chisolm nodded. 'Quite so. With regard to their…' He paused, frowning. '…activities, Sam and Debbie, what did you get?'

'Where the escort work is concerned, Sam's an old hand, it transpires, has been at it since her marriage broke up. It's what funded the gambling, that and whatever she could cadge off the current boyfriend. When the gambling got out of hand, she stepped the escort work up. But, what with one thing and another – the oil downturn was one factor – she couldn't make enough to fund an escalating habit. That's when she got in hock with Albanians.'

'And Debbie? How did she get embroiled?'

'Started out as a dare, so she says. Debbie was smitten by Sam Clark: the bling clothes, the racy lifestyle. And she was in a receptive frame of mind: worn down by the house move, but still channelling the domestic goddess. I think the burden of expectation – on herself, never mind from the husband and kids – got too much. As for Sam, I reckon she was envious of Debbie. She had everything Sam didn't: the solid marriage, the two kids, and, now, the forever home.'

'You're saying Sam Clark involved Debbie Milne in prostitution out of spite?'

'Not spite, sir, no. More…' Brian struggled to find the right word. '…payback, I suppose. I think Sam saw it as a bit of sport, tempting Debbie out of her comfort zone. Although there's no evidence Debbie crossed the line, actually offered sexual services. Quite the reverse. When she was interviewed, Debbie was adamant she never went further than have drinks or dinner with any of those men.'

Chisolm snorted. 'Well, she would be, wouldn't she? And we'd be toiling to prove otherwise. Who's going to testify to that sort of activity? Neither the punters nor the hotels, I'm quite sure.'

Brian knitted his brow. 'I believe her. When you think about it, even if Debbie had the inclination, she didn't have the opportunity. How could she? The woman only got off the leash a couple of evenings a week. Plus, she had to be home by a decent hour to get her kids up for school in the morning.'

'That's easy enough to say, but…'

'…Debbie was genuinely shocked when she was told the women in the Ferryhill flats were on the game. She'd only been there a few times with Sam and thought the tenants were Polish domestic workers lodged there by an agency.'

Chisolm sighed. 'Either way, we'd have a hard job putting a case together. We have witnesses to the fact Sam had been threatened, though whether they'd go as far as to testify in court…' He broke off. 'These Albanians are bad buggers. Treat women as a commodity. Take away their identity, their freedom of choice, of movement. Trade in them, sell them on. Tayside have been investigating this network for I don't know how long., and it wouldn't be the first time they've slipped the net.'

'Oh, well,' Brian responded. 'At least it's their problem, not ours.'

Chisolm grinned. 'Not anymore. Since Debbie Milne gave you her statement and a description of the man who threatened Sam Clark, we've been able to issue an E-Fit. All units are on the alert as we speak.'

'Wow!' Brian's jaw hung open. 'That was quick work.'

'Goes to show…' Chisolm assumed his stern face. '… solid policing brings results.' With a favourable wind, Aberdeen Division would nail the Albanian and his cohort before Tayside had time to sort out the politics.

Brian's face was a study in consternation. Was there something he didn't know? He racked his brains, came up with nothing.

'Wouldn't you agree?' Chisolm prompted.

'Oh,' Brian jerked to attention. 'Yes. Of course.'

Chisolm didn't mention Maggie Laird. If, as he suspected, Burnett had renewed intentions in that direction, he didn't intend to make life easy for him.

Debbie

Noiselessly, she slipped into the bedroom. 'Time that light was out,' she said.

'Oh,' a small head surfaced from under a tent of duvet, 'Mum.'

'Never mind, "Mum", she tousled the blond head, laughing. 'If you don't go to sleep you'll never get up for school in the morning.'

'But…' Innocent blue eyes engaged her own.

'Don't give me that look, Jack. You know perfectly well I'm right.'

'But, she…'

'And don't throw your sister at me. Chloe put her light out an hour ago.'

She tugged the duvet straight. 'Have you been to the bathroom?'

'A minute ago.'

'Brushed your teeth?'

By way of answer, he bared his gums, displaying a gleaming set of incisors.

'Well, snuggle down.' She bent, tucked the duvet around the small figure, brushed hair from his eyes.

'Night-night.' She turned from the bed.

'Night, Mum.' Muffled voice. Then, 'Don't shut the door.'

'I won't.' Not that her son was afraid of the dark. Not now. But the thought of going up to 'big school' after the summer was worrying him, she knew.

There was a long pause. Then, 'Thanks.'

'Sweet dreams.' Her voice was imbued with a confidence she didn't feel. 'I'll look in on you later.'

'Okay.'

Debbie was smiling as she started down the stairs. Halfway, her smile faded. The family liaison officer was still in place, a police team working with her and Scott to protect their family. But until

Sam was laid to rest and the men who'd murdered her friend behind bars, Debbie would never find peace, nor would she see Belvidere Street as her forever home.

Here's Looking at You

'Here's looking at you.' Wilma raised her glass.

'You, too.' The corners of Maggie's mouth twitched as she mirrored the gesture, for Wilma's *bon mots* never failed to surprise.

They were in the Dutch Mill, a long-established hotel and bar on the Queen's Road and something of an Aberdeen institution. Following on from Maggie's success in bringing Debbie Milne home safe and well, Wilma had persuaded her that a celebration was in order.

Maggie had demurred. *We don't have money to burn.*

Wee spot of supper, Wilma came back. *Couple of drinks.*

Who'll be driving? Maggie countered

Neither one of us. We'll go somewhere in the West End.

They're expensive, those places.

There's the Dutch Mill. It's not too fancy.

Now, the pair were installed at a table on a raised dais, its fretted cast-iron supports fashioned so as to resemble an old-fashioned treadle sewing machine. From their padded grey flannel banquette, they had a birds-eye view of the bar proper with its wooden floor and dark-painted panelling. Blue and white Delft plates depicting tulip fields and windmills lined the walls.

'What's the news on the Milne case?' Wilma bit into her Big Mill burger: two beef patties with coleslaw, salad and French fries. Her boxing gym sessions had gone to the wall and she'd been piling on the pounds. She vowed to start another diet once things calmed down. 'Has Scott taken Debbie back?'

Since she'd burst upon Debbie Milne and Allan Chisolm in Maggie's sitting-room, the two PIs had found precious little time for conversation. Chisolm had driven both Maggie and Debbie Milne – under protest – to Queen Street, and he'd warned Wilma that she, too, would be required to give a full statement on the agency's involvement in the police investigation.

'I gather so, although according to Brian they've signed up to a course of counselling.'

'Making promises they can't keep: to be more open with one another, all that guff,' Wilma scoffed through a mouthful of food. 'Won't last. Me and Ian, after all the noise he made over the agency's hours, we weren't five minutes back together than I was out on the ran-dan and he was back to being an old pussy-cat.'

'Don't mock,' Maggie cautioned. 'Many a true word is said in jest.'

'You sound like my ex-schoolmistress,' Wilma pooh-poohed. 'Old before your time.'

'Wish I was,' Maggie retorted, sighing. 'Instead of the school dogsbody. Still...' She speared a sliver of iceberg lettuce. She'd settled for a Caesar salad with added chicken. '...Ian could surprise you yet.'

'You haven't mentioned the bairns.' Wilma took a greedy slurp of Merlot. Overriding Maggie's protests, she'd ordered a bottle. *Works out cheaper than buying by the glass.*

'No.' A frown creased Maggie's forehead. 'On the face of it, they seem okay, but who knows what's going on in their heads.'

'They're young, yet.' Wilma demolished a forkful of coleslaw.

'Yes, but these early traumas can shape a child for life.'

'You don't need to tell me.' She dabbed a dollop of mayonnaise from her chin.

Maggie wondered – not for the first time – if Wilma had been abused as a child. Thought it prudent not to go there. 'I wonder how Mika got on?'

'There's no happy ending there,' Wilma said, emphatically. 'Even if Tayside's team catch the perps, there's bound to be a long line of other bad guys waiting to fill their shoes.'

'So Mika's mother...' Maggie took a cautious sip of her wine.

'Not a chance she'll ever see that girl again.'

'You reckon.'

'Think on it, if you'd experienced what she's been through,'

Wilma took another huge bite of her burger. 'Would you want to visit that on your wee sister?' She spoke with hamster cheeks.

Maggie frowned. 'I haven't got a sister.'

'No,' Wilma swallowed noisily. 'But say you had.'

'I suppose not,' Maggie responded with a sinking heart. 'What a tragedy: a beautiful young girl like that plucked from her home and traded like a piece of meat. Small wonder she was scared.'

'Aye. Can you imagine: no papers, no way of paying for anything? Is it any wonder those girls don't run? They've no alternative. The gang-masters might not be killing their victims, but they're as good as taking their lives away.' She sniffed. 'At least it won't happen to your daughter.'

'I sincerely hope not. What I don't understand...' Maggie broke off.

Wilma regarded her with amusement. 'What don't you understand?'

'The set-up in Ferryhill. I mean, if those girls aren't on the street, how do they meet their customers?'

Wilma started to laugh.

'I get it.' Maggie stabbed a piece of chicken with her fork. 'They put cards in shop windows, like you used to get in telephone boxes.'

'Numpty.' Wilma was in full guffaw. 'That went out with the ark. It's all done on social media these days.'

'Facebook?' Maggie echoed, swallowing her chicken. She wondered if Kirsty was safe.

'Yup. That and the rest. Post their services online, and Bob's your uncle.'

Maggie's eyes widened. 'That can't be safe. Anyone could contact them.'

'Yes, but women who aren't trafficked or controlled by a pimp are free to choose. It's no different from a dating site in that regard. And a whole lot safer than standing on a street corner. Plus, it keeps their activity under the radar.' Wilma nodded, knowingly. 'Trust me, Maggie. Pop-up brothels are the way to go.'

Hastily, Maggie changed the subject. Wilma was queening it again. 'Do you think Sam was killed because she messed up with the bookies?' Her business partner had filled her in on Dave's intel.

'Could be. Maybe she took a beating to bring her into line. There again, could be they didn't mean to kill her.'

'I don't think that's likely, do you?'

'Probably not. These guys have beatings down to a fine art.'

'Do you think she could have been murdered because she helped Mika escape?'

'Fits.' Wilma topped up both their glasses. 'Didn't Mika tell us Sam had been kind to her? Doesn't take a leap of imagination to think she pointed Mika in the right direction, so to speak. Would only take one of them girls to get free and clear and others would follow. And then,' she took a swig, 'you've opened a whacking great can of worms.'

'Poor souls,' Maggie chewed, reflectively, on another piece of chicken.

'Aye. That's a whole other side to sex work.'

'I can't help but feel sorry for Sam, too.'

'You're too soft, Maggie. Sam Clark chose the life she led, nobody forced it on her. She took a gamble. Lots of gambles. But this last one she lost. Do I not keep telling you: play with fire, you run the risk of getting burnt?'

'Who are you calling "soft"?' Maggie retorted. 'Weren't you the one banging on about Debbie Milne's "bairns"?'

'Aye,' Wilma stuffed a few French fries into her mouth. 'Got it wrong, this time. Still,' she dispatched the fries with alacrity, 'we got a result.'

We? Along with a mouthful of chicken breast, Maggie nearly swallowed her tongue. Wasn't it all on her? It was she who'd driven all over the country, burgled a farmhouse, and found Debbie Milne, all on the strength of a hunch.

'What a team!' Wilma continued, unabashed. 'Fair beat the polis at their own game, huh?'

She raised her glass. 'Toast?'

Maggie drew a deep breath. Her success in cracking the Milne case had proved her worth as a PI. More, it had restored her faith in herself. She'd already resolved to put the past firmly behind her. The agency was her business, now, not George's. She'd restore the Laird good name for her own sake, hers and the children. As for Wilma, Maggie could keep her distance, compartmentalise till she was blue in the face, but she'd never keep her partner down.

'To us!' she replied, a twinkle in her eye.

Acknowledgements

Heartfelt thanks go to my publisher, Sara Hunt at Contraband, and to my editor, Russel D. McLean, for their advice and support.

I am grateful for the specialist input of Sergeant Teresa Clark of Police Scotland and my first reader, former Detective Sergeant Bill Ogilvie.

To my family and friends, a huge thank you for your patience!

My sincere appreciation extends to the reviewers, bloggers, booksellers, festival programmers and librarians who have brought Maggie and Wilma to a wider audience, and to the many readers who have taken this unlikely crime duo into their hearts. Thanks, too, to Swaksha Krishnakumar for proofreading.

And lastly, to the good folk of Aberdeen and the dedicated staff of Seaton School, my apologies. I have taken liberties with accuracy in the pursuit of a good story!

The events in this novel are entirely fictional and errors wholly mine.